SOUR GRAPES

BLUE PLATE SERIES

RACHEL GOODMAN

PRAISE FOR RACHEL GOODMAN

"Goodman's debut Southern contemporary is smart, sexy, and funny. [She] piles on the Southern charm to make this story a winner." --Publishers Weekly on *From Scratch*

"Debut author Goodman enters the world of foodie fiction with a "bam" that would make Emeril proud." --Library Journal on *From Scratch*

"The chemistry between Ryan and Margaret is genuine, and the quaint vineyard backdrop and small-town atmosphere Goodman creates will enchant readers." --Library Journal on *Sour Grapes*

ALSO BY RACHEL GOODMAN

Blue Plate Series

From Scratch

Sour Grapes

This book is a work of fiction. Any references to historical events, real people, or real places are used fictitiously. Other names, characters, places, incidents, and events are products of the author's imagination, and any resemblance to actual events or places or persons, living or dead, is entirely coincidental.

Copyright © 2016 by Rachel Goodman

From Scratch excerpt copyright © 2015 by Rachel Goodman

All rights reserved. No part of this book may be reproduced in any form or by any electronic or mechanical means, including information storage and retrieval systems, without written permission from the author, except for the use of brief quotations in a book review.

First paperback edition 2019, ISBN: 978-1-7342198-1-4
Second ebook edition 2019, ISBN: 978-1-7342198-8-3

First Pocket Star Books/Simon & Schuster ebook edition 2016, ISBN: 978-1-4767-9290-3 (out of print)

Cover design by Najla Qamber, Qamber Designs

For Elizabeth Dyer, who believed in Marge from the beginning and who has never steered me in the wrong direction

1

Bitterness is as classic as Chanel.

Tonight I'm wearing it as armor under my black flowing silk chiffon gown. At any moment guests will start arriving for Baylor Medical's annual gala—the hospital's biggest fundraiser and the most ambitious PR/event planning project I've ever tackled. After ten months of intense preparation, I'm ready.

Nick should be celebrating the success of the evening with me, but I'm here alone after he tossed me aside for his first love like last year's Christmas present. Tonight is my chance to prove to everyone that a failed relationship won't keep me down.

It's be hurt or be hardened, and I pick the latter.

I adjust my headset and glance around. The modern concrete building of the Dallas Museum of Art is bathed in jewel tones, complemented by the mosaic wall opposite the entrance. The Moroccan music playing in the sculpture garden drifts on the wind, carrying the scent of incense and fruit from the hookah lounge. Photographers flank the red carpet leading into the main atrium, and valets surround the rectangular drive in preparation.

As if on cue, a train of limos and luxury vehicles pulls up. A fluttering sensation ignites in my stomach. Gathering my bearings, I inhale a deep breath and say, "All right, everyone. Look sharp."

I polish off a glass of Dom Pérignon, the taste light and crisp with a dry finish. Life should never be wasted on unremarkable champagne. Hiding the flute in a manicured bush, I click on the headset and ask my assistant, "Is everything finalized for the live auction and dinner?"

"Yes, Captain," she says, as though we're some ridiculous crew at sea. "Can I take a breather now? My feet are *killing* me." She's a psychology major straight out of college with no experience or work ethic—she's chronically late, frequently leaves early, and spends most of the day fighting with the coffee machine. Last week she barged into my office complaining about the workload and begging for an assistant, not even comprehending that she *is* the assistant. I only hired her because our mothers are tennis partners at the club and my mother demanded I do her a favor. Never again.

Only if you'd rather be unemployed, I think as a valet opens the first car door. To my shock, Dr. Greg Preston, Nick's father, steps out.

I knew Dr. Preston would make an appearance this evening—he's the head of cardiology at Baylor Medical—but I thought I could avoid him in the throng of the three hundred people attending the gala. Panic builds in my chest, my heart thumping an erratic rhythm. Cameras flash as he walks the red carpet, talking and shaking hands with the other benefit goers all dressed in their finest formal attire. His resemblance to Nick makes my stomach tighten—the tousled hair, the eyes so blue I could dive into them, the movie-star features.

Nick was supposed to be mine, I think, as resentment latches on to me, strengthening my suit of armor. When everyone else abandoned him—his family, his friends, his *fiancée*—during the darkest point in his life, it was *me* who picked him up off the floor and helped him rediscover his passion for songwriting. *I* saved him. *I'm* the one who deserved his trust, loyalty, devotion. Yet Nick chose Lillie, the girl who destroyed him when she ran off, only to return five years later to steal the man I had rightfully earned.

Dr. Preston turns in my direction, but I duck out of sight before he can see me. I sneak behind the receiving line of belly dancers greeting guests to the festivities and move past the check-in area overflowing with the event programs and promotional materials I'd spent months creating.

The atmosphere in the main atrium feels as warm and exotic as the spices in Marrakech. Luxurious silk fabrics in vivid shades of teal and purple are draped across the ceiling, the walls lit up to match. A Moorish tile pattern is projected onto the floor, while pierced iron lanterns adorn tallboy tables covered in linens the colors of precious gemstones. Servers in traditional dress, from fez-capped heads to feet in heelless leather slippers, offer mint tea mojitos and caramel-fig martinis to attendees when they enter the cocktail reception. Several people gasp as they scan the room, and I hear a woman comment that it feels as though she's been whisked away on a flying carpet.

I spot my parents near the stage set up in front of the windows framed by beautiful Chihuly glass. My father looks regal in a tuxedo and my mother sparkles in a beaded couture gown, exuding confidence and feminine sophistication with impeccable posture. Her red hair, identical in color to mine, is styled in an elegant French twist, and diamonds are dripping off her neck.

When my mother notices me, her megawatt smile disappears into a thin line and her eyes narrow, displeasure evident in her features. It's an expression I'm all too familiar with given that I'm always on the receiving end of it, though she's typically more conscientious than to show it in public for fear someone may see past her perfectly constructed persona. Knowing it'll only make her more upset if I delay, I pull my shoulders back and go greet them. My mother embraces me in a hug, her nails digging into my shoulders.

"Margaret, sweetheart, you decided on a black dress. How lovely," she says. To a bystander, her tone sounds smooth and inflectionless, as though she's doling out a compliment rather than thinly veiled criticism.

My mother thinks black is too harsh for redheads and our fair skin. She prefers midnight blue or emerald green. *To accent the gray in your eyes*, she reminds me often. But tonight? Tonight is *my* time to shine, so I'll wear whatever I want, even if I'll be admonished for it later when we're behind closed doors.

"Thank you," I say with a grin so believable it could pass as an authentic Birkin handbag in Chinatown.

She tucks a loose strand of hair into my updo. "That's better. I wouldn't want you mistaken for a slob." She raises an eyebrow, daring me to respond. When I don't, she laughs, but there's an edge to it. "Your father and I were just talking with the Westways. You remember their daughter Harper? I think she was three years behind you in school. She got engaged last night. Yale educated, investment banker, comes from a long line of politicians. The wedding will be next summer at his family's estate in East Hampton."

It's her subtle way of reminding me that I've embarrassed her, marred her pristine reputation, for wasting years of my life on an inappropriate man who, despite his sterling upbringing and pedigree, abandoned his family legacy of medicine to pursue such a tasteless ambition as songwriting. No amount of success—monetary, awards, or otherwise—could change my mother's impression of Nick. To her, he'd always be an indiscretion. That he then chose a *waitress* over me, thus subjecting our family to a fresh round of gossip and scrutiny, has only fueled her anger.

If only my mother could understand that I never expected Nick to be a lesson I had to learn, or that I would be the one left standing on the sidelines.

"Do let me know if they need an event coordinator," I say, refusing to let her elicit a reaction from me, then turn toward my father and peck him on the cheek, careful not to leave a lipstick mark. "Daddy."

"Hello, honey." He brushes a kiss against my forehead in return. "The food so far has been delightful. Particularly these tasty little things," he says, snatching a bacon-wrapped date off a passing tray.

"Don't be ridiculous, Roger," my mother chides.

He pops the date into his mouth, blithely ignoring her —something he excels at. There's a reason he's one of the best family law and divorce attorneys in Dallas—he spends the majority of his time at the office and away from home in order to avoid my mother. I've often wondered why they're still married, or how they ever got engaged in the first place. If their current relationship is any indication, I imagine the whole thing was more of a business transaction my mother probably suggested—"It's the next logical step in our courting," she'd have said— than an over-the-top romantic gesture. Perhaps the reason my father stays with her is because he's witnessed firsthand how vindictive and cruel people can be when it comes to dividing assets.

"I'll have a box of dates delivered to your office," I whisper to him with a conspiratorial wink. "I'll even include some fig and pear pastilla for dessert." He smiles and pats my shoulder.

"Margaret, your father and I were discussing tonight's theme—Arabian Nights. Interesting choice," my mother says. Her voice is breezy, but the underlying reprimand is obvious.

"Moroccan," I correct.

"What's that, sweetheart?"

"The theme is centered around Morocco," I say, the fragrant aroma of turmeric and cinnamon heavy in the air.

My mother waves me off, the diamond tennis bracelet on her wrist glinting in the light. "Same thing."

"Arabia is in the Middle East. Morocco is in Africa. Different continents," I say.

"Either way, we wondered if you'd considered its appropriateness for a hospital gala. Isn't that right, Roger?" she says to my father. He's staring at a group of people admiring their newly applied henna tattoos, not even pretending to listen.

I don't bother to tell my mother that I selected the theme to separate the benefit from every other bland black-tie fundraising event so I could give people a night they'd remember. Once she's cast judgment, any attempt at explaining is as futile as waiting for a Louis Vuitton sale.

"Roger," my mother says again, touching his arm. "Explain to your daughter the importance of fulfilling client expectations."

My father glances at her, then over at me, and shrugs. "In my experience, it is important to consider all sides of an issue before moving forward," he says noncommittally, finishing off his scotch. After a lifetime of conversations with my mother, he's built an entire arsenal of platitudes. It's unfair how he gets stuck in the middle of us, how he often has to act as Switzerland in the battle between my mother and me. "When is dinner served? The small bites are great, but not nearly enough to hold me over."

"Soon," I say. "I hope you're ready for an authentic feast."

My mother opens her mouth with no doubt another jab, but I cut her off. "Speaking of which, I should go check on the meal. Please excuse me," I say, striding away at a speed just shy of fleeing. *Where did I put that flute of champagne?* A server balancing a tray of mint tea mojitos brushes past me. I swipe a glass and take a few sips. The alcohol burns my throat, the hint of lime tart on my tongue.

While attendees mingle and nibble on lamb skewers and beef phyllo cigars, I ensure everything is still on schedule and running smoothly. So far no issues, apart from my mother's condescending voice echoing in my head. The invite list is completely crossed off. It's go time.

Not surprisingly, my assistant has vanished. I try reaching her through the headset, but all I get is silence. I find her in the sculpture garden smoking a hookah with a group of her friends from the country club whose parents paid for their tickets.

My expression must reflect my annoyance, because when she sees me, she stands so fast her knees bump the center table, nearly causing the hookah pipe to topple over.

"The last guests have arrived," I say, sharp enough to bite.

She mumbles a *sorry* and quickly shoves her heels back on.

"I don't want your apology. Just do your job. I need you with catering to make sure the food service is expedited properly. Can you please handle that?"

"Yes . . . I mean, no, I mean—I'll take care of it."

"Good." As I turn away, I hear her mutter what sounds like *bitch* and *slave driver*. The rest of the group snickers. *Tomorrow you can fire her.*

I paste a smile on my face before returning to the atrium and motion the mistress of ceremonies, the Medical Center Foundation director, to start. She nods, adjusts the microphone on the podium, and calls for attention.

"Ladies and gentlemen, it is with great pleasure that I welcome you to 'A Faraway Land,' Baylor Medical's annual gala, benefiting programs and services for the hospital. I'd like to express my sincere appreciation for your support and generosity, which help ensure our patients and their families have access to outstanding care and facilities. Thank you for being a part of this special event. Please enjoy your evening of enchantment."

The audience applauds as cameras flash. The woman from Christie's leading the live auction steps behind the podium and begins introducing the first item. People sink into plush velvet banquettes, cocktails in their diamond-adorned hands, ready to bid. As the prizes—the VIP luxury suite season tickets for the Dallas Cowboys; a long weekend of golf at the exclusive Shadow Creek in Las Vegas; a ten-day yacht cruise in the Caribbean—go quickly and expensively, I breathe easier. The paddle-lifting concludes as the final item, a magical three-week getaway to Morocco, sells for the price of a Lamborghini. My heart swells with pride. Between the auction and the donations, the gala raised more than two million dollars—nearly double last year's amount.

Staffers escort the guests to the Chilton Galleries for an

authentic Moroccan feast served family style, save for dining on the floor and eating with their hands. Little bowls of olives, hummus, smoked eggplant, and harissa are scattered around the table to accompany flatbread. Red wine is poured into colorful tumblers, while platters arranged with roasted vegetables in flavorful marinades are passed around. I watch as faces transform with delight at the first bite of carrot and chickpea salad, and grin. Keeping the menu consistent with the theme was a risk, but it seems to have paid off. Soon the museum is filled with sounds of people sharing good food and conversation.

As the second course is served, a waiter taps my shoulder. "Excuse me, miss," he says, shifting on his feet. "There's a problem at table fifteen."

Great.

I follow him into an adjacent gallery, where Mr. Dugan —Dallas's most successful car dealership owner—has wedged himself between two women, one on the verge of throwing a clay pot of basmati rice, the other gripping a fork, armed for combat. My earlier excitement fizzles. *Shit.* How did I put his wife of thirty years in the same vicinity as his thirty-year-old mistress? The tension in the room is thick, everyone transfixed by the scene.

"Let's move this outside," I say, approaching with caution. The women don't hear me, each focused solely on the other.

"He bid on the trip for me, you saggy old hag. Do you really think he'd spend ten days in the Caribbean staring at *you* in a bikini?" the mistress hisses at Mrs. Dugan, slashing the fork in the air. Mr. Dugan grabs her wrists and pins them against him.

Mrs. Dugan's mouth opens and closes like a fish, but no words come out. She looks at her husband, but he won't meet her gaze.

"Ladies, please. This is neither the time nor the place." I keep my voice calm but don't dare intervene for fear of getting stabbed.

The mistress flings out a graphic comment about her favorite sexual position with Mr. Dugan, and the cord snaps. Mrs. Dugan hurls the clay pot at the mistress's chest, nearly knocking her off her feet. The pot crashes to the ground and shatters. Basmati rice flies everywhere. Then, as if she were doing nothing more than brushing away a speck of lint, Mrs. Dugan adjusts the shawl on her shoulders and strolls away.

The air feels thin in the sudden silence. The mistress clutches her chest, rage burning hot in her eyes. Mr. Dugan stands frozen like an ice sculpture. A staffer rushes around me to wipe up the mess. Someone giggles and hiccups, and the fog around Mr. Dugan evaporates. He glares at me with a coldness that causes a prickle to run down my spine, then whispers to his mistress and guides her to the exit with his back straight and head held high, as if determined to ignore the awkward hush around him and the people gawking.

I don't manage to be so collected—my heart is lodged in my throat and my stomach is tangled into knots—especially under the weight of my mother's deprecating stare. I know she'll say this entire scene is my fault, that I'm in charge so it's my responsibility to have my finger on the pulse of our social circle's ever-evolving spats.

Desperate to get the evening back on track, I instruct the waiters to immediately start serving the main course. Still, even as the guests enjoy steaming tagines of lamb chops with pomegranate molasses, roasted chicken with preserved lemons and olives, and couscous with raisins, almonds, and saffron, they continue to discuss and dissect what transpired.

No doubt it'll make the rounds in the next few days, ensuring this event will be the talk of the town, though not in the way I'd hoped. Still, if this is the worst thing to happen tonight, I'll consider it a success. After all, when money, alcohol, and society mix, something is bound to go wrong. And the only thing worse than a scandalous event is one no one talks about.

The lights dim and the music rises, signaling it's time for the real party to begin. After the last person leaves the galleries in search of the hookah tents and dance floor and I'm alone with only the servers and cleaning crew, my heart returns to my chest and the knots in my stomach loosen. The hard part is over. I survived.

I allow myself one more moment of solitude before I rejoin the guests back in the main atrium. My mother intercepts me as I enter, pulling me off to the side by the fleshy part of my arm. Pain shoots into my fingers and tears sting my eyes. I remember during my sixth-grade cotillion dance when I removed my white gloves because my hands broke out in a rash, my mother dragged me out of the ballroom away from the other attendees, squeezing the skin so hard the bruise took weeks to fade, and scolded me until my eyes were bloodshot and snot ran down my nose. Since then I've learned it's better to swallow the pain and the scolding.

"You sat Mrs. Dugan at the same table as her husband's mistress?" she hisses. "How could you be so incompetent? These are our family's friends and your father's colleagues!"

I don't respond. Answering will only prolong the torture.

A belly dancer takes position in the center of the floor, and a hush falls over the room. The music changes, and the dancer's hips begin to sway. My mother *tsk*s in disapproval even as guests create a large circle around her, clapping in rhythm with her movements.

"The whole gala has been a disaster. First the theme. Then your inability to handle something as *basic* as a seating chart. Now this?" she continues, gesturing to the performance. "And the menu! Did you even consider people's food sensitivities? The foundation committee trusted you to plan an elegant affair, but all you've managed to do is embarrass yourself and this family." She glances over her shoulder, scanning for nosy eavesdroppers. "You've been slow to understand this, so let me spell it out for you, Margaret. You're only as meaningful and valuable as others perceive you to be. And tonight no one envies me my daughter. An experience I expect not to repeat in the future—" She breaks off, ordering me through clenched teeth to smile as the newly appointed Junior League president approaches us. I rub the tender spot on my arm where I know a bruise is already blossoming.

The League president greets my mother and faces me, kissing my cheeks. The scent of caramel-fig martinis is heavy on her breath. "Margaret, you outdid yourself! What a memorable event. Truly spectacular."

"Thank you," I say.

"Nancy, you and Roger must be so proud," she says to my mother. "This night is going to be all anyone talks about."

My mother loops an arm around mine, the megawatt smile ever present, and pinches the soft skin above my elbow. I bite my tongue to prevent myself from wincing. "Of course. We're proud of everything Margaret does."

A coldness rushes through me, as if I've been doused with ice water. At thirty-two and a professional businesswoman, I shouldn't feel such crushing disappointment at her words. After all, my mother hasn't been proud of me since I was a little girl, before I could form my own opinions and dreams. Still, I'd hoped this time would be different, that she would recognize how important this night is to me, how hard I've worked even if it isn't the event she would've planned. How idealistic and foolish of me to assume I could ever be good enough.

The League president starts to speak as my earpiece crackles. "Margaret, we've got a man out here trying to reach one of the guests inside. He's insisting on entering the gala, but he's not on the list. Can you come talk to him?"

I sigh. It never ends. Why security can't turn away some party crasher is beyond me. I click on the mouthpiece. "I'll be right there." Wiggling out of my mother's grip, I walk away without a good-bye or second glance. Later she'll reprimand me for my rude behavior, but I don't care. Not tonight, anyway.

Weaving through the crowd, I step outside and come face-to-face with Nick.

2

"There are oil splatters on your shirt."

After ten months of no communication, this is the first thing I say to him? *Honestly, Margaret.*

His hair is shorter, his eyes are a darker shade of blue than I remember, and there seems to be a glow around him. My memory hasn't done him justice.

"Hello, Margaret," Nick says with a pleasant smile, as if I'm nothing more than an acquaintance. "I'm sorry they had to pull you away like this. From what I can glimpse, the gala looks like a huge success. Congratulations."

I'm sure his words are meant as a compliment or some kind of olive branch, but a fresh wave of anger and bitterness washes over me—for being cheated out of a love I earned, for the future Lillie took from me, for how things can never return to what's supposed to be. The feelings weld on to my armor, now an indestructible layer, so nothing can touch me.

"What are you doing here, Nick, since it's obvious you're not dressed for the occasion?" I ask, referring to his casual jeans and plaid button-down.

He opens his mouth to answer, but the head of security approaches us and cuts him off. "Excuse me, Ms. Stokes, this is the man—"

"Thanks. I've got it handled," I say, then turn to the other tuxedoed guards and valets milling around. "Can we have some privacy please?"

I wait for them to scurry away and refocus my attention on Nick. "Did Lillie bail on you and now you're expecting me to salvage the pieces *again*? Is that why you're here?"

"Margaret, stop," he says, shaking his head, as if I'm the one who's in the wrong, which only fuels my anger. After I devoted myself to his recovery, his happiness, the least he can do is pretend he ever needed me in the first place.

"So how are things between you two?" I'm baiting him, watching for a spark of irritation to cross his face, but his expression remains impassive.

"Come on. Don't act like this." He stares at me with pity in his eyes, and I stare back, unflinching. I refuse to show him that he holds any power over me.

"Like what? I'm simply asking about your life, which includes Lillie."

"I'm not discussing her with you," he says in a tired voice.

"How typical," I say. Not once, even after four years of friendship and five months of dating, did Nick ever confide in me any personal details about his former life with Lillie, the reasons she ran off to Chicago without him, or what happened between them to ruin him so completely. "Yet when it came to me, you had no problem using my friendship and support for your benefit."

My stomach twists as I remember dragging Nick, drunk with the bourbon bottle on his lap, off the kitchen floor and into the shower, clothes and all; cleaning his shredded knuckles after his fight with Wes, his best friend of twenty years, because inflicting pain on someone else was easier than confronting his demons; acting as an anchor when his mother disowned him for abandoning medicine to pursue his dream of songwriting; believing if I *saved* him, I'd earn his love. Except I did save him and look how well that worked out.

Nick rakes a hand through his hair and exhales a deep breath. "Margaret, I know I hurt you, and I'm sorry for that. Truly. But can we please not do this?"

I snort. *Sorry*. The most useless word in the world, void of all honesty, as insincere as falling in love.

"You didn't hurt me, Nick," I say, as I silently repeat the mantra that it's be hurt or be hardened. "Though you did show me your real character when you didn't have the decency to break things off between us before you slept with her—"

"Lillie and I didn't sleep together before you and I talked. I wouldn't do something like that to you, Margaret."

"So you claim, though you can understand how I have trouble believing you."

He nods, granting me that point. I want him to say more, convince me that I wasn't a placeholder for Lillie, but he remains quiet.

Finally, I clear my throat and say, "What do you want, Nick? I need to return to my duties inside."

"I've been trying to reach my father on his cell, but he's not answering," he says. "Can you tell him I'm here? I'm headed out of town and need to drop something off with him before I leave."

I sigh, long and drawn out, as if this is a huge imposition, and click on my headset. It takes three tries before I reach my assistant to instruct her to retrieve Dr. Preston and bring him out front—I suspect she was in the hookah lounge again by the snippets of conversations and Moroccan music that crackled through my earpiece. I hope she enjoyed the experience, since she's about to be unemployed.

"Your father should be outside shortly," I say to Nick.

"Thank you," he says, shoving his hands into his pockets.

The sounds of Dallas traffic fill the awkward silence between us. I should walk back into the gala, forget Nick the way he's forgotten me, but my feet won't move. There's something unfair about still wanting someone who once belonged to you—or at least who you *thought* belonged to you. And standing in front of Nick, it's all too easy to remember everything that's been taken from me, to feel the reminder that, in his eyes, I just wasn't what he wanted.

I start to break the silence before it stretches on too long when the museum doors burst open and Paulette Bunny and Sullivan Grace Hasell spill onto the red carpet. Both women are friends of my mother and reside over me on several Junior League planning committees. They're normally the epitome of poise and grace in their St. John knit suits and sheath dresses, but right now they're behaving like two drunken sorority girls stumbling out of a frat house, holding on to each other and talking in overloud voices as they stagger toward the valets lined at the curb. If I could remember how, I'd laugh, witnessing them in this state.

Paulette Bunny doesn't seem to notice us—she's too busy slurring her request for someone to fetch their limo driver—but Sullivan Grace spots us immediately. "Margaret, dear, the fundraiser was fabulous," she says, her

South Carolina accent thicker than usual. "The most fun I've had in ages."

If only my mother could offer such praise.

Sullivan Grace attempts to kiss my cheeks but ends up landing on the corners of my mouth. Her hands are decorated with henna tattoos and the smell of incense surrounds her. She turns to Nick, swaying a bit, and embraces him in a hug, something I've never seen her do with him.

"Hello, Ms. Hasell," Nick says, grinning, clearly amused at her level of intoxication.

"Sweetheart, how many times do I have to tell you to call me by my first name? I'm practically your mother-in-law," she says. "Jackson will be thrilled to hear we bumped into each other." She's referring to Jack Turner, her "gentleman friend" who happens to be Lillie's father. He owns Turner's Greasy Spoons, a diner across town, which for some reason people think is delicious, though Lillie's the one managing it now.

"He didn't join you this evening?" Nick asks.

Sullivan Grace laughs. "Don't be foolish. You know Jackson wouldn't attend one of these events if it were free and the entire Texas Rangers roster was invited. But enough about that," she continues. "Shouldn't you be on your way to the airport? Paris in late summertime. Absolutely spectacular! I can't imagine a more romantic honeymoon."

At first I'm certain I misheard her, but then I glance at Nick's ring finger. There, shining under the jewel-toned lights illuminating the entrance, is a simple platinum band. Icy talons grip my chest. I finally understand why he appears so content and utterly unaffected by my presence. I look at Nick, and once again his eyes are full of pity and a tenderness that makes me want to throttle him.

The resentment of the past several months bubbles up inside me and I blurt out, "You married her," interrupting Sullivan Grace, who's been droning on about the Louvre and the view from the Eiffel Tower. My voice sounds strange, mechanical, like the rotor spinning in my Rolex watch.

Sullivan Grace stands there with her mouth hanging open, as if my history with Nick has escaped her memory, while Nick says softly but with conviction, "I did."

In that moment I hate him.

Before Nick can say anything more, I abruptly turn around and rush back into the gala. It's only as I'm stepping inside the atrium that I realize a small part of me has been clinging to one last ounce of hope that he'd change his mind, recognize that we could be something special. I guess that's the difference between logically knowing something and deep down believing it, because while I *know* Nick's fully, irrecoverably committed to Lillie, in my heart of hearts, I still can't *believe* he picked her over me.

I NEED A CHANGE.

That's the only thought I have the next morning as I enter the restaurant Villa-O. A blast of air-conditioning envelops me. Its cerulean blue walls and Mediterranean nautical decor remind me of the semester I studied abroad in Greece before my junior year at Southern Methodist University. The place is buzzing with the typical brunch crowd of Dallas urbanites—well-groomed men who hide their hangovers behind aviators and bottomless Bloody Marys and former sorority girls turned stay-at-home wives with perfect volumized hair and decked out in designer clothes or overpriced spandex disguised as luxury sportswear that's never absorbed an ounce of perspiration.

All around me people play on their smartphones, texting, posting on social media sites, snapping pictures of themselves and their food. I imagine half of these people don't even remember what it's like to have real-life relationships anymore.

Yet here I am, right alongside them, week in and week out. Perhaps this is the first habit I'll change.

Or maybe I need a break from the Dallas social scene altogether, some room to breathe, where my entire life isn't being examined and dissected under a microscope.

Winding my way through the dining room, I spot the girls—Piper, Samma, and Faye—laughing and chatting on the patio. Bellinis, antipasti plates, and a basket of focaccia are scattered around the table. Of course they wouldn't wait for me to arrive to start the festivities.

I walk outside through the open floor-to-ceiling windows, the humidity sticking to my body like a second skin.

When the girls notice me, they abruptly stop talking and plaster on smiles loaded with more fake sugar than the artificial sweeteners they dumped into their coffees. I tense, knowing what's coming. Rumors fly faster than Highland Park real estate among our social scene, so I shouldn't be surprised they know about my encounter with Nick last night, but right now that's the last thing I want to talk about.

Forcing a smile of my own, I greet each of them with a kiss on the cheek. "Sorry I'm late," I say, draping my purse on the back of a chair and sitting. "I had to deal with a situation at the office."

"Taking out the trash again?" Piper asks, popping an olive into her mouth. She's constantly eating despite not weighing more than a hundred pounds. Piper claims she stays so thin because she works out with a trainer, but everyone knows she uses laxatives to maintain her figure. She also happens to be one of the worst offenders of wearing lululemon apparel as everyday attire.

"I swear you shuffle through assistants as often as I shuffle through shoes," Faye says. Her lips are puffy and slightly bruised—I'm betting she's three days post injections. She has the looks of a supermodel that rivals the greatest '90s divas, but by fashion standards she's last year's sloppy seconds.

A waitress extends a menu to me. Waving it away, I order a glass of prosecco and my usual egg-white omelet. "This one was worse than the others," I say to the girls. "I had to do her job for her. It was like dealing with a toddler."

"I think you're incapable of relinquishing control," Samma says. She flips her hair, mainly comprised of extensions dyed to match her natural deep brown color, over her shoulder. Her five-carat diamond solitaire sparkles in the sun. She's been married less than a year and has already upgraded the stone twice and taken numerous solo trips to the spa to deal with "stress." If I were married to her husband, Alan, with his comb-over, potbelly, and onion-smelling breath, I'd self-medicate with retail therapy and beauty treatments, too.

"Don't forget asking for help," Faye adds.

"And apologizing," Piper mumbles around a mouthful of bruschetta.

"You're confusing capability with willingness," I say. "I'm quite able to do those things. I just don't believe in them."

Before they can argue, the waitress delivers their entrées and my much-needed glass of prosecco. I take a sip, the taste bright, crisp, and lively with a subtle amount of sweetness. While this sparkling wine is great for Dallas patio weather, my favorite way to enjoy it is straight from the source at a vineyard nestled in the verdant rolling hills of northeastern Italy.

As they eat, Piper gushes about attending New York Fashion Week this fall, Samma rants about the general contractor in charge of renovating her Florida beach house, and Faye complains about the service department at the Mercedes-Benz dealership. None of the girls mentions the gala or offers me her congratulations, even though they were there. Not that this is unexpected. Instead of celebrating the good things that happen in our lives, we treat them like dirty secrets and pretend they don't exist. It's been this way since we met in sixth grade.

The waitress drops off my dish. I'm midbite when Samma fires off a question that catches me so off guard I nearly choke on a mouthful of omelet. "So, Margaret, how are you *really* feeling about Nick marrying Lillie?"

Piper and Faye exchange a conspiratorial look, and I wonder how many conversations they've had about this behind my back, how many jokes they've made at my expense.

"I didn't realize you all were aware of it." It's strange how my voice sounds neutral and steady when it feels as if a fist has punched my chest.

"Oh, honey, of course we knew about the wedding," Samma says with a laugh that's as genuine as a cubic zirconia. "It happened *months* ago. As I understand it, Nick and Lillie have been waiting until after the Food Network filmed a special about the diner to take their honeymoon."

Months ago?

"We would've mentioned it, but we didn't want to spoil

the fun of you discovering it for yourself." Faye smiles, but it's anything but kind.

"See, your reaction is priceless. You look like a kid who just found out Santa Claus isn't real. I can only imagine what it looked like last night after you ran into Nick," Piper says, pointing at my face, which clearly betrays the unaffected air I'm trying hard to project. She nonchalantly steals a piece of cantaloupe wrapped in prosciutto off my plate, as if we've casually been discussing if ankle boots are a fading trend or a classic style.

My stomach clenches so tight I worry my breakfast may ride up my throat. I know what I'm feeling is shock, but I'm not sure if it's *Surprise, you've been punked,* or *Surprise, these women are even more vindictive than you suspected.*

I gulp down the remainder of the prosecco and toss my napkin onto the table. "I'm glad this situation amuses you all so much." My tone is dry, stripped of all color, despite the anger bubbling up in me.

"Sweetie, we know it hurts that Nick married a waitress, but for God's sake you need to put this whole mess behind you," Samma says, patting my hand. "Though it is unfortunate you ran into Nick the way you did." Her expression is smug, and the undercurrent of superiority in her words is unmistakable. She's enjoying watching me fall.

Nick may come from the same background as us, but he's never cared about wealth and the privileges it afforded. There's always been something different about him—something deeper and utterly unattainable in its rawness—that puts him in a separate category. It's these differences that make people like Samma, Piper, and Faye seethe with jealousy. While they're stuck in predictable, cookie-cutter marriages that were entered into for status, ego, stability, Nick is living an adventure, something I'd once been a part of, if only for a little while.

"Besides, it's obvious Lillie's trash and Nick enjoys slumming it," Faye says. "You shouldn't want to associate with someone like him even though I know you can't help yourself."

I glance around the table at these women who have clearly never been my friends, merely appropriate social contacts my mother approves of, and the anger finally bursts out of me.

I'm done. With *all* of it.

"Oh, you want to talk about what we can't help doing?" My voice is loud and unrecognizable, filled with something feral. "Let's start with you, Faye, and your pathetic Botox addiction. I know you think you're preserving your youth for inevitable husband number *three*, but the only thing you seem to be preserving is your total inability to fake anything. So how do you fake your orgasms?" I focus my attention on Samma sitting beside me. "And, *sweetie*, Nick may have married a *waitress*, but are you really one to throw stones when you're sleeping with the lawn guy? You should probably wash your clothes before Alan notices the grass stains."

Pushing up from the table, I gather my purse and begin to walk away when Piper calls behind me, "What about your portion of the check?"

I stop and turn to face her. "Use your allowance. That should more than cover it, don't you think?" Then I exit the restaurant and brush past the valet, yanking open the door to his stand and retrieving my keys without asking permission.

I don't know where I'm going, but I can't wait another second to be gone.

3

Five hours later, I arrive in Wilhelmsburg just before dusk. After brunch, I returned to my condo in Uptown Dallas, pawned off all my work obligations to other firms without a second thought, and packed my bags. I was driving to my grandmother's bed-and-breakfast in the middle of nowhere before most people had indulged in an afternoon nap.

As I enter the central strip of town, the satellite radio finally acquires a signal—it's been nothing but static for the last hundred miles—and the voices of the Randy Hollis Band fill the car, blindsiding me so I nearly ram into a carriage ride. My throat tightens with every verse, every note. Yet I can't shut it off.

Memories surge up: the band playing at a dive bar to a small but captivated audience, me singing along in the front row; the guys—Matt, Karl, Jason, and Tim—writing music and lyrics for their debut album *Resolution* with Nick, the genius behind the band's most popular songs that put them all on the map; the group of them sitting around a campfire, strumming a lazy melody on guitars while I listened, fireworks exploding over Lake Travis on the Fourth of July. Friendships I lost when they became country music superstars and left me behind, when they chose Nick over me.

I force the memories away and bury them deep. The past doesn't matter anymore.

I drive down bustling Main Street—the center of historic downtown that offers shopping, restaurants, art galleries, and wine-tasting rooms—and fight my way through evening traffic. It's the most direct route in and out of Wilhelmsburg, a design I imagine the town council vigorously protects because it forces the throngs of tourists to pass by the locally owned businesses. The air outside is heavy with the smell of impending rain and sweet German pretzels baking at the Ausländer, the local pastry shop.

It's impossible to picture my mother growing up here—a typical small town in Texas Hill Country with nothing but gossip to feed it. Where everyone attends the same church on Sunday and privacy is a foreign concept and teenagers cause trouble because what the hell else is there to do besides work in the vineyards or on a farm? Where the locals never venture beyond the county line but think they know the world.

Where you can escape and not be found.

But perhaps back then she wasn't so tightly controlled the way she is now. Or maybe she never felt like she fit in here and that's why she left at the first opportunity.

I'm watching a woman wipe chocolate ice cream off a kid's face when the light turns red. I slam on the brakes, jerking my neck. Ugh, I could use a glass of Silver Oak Cabernet.

Thankfully, I stumble upon The Tangled Vine, which seems to be a local hangout in a limestone cottage a block off Main Street, and park my Audi coupe. As I'm walking to the entrance, one of my black patent Louboutins gets stuck in the many cracks marring the cobblestone path.

"You've *got* to be kidding me," I mutter, along with a string of expletives. Slipping out of the shoe, I kneel and work on dislodging it. By the time I manage to yank the heel free, I'm sweating through my silk blouse, little pebbles are indented into my skin, and the signature red sole has been scuffed beyond repair. Eight-hundred-dollar pumps ruined. Screw the glass of wine, I'll take the whole bottle.

Something cold and wet hits my face. The sky is streaked in shades of darkening gray and purple as the storm blows in. A gust of wind whips the trees. Another drop strikes my cheek, and two more land on my arm. Then, all at once, lightning cracks, thunder rumbles, and the swollen clouds burst.

I run for the covered porch as rain hammers down and shove the stubborn wood door open with my hip. The crowd quiets as I step into the warm, dimly lit room filled with plush couches, shelves stacked with wine bottles, and oak barrels serving as tables. Ignoring the stares, I head for the copper-clad bar flanking the side wall. I shake away the water dripping off me and settle on a stool.

"Excuse me," I call to the bartender. He glances my way but makes no move to come over, too busy chatting with some guys about grape yields and this year's harvest. I try again to get his attention, but this time he doesn't even acknowledge me. Irritation coils around me like a snake ready to attack.

I walk over to the group and wedge myself between them, ending the conversation. Two guys raise their hands as they retreat a few paces, while another stands firm. A challenge gleams in his eyes, which heightens my aggravation, though I can't deny he's sexy in a dangerous way that invites trouble and advertises he's up for anything—all things I'm not interested in. I've given up men.

"A bottle of Silver Oak Cabernet," I tell the bartender—Possum, according to the tag clipped to his black button-up shirt. *What kind of name is Possum?*

He cocks his head, giving me a good look at his big ears, freckled nose, and mop of shaggy curls dyed bright orange. He squints, as though I'm speaking in tongues. "We only stock varietals from the area."

"Figures," I say, my tone clipped, because the universe hasn't had enough fun with me yet. "I suppose you serve your wine in a Solo cup as well. I'll just take a water when you can squeeze in a moment."

I stride back to my seat and power on my cell. The message icon pops up in the corner. I steel myself, confident it's my mother. Sure enough her voice pierces my ear. I wince.

"How could you be so irresponsible, Margaret?" she says by way of preamble. "Where are you? Enough of this nonsense. Stop acting like a child." I quit listening, deleting the message before I switch my phone back off and toss it into my purse. I massage my temples, but the throbbing doesn't let up. At least Possum is capable of following directions, because a glass of water appears, and I drain it in seconds. Rain taps against the windows, and I focus on its methodic rhythm, which has the welcome effect of dulling my headache.

Someone slides in next to me—Mr. Roaming Eyes from the other end of the bar. *Fantastic.* He wears an easy smile and a smudged T-shirt with holes in the sleeves. He places something resembling red wine in front of me.

"It's called No Regrets, a Malbec and Petit Verdot blend," he says.

The cracks in his hands are stained reddish purple, and

there's dirt underneath his fingernails. His skin has the kind of tan possible only from a lifetime of outdoor work.

Wrinkling my nose, I push the glass toward him. "No thanks. I don't enjoy the taste of longhorn manure."

His face drops, all humor gone. "I see you've still got that silver spoon stuck up your ass," he says with an edge that instantly recalls my mother, who proudly displays her condescension like an heirloom china set.

"Excuse me?" I say as I take in his strong, stubbled jaw and defined cheekbones, broad shoulders, and honey blond hair that looks as if he's been running a hand through it. "Do I know you?"

"Hardly." He assesses me, as though searching for something. "Maybe if you *tried* the wine before insulting it, you'd discover how much you like it." His accent has the clipped rhythm of central Texas—a mixture of a slow, musical drawl and a flat, nasally twang.

I flip my hair over my shoulder. "Doubtful."

"So you're close-minded and a snob."

"Standards aren't the same as snobbery. You'd know this if you had any. Perhaps you should refine your palate," I say, crossing my legs, my pencil skirt riding up. His gaze locks on my exposed skin. Typical.

Over his shoulder I see Possum and his friends observing our exchange like we're zoo animals. One of the guys—the bulky one with short, dark hair, a cherub face, and a cartoon moose tattoo on his forearm—notices I've caught him gawking and waves. *Cute.* I don't reciprocate.

"My palate's just fine. Go ahead. Take one sip and tell me it's not good." Mr. Roaming Eyes sets the wine in front of me again. His eyes dance with mischief, even as his expression remains neutral. "Prove me wrong. Hell, prove *Wine Spectator* wrong," he says, referring to the magazine that's the authority on the wine industry.

Irritation sparks in my chest, the challenge in his words coaxing it to the surface. *What a pain in the ass.*

"Fine." I take a drink without flourish. Immediately flavors of black cherry, chocolate, and espresso flood my mouth, followed by a smooth tobacco finish. Hints of violet linger on my tongue. *Shit, that's delicious.*

The smug grin on his face makes me want to slap it off, then tug him toward me and kiss those full lips. *Wait, what?* Pulling my shoulders back, I clear my throat and say with an air of boredom, "It's passable, which isn't saying much, since I expected grape-flavored vinegar."

He laughs, and it stirs something inside me. He smells like spice and fresh-turned soil and a sweetness I recognize but can't pinpoint.

"Fair enough," he says, then signals to the bartender. "Hey, Possum, bring over the bottle and some more water." He rakes a hand through his hair and turns to face me, his arm brushing mine. Up close, I realize how striking his features are—the slope of his nose, his full lips, his hazel eyes flecked with green and gold staring intently at me. My skin prickles as something electric grows between us, dangerous and uninvited. Then Possum refills my water, sloshing an ice cube on my wrist, and the thread breaks. Shaking my head, I draw away from him.

Mr. Roaming Eyes gestures to the bottle. "For you, in case you're interested in any more vinegar." His voice is as relaxed as a ratty sweatshirt, but it's obvious he's taunting me by the cocky smile still on his face. He flicks the water glass and says, "This is to wash it down."

I open my mouth to retort, but he winks and walks away before I can fire the parting shot.

Mr. Roaming Eyes grabs a bottle of wine for himself and joins his friends in an adjacent room with a pool table in the center. Pouring a glass, he swirls the ruby-colored liquid, sniffs, and sips, watching a game already in progress. A girl dressed like the lead in a country music video—cutoff jean shorts, tight plaid shirt tied to show off her midriff, and cowboy boots—yells something to him about fixing her mess and throws him the cue stick. He captures it in midair and laughs. Once again I'm struck by the sound of it—deep and rough, yet threaded with warmth—and the conviction that I know it somehow. He stalks around the table and surveys the situation, studying the angles. After another drink of wine, he bends over and shoots, sinking the blue two ball into the right corner pocket. I can't help but stare at the way his jeans fit his body perfectly, as if they're old friends.

With his attention diverted, I sneak a sip of the Malbec and Petit Verdot blend, certain the previous one was a fluke. The taste is just as complex as before. Tipping the glass up to my nose, I inhale the aromas of red fruit and vanilla. No way this is made in the area. I inspect the label, which, along with NO REGRETS in block print, has an icon of a winking eye on it. I spin the bottle around and read the back.

We created this wine for all the insane people who rush headfirst into reckless decisions and crazy, blinding love. Enjoy it while disobeying society's expectations and common sense.

Childish and yet an apt description of my life this past year. It was produced by Camden Cellars, an estate winery from right here in Wilhelmsburg. *Damn.*

I'm in the middle of another sip when Mr. Roaming Eyes looks straight at me. I swallow quickly and grimace, refusing to give him the satisfaction. He points to the water and mimics guzzling it down. Bastard.

His gait is slow and easy as he walks around the table,

calculating the angles again. There's an unhurried way to his game, like he prefers to take his time and focus on the details, and I wonder if he's this way in all areas of his life. It's enough to make me curious what that sort of attention would feel like when focused on me. I suspect it'd be a great deal more intense and satisfying than the obligatory foreplay I'm accustomed to.

"Thirteen ball, left side pocket," I hear him call. He lines up and shoots. There's a loud smack as the cue ball sends the orange-striped ball spinning off the rail and into its destination with a thud. He pauses for more wine before leaning against the edge, bridging, and tapping the cue ball into the maroon seven ball, which glides effortlessly into the back corner pocket.

The group whistles and applauds. Moose Tattoo bumps fists with him, while Big Boobs McGee wraps her fingers around his bicep and whispers in his ear. He nods at whatever she says, but by the way his gaze drifts around the room, I sense he's not really listening. Perhaps they're involved, or maybe he's using her like Nick used me.

Enough. He's in the past, I remind myself, blotting out the memories, cutting a black line through each one.

I empty the wine glass and pour another, filling it until the dark burgundy liquid is just below the lip. This time I take a gulp, then another, not even bothering to savor it. The alcohol burns my throat. I keep drinking until my body tingles and my head feels as fuzzy as a cotton ball.

"Careful, or you may convince Ryan you like it."

I jump, almost spitting out the last of the wine. Possum stands across from me drying a decanter. There's a high-pitched squeak each time the towel rubs against the surface. Under the lights, his hair seems to glow, as if lit from within. Too bad he claimed the name Possum, since Orange Crush would be more suitable.

I take a sip of water. "What?"

"The wine." Possum jerks his chin toward Mr. Roaming Eyes—Ryan, I guess. The name doesn't register, but the feeling that I somehow know him doesn't dissipate. Ryan is hunched over the pool table, deep in concentration, the corners of his mouth turned down. I bet he's the sort of guy who craves competition but hates to lose. The sort of guy who demands a rematch until he emerges victorious because losing is for losers, as my mother likes to say—one of the only sentiments we agree on.

"It's tolerable," I say, hoping the slur in my voice doesn't betray my words.

Possum holds up the decanter, wipes off a mark, and adds it to a shelf with several others. "Right, that's why you polished off the bottle," he says, then strolls away without waiting for a reply.

If I'd wanted a passive-aggressive lecture, I'd have stayed in Dallas with my mother. I dig in my wallet and slap a fifty on the bar. The wine probably costs less than a fast-food hamburger, but it's the only cash I have and I need to get on the road to Grammy J's before she locks up for the night. Gathering my purse and keys, I head for the door, blaming my mangled stiletto for why I'm swaying and not the bottle of wine I've consumed.

"So much for grape-flavored vinegar."

With my hand on the knob, I spin to face Ryan. He's holding my empty bottle, that shit-eating grin ever present, and dammit, why hasn't it become any less sexy?

"When the only thing in this place are sorry excuses for wine, I'm not left with many options," I say, hoping he can't detect my lie.

He chuckles and says, "Come on, Stumbling Shortcake, I'll give you a lift." He steals the keys from my grasp and steps outside, leaving me with no choice but to follow.

4
***

The rain has turned into a mist that hangs in the air like a sheer curtain, the annoying kind that gets you wet but not to the point of needing an umbrella. I can feel the mosquitoes rising, ready to bite.

Ryan hits the remote lock button until my trunk pops open and grabs my Louis Vuitton luggage. "This way." Crossing the lawn, he walks to a rusted navy and gray Chevy Blazer manufactured in what had to be the eighties.

"Excuse me. What're you doing?" I ask, trailing behind him. My patent pumps squish in the grass, mud oozing up as my heels sink into the earth.

He tosses my bags into the back cluttered with random junk—an extra large funnel, buckets stacked eight deep, a half-zipped bag with bandanas poking out. As he slams down the hatch, a few peacock feathers escape and flutter to the ground. He jogs around to the passenger side and opens the door, empty wine bottle still in hand. "Hop in."

I frown and fold my arms over my chest, my purse tucked against my side. "I'm not getting in there. You could take me into the woods and hack me into pieces."

He shrugs, as if my actions make no difference to him, and settles into the driver's seat. I lean inside the door. The world tilts, and I lose my balance. My forehead bumps against the frame. *Crap, that hurt.*

"I need my keys," I say, massaging the tender spot. Ryan ignores me, tuning the radio until he finds a semi-clear station. "Hello? Can I have my keys please?"

He sighs like I'm an exasperating child who won't quit begging for an ice-cream cone. "Are you staying on Main Street?"

"No," I say, somehow managing to slur a two-letter word.

"Then have fun hitchhiking." He sticks the key into the ignition and starts the rust mobile, the engine turning over and over until it wails to life. "Wilhelmsburg doesn't have taxis and we're all out of drunk drivers. Unless you'd rather I chauffeur you around in your Audi?"

I give him a glare that screams, *Not a chance in hell.*

"Well, Stumbling Shortcake, it's either huff it on foot or accept the ride. What's it gonna be? The offer expires in five, four, three—"

"Fine," I say, throwing up my hands.

Hugging my purse, I climb in, careful to touch as little as possible. The SUV smells of coffee and gasoline, and dog hair and dirt cover the dashboard and ripped leather seats.

"How do you not have a disease?" I say, wiping my palms on my skirt, leaving a brown smudge on the fabric. Disgusting. I crack the window in an attempt to flush out the fumes, even though I know it's futile —my clothes will reek of exhaust and be coated in filth.

"I'm immune from long exposure. Hold this," he says, dropping the empty wine bottle on my lap. "Wouldn't want you to lose it." He puts the car in gear and pulls away from the curb.

We drive out of town in silence, the road empty and dark except for the pale glow of the headlights. The fine mist of rain coming in through the window seeps into my hair, causing the red wavy strands to curl. I peer out at the countryside as we pass, but all I see are shapes, the fields and rows of grapevines shrouded in blackness. The moon dodges in and out of clouds, and a few stars light up the inky sky. So different from nighttime in Dallas, with its skyscrapers outlined in neon lights and the constant *whoosh* of traffic on the highways. Where the stars aren't visible for miles, obscured by the pollution hovering over the city.

Ryan hums along to the radio, his thumbs tapping a rhythm against the steering wheel. The opening chords of Fleetwood Mac's "Rhiannon" filter through the speakers—one of Nick's favorite songs—and it's like a whiff of ammonia under my nose. It's amazing how something as simple as a song, something that once felt like a shared, intimate secret, now floods my mouth with the bitter taste of the knowledge that Nick never truly shared himself with me at all.

I shut off the music and continue staring at the dark, unchanging landscape. Ryan mutters under his breath and rakes a hand through his hair. I feel his gaze on me, goose bumps pricking up on my arms.

"What?" I ask, harsher than I intended. My buzz is fizzling like a wet sparkler. I need out of this car and to get someplace where I don't feel like a guest who's long outstayed her welcome.

"Just curious as to what Stevie Nicks did to offend you," he says.

"An illicit affair and a string of bad choices." I keep my

voice even, but I wonder if he can sense there's a story behind my words.

A small smile plays on his lips. "Messy can be fun."

"So you have the maturity of a three-year-old. Lovely."

"Ah, I get it. Stumbling Shortcake's had her heart broken," he says.

I cast an irritated look in his direction. "Hardly. If anything I put them back together. Not that my efforts are appreciated."

"So this is an issue of wounded pride."

"Yes, well, I'm sure you'd feel the same way if you'd painstakingly helped someone rebuild their life only to have him choose the woman who broke *his* heart," I say, swatting away a dog hair tumbleweed rolling on the dashboard.

The headlights sweep over a tall sign for Camden Cellars, the culprit responsible for my tipsiness. Ryan turns down a dirt path that seems to snake on forever. At first I think he's messing with me, but then I notice a smaller sign pointing to the Bluebonnet Inn. The winery must border the bed-and-breakfast.

The Blazer rocks over bumps and depressions, muddy water splattering everywhere. Trees envelop us on either side, and occasionally branches scrape along the doors with the ill-mannered sound of forks dragging across fine china. My purse and the wine bottle bounce around in my lap. I press my hand against the roof of the car to prevent banging my head on it. The spot where I hit my forehead is still sore and probably swollen. He shifts gears and the SUV jolts, his fingers grazing my leg. I jerk like he's burned me.

"Easy there, jumpy," he says.

"You groped me."

He barks out a laugh so loud it echoes. "You're drunk."

"You're a wart."

"Should you be insulting someone who's doing you a favor?" he says as he pulls onto an even narrower dirt path that serves as the entrance to Grammy J's.

"A favor? More like an abduction. You're a kidnapper. A kidnapper with small ears."

"Your flattery is quite endearing. Please keep going," he says, his eyes flickering with amusement.

I shake my head, biting my tongue, and watch as the trees fall away and the bed-and-breakfast emerges like a life-sized dollhouse at the top of the hill. A wooden sign announcing BLUEBONNET INN dangles from a post sprouting from the ground like the wildflowers surrounding it. Ryan drives around to the rear and parks near Grammy J's truck. The B&B is dark, save for a lamp lit downstairs.

He moves to open his door, but I stop him with a "Don't bother." He mumbles something too quiet for me to hear. Abandoning the wine bottle on the seat, I grab my bags and haul them to the base of the back porch, then walk over to his window, where he's twirling my key ring around his finger. I hold out my palm.

"Still maintaining the wine tastes like vinegar?" he says, my keys whipping around and around in a taunt. I'd wear a cheetah print bodice and pleather pants before I'd admit otherwise. Why does he care so much anyway?

"Maybe I exaggerated." I grab the keys midswing and tug them off his finger. "The wine tasted like grape cough syrup."

Ryan captures my wrist, drawing me closer to him, and leans out the window. For a second I think he's going to kiss me good night, and my heart stops. Clearly, I'm drunker than I thought, because why on earth would he do that and why would I want him to? We just met. Instead he raises a hand to my face and removes a leaf tangled in my hair before putting the SUV in reverse. "Joy's a light sleeper and keeps a shotgun under her pillow. Don't let her mistake you for a burglar," he says with a chuckle. Only after his taillights have retreated down the hill does it register that I never told him where I'm staying.

I'm too tired to focus on that right now. Today has dragged on worse than a soap opera, my clothes are sticking to me like cling wrap, and the alcohol flowing through my veins weighs down my limbs. With the promise of a bed, I gather my belongings and fumble up the steps.

One second I'm reaching for the doorknob and the next I'm splayed out on my back, my stuff scattered everywhere. My ankle throbs and my body is contorted in an unnatural way, but I'm so stunned from the fall I can't move. A few beats later, the porch light clicks on and the door swings open, banging against the siding.

I squeeze my eyes shut, bracing myself for the distinctive sound of a gun being cocked. Only instead of a loud *pop* there's a drawn-out sigh. I peek and see Grammy J standing in the doorway, the shotgun propped under her robed arm, fingers fiddling with some kind of object. She's staring at me with her mouth set in a hard line. The rocking chairs on the porch creak in the wind like in a horror movie.

"On your feet, child," she says, nudging my hip with her toe. "Come sunrise you've got work to do." Without a second glance, she tosses the object over her shoulder before stepping back inside. It lands on my stomach.

I hold the object up to the moonlight. It takes me a moment to comprehend that my mangled stiletto has snapped clean off the shoe.

The wind howls, and I swear it's the universe cackling at me.

I WAKE the next morning to the scent of fried eggs and the sound of feet creaking on the hardwood. It tricks me into believing I'm in Nick's tiny bungalow, snuggled in his bed, while he fixes us breakfast. Soon he'll call me into the kitchen and greet me with a kiss and a cup of coffee.

Except in the months we dated that scene happened only once.

The hard knock on the door plunges me into reality, and I remember I'm in Grammy J's spare room. Everything hurts, made worse by the fact that the mattress has more springs than foam. It's been years since I've been hungover. The door opens, and I drag a pillow over my face, smothering my moans. My head feels as if it's stuck in a vice. The wine from last night sloshes around in my stomach, ready to ride up my throat.

The queasiness builds as I hear drapes *swoosh* aside and Grammy J's squeaky steps move closer to me. Clinging to the blankets, I pray she'll change her mind, leave me alone, but my efforts are as helpful as using a bowling ball for a flotation device. She rips away the covers and cold air assaults me. I grunt, curling into myself as though it'll protect me. From somewhere in the house, the sound of high-pitched laughter pierces my ears. *Why are people in this town always so chipper?*

"Up, up, up," Grammy J says, punctuating each word with a clap. She snatches the pillow off my face and flings it away. "Lazy hour's over, child."

"Time is it?" I croak, my mouth dry as coffee grinds and just as bitter. I try to open my eyes, but they're crusted together from the mascara I forgot to wash off. Rubbing away some of the gunk, I squint as sunlight streams in through the window, a spotlight on me. I miss the rain and the gloom and the thunder—they complemented my mood so much better.

"Late. The rooster crowed ten minutes ago," she says. "Linens need washin', the silver needs polishin', and the back porch needs paintin'. More wrinkles are carvin' into my face every second you lie there." Her voice is impatient, but somehow she still manages to stretch out the vowels and meander around the consonants.

I groan. I came to the bed-and-breakfast for escape, not to do manual labor. Besides, this is why cleaning services and contractors exist.

"The laundry isn't goin' to fold itself," Grammy J says. "Out of bed."

"Tomorrow." I need one day without people barking orders at me or telling me how to act, one day where I can just forget everything and relax. "I'll do it all tomorrow." I pat around for something to shield my eyes from the sun but come up empty.

Grammy J sighs, one hand on her hip, the other clutching a garden spade. She taps a foot on the floorboards, loosening some of the soil caked on her galoshes. Dirt footprints mark a trail from the hallway to the bed. Her pant legs are soaked, the denim bleeding from a navy to a crisp blue. Perhaps she was planting vegetables. In the midst of my tripping incident last night I didn't get a good look at her, but now I see the years have aged her, made her skinnier and frailer, with a freckled nose and rosy cheeks that wished they could tan if not for her fair complexion. Her once-vibrant red hair has faded into strawberry blonde.

She scrutinizes me, her expression sharpened by the creases around her green eyes and mouth. For a moment, I swear I'm staring at my mother in twenty years—well, if I ignore the fact that my mother wouldn't be caught dead with a bandana around her forehead or with dirt beneath her fingernails; gardening is only fit for the hired help. I brace myself in preparation for the onslaught of criticism coming my way. *What were you thinking causing all that racket? You behaved like a drunken fool, Margaret. An embarrassment to this family.*

Only Grammy J says none of this. "You want to stay here, you earn your keep." She turns and heads for the door, pausing beside my luggage heaped in a pile in the middle of the floor. She purses her lips. "And take a shower, child. I can smell you from downstairs."

She disappears before I realize she didn't ask why I'm here or seem surprised, despite not having seen me since the day of Poppa Bart's funeral sixteen years ago. The same day I was cuffed and thrown into the back of a cop car for a stupid lapse in judgment. The same day my mother and Grammy J had a falling-out nobody discusses, the secret they share the only lifeline connecting them.

I once asked my mother what happened. It's the only time I can recall unguarded, raw emotion on her face, but rather than a verbal attack like I expected, she simply walked away in an intimidating way that was worse than yelling. In that moment, I remember wishing my mother would berate me. At least then I'd know how to act, given all my years of experience. Later, after she'd gone to bed and my father and I were alone, he told me that sometimes there's a reason people change and why they keep secrets and not to bring up the subject again. It wasn't a surprise when he promised to smooth things over with my mother the next morning—my father had practically made a second career of keeping her happy—but the fact that he looked troubled as he did so, as though whatever bothered her was something deep and painful, got my attention.

I wonder now, if my mother discovered I'm in

Wilhelmsburg, if she'd cut me out of her life as effectively and efficiently as she did Grammy J, but more important, would I want her to?

As I listen to the sound of Grammy J's footsteps growing fainter on the stairs, I stare at the trees outside, a chorus of birds darting off into the sky, and contemplate going back to sleep. But Grammy J's worse than a telemarketer when it comes to pestering people, so ignoring her is futile. My body refuses to obey as I struggle to sit up. The ceiling spins like I'm on a teacup ride, and I collapse back onto the bed.

Pieces of yesterday flash through my mind. I owe Ryan, his taunting words, and that bottle of No Regrets a harsh talking to. I haven't consumed that much alcohol since Nick ended us, after he confessed to always loving Lillie with such heartfelt, sickening sincerity I almost choked on it. *I've been unfair to you*, Nick said. *You've been a great friend to me when I didn't deserve one and helped me through the darkest point in my life. I thought I could make this work between us—that I could be that man for you—but I can't. I don't love you in the way you need. I'm sorry.* I remember how he had the audacity to appear stricken by his admission, as if it was hurting *him*.

After a few more failed attempts, I haul myself into a seated position, holding the headboard for stability. Touching the spot where I bumped my forehead on Ryan's SUV, I wince, the knot tender and larger than I expected. My blouse and skirt have bunched and twisted so they feel as though I'm wearing a full-body straitjacket that reeks of sweat and gasoline. I'm never passing out without changing into pajamas again.

I look around. The spare room is like that optical illusion with the young girl and the old woman. At first glance it looks unchanged since the time I spent growing up here:

the four-poster queen bed flanked by windows decorated with silk draperies, the quaint sitting area featuring armchairs to enjoy the fireplace, the antique writing desk against the far wall. But on closer inspection, the floral wallpaper has yellowed and is peeling in places, the brass light fixture has tarnished and hangs at an awkward angle, and the crown molding is cracked and separating from where it meets the ceiling. The air smells as musty as an old book, thick with dust.

I stand, and a knife-like pain shoots up my leg. My ankle is puffy and bluish purple, and my knee is scraped from where I landed on it. Limping over to the desk, I grab my cell phone and power it on. A text message from Piper pops up. *You skipped the Chanel private showing? After your display at brunch, people are talking, Mags. Call me.* I sigh. When are people *not* talking?

The icon in the corner shows six missed calls and messages, all from my mother, with more disparaging remarks no doubt. I glimpse at the date.

Crap.

My father's birthday dinner. I've never missed a family gathering, so while it's not unusual my mother has called so many times, it's strange my father hasn't reached out at least once. "We're in this together, Margaret," he always says.

How could I forget?

I picture my parents seated at our formal dining table, my place setting untouched, their conversation stilted without me there to bridge the gap. I picture my father eating his baked potato plain because I wasn't there to pass him the butter and sour cream, my mother refusing to do so in my absence. I picture my father blowing out the candles on his favorite German chocolate cake, wishing his daughter had remembered.

I'd been so caught up in my desire to get out of Dallas that his celebration slipped my mind. My father expects so little of me beyond not upsetting my mother. And while he's rarely home, we both rely on each other to get through the awkward family occasions my mother insists on observing.

Grammy J appears in the doorway. She walks to where I'm leaning against the desk and presses a mug of tea into my hands. The aroma of jasmine blossoms and orange peel hits my nose. My stomach rolls, but my throat feels as though I've swallowed steel wool, so I'm willing to risk it. I take a tentative sip, and the hot liquid brings such relief I could cry.

Appraising me, Grammy J shakes her head and hands me a paintbrush. "You're not going to fix your life moping around a rickety old bed-and-breakfast," she says, patting my arm in a way that feels reassuring despite her authoritative tone. "You'll deal with your troubles the same way you'll deal with painting the porch—one rotten board at a time."

5

Scalding water beats against my shoulders and loosens my muscles. Steam encases me in a bubble, and the steady sounds of the shower fill the bathroom. But I can't avoid Grammy J or the fact I forgot my father's birthday celebration forever.

I shut off the water and wrap myself in a scratchy, threadbare towel. Climbing out of the tub, I step onto a mat as thin as a pillowcase, and shiver as the coldness of the tile seeps through. This bathroom is nothing like mine in Dallas, with its heated marble floors and rugs so plush my toes disappear. Wiping the fog off the mirror, I examine my reflection, hardly recognizing the person staring back at me, the resentment in her eyes, the hard set of her jaw.

I style my hair, put on makeup, and slip into white skinny jeans, a Kelly green blouse, and ballet flats, careful not to aggravate my still-throbbing and swollen ankle. Like the rest of my closet, my daily wardrobe is crisp and polished. My mother says worn-in, comfortable clothing belongs on slobs or in the children's department. *Sophistication is everything*, she reminds me at least once a week.

Outside an engine growls, and I remember my Audi is still at The Tangled Vine. *Thanks again, Roaming Eyes Ryan.* Maybe after I conjure up a painter to deal with the porch, Grammy J will drive me into town to get it.

Tucking my car keys and cell phone into my pocket, I hobble downstairs, past the dining room arranged with individual white-clothed tables with flowers at the center of each. Carafes of various juices, bowls of fresh fruit, and platters with pastries crowd a sideboard that could use more varnish.

At a large round table, a group of twentysomething girls chat and laugh while they eat omelets off fine china and drink mimosas out of crystal goblets, fueling up for a long day of wine tasting. The brunette nearest the French doors wears a glittery plastic crown and a sash over her eyelet dress—a bride-to-be surrounded by her closest friends for a bachelorette weekend. I wonder how long her happy ending will last.

In the adjoining sunroom, an older couple sips coffee and reads the newspaper, admiring the rolling countryside of Wilhelmsburg, a yellow-green patchwork of vineyards and farms and wildflower fields that remind me of a Van Gogh painting.

Grammy J wanders in from the kitchen and peers at me over her glasses. "Child, I hope you've Scotchgarded that outfit."

More like Teflon-coated.

"Not to worry. I've got it under control," I say, waving the paintbrush in the air to assure her the porch will be painted, just not by me. Where I come from, we leave home improvement to hired experts, so I'll make a phone call.

Grammy J nods, though her expression indicates she's certain I'm about to learn an obvious, unwanted lesson, and delivers a tray loaded with pancakes to the couple.

From somewhere upstairs, I hear a door open and cheerful voices. The Bluebonnet Inn has seven rooms—five available for guests, the spare I'm occupying, and Grammy J's modest suite off the rear entrance. During high season visitors flock to Hill Country to tour the wineries, pick apples and peaches in the orchards, and enjoy the many festivals and historic sites. Late summer means the bed-and-breakfast should be booked solid, but the few cars I saw parked out front last night indicate otherwise. So different from the summers I spent here as a kid. I wonder what Grammy J does to promote the B&B or if there's a website for people to make online reservations. Maybe it's something I can help her with while I'm here.

I move onto the back porch, which looks like it should be attached to a run-down, abandoned house. The wooden floorboards are cracked and pulling up in places, crying for a face-lift. The white paint is peeling away and is gone entirely on the top of the railing, and a layer of dust and dirt covers everything. Cobwebs hang under the eaves and in the corners—I guess the Haint blue color didn't fool the spiders into believing the ceiling is the sky.

Grammy J must be delusional to think the porch only needs a fresh coat of paint. I don't know why she doesn't sell the Inn and buy something more reasonable for herself. She's getting older, and the number of things needing repair will only continue to grow.

I take my phone out of my pocket and sit in a rocking chair. The air feels as hot and thick as a dog's tongue, the wind like a warm breath across my arms. Sweat pricks up along my hairline. The muddy spots dotting the yard have dried in the sun, all traces of yesterday's storm gone. My thumb hovers over my father's office number before I hit send, pressing the phone to my ear.

"Law offices of Stokes and Ingram. How may I assist you?" his receptionist answers.

"Hello, Thelma. This is Margaret. Is my father available?"

"Let me check, sweetheart."

She puts me on hold, and classical music plays in the background. A breeze sweeps through the garden and rustles the magnolia and pecan trees dotting the property. My knee bobs erratically, the paintbrush bouncing around as though my lap is a trampoline. I fling it at the painting supplies stacked against the side railing. Near the heap of rollers and cans of primer, I notice scrapers and a belt sander. Two more reasons why I'm hiring a contractor once I get off the phone with my father.

Thelma comes back on the line and says, "He has some time before his next meeting. I'll transfer you." There's ringing and a click.

"Hello, Margaret," my father says without the usual joviality he reserves just for me.

My stomach clenches with guilt. I clear my throat. "Daddy."

"You left me to fend for myself at dinner last night." He doesn't sound mad, just a little hurt. I don't think I'll ever understand why his disappointment stings far worse than my mother's anger and disapproval. Perhaps it's because I actually have a relationship with my father. I've shared pieces of my life with him, sought out his advice when I needed guidance. He's the person I went to after Nick cast me aside—unlike my mother, my father has always trusted my judgment and allowed me to find my own path, even when that path led me somewhere it shouldn't.

"I know." I can't quite bring myself to say I'm sorry. Apologies are for the weak and impressionable.

"You've upset your mother," he says, getting to the heart of what's bothering him most.

When don't I upset her? I press a finger to a bruise marring my arm to distract me from my own frustrations simmering below the surface. With my mother, being a disappointment comes naturally, but letting down my father is something I work hard not to do.

And I failed.

"I know," I say again, like I'm a recording on repeat.

A hint of humor enters his voice as he says, "I hope there's an appropriately contrite gift heading my way."

I smile into the phone. "A titanium driver, of course. It'll be waiting for you at the club before your next tee time." My father claims to love golf, but really I think he loves that it gets him away from home.

"In any case, this isn't like you. I assume there's a reasonable explanation. Come by the house tonight to talk it over with your mother. She tells me you've been unreachable since the benefit. I must go—I have a full schedule today," he says with no further mention of his birthday celebration. That he so easily forgives my transgression makes it hurt that much worse, and the frustration and guilt surge up in full force. I should have remembered, been there for him the way he's been there for me, if in his own distracted way.

"I'm not in Dallas," I confess.

"Where are you?" I hear papers shuffling and the sound of a chair squeaking.

"I'm staying at the Bluebonnet Inn . . ." I don't need to clarify with whom—he knows perfectly well I've gone to the one person my mother doesn't dare interfere with.

There's a long pause, his silence crushing me under its

weight. "I see," he says in a tone that verges on angry, and I wonder if he's thinking about how my mother will react to my whereabouts. My father avoids arguments with my mother the same way he avoids discount stores and restaurants with pictures of food on the menu, and this is bound to spark one. "When do you intend on returning?"

I bite my lip. "I'm not sure . . . I'm taking an extended vacation."

"And what about your professional obligations?"

At least for this question I have a concrete answer. "I've delegated all projects to other reputable firms while I'm away." I don't tell him that several of the PR campaigns are in their most crucial stages or that a large number of the company presidents are his golfing buddies and clients. Nor do I tell him that I have no real plan for the future—I'm not thinking that far ahead. I've spent too much time acting like a windup doll—crank my key and watch me perform.

"I assumed you knew better than to do something like this, Margaret," he says. "I'm not sure what's gotten into you, but you need to call your mother." Then, in a move he's never done, he hangs up on me.

Wonderful. I've managed to infuriate my father for only the second time in my life. Will I *ever* do anything right?

I throw my cell on the porch. It hits the edge of the steps and lands faceup on the ground, a hairline fracture running across the screen. *Figures.* I should teach a course on how to be a constant source of disappointment, I'm so skilled at it.

As I stand to retrieve the phone, my eyes lock on a rusted, twisted nail poking out of a board. A part of the red leather sole of my destroyed Louboutin is caught around the nail head, mocking me. The frustration finally boils over.

Searching the painting supplies, I find a hammer buried under some drop cloths. Sliding the round top between the claw, I rip out the devil nail responsible for my swollen ankle and scraped-up knee. The old wooden board groans in response. Bits of rust fall onto my once-pristine white jeans as I wrench the nail from the hammer's grasp. I attack another nail that's even more corroded and crooked. Then another. And another.

The heat and humidity shimmer in the sun. My blouse sticks to my skin, my hair is in tangles and matted against my cheek, and sweat trickles down my forehead, mixing with my mascara and stinging my eyes. My palms are so slick I can barely grip the hammer, but I continue to yank out nails. I position the claw around another rusted head and *crap* . . . I've completely ruined my manicure—something I'll have to rectify before Sunday brunch at the Ritz with my parents. I jolt at the realization that for the first time in recent memory I won't be in attendance for our weekly ritual. That there won't *be* a reason to have my nails sculpted and covered in the same boring, predictable shade my mother deems appropriate. That there's no need for me to be appropriate at all.

Reveling in my newfound liberty to do whatever the hell I please, I stack the rocking chairs on top of the painting supplies and work on pulling up the floorboards. Some planks come off easily, while others require my whole body weight to tug them free. My shoulders ache with a satisfying burn. The air tastes gritty from the dirt and dust floating around and carries a metallic, flowery odor. My arms tremble to the point where I can't lift them to wipe the grime off my cheeks. *You're disgraceful, Margaret*, my mother's voice admonishes in my ear. *You resemble something that belongs in the garbage and smells just as foul. It's no surprise Nick left you.* I pry away another board. With each one I add to the pile, thoughts of Nick and my mother—my frustrations—flake off me like the rust and old paint clinging to my clothes and skin. The splintered, weather-beaten wood scratches the soft flesh of my hands that's now covered in blisters.

As I stand in the hole I created, my ballet flats sink into the moist earth. The pressure on my ankle makes it feel like a water balloon about to burst. The porch framing is warped and stinks of rot, like teeth that have never touched toothpaste. I'm fighting with a plank that doesn't want to budge when a long, slow whistle captures my attention. I squint against the glare of the afternoon sun. Ryan leans against the railing at the base of the stairs, holding a box with CAMDEN CELLARS printed across the side.

"I'll never understand the latest fashion you city girls wear. What is that? Garden gnome chic?" he says, referring to the disaster I'm presenting to the world.

"Oh, it's you, Mr. Roaming Eyes," I say as sweat drips down my nose. I try to swipe it away, but my arm is so weak I end up smacking myself in the mouth.

He cocks his head to the side, a curious expression on his face. "Just Ryan, actually."

Setting the box down, he rummages through the porch debris. I watch how his lean lines and corded muscles move beneath his T-shirt and ripple in his tanned biceps and forearms. I avert my gaze before he catches me ogling him. I form a fist, and with a hard upward hit, manage to dislodge the stubborn plank.

"Roaming Eyes Ryan, got it," I say, as he rights himself, my cell in hand. When he places it on the railing, his shirt rides up to reveal a flat, toned stomach. This time, he busts me staring.

"Would you prefer if I just stripped down?" he asks, raising an eyebrow.

"Don't flatter yourself," I grumble, even though my thoughts are running rampant. Squeezing the rough wood, I imagine sliding my fingers over his broad shoulders, down his torso, lower and lower, eliciting a groan from deep in his throat when I reach where he craves it most.

I can't help but notice the similarities between him and Nick—they both have a square jaw, unruly hair begging for fingers to rake through it, features carved from stone—but there's an elegance in Nick's ruggedness, a product of being born into privilege and money, that Ryan lacks.

"Don't you think you should be a little nicer, Stumbling Shortcake, given that I just delivered a case of the cough syrup you like so much for the Inn's evening social hour?"

I toss the board into the yard. "Margaret," I grind out, instantly regretting it. The playful twinkle in his eyes, the smirk on his face tells me he's baiting me. "Are you a spokesperson for the winery or a pathetic groupie?" I ask, pointing to the box at his feet.

I don't tell him that if a bottle of No Regrets—with its rich garnet color, sweet tannins, silky texture, and floral aromatics—were a famous rock star, I'd travel around the country for every show, and after the concert ended, sneak backstage for some private time. My mouth waters as I envision the flavors on my tongue—the taste of perfection.

"Both," he says. His honey-blond hair glints like a gold coin in the sunlight, curling just behind his ears. "I work for the vineyard."

"Figures." I maneuver around the wreckage to an area of the porch still in need of demolition. "Why else would you force that crap on unsuspecting people?"

"Speaking of which, you forgot your empty bottle in my Blazer last night. I put it in the kitchen since I know you want to keep it as a memento." His voice is rich and strong and so smooth, as though it's been aged like fine bourbon.

Ignoring him, I tug on a board but it stays put. More wavy red strands of hair plaster themselves to my forehead each time I yank on it.

Ryan steps onto what remains of the porch and asks, "Want some help?"

"Nope," I say through gritted teeth. Crouching down, I lay my palms flat on the underside of the wood and, with a grunt, push up using all my strength. My skin glistens with sweat and my arms shake so hard I'm sure they're about to give out completely, but I refuse to surrender. The plank pops free with such momentum I lose my balance. My butt whacks something hard as my already hurt ankle twists unnaturally. Sharp pain zings up my leg, and white spots blur my vision. I stand and put weight on my foot, wincing.

Ryan offers me an outstretched hand. I swat it away as if it's a fly. "I said I don't need your help." I climb out of the hole, albeit unsteadily.

"I see that," he says. "But you've got me wondering how you're going to rebuild this mess since there's no replacement lumber anywhere, and you don't strike me as the power-tool-wielding, do-it-yourself type."

"Worry about yourself." I limp over to the pile of supplies to grab a crowbar, intent on prying free a stubborn nail still wedged in the framing, but Ryan steps in my path. As I try to move around him, a fiery bolt shoots through my leg. I bite the inside of my cheek to prevent a cry from escaping.

The pain must be obvious in my expression, because Ryan says, "Marge, stop acting like a mule and let me look at your ankle. It's starting to resemble a marshmallow."

I consider disregarding him—I'm not weak or a quitter —but he's right, and the pressure only seems to be worsening. I nod. Kneeling in front of me, Ryan gingerly removes my ballet flat. I grip his shoulders for support, the muscles firmer and more solid than I anticipated, as he inspects my ankle. His calloused fingers feel rough against my skin, and I shiver despite my better judgment.

"Well, you've got a slight sprain, but nothing an ice pack and rest can't fix. For now, I'll wrap it to lessen some of the pressure," he says, pulling a bandana from his back pocket and tying it around the puffiest part. "How's that?"

"Marginally better," I say, torn between relishing the fading throb and appreciating Ryan's thorough attention. I don't understand how such basic care can set me so on edge. The man is too handsome for his own good, that's undeniable, but if this is mere attraction, it's a variety I've never sampled before.

"Always so shy with praise," he says with a grin, putting my shoe back on, though not before he trails a finger down my calf that causes my breath to lodge in my throat. "You really should be thanking me. I doubt Joy wants the rear entrance of the Inn torn up for the foreseeable future."

At the mention of Grammy J's name, my heart freezes. One look at the porch and she'll bury me alive in the vegetable garden. All I had to do was hire someone to slap on a fresh coat of paint. *How did I get so carried away?* Then I remember the rusted devil nail, the conversation with my father, and the frustration flares up again.

There's still time to fix this. I'll get a contractor over here for a quote tomorrow, and by the end of the week, the bed-and-breakfast will have a shiny new porch.

"How about you mind your own business?" I say, snatching my cell off the porch railing. The screen has shattered—I guess too many rotten boards landed on it. I press the center button, but the display remains black. "Come on," I mutter. I hit the phone against my leg, then press the button again, but nothing happens. "Turn on, dammit."

"Joy didn't give you permission to rip up the porch, did she?" Ryan says, crossing his arms over his chest. "I have a buddy who's a carpenter. Want me to introduce you?"

"What I want is for you—" I stop when I hear squeaky footsteps approaching from somewhere inside the house. Grammy J. My eyes grow large as saucers.

He laughs, a low rumble that reminds me of thunder on a hot summer day. "You better pray she isn't carrying the shotgun."

Crap.

I'm dead.

I glance around frantically and spot Ryan's Blazer parked beneath a pecan tree. *Grammy J can't shoot me if I'm not here.*

"Why are you moving like a slug?" I hiss to Ryan, grabbing his hand and hobbling down the stairs, careful to avoid the broken boards and nails scattered everywhere. The pain in my ankle has returned, but I don't stop my pathetic attempt at running toward his SUV as I drag him behind me. Flinging open the passenger door, I hop inside and honk the horn. Ryan saunters over to the driver's side without a care in the world. I lean across the center console and pull his handle. "Hurry up. Get in."

"You really need to work on your bedside manner," he says, climbing inside. He starts the engine just as Grammy J appears in the doorway.

"Go, go, go," I say, tapping his leg, watching as Grammy J surveys the porch with both hands on her hips, a murderous expression on her face.

Ryan shifts the car into gear, throws an arm behind my headrest, and looks over his shoulder as he reverses down the hill. Tree branches scrape against my window. When we're safely out of sight, he pulls off to the side, puts on the brake, and stares at me expectantly.

"What? Town is that way," I say, gesturing in the general direction. "Drive already."

He lifts an eyebrow. "Any time now."

I frown, not understanding, then it clicks. I sigh. "Ryan, would you please introduce me to your carpenter friend?" The question tastes like acid on my tongue.

"See, asking for help wasn't so hard." He gives me an I-always-get-my-way smile, and it touches me in a way I'm not sure how to process. Then he moves his arm from behind my head and veers back onto the dirt road. "You even said please," he says, the grin still glued to his face.

I bite the inside of my cheek, letting him have the last word. This time.

6

Ryan parks the Blazer in front of a large building that looks patched together like Frankenstein's monster. The structure itself is limestone, consistent with the German architecture of the area, but the shutters and gambrel roof belong on a Dutch Colonial, and the intricate, superfluous exterior trim appears stolen from a Victorian gingerbread. A sign with H.P. painted in sloppy letters hangs above the door.

"What does H.P. stand for?" I say, unbuckling my seat belt.

"Hodgepodge," Ryan says.

"Why? Because this place can't decide what it wants to be?"

"Something like that. Let's go." He shuts off the engine and gets out. A beat later, he's opening my door and holding out a palm, which I begrudgingly take, if only so I don't further irritate my ankle. My arms stick to the leather seat as I climb out, a flurry of dust and dog hair following me as if I'm Pig-Pen. I'm desperate to wash away the layers of grime, to relax in a bath with a glass of Pinot

Grigio and cucumber slices on my eyes. If I can manage to peel the sweat-soaked denim off my body without also taking off a layer of skin, that is. Chafing—it's nobody's friend.

I hobble behind Ryan, working hard not to stare at his ass in jeans that shouldn't fit as well as they do and failing miserably. A breeze blows hot on my face, offering no reprieve from the heat and humidity.

A bell rings as I enter the store, the inside just as much of a mishmash as the outside—the shelves stocked with everything from groceries and toiletries to fishing gear and car parts, home improvement supplies to gardening equipment.

Ryan walks to the guy operating an ancient cash register. I recognize him as Ryan's friend with the moose tattoo from The Tangled Vine. They bump fists, and Ryan places a hand at the small of my back, pushing me forward. "This is Moose, co-owner of Hodgepodge and carpenter extraordinaire."

I snort. *Of course* that's his name. Ryan stares at me, steady, hard, but Moose smiles, a dimple appearing in one cheek.

"It's better than Marvin," Moose says, his voice warm and light despite his size. "Don't tell my granddad I said that. He thinks the family name is the equivalent of an Aston Martin rather than a rust bucket that coughs blue smoke when it backfires."

I laugh—the first genuine one in months—the sound shaking something loose in my chest. I bet Moose collects friends the way I collect Hermès Kelly bags. I instantly like him.

"So what can I help you with?" Moose says, ripping a receipt off the printer and tossing it into the trash.

Ryan rests an elbow on the counter, dirt rimming his

cuticles and a reddish-purple hue still staining his fingertips. I wonder if they're permanently colored that way, if they're as skilled as I envision.

"This is Marge—"

"Margaret," I say.

"—Joy's granddaughter. The Bluebonnet Inn needs its rear porch rebuilt. Half of the demo has been done for you already, courtesy of Marge."

"Margaret."

Ryan winks and gives me a grin that strikes like lightning. A lock of honey-blond hair has fallen over his forehead, and my fingers twitch to brush it back. I glance away, refusing to be sucked in.

Moose retrieves a pen and a legal pad from a drawer beside the register. "What exactly are you looking for?"

I'm in the middle of explaining the situation, Moose scribbling notes, when a burly woman interrupts me, hip-checking me to the side and dumping the contents in her arms onto the counter—a tackle box, a flashlight, three bags of chips, and a six-pack of beer. I open my mouth to lay into her, but Ryan runs a single finger down my arm and shoots me a pointed stare that says, *Behave*. I obey, since her body odor is so strong the air around her feels thick and textured like cheap polyester.

Moose rings up the items and hands her a penny from the cup of spare change. "For luck," he says. She pockets it and leaves without a word.

"Charming," I say.

Moose shrugs. "Her husband skipped town with a waitress from Earl's last month. She's having a rough time."

"Your foot must taste like chocolate with how often you put it in your mouth," Ryan says, fiddling with a bowl of crocheted Hacky Sacks beside the register. A trio for ten dollars.

"Would you be quiet?" I snap, my stomach bottoming out as I remember when Nick ran off to Chicago to find Lillie, to confess to her whatever secrets he guarded so close. Like a supportive, dutiful friend, I let him go, keeping quiet, because I was tired of competing with her ghost. Where was she when Nick's life fell apart? Where was she when he fought his way out of the dark, picked up a guitar, and pieced himself back together again? I let Nick go so he would finally move on, shed Lillie like a second skin, embrace what was right in front of him, and realize I was so much better suited for him. Nick came back to Dallas alone, as I expected. Still, it took years of prodding before he finally agreed to a relationship with me. I should've known then I was simply a placeholder.

I push thoughts of Nick aside. "When can you start?" I ask Moose.

"She's on a deadline," Ryan says. "Joy didn't exactly grant her permission to rip up the porch." He drops a Hacky Sack on the toe of his shoe, kicks it so it sails high into the air above his head, and catches it on the back of his neck. Show-off.

"I did the rotten thing a favor," I say, snatching the Hacky Sack away from him and returning it to the bowl. "In fact, the entire bed-and-breakfast looks rotten. It should be bulldozed and the land underneath used for something else."

Ryan frowns and scratches his jaw, the stubble creating a raspy sound. "I think Joy would disagree. People have been interested in the land for years, and she won't sell."

"That's unfortunate," I say.

Moose pulls a business card from his back pocket and slides it across the counter. "I'll stop by the Inn tomorrow morning to give you an estimate. Then we can discuss the schedule. Work for you?"

I nod and say, "My cell phone broke earlier. Is there somewhere I can buy a replacement?"

"Nearest electronics store is two towns over. We've got a computer with Internet access next to the coffeepot," Moose says, jerking his chin toward the back wall. "You can find something online and rush deliver it here."

Thanking him, I turn to leave, but he calls out, "We've got aspirin, ice packs, and compression bandages in aisle five." I look at him, confused. "I saw you limping earlier, and I don't think that bandana will cut it long term. Plus, that's quite a golf ball you've got there," Moose says, pointing to the knot on my forehead from where I bumped it on Ryan's car.

"A casualty from too much good wine," Ryan says, then meets my gaze, his amusement like a feather-soft stroke I shouldn't enjoy. "Bonus for you, I included some of it in the delivery I made to the B and B earlier so you can have some when you get back. Assuming Joy doesn't kill you first."

Shaking my head, I mutter, "It's as if you *want* me to hit you," and stalk off.

I gather the supplies for a homemade first-aid kit and sit on the floor, ignoring the grumbles from the man standing by the allergy medicine. He's not the only one who'd condemn my behavior—my mother would have a conniption if she saw my current state. Twisting open the aspirin bottle, I swallow a few pills, not even bothering with water. Then I untie the bandana, wrap the bandage around my ankle, the compression alleviating the pressure instantly, and carefully slip my foot into my ballet flat.

The computer reminds me of the old, clunky machine I used in elementary school to play Oregon Trail. I click on the Internet icon and the dial-up connection screen appears. Beeps and crackles fill the air. *Who still has dial-up?*

An eternity later, I'm finally able to order a new phone. I return to the register and put the items on the counter.

"Any troubles?" Moose asks, picking up an ice pack and ringing it in.

I tell him no as Ryan inspects the ripped package of the compression bandage and the open box of aspirin. "You're the type of person who snacks while grocery shopping and then scans the empty wrappers at checkout, aren't you?" he asks me.

Sometimes. "None of your business." I search my pockets for money only to realize I don't have any on me. "Crap."

Ryan fishes some cash out of his wallet and gives it to Moose. "You can pay me back tomorrow night when you come to Camden Cellars."

"That's presumptuous," I say.

"There's going to be a small get-together for staff and friends. A celebration of sorts. Since you're new to town I thought you'd be interested." His voice is casual, but there's an underlying edge to it. As if offering me a pity invitation somehow helps him, for what I don't know, but I won't be used again.

"Not happening," I say.

Ryan leans against the counter. A muscle ticks in his jaw. I wonder if I pegged him wrong. Maybe he's not the sort of guy who wants a challenge. Maybe he's like my mother in that he prefers people who dish out approval for three square meals a day.

"Still refuse to lower yourself?" he asks.

"I just prefer to refrain from situations where keg stands, beer pong, and body shots are the evening's entertainment," I say. My eyes flick to the dip and hollow of his well-defined collarbone. He catches me gawking and arches an eyebrow. He could call me out, but we both know it's unnecessary.

"You don't like someone licking tequila out of your belly button?" he asks.

"No."

"Maybe you just haven't been licked properly," he says, his voice dripping with innuendo. Ryan flashes a wicked grin that sends a rush of heat through me.

Oh, that smooth bastard.

Before I can respond, Moose cuts in, handing me a paper bag with my items and Ryan his change. "You should come, Margaret. We'll all be there." By "we all," I assume he means their friends, none of whom I have any desire to meet. "The winery throws a great party, especially when Cricket breaks out the private reserve Cabernet from the cellar."

My heart stutters at the name Cricket. "What did you say?"

Moose slaps Ryan on the shoulder and says, "This guy keeps the good stuff under lock and key except for special occasions. You don't want to miss it."

Moose continues talking, but I don't hear him. My skin tingles, sensing Ryan's gaze on me. I look at him. The intensity in his expression steals my breath as I recall the familiarity of his laugh, the certainty that we've met before. I study Ryan's face, trying to find the resemblance between him and the boy I remember from that crazy, stupid night long ago, but my brain can't make the connection.

Then Ryan smiles, his hazel eyes alight with mischief, and says, "If you come to the party, I promise the cops won't make an appearance this time. Scout's honor."

And it's like I'm sixteen again, reliving the night Cricket—Ryan—got me arrested.

I'd STUMBLED upon the party by accident. I'd been walking aimlessly, picking wildflowers along the dirt road that led to the bed-and-breakfast, the sun sinking below the horizon, when I'd heard faint music from somewhere on the other side of the hill. Following the sound and the scent of smoke so heavy in the air it scratched my throat, I found a clearing crammed with what I'd guessed was the entire student body of Wilhelmsburg High School—maybe a hundred people in total—all getting drunk off moonshine and cheap beer.

Mud-caked trucks were backed into a wide circle around a bonfire. Couples lounged in the beds, smoking cigarettes, talking, making out, their bare feet swinging off the tailgates. One of the radios was blaring a twangy country song that thumped under the pulse of conversation.

"Shit. Who called the feds?"

The voice came from behind me, and I jumped. I'd been watching the crowd from the field surrounding the clearing, and I thought I'd done a good job of blending into the darkness. I spun around, the tall native grasses brushing against my legs. A boy a couple of years older, maybe a senior, stood a few paces away, head cocked to one side, a Solo cup in his hand. A small smile played on his mouth. Like most of the other boys, he wore faded jeans and a T-shirt.

"Excuse me?" I said, pulling my black cardigan tighter around me. Funerals, according to my mother, were the only occasion deemed acceptable for me to don such a color.

His gaze scanned over me in a way that caused my stomach to flip. "Black dress. Modest shoes. Expression in a scowl. You must be FBI."

I narrowed my eyes and clenched my jaw, ignoring the

whine of mosquitoes in my ear and the itchy, swollen welts spotting my skin.

"No?" he said. "How about a spy? You *are* lurking in the shadows."

I continued to glare at him. He glanced away for a moment, cheeks sucked in, as if he were fighting a laugh. A breeze blew a lock of honey-blond hair in his eyes, but he made no effort to smooth it back. When he looked at me again, he was full-on grinning.

Near the bonfire, a girl squealed and giggled as one of the boys picked her up, threw her over his shoulder, and vanished into the field. At least at the parties in Dallas we had pool houses stocked with top-shelf liquor and plenty of bedrooms to sneak off to for sex, while parents "supervised" in the main house, hosting a gathering of their own and becoming as overserved as the teenagers. But I wasn't dumb enough to get caught half naked with a boy in a compromising position—my father would ship me off to a convent.

The boy stepped closer and took a sip of his drink. "I figured it out," he said. "You're either an uptight magician or someone died."

"My grandfather," I snapped, crossing my arms. Hours ago, Grammy J had said good-bye to Poppa Bart, her partner of forty years, and my mother had buried her father. He was more of a distant relative to me—my grandparents never ventured north to Dallas and we visited Wilhelmsburg only once every few years—but still my heart hurt for Grammy J and all she'd lost. Now who'd trim the trees or fix the banister when it needed repair? Who would help Grammy J manage the bed-and-breakfast?

His smile faltered. He raked his fingers through his hair. "Okay, I'm a jerk," he said, then offered me his drink as some kind of apology. I sniffed it, and to my surprise, the moonshine smelled like fresh-baked apple pie. I gulped some down, squeezing my eyes shut as the alcohol burned my throat and sent a rush to my head. The cinnamon aftertaste reminded me of the Red Hots candy our live-in chef used to decorate Christmas cookies. I gave the cup back to him and introduced myself.

"Cricket," he replied.

I wrinkled my nose. "That's awful if that's actually your name."

He laughed, the sound low and rough but threaded with a lilting warmth. "It's because I'm fast and squirmy."

When I furrowed my brow in response, he clarified, "On the football field."

I studied him and tried to imagine him dodging and cutting and slipping through the defense into the end zone. Silence stretched between us. The wind shushed through the field, birds trilling from somewhere above. The air felt cool and dry, uncommon for Hill Country.

"So, Margaret, what are you doing out here all alone?" he asked after a while.

I shrugged, tucking a stray hair behind my ear. "Erasing the day."

All throughout Poppa Bart's service and wake, my mother had pecked at me like I was a corn kernel. Stand up straight, Margaret. Slouching is a mortal sin against poise and makes you look unattractive; if you insist on sitting around rather than mingling with visitors or helping your grandmother, then cross your legs at the ankle, place your hands together on your lap, and smile; for Heaven's sake, Margaret, the deviled eggs aren't going to run away. Take smaller bites and use a napkin. You're not some backwoods inbred.

After the last guests had left and the bed-and-breakfast was eerily quiet, I thought we'd all settle into the rocking chairs on the porch and tell stories about Poppa Bart.

Except my mother had been insistent that we sort through my grandfather's belongings that very moment, and Grammy J had seemed too drained to argue. My mother had put me in charge of emptying his closet and packing the items into boxes. When she started in on my inability to properly fold the dress shirts I doubted Poppa Bart ever wore, I had to escape.

Cricket rocked on the balls of his feet. "You're not going to have much luck with that if you keep hiding away from everybody. Come on. Join the fun." Capturing my hand, he tugged me toward the crowd. His palm was rough as tree bark, and I wondered if his summer job involved manual labor. Ordinarily I hated it when people dictated my actions—I got enough of it from my mother—but I was already feeling hazy from the liquor, so I let him lead me to where some boys were strumming guitars by the bonfire.

"Guys, this is Margaret," Cricket declared. "Margaret, this is everyone."

People said hello or nodded, not appearing to care that I crashed their party. I planted myself in a plastic folding chair and listened to the slow, easy melody and the wood crackling. Cricket rummaged in a cooler and retrieved a mason jar of amber-colored liquid. Unscrewing the lid, he handed it to me and sat in the empty chair beside me.

I sipped the apple pie moonshine and stared at the group of girls across from us whispering to one another, casting glances between Cricket and me. The one with her cleavage on display sneered at me. I rolled my eyes. She'd have to work harder than that to intimidate me. Her hair was bleached so blond it was almost translucent and probably had the same texture as hay, while mine was like a flame—even in the dark it radiated light. I heard one of the other girls call her Bonnie, but I bet her mother referred to her as Bon Bon or something equally ridiculous. Unlike her, at least I was on my way to bigger, better places, and not stuck in this tiny town forever.

An hour passed, filled with music and laughter and overloud conversation that jumped from topics like prom to next season's football schedule to the group of seniors who had snatched three barrels of Merlot from one of the local wineries for kicks—how they'd managed to lift the barrels onto the getaway truck with only their brute strength was something of an urban legend now. Cricket stayed near me, shooting glimpses in my direction, but he didn't touch me again.

At one point, Cricket mentioned the long-standing dare to break into the Gansey house, an abandoned cottage that was supposedly haunted by the spirit of Mr. Gansey, the crazy old man who had sliced off his wife's head with a carving knife and dangled it from the ceiling. To win you had to survive for ten minutes inside and steal something as proof. I wasn't exactly sure what the prize was—glory? Respect? Eternal adoration?—but that didn't seem to matter.

"So who's going to do it?" Cricket asked, his gaze darting around the group. When no one volunteered, he faced me. "What about you? Wanna go for it?"

Bon Bon and all her cleavage leaned forward. Her eyes were glassy and her cheeks were flushed. "No way she has the guts. Most people don't make it past the front door before they get spooked and bolt." Her words contained a hint of laughter, as if this whole thing were a joke.

Cricket kept his focus on me. A sly smile tugged at his lips. "I'll come with you. What do you say? You in?"

I'd never done anything like what he was suggesting—trespassing, breaking and entering. I was the popular girl, the good girl who earned perfect grades, played it safe, abided by the rules. Before I could talk myself out of it, I nodded, a thrill surging through me.

"I'm not afraid of ghosts," I said to Bon Bon. "I'm in."

Hollers and whistles erupted as Cricket pulled me to my feet. The ground lurched under me, and my head felt weightless and fuzzy as dandelion fluff floating on the breeze. There was a tingling from my fingertips all the way down to my toes, and my whole mouth tasted like a cinnamon stick. I was drunker than I'd thought, but Cricket was sober as he guided me to a pickup truck. After I hopped in, he slid behind the wheel and drove us into town. A line of headlights followed behind us—we had an audience. Or perhaps everyone wanted to ensure we didn't cheat. Cricket turned onto a deserted road that sloped upward. When we reached the top, the sagging, gaunt structure rose out of the ground before us, the limestone crumbling and coated in grime. The moon shone on an overgrown tree that pressed against one side, its branches jutting through the holes in the roof.

Cricket parked and killed the engine. "Ready?"

A fist tightened around my chest, my bravery gone with my buzz. The house didn't look scary or even haunted, only dilapidated, but what if Mr. Gansey was real? As if sensing my apprehension, Cricket said, "The story's just a story. Nothing's gonna happen."

He grabbed a flashlight from the glove box and jogged to the porch. I trailed after him, my stomach knotting like a gold chain in a jewelry drawer. A small crowd had gathered in the weed-infested yard, watching, waiting. The air felt charged in anticipation.

We reached the front door too soon, and I hesitated, clutching Cricket's shoulders.

"All we have to do is rip off a piece of wallpaper or something and make it the ten minutes. It'll go by fast, I promise," he said to me, then yelled to the spectators, "Time starts now."

He heaved open the door with a calm I didn't understand, as if he did this sort of thing regularly. Cricket stepped into the dark, floorboards creaking beneath his shoes. The wind howled through the gaps in the stone. I stuck close to him as I entered. Instantly the stench of mold and rot assaulted my nose, and I had to force the alcohol from coming back up. Blackness swallowed us, and the noises from outside vanished as if we'd been sucked into a vacuum. Something scurried across my ankle, and I bit down a scream. My heart pounded in my ears.

Clicking on the flashlight, Cricket reached up and squeezed my hand clenching his shoulder. "You all right?"

"Fine," I whispered, imagining the rats and insects crawling everywhere, the spiders that could drop on me.

We advanced deeper into the shadows, the flashlight beam bouncing as we walked. The cottage was littered with dead leaves and trash—cigarette butts, tin cans, flat cardboard boxes squatters had probably slept on.

"The kitchen should have something we can swipe," Cricket said, directing the light ahead of us, like he'd been inside before and knew exactly where to go.

"Okay," I croaked, even though the room felt as if it were shrinking around us.

As we moved forward, I swore I heard a faint moan from somewhere behind me. The hairs on the back of my neck stood up. *It's nothing. Probably a gust of wind*, I told myself, refusing to look anywhere but in front of me. Cricket was so calm, so at ease, it made me want to match him.

"Here we are," he said, sweeping the flashlight across gutted cabinets and a hollowed-out ancient refrigerator with an unhinged door.

As we crossed the threshold, the floor shifted from wood to chipped tile, and I tripped. Cricket wrapped an arm around my waist to stop my fall. "I've got you," he said, his breath tickling my ear. A shiver traveled down my spine but not in fear. He tightened his grip, and I focused on the warm strength of his hand.

"How much longer?" I asked.

"Not much," he said, his nose skimming my cheek. He smelled like smoke and apple pie moonshine and new soil.

My heart thudded against my ribs as I said, "This was a bad idea."

"Aren't the messiest decisions the most fun?"

"No," I said, but I wasn't sure I meant it. My buzz was returning in full force, but not from the alcohol.

"You sure?" His mouth brushed against mine, and for a moment, everything went still.

Then he was kissing me, soft but strong. A small sound escaped from my throat when he licked my bottom lip. He used my cardigan to pull me tight against him, his palm flat on my back. My hands found his chest, his heart beating like a drum beneath my touch. When he deepened the kiss, his tongue brushing mine, I let myself go, lost in his taste and the sensation of his mouth on mine. I'd never felt anything so good.

Suddenly the room whirled with red and blue lights.

Cricket broke away. "Shit. We lost," he said, his voice hoarse.

"What?" I asked, missing the pressure of his mouth and body against mine.

"The cops showed up before the ten minutes were over," he said, pointing to the kitchen window, where two figures in beige uniforms were approaching the cottage. I noticed the crowd that had been gathered outside was gone.

"I don't understand."

"We got beat."

When I didn't reply, he said, "Old Mr. Gansey is harmless—everyone knows that. The dare is outlasting the cops. Once you announce you're entering, someone calls the cops about the break-in. You win if you make it the total time and steal something from inside before they get here."

Anger rose like a tide in my chest. "You tricked me."

"It wasn't like that." He reached out to put his hands on my shoulders, but I stepped away. "It's just—I knew you wouldn't come in otherwise."

"No crap I wouldn't have come!" I shouted.

Cricket shook his head. "We don't have time for this. We need to get outta here before they catch us." He grabbed my arm to pull me toward the doorway, but I refused to budge. "Margaret, come on, there's no—" The rest of his sentence was interrupted as the two policemen entered the house, blocking our exit.

They slapped handcuffs on us and threw us into the back of a cruiser. My parents were going to murder me, but I didn't care. My anger was growing like a cancer, but there was something else, too—a betrayal so thick I nearly choked on it. Cricket had kissed me, took advantage of the situation with my grandfather, and I'd completely fallen for it. How stupid could I be?

With his hands bound behind his back, Cricket scooted closer to me. "Margaret, listen, it's gonna be okay. It's not that big of a deal. It's supposed to be fun—"

"Fun?" I said with a bitter laugh. "You consider this *fun*?"

"No, not this. Just let me explain—"

"Shut up." I turned away from him and stared out the window at the officers talking into their radios. "Of course this isn't a big deal to someone like you who'll be stuck in this town forever, but I plan on doing something with my life. Like go to college, which has now been jeopardized thanks to you."

"I plan on going to college." He actually had the audacity to sound offended.

"Yes, I'm sure whatever trade school you end up at is waiting in anticipation for your application. No doubt getting arrested is exactly the sort of extracurricular activity that earns full-ride scholarships, as is perfecting the varying flavors of moonshine."

He muttered a few choice words under his breath, but I ignored him and continued to watch the officers, who were now filling out paperwork.

A pair of headlights rounded up the hill. My stomach dropped when I saw it was my father's BMW. It rolled to a stop next to the cruiser. One of the police officers opened my door. "You're free to go, little lady. You can thank your Grandma Joy for that, though I'm not obliged to comment on what your Grandpa Bart would say 'bout your behavior, God rest his soul." He helped me out of the cruiser and unlocked my cuffs. Cricket leaned across the seat to say something to me but the officer cut him off. "You, son, aren't quite so fortunate. It appears your winning streak has finally ended." Then he shut the door in his face.

I rubbed my sore wrists as my parents stepped out of the BMW, my mother crushing a weed under her foot. She refused to acknowledge me, but I could feel the displeasure rolling off her in waves. She looked as though she'd been crying, which she hadn't done at all during Poppa Bart's funeral or at the wake after. Perhaps something happened between her and Grammy J after I snuck out—I knew she wasn't worried about me.

"Get in the car, young lady," my father said. "We'll deal with you when we get home."

I hesitated—we were supposed to be staying in Wilhelmsburg for a few more days. I glanced at Cricket through the foggy police cruiser window and noticed he was staring intently at me.

"*Now*, Margaret Ann," my father barked. I'd never seen him so angry, and never at me.

I hurried into the backseat and kept silent for the entire four-hour drive back to Dallas.

After all, I always did as I was told.

7

The memory fades and Hodgepodge comes back into focus. I look at Ryan. All traces of the boy are gone. Now he's all man and devastatingly sexy, and damn if it doesn't suit him.

"You told me we didn't know each other," I say, tucking the bag under my arm.

"No, I said we *hardly* know each other. Which is true." Ryan swipes a package of gummy bears from the row of junk food displayed beneath the register, tucks it into his back pocket, and tosses a five-dollar bill on the counter near Moose, who's assisting another customer. "Though I'm offended you didn't immediately recognize me. I thought I made quite the memorable impression."

"Yes, so memorable I blocked out that entire night," I lie.

"You know, Marge, us getting arrested was really your fault," he says with humor dancing in his eyes. "If you'd listened to me when I told you we needed to leave, we never would've been caught." He steps into my personal space, issuing a challenge I shouldn't want to meet. "Or were you still too dazed from kissing me to move? I tend to have that effect on women."

I had been dazed, but I'll never admit that to him. Even as a teenager he'd known exactly what to do with that mouth, and I can only imagine the things he's capable of doing with it now after sixteen years more experience.

"I'm surprised you even fit in this store with that ego," I say. "Perhaps *that's* the reason we got caught."

"Hey, wait," Moose interjects, joining our conversation. He opens the cash drawer and slides in Ryan's five-dollar bill. "It was you with Cricket that night at the Gansey house? Did you two share a jail cell?" He glances between Ryan and me.

"No," Ryan says. "Joy sweet-talked the police into letting Marge go."

"Margaret," I stress.

"Too bad. You two could've cuddled," Moose says. A man with a leather-brown neck, deep creases in his face, and a crimp in his hair, probably from a hard hat, sets a basket on the counter. Moose waves. "Howdy, Hank. How are things at the reno site today?" He moves off to ring up the man's items.

"The officers threw you in jail?" I ask Ryan.

"Only until morning."

"That's a shame," I say. "You probably felt at home there."

Chuckling, Ryan says, "I've only been arrested once, thanks to you."

"You're that talented at skirting the law? I'm glad to see you lived up to my predictions."

He clenches his jaw and gives me a hard stare. "There you go again with your silver spoon bullshit," he says, crossing his arms, his shirt stretching tight across his chest.

"It's like I already told you, standards aren't the same

as snobbery." I keep my expression neutral, determined not to show how exposed he makes me feel.

He steps closer, his expression darkening. "You know, your abrasiveness should be a turnoff, but somehow it's . . ." He pauses, as if carefully picking his next words. "Fucking alluring." His voice, deep and low, vibrates across my skin like a caress, igniting senses I was certain had died and making me crave a much bolder, firmer touch.

"You call me abrasive, but I'm sure you mean direct," I say, steady and strong, even though my heart continues to thrum like a hummingbird. "I won't fault you for your confusion. No doubt you're accustomed to passive women who exist solely to satisfy your needs and ego, so I understand it's difficult for you to identify the difference."

"You know what?" Ryan moves forward another step, his eyes shining with a predatory light, as if I'm something he's about to devour. "I think you're bored. I think you've been waiting your whole life for a guy like me to come along and wake you up, show you just how fun messy can be."

I suck in a breath, my entire body tightening. I don't want to be drawn to him like this, especially after the way he tricked me, *lied* to me, but it's as if I'm being pulled by an outside force. I swallow, the paper bag tucked under my arm crinkling as I press it firmer against me. "You're wrong."

Bracing a hand on either side of me, he pins me against the counter. "So this doesn't affect you?" he asks.

"No," I say, hoping he can't sense the way his nearness is knocking me off balance.

Ryan leans in closer so I feel the warmth radiating off his body, smell his natural scent—earthy yet slightly sweet. We're close enough that we're sharing the same air, and if I were to tilt my chin up, my lips would graze his. "How about now?" he asks.

"No," I say again. I ball my hands into fists to prevent myself from doing something reckless, like curling my fingers into his shirtfront and finding out if he tastes as delicious as I remember. His eyes drop to my mouth, and after a painfully long beat, he dips his head. Alarm bells blare in my mind, but they're drowned out by the roar of blood in my ears and the slow, heavy ache spreading inside me. Right when I'm certain he's going to kiss me, he pulls away.

He pulls away.

"You're a horrible liar," he says.

For a moment, I can't do anything but blink and try to steady my breathing. Ryan smiles at me with smug satisfaction, as though he's proven something. He's playing with me, and I'm letting him, just like before.

The anger flares up again. Good. I need to be angry and stay that way. It's easier to fight this attraction I feel toward him, to maintain my control. I let Nick fool me once, and I won't allow Ryan to fool me twice. *It's be hurt or be hardened*, I remind myself.

I square my shoulders and clear my throat. "And it's horribly predictable that you'd equate a mess with a fun time." I squeeze past him, ignoring the way my chest brushes against his, and head for the door.

"You're already falling in love with me, Marge, and you're not even aware of it," Ryan calls after me.

Except that's where he's a misguided fool. I don't believe in love.

I MANAGE to hobble the four blocks to The Tangled Vine to

retrieve my Audi and find my way back to the bed-and-breakfast in one piece. I park under a magnolia tree that I hope will offer shade come tomorrow afternoon, but with my luck, my car will probably end up littered with leaves and bird shit.

Grammy J has relocated the rocking chairs from the pile of painting supplies to the middle of the yard and is now rocking back and forth in one, staring at the rotted floorboards still scattered on the ground and drinking a glass of wine. I inhale a deep breath and walk toward her.

"A carpenter is stopping by tomorrow morning to give me a bid for the porch. I'll pay for the rebuild out of my savings," I say before she has a chance to speak. If I take charge of the conversation, maybe I can control it.

Grabbing the wine bottle resting at her feet, Grammy J tops off her glass and nods at the empty rocking chair beside her. "Make yourself comfortable."

Despite the way she drags out her words and decorates them with an easy Texas drawl, there's something assertive in her tone that makes me follow her command. My posture is rigid as I sit, my nerves frayed like the hem of my ruined blouse. I thought only my mother had the power to reduce me to a wary, obedient child.

"Appears the Scotchgard worked wonders. You're a disaster," Grammy J says, scrutinizing the bits of grime, rust, and paint stuck to every inch of me. She has this way of studying me as though I'm transparent.

"I'll make sure none of the guests notices me when I head upstairs," I say, certain she'd rather I not embarrass her with my unprofessional appearance on top of everything else.

A wrinkle appears between her eyebrows. "What are you ramblin' on about, child?" Grammy J lifts a hand to my face and rubs a spot below my left eye, the skin of her thumb surprisingly soft for how much she slaves in the garden and around the Inn. "Hard work's never looked bad on anyone and definitely doesn't on you."

Her response catches me off guard. I search her eyes for signs of amusement, but all I see is sincerity in the depths of green. "I'm not sure my mother would agree with you," I say.

"Yes, well, there are a great many things Nancy and I don't agree on."

"Has she always been this way? So . . . so . . ."

"Controlling? Impossible to please?" Grammy J sips her wine and sighs, the sound far too world-weary. "Not always. If anything, Nancy used to be more reserved. Private."

My mother, reserved?

She's quiet a moment. Finally Grammy J smiles, but it's loaded with a sadness that pinches my heart and something else I recognize but can't pinpoint. Regret, maybe?

"Nancy never felt she fit in Wilhelmsburg and was always searchin' for a way to define herself outside of it," she says. "Always wanted to make somethin' more of herself. A trait she passed on to you, I reckon."

Before I can decide if I'm insulted or intrigued by the idea I have anything in common with my mother, Grammy J adjusts in her seat, the joints of her rocking chair creaking the way Poppa Bart's knee used to, and continues. "Problem was, your mother never understood that buildin' herself up didn't require tearin' others down. She was in such a hurry to trade the small-town rumors for big-city livin' that she never noticed she traded one fishbowl for another."

I glance around at the worn-down B&B and try to envision myself growing up here, to see Wilhelmsburg through my mother's eyes. It all seems so . . . uncomplicated.

"It's difficult to picture what could be so awful about this place," I say, especially given my upbringing in Highland Park and the never-ending quest for social standing and approval.

"That's a matter of perspective, isn't it?" Grammy J says. "It's no easy thing, child, knowin' yourself well enough to decide what future you want. And even harder to risk everythin' for somethin' that may not happen. I think your mother, in her own way, chose the more familiar road when she went to SMU and married your father. Though I doubt she'd agree."

"No, I suppose she wouldn't," I say. It's strange hearing Grammy J speculate that my mother took the easy way out, because nothing about my mother is ever easy. Straightforward, perhaps. But not easy. Then again, if you're like my mother, who sought out an entirely new life, I guess you'd do everything necessary to not only keep it but ensure it appeared effortless.

"Speakin' of, your mother know where you are?" she asks, placing a hand on my wrist. She traces a pattern with her finger. The sensation is so utterly foreign and nurturing I'm momentarily stunned.

"I don't care if she does or not." My voice sounds strong, full of confidence I don't feel. Grammy J levels me with a hard stare identical to my mother's, except it comes off less threatening. The assuredness crumbles. "Maybe. If my father told her."

"Before you get too settled, call her. I imagine she won't be too thrilled you're here."

"Because of what happened between you two?"

Most people shy away when asked a difficult question, but not Grammy J. Her gaze remains steady on mine. "Yes, because of what happened." She doesn't elaborate and I don't press for more. There's an edge in her tone that tells me to leave it alone. Or maybe whatever secret they share is something I need to hear from my mother, if only I could gather the energy to talk to her.

"Now, after the day you've had, I think you need this more than I do," she says, passing me the bottle of wine—a Tempranillo from Camden Cellars. "It's from my private collection."

I take a sip and immediately taste the essence of deep red plum, tobacco, and clove. The finish is slightly acidic with added notes of vanilla and almond, the flavors trailing smoothly on my palate. There's a mixture of bold and refined elements to the wine I'd expect from my favorite Spanish Rioja, but never from grapes harvested in Texas Hill Country. A fact I would never admit to Ryan even if I were forced to endure a cross-country road trip sharing the backseat of a subcompact car with a gassy Saint Bernard.

Leaning back, I peer at the grass and wildflowers that stretch out around the Bluebonnet Inn, and beyond that, at the hills populated with rows of grapevines. Perhaps those acres, once raw land and fallow fields, now belong to Camden Cellars. The sun is descending like a blazing copper token, the sky streaked in pinks and oranges.

"I got carried away," I say, waving at the porch, but damn if it didn't feel good ripping it apart, sweating out my frustrations. Worth every bit of soreness and exhaustion that's dragging me down now.

"I've seen worse ways to deal with pent-up emotion, and from the sheer amount of wreckage, there seems to be a whole lot inside you," she says. There's no sarcasm in her voice, just pure honesty. We're family and practically strangers, yet she knows exactly how to read me. "But finances are tight these days, so next time work with what we have. I can't afford for you to destroy everythin' around here and neither can you."

"The B and B isn't as busy as I remember," I say, glancing at Grammy J. Her eyes are locked on some spot off in the distance, and I wonder if she's happy residing out here in the quiet with only the brief conversations she has with guests to keep her company.

She swallows more wine and says, "Business has been slow for several seasons now. Most of the larger commercial vineyards built lodging on the property and folks are choosin' to stay there instead of at independently run places. Hard to compete with convenience, I suppose, though I reckon quaintness and charm should count for somethin'."

"I'm in public relations. If you'd be open to it, I can develop some promotional materials for you, overhaul the website, help generate buzz about the Inn outside of the area," I say, ideas already swirling in my head. The B&B could partner with other small local vendors—boutique wineries, family-owned farms and orchards, restaurants and markets—to create vacation packages that showcase hidden gems around Wilhelmsburg. Napa has been successfully doing that type of thing for years. It's about time this one-horse town caught on. Except the Inn needs more than just PR to salvage it—more like a total renovation, but I would never say that to Grammy J. She'd have her shotgun cocked before the words left my mouth.

"I wasn't aware you'd be stickin' around long enough to accomplish all that." Grammy J looks at me. Her lips have taken on a purplish hue thanks to the wine. "Not that I'm unhappy to see you, but want to tell me what prompted this little visit?"

Brushing flecks of paint off my dirt-stained white jeans, I sigh and say, "I needed a break. Some time off." From

Nick and my mother and life. From *everything*. I've been here a day and already it's as if the weight that's been pressing on my chest has lifted a fraction so I can *breathe* again.

Grammy J shakes her head, now a darkening silhouette against the sunset. "Then you're a fool, child. I already told you I'm puttin' you to work, and while I appreciate whatever you can do for the Inn, there are no free passes—even for family."

"Noted," I say, tucking my feet under me, the low drone of cicadas a relaxing chorus around me. I close my eyes. A breeze washes over my face, and I inhale the scent of soil and ripe fruit growing somewhere nearby that instantly reminds me of Ryan. The image of him pinning me against the counter in Hodgepodge flashes behind my eyelids. "But right now I'm off to soak in a bubble bath." Standing, I stretch my arms above my head and offer the bottle back to Grammy J.

"Keep it," she says. "I reckon you're goin' to be in that tub awhile with the amount of scrubbin' you need. May as well drink some great wine while you do it."

A small laugh escapes. "You're probably not too far off, but don't say anything to Ryan about me liking it, okay?"

"You know, after that debacle between you two at the Gansey house all those years ago, I never thought I'd see you runnin' off with him again, but you sure were quick to get in his car this afternoon." A conspiratorial half smile forms on her face.

"I panicked. I have no interest in Ryan," I say, trying to ignore his words playing in a loop in my head. *I think you've been waiting your whole life for a guy like me to come along and wake you up, show you just how fun messy can be.* I've already done messy. What was Nick, if not the biggest mess of my life?

"Mmm-hmm."

"Absolutely no interest. None."

"And yet you're the one who brought him up in this conversation," Grammy J says, confirming that I don't know why I bother lying because I'm not convincing anyone. She hides her mouth behind her glass, but I can tell she's grinning—it's the way deep creases appear in her cheeks and her eyes dance with something playful. She's enjoying this way too much.

"I really am going to soak in a bath now." I lean down to kiss her cheek, then start to head for the Inn, but Grammy J's voice stops me.

"Next time you see Ryan be sure to congratulate him. That bottle in your hand ranked in *Wine Spectator*'s Top 100."

My first thought is there's no way a Tempranillo from Texas Hill Country made that list, but then I register the rest of her words. I turn to face her, my brow furrowed. "What does he have to do with it?" I ask. "He just works for the vineyard."

Grammy J cackles, the sound overloud and too high-pitched, and I wonder if before I arrived she'd indulged in one too many glasses of wine during the Inn's evening social hour. But what she says next leaves me dumbstruck.

"Oh dear Lord, child," she says. "Ryan doesn't just work for the vineyard—he owns the damn thing!"

8

Moose loads the last of the mangled boards onto his truck bed as the sun edges completely over the horizon. The world is a kaleidoscope of grays and purples and pinks. When he said he'd stop by the bed-and-breakfast in the morning to provide an estimate for the porch, I thought he meant when it was fully daylight. Instead he arrived an hour ago with a tool belt around his waist, a clipboard propped against his side, and a grin on his face that was annoyingly cheery for the crack of dawn.

At least the bump on my forehead is down to the size of a gumball, the swelling in my ankle has lessened so I can almost walk normally, and my muscles, while stiff, are still functional. Thank God for aspirin, a bubble bath, and a solid night's sleep.

"That should do it for now," Moose says, latching the tailgate and wiping the dirt from his hands.

I find another rusted nail in the grass and toss it into the bucket that's weighing down the already-sagging porch steps. "How long will the rebuild take?"

"I'll buy the lumber and other materials this weekend.

My team works fast, so I'd guess about a week, especially since you did much of the demo for us." He writes some notes on a form, then rips away the carbon copy and hands it to me. The rebuild is going to cost as much as a weekend getaway to the Ritz Carlton Grand Cayman resort. Still, it's worth it.

"Because of the significant structural damage," Moose continues, "I won't know for sure until we get in there and determine the full extent of what we're dealing with, but I'll keep you informed."

I nod, gazing out at the view. From my vantage point, I see groups of people picking grapes in the vineyards in the distance. A tractor trails each crew, hauling plastic bins to collect the clusters. I pull my hair into a ponytail, allowing the breeze to blow across my neck. It's already hot enough to make my shirt stick to my back.

"It's been awhile since I've been here, but glancing around at the exterior, I can tell you the Inn isn't up to code," he says, opening the driver's door and placing the clipboard on the dash. "The roof needs replacing. The walls are leaning slightly, meaning there's probably foundation problems, and the egress windows in the bedrooms don't meet the size requirements. You may want to speak to Joy about fixing those things first. Otherwise, renovating the porch will be a waste of time and money."

"I've been informed the budget only allows for the bare minimum."

"Then you have quite the chore ahead of you."

"Don't remind me. Today I've been tasked with organizing the shed and vacuuming the curtains and furniture." Though anything is better than returning to Dallas to face my mother and everyone else who thinks I'm a failure.

"All right, I gotta open the store." Moose grabs the bucket filled with nails and sets it on the passenger-side floor. "I hope you'll come to the party tonight. At least for the free food and wine."

"You inviting me to be your date?" I ask, nudging his arm with my elbow. There's something warm and welcoming about Moose that brings out the playful side of me. Maybe it's his lack of pretense. Or perhaps it's the way he doesn't seem to pass judgment.

Climbing inside the truck, he drops into his seat and says, "As much as I'd love to, I doubt Cricket would like it. He's sweet on you."

"Fortunately, I'm not attracted to insects," I say. Sure Ryan's sexy in a rough-around-the-edges kind of way, and those hazel eyes draw me to him like a bee to a flower. But even beautiful flowers can hold hidden dangers, be as lethal as belladonna berries.

"You know, you could always approach the situation differently," Moose says. "Have some fun with it."

"How do you mean?"

He secures his seat belt and turns the engine over a few times before it catches. "Ever heard the phrase, 'Don't get mad, get even'?" he says, winking conspiratorially.

As Moose drives away, I remember the secret cave tucked into the hillside on the far edge of Grammy J's property. He's a genius. I know how I'm going to beat Ryan at his own game, demonstrate that he's the fool. It's exactly what I need to regain control. With a skip in my stride, I head for the shed to start cleaning, feeling upbeat for the first time in months.

I have a plan to execute.

THE PARTY IS in full swing when I arrive at Camden Cellars that evening. Music, loud voices, and laughter pour out of an old German stone barn I assume acts as the tasting room and winery, which is surrounded by a Provençal-style landscape of lush trees, lavender fields, and acres of grapevines covering gently sloping hills. I can't believe all this belongs to Ryan. When Grammy J said he owned Camden Cellars, I was expecting a modest operation. I've vastly underestimated him, but I refuse to focus on that. I'm here for one purpose—retribution.

Walking up the paved path, I'm careful to hold the fruit basket steady despite my slight limp. Wearing wedges with a still-sore ankle wasn't my smartest decision, but since I wasn't apprised of the attire for the evening, I erred on the dressier side of causal. My mother, of course, would not approve. Pain should be no hurdle to beauty or propriety.

A peacock saunters past me, its jewel-toned tail brushing against my leg. That explains why a few feathers fell out of the back of Ryan's Blazer.

I step through the arched doorway and immediately into a room packed with people gathered around a massive bar in the center, wine flowing in abundance. I glance around for a place to set the fruit basket, except there doesn't appear to be a spot designated for host gifts. *Apparently proper party etiquette is optional here.* I stick the basket on a built-in cabinet and try to blend in.

Many attendees look as if they've come straight from working in the vineyards—sunburned noses, dirt-stained clothes, unkempt hair. Based on bits of conversation, I piece together that tonight's festivities are in honor of a successful harvest, early in comparison to other domestic grape-growing regions because of the intense late-summer heat.

I scan the crowd for Ryan, but I'm interrupted when my cell phone vibrates in my pocket—this afternoon I finally managed to get the display to turn on, though the new one I ordered can't get here quick enough. I pull it out, and dread clutches my chest when I see my mother's name, but I retreat to the parking lot to take the call anyway. The sooner I get this over with, the sooner I can forget the conversation ever happened.

"How lovely of you to pick up," my mother says in her usual biting tone when I answer. "Given your recent childish actions, you can't afford to ignore me."

"Hello, Mother," I say, hoping the determination in my voice conceals my apprehension, though I'm sure she can sense it. My mother has the innate ability to detect my true emotions, no matter how well hidden, and twist them into something ugly, then use them against me. One of her many talents.

"Imagine my shame when I discovered from your father that you've not only dropped all of your professional and social commitments to wallow over an entirely inappropriate man, but you've chosen to do so in Wilhelmsburg with *that woman*." I envision her sitting in the formal living room, encircled by oil paintings and family photos in sterling frames flaunting our enviable, fake life.

"That woman is *my grandmother*," I say, putting the phone on speaker and strolling up and down the path, running my fingers through the wildflowers that edge it.

"Yes, and as such, she should have told you to return to Dallas and tend to your responsibilities, though why I'd expect such a thing from her, of all people—"

"Maybe if you'd told me what happened between you and Grammy J, I wouldn't have come here." But that's not exactly true. While Grammy J and I have never been close, I've always been curious about her and wondered how much of my mother is a reflection of her. Except now that I'm here, I realize they're entirely different people and that perhaps Grammy J could be someone special, someone I never knew I needed.

"This conversation is about your juvenile behavior," my mother says, glossing over my statement. If I want answers, I guess I'll need to get them from Grammy J.

"I'm just taking some personal time. The situation isn't permanent," I say, but the wind causes the words to sound small, almost lost.

"In this household, we don't run away from our failures or obligations, and I won't have rumors spread about our family because of your inability to make rational decisions. As it is, I've already had people inquiring after your whereabouts, one being that nosy Bernice Rimes who can't keep her blubbering mouth shut. I had to hear from her that you passed off the Make-A-Wish Foundation fundraiser to Bill Heacock's firm. How could you do that? You know the president of the foundation is one of your father's biggest clients. And she's telling everyone about how you backed out of the Scottish Rite Treasure Street benefit. It's as if you're happy committing professional suicide."

Of course all my mother cares about is me tarnishing our family's reputation, not my mental or emotional well-being.

"You need to return home and stop acting like a brokenhearted teenager," she continues. "Until you do, you won't receive anything from your father and me in terms of support."

"Then I guess I'll be destitute, because I'm not leaving here until I'm ready," I say, then abruptly end the call. Squeezing my eyes shut, I force several deep breaths into my lungs and, not for the first time, think about cutting my mother out of my life completely. I don't know why I grant her so much authority over me or let her reduce me to feeling like a child.

Slipping my phone back into my pocket, I turn to head back into the party but freeze when I realize I've had an audience. Ryan leans against the limestone facade a few feet away, studying me. There's a strange tightening in my stomach, a mixture of self-preservation, panic, and anger I know is misplaced but present nonetheless.

"How much of that did you hear?" I ask.

He pushes off the wall and saunters toward me. In three strides he's in my space, and my heart trips over its own beat. It's all I can do to stand my ground and try to ignore the smell of him—soap and aftershave and the hint of green things. "How much do you want me to have heard?" he asks, brushing a wayward strand of hair off my cheek.

None of it.

I wish I could remember if you're supposed to swim parallel to the shore or against the strong rush of the ocean when swept away by a current, because that's what standing exposed in front of Ryan feels like.

We stare at each other, the silence clotting around us in the hot evening air.

"So all of this is yours," I say after a bit, gesturing at the estate that appears never-ending. "It's adequate, I suppose."

A smile tugs at the corners of his mouth. "I guess trade school taught me something besides how to concoct different flavors of moonshine."

"Like how to make wine that tastes like cough syrup?"

"Among other things. But just like you had no interest in attending tonight, I'm sure you have no interest in finding out what those things are." The suggestive tone of his words, rich and enticing, flows through me like a finely crafted port.

He's wearing dark jeans and a checkered dress shirt

with several buttons dangerously neglected. The reddish-purple color staining his hands is absent, and his honey-blond hair, even more golden in the evening sun, is wet and raked back—with fingers, not a comb. It's all too easy for me to picture him fresh from the shower, towel slung low on his hips, water dripping down his smooth, tan neck, his hard, well-muscled chest, his impossibly defined abs. The image is enough to send an ache to places that have no business aching.

My thoughts must be plastered all over my face, because Ryan flashes a the-reality-is-even-better grin and says, "Keep mentally undressing me and you'll owe me dinner."

It's nice to see his reserve of smug charm hasn't dried up yet. He's more skilled at this game than I initially gave him credit for, but that ends now. *You're here for payback*, I remind myself. "If impressions are any indication, you're worth the price of a Happy Meal," I say. "Toy not included."

For a moment he looks astonished, an expression I intend for him to wear more than once tonight, but he quickly recovers. Shaking his head, he turns toward the entrance and says, "Come on, Marge, I'll give you the grand tour and show you how we create that wine you hate."

He throws an arm around my shoulder, gently pulling me against him in a way that feels too intimate for such a simple gesture, and leads me back inside. I try to hide my scowl—it's annoying how he so effortlessly trades verbal blows with me. What will it take to have the last word with this man? As we enter the tasting room, I vow to find out.

The interior is breathtaking in its construction and true to the architectural style prevalent in Hill Country. "Is this an original late-nineteenth-century German stone barn?" I ask.

"You know your Wilhelmsburg history," he says, glancing at me. "It's a reproduction. We built the barn two years ago to accommodate our growing customer base. It houses the tasting room, barrel cellar, and winery."

"How much are you producing annually?"

"Between twenty-five hundred and three thousand cases, depending. Most of it is sold to our wine club members and restaurants, but I'm getting ahead of myself. Tour starts after we eat. Follow me."

We step out onto the veranda where most of the guests have migrated. Immediately I spot Possum, the bartender from The Tangled Vine, his hair still brighter than a traffic cone. He has an arm draped around a woman who exudes personality despite not being taller than five feet in heels. The pixie cut, the half sleeve of pirate-themed tattoos and full color chest featuring intricate artwork, the cat-eye glasses, and the bright red lips all scream confidence.

Hundreds of white lights are strung in the trees, and the air is thick with the scent of steaks charring over the applewood-fire grill on the far side of the patio. While I stand idle beside Ryan, people slap him on the back and offer their congratulations on another fantastic crop of grapes.

"This is going to be our best vintage yet."

"Yields for Petite Syrah were lower than normal, but the quality is there."

"The Cab Sauv took her sweet time getting into rock-and-roll mode, but she came through," says one man with bushy eyebrows and purple-tinted fingertips. "The extra hang time on the vine should really enhance her flavor development."

Ryan answers them with praise of his own for their

efforts and dedication. He's good at working a crowd. Almost too good. For an instant, I get a glimpse of someone else—someone polished and educated and who knows how to win—and I realize there's more beneath his rugged exterior than I thought.

Ryan slips behind the outdoor bar and fills two glasses with white wine the color of hay bales, and passes one to me. "It's a Viognier. To wake up your palate."

"Really? I thought it was cat pee," I say, smiling sweetly at him.

"Do you ever stop being a pain in the ass? Just drink it."

I'm getting under his skin. Perfect.

I swirl the glass, holding it up to the slowly fading light, and sniff the wine, inhaling the aroma of overripe apricots, melon, and orange blossoms. I take a sip, letting the liquid rest in my mouth a moment. Having never tried Viognier before, I expected a syrupy, sappy flavor to match the bouquet, but instead it's crafted in a dry style with a creamy texture and tastes of tropical fruits and a touch of spice.

Ryan watches me the entire time, waiting for the verdict.

"It's no Chardonnay, that much is obvious," I say, which of course is a positive thing, because I hate Chardonnay and its oaky, buttery profile, but he doesn't need to know that.

"I thought you'd appreciate this varietal of grape since she's so much like you. Difficult to handle. Finicky about her growing conditions. You have to pick her at just the right moment or else she throws a fit and the wine turns out wrong."

Cheeky bastard.

I start to respond when sixty pounds of white-and-gray

canine barrels up to me, paws landing on my chest, tongue licking all over my cheeks. I stumble in my wedges, and a split second before I'm about to fall over, I grab the edge of the bar. Wine sloshes out of my glass and onto my blouse and neck, which causes the dog to lick harder and more frantically. I gag as I try to push it off me.

Ryan snaps his fingers. "Bordeaux, off." His voice is deep and commanding and a little bit rough, and I bet it'd sound even better when spoken in my ear. The dog sits and stares at me with an eager look, as if she wants me to pet her.

I prefer goldfish.

"Cute," I say, wiping off the saliva on my clothes. The dry cleaner is going to love me.

Ryan pats his leg and the shaggy beast struts over to him like a model on a runway. "She's a bearded collie puppy. Eventually she'll settle down."

"Except Bordeaux is almost four years old, so it's not likely," Moose says, approaching with a plate crowded with what appears to be every offering from the grill.

"Ignore him. Moose is envious of your spirit," Ryan says to Bordeaux, scratching behind her ear. Without warning, my mind conjures up all the ways those capable hands and rough fingers could make me melt, causing heat and anticipation to rush through me and settle low in my stomach.

Moose elbows me in the arm, knocking me back into my good sense. "I'm glad you came tonight," he says, plucking a spear of asparagus off his plate and eating it in two bites.

"I had to thank you in person for your suggestion. And you'll be happy to know I figured out a way to accomplish it."

A grin crosses Moose's face that tells me he understands my meaning. "Excellent. I hope there's a little something in it for me if it's successful. I'm partial to sweets."

"I wouldn't stress it, Marge," Ryan interjects, winking at me. "Moose has a very loose definition of sweet. He seems to like you well enough." He thinks he's so witty. I bet if he knew what Moose and I were referring to, he wouldn't be so proud.

I sneak another sip of wine, summoning up a quip of my own, when Big Boobs McGee, the blonde who was hanging off Ryan during the pool game at The Tangled Vine, joins us. Tonight she's dressed more appropriately in jeans and a form-fitting T-shirt with the Camden Cellars logo printed across the chest. She carries a plate of food and the attitude of a jealous ex-girlfriend.

"Well, who do we have here?" She sidles up to Ryan so her chest presses against his arm. It's a subtle claim of ownership, yet I feel the move more acutely than Ryan seems to. The manipulation, the passive aggressiveness reminds me of all the times I pulled similar stunts on Nick, and for what? He still chose Lillie. "We haven't been introduced. I'm Bonnie Cantrell. I work in the tasting room. Are you new to town?" she asks me.

"Margaret," I say. "I'm . . . visiting."

"You two have met before," Ryan says, stepping away from her, closer to me, and I wonder if the move was conscious on his part. "The night of the Gansey house prank."

I should have guessed Big Boobs McGee is Bon Bon.

"Funny. I remember that night, but I don't remember you," she says, inspecting me as if I'm invading her territory. It's possible that even back then, while Ryan and I were kissing in that dilapidated kitchen, they were a thing. Or maybe it was an unrequited crush. After a pause, recognition lights up her eyes. "You're Joy's granddaughter. So that means . . ." She faces Moose, then Ryan. "Well, your family certainly knows how to grease the wheels of the gossip mill. You were the hot topic for weeks after that, which of course just brought old rumors and gossip back to life."

Ryan shoots her a glance and she quiets under his subtle head shake.

"How sad that I was the focus of such interest. Life here must be terribly boring for those of you who never manage to leave," I say, showcasing my signature bitchy smile.

"All right, I'd better feed Marge before she reaches a new level of snarky." Ryan steals my wine and polishes it off in one gulp before finishing his own. What a wart. I was intending on drinking that. He sets both empty glasses on the bar and places a hand on my lower back. As he escorts me over to the food area, I catch the sour expression on Bon Bon's face.

"Is Bonnie your ex-girlfriend?" I ask.

"Not that it's any of your business, but no," Ryan says, then greets the chef manning the grill. They spend a minute chitchatting about the upcoming wine dinner at the chef's restaurant. Finally, Ryan glances at the chalkboard menu and orders the center-cut filet served with a Zinfandel demi-glace, Boursin mashed potatoes, and roasted vegetables.

After I order the same, I turn to face Ryan and ask, "How about your paramour?" He stares at me like I'm talking in some secret fairy language. "You know, your occasional sex partner?"

"Leave it to you to make a fuck buddy sound snotty. And, no. Not recently."

"So you're sticking to second cousins for pleasure these days?" I ask. "That's how you country boys do it, right?"

Ryan shakes his head, as if I'm an infuriating creature he can't make sense of. "Please never change."

He's joking—I know this—but still his words spark something inside me. A hope, a possibility, that maybe someday someone will accept me for who I am and deem me worthy all the same.

But there's a reason people say hope, like love, is fleeting.

9

After we eat and bottles of private reserve Cabernet are passed around and toasts celebrating the harvest have concluded, Ryan whisks me away for the official tour. It's time to put my plan into action and amp up the charm, enough so he thinks I'm interested but not to the point I get carried away. Coaxing him to the bed-and-breakfast's property will be tricky if he suspects I'm up to something, so I have to play this right.

He guides me through an arched doorway and into the wine production area. The air in here is cooler and less humid, a sharp contrast to the sweltering heat outside. Goose bumps pop up all over my skin.

While Ryan adjusts some controls on the wall, I sneak several sips of Cab and stare at the way his upper body tapers into a V-shape, how his broad shoulders and back muscles are defined and visible beneath the fabric of his shirt. I have a flash of me wearing nothing but that shirt, my hair a mess, and his scent all over me. Ryan turns around before I can cut my eyes away or rearrange my expression, and the smile that spreads across his face is so wide and self-satisfied I'm surprised canary feathers aren't stuck in his teeth.

"Marge, I think we can both agree I'm worth more than a Happy Meal," he says. He glances at my near-empty glass without comment, but no doubt there's a pompous remark waiting on the tip of his tongue. "This way." He practically skips backward between the two rows of tanks on either side, swinging the wine bottle in his hand. "This room is where the magic starts to happen. After the grapes are picked, they're brought here to be sorted and destemmed. The fruit is placed whole into these tanks to cold soak for several days before fermentation."

Ryan speaks with such passion and authority I can't help but wonder how a trouble-seeking teenager with the nickname Cricket transformed into someone who owns and operates a boutique winery.

"So we've already reached the part of the tour where you spout off facts like a brochure," I say.

He stops beside a large egg-shaped thing I've never seen before and slaps the side, the resulting noise loud and harsh and with a slight echo. "We've recently switched to using concrete tanks to age our private and special-reserve wines, specifically our Tempranillo and that Cabernet you're pretending not to enjoy. We believe the concrete provides a truer taste of the vineyard without oak flavoring hiding flaws in the fruit. It's brought the final product to a whole new level."

I sniff my wine, breathing in the aroma of plum and cranberry, then take a sip, paying closer attention to the flavor profile. Now that Ryan mentions it, I taste none of the vanilla or toffee notes commonly found in wines exposed to oak barrels, but rather a concentration of dark ripe fruits framed by silky tannins that give way to a lingering cherry finish.

"Very unique," I say, but it's also smooth and pronounced and impeccably crafted. The intense climate, difficult soils, varying landscapes, and presence of pests and vine diseases should make grape-growing conditions harsh and unpredictable in Texas. And yet Ryan has managed to create a range of wines that prove anything is possible. How does he do it?

"The Cab is more than unique." He steals the glass out of my hand, the calluses on his palm brushing my knuckles, and a tingling sensation vibrates through my body. Drinking some of the wine, Ryan moves closer to me, his gaze roaming over my face. He slides a hand around my waist, his palm coming to rest on the small of my back. "She's like an enticing redhead playing hard to get. At first she's standoffish, but then slowly you catch a glimpse of what's underneath. Before you know it, you're in deep, a slave to her allure."

Had he thrown a live grenade at me, it wouldn't have felt more dangerous than his words just then. My heart is pounding like a jackhammer, and my common sense is crumbling in a way I've never felt with anyone. Lust I'm familiar with. But this . . . this is something different.

But that kind of temptation can only lead to trouble. I reclaim my wine glass and put enough distance between us to lessen the uncontrollable tug I feel toward him. "Or perhaps you're confusing playing hard to get with uninterested." I try to keep my voice strong and even, but I've learned that Ryan is unnervingly perceptive, so I'm sure he hears the warble in it, hears how absolutely terrified he makes me. He has this way of spinning me off course, pushing me out of my element, and even worse, I'm beginning to enjoy it.

He barely reacts, save for the muscles tightening in his jaw, as if he sees right through me.

I clear my throat and gesture to the egg-shaped tank. "How do you handle pump over in this thing?" I ask, referring to the technique where a portion of the juice is pumped out from the bottom of the tank and sprayed over the mass of grape skins, stems, and seeds floating at the top.

Ryan continues to stare at me with an all-too-invasive look. Finally he says, "The shape allows the wine to circulate naturally during fermentation, reducing our need for punch down." He pauses a moment. "Not only are you a contradiction, but you're quite the enigma. How do you know so much about winemaking?"

I shrug. "I've toured countless wineries and vineyards all over the world—Napa, Châteauneuf-du-Pape, Rioja."

"Then you won't mind a little competition in the form of wine trivia," he says. "Let's make this more interesting. I'll ask you a question. If you get it wrong, the tour ends. But if you get it right, we move onward."

Calculating, bluff-calling wart. If I refuse to participate, it means I'm not up for the challenge—and I *never* back down from a challenge—but if I agree and answer the questions correctly, he's proven a part of me wants to be here with him. Except Ryan doesn't realize that engaging in his little game also brings me closer to my goal.

"What's it going to be?" he asks.

"I'm in, but only if you answer some personal ones of my own."

"It doesn't take much to figure out a simple country boy like me. I'll grant you three. Make 'em count."

"Ditto for you," I say, back on track, though it's unclear which one of us has the upper hand.

"Then let's discover how smart you really are," Ryan says, walking backward again. "What's the name of the process of siphoning wine off the dead yeast into a clean container?"

"There's easy and then there's insulting," I say, following him. "The answer is 'racking,' and it's something that should be repeated several times during the various winemaking phases in order to soften tannins, clarify the wine, and enhance its aromatic characteristics."

"So you are up for the challenge." Ryan opens another arched door, exposing a steep stone staircase, and signals for me to go ahead. "Tour continues below. I'll hold this," he says, grabbing the wine glass from my hand again. "It'd be a shame for you to trip and fall face-first."

"I assumed you'd relish the opportunity to bask in the view," I say, descending the steps, careful of my foot placement so I don't reinjure my ankle or twist the other one. "And it's *my* turn when we reach the bottom."

"I'm shaking in anticipation," he says, trailing after me.

The stairwell leads to a cave-like cellar with barrels lining the walls. It's not hard to spot the ones that have been aging the longest—sections of the outsides are stained a burgundy color where the red wine has seeped into the oak. Rustic iron chandeliers run along the ceiling, creating an inviting and romantic atmosphere. The air is dank and still and smells slightly of minerals and Herbes de Provence, something I've always found refreshing.

Ryan corks the bottle of Cabernet and sets it, along with my glass, on a hand-carved wooden bar perfect for wine tasting. "This is our barrel room—"

"Thank you for stating the obvious."

"—where we age everything but our reserve wines in French oak for two years with an additional year in the bottle before being released to the public."

He retrieves two fresh glasses and a bottle of wine from a rack fastened to the stone wall. The label has Wild

Abandon printed in script around an icon of bright red lips, similar in tone and style to the label on the bottle of No Regrets I drank at The Tangled Vine. Pouring some for each of us, Ryan passes me a glass and says, "For when you want to live on the edge. It's a Grenache, Syrah, and Mourvèdre blend."

The enthralling look in his eyes momentarily knocks me off-kilter and makes me want to do something stupid like swim naked in a public fountain. I imagine he's caused quite a few women to throw caution to the wind and lose themselves in his brand of reckless love.

"I favor the straight and narrow," I say.

"Sure you do. Which is why you're here with me right now," he says. "Hit me with your worst, then."

Leaning against the bar, I take a sip and study him. I shuffle through a list of questions in my head but settle on the all-encompassing one I was contemplating before. "How did the boy I remember from that night become the owner of an award-winning winery?"

"That's the best you can do? I thought you'd go for the jugular." His tone is lighthearted, almost flirtatious, but I catch a hint of something cautious and guarded underneath, and I know I've touched on a sensitive subject and this is his attempt at deflection.

"I thought I'd let you warm up first. But take your time if you need it," I say, curious as to how much information he'll share.

He swirls his glass with a flick of his wrist, the red liquid climbing up the sides. Finally he rakes a hand through his hair and sighs. "When I was twelve my dad ran out on my mom and me. He was never around much to begin with, and when he was there he used his fists more than anything else, but I still didn't handle his departure well." He hesitates, his relaxed demeanor slipping for a moment, so quick I would've missed it if I hadn't been staring closely at him. "I was a handful for my mom and constantly in trouble, so she arranged for me to help Fred Baxter, an older man who lived on this hill surrounded by thirty acres of land perfect for grape growing. His wife had died years prior and he'd let things become overgrown and run-down. My mom thought offering me as manual labor to fix the house and get the property in order would set me straight. And it did."

At first I think that's all Ryan's going to say, but he strides over to one of the barrels, checks the seal on a stopper covered in burlap, and continues. "I discovered I enjoyed working the land and felt connected to it in a strange way I've never been able to articulate, but never once did I consider someday owning a winery. That concept was so far out of my realm of possibility, but Mr. Baxter encouraged me to apply to UC Davis's Viticulture and Enology program anyway. When he passed away a few years after I graduated, he willed his entire estate to me on the condition I used the acres for a vineyard. I was living in Provence at the time but moved back to Wilhelmsburg after his attorney contacted me with the news. I planted the first grapes that spring, almost a decade ago, and I owe it all to an old man who gave me a chance."

His words blow open a hole inside me. Apart from being a troublemaker as a kid, nothing about him is what I expected—educated, cultured, a successful businessman. More questions swirl in my mind, but all I manage to blurt out is, "Do you speak French?"

Ryan imitates the sound of a buzzer. "It's my turn now."

I gesture for him to get on with it while I drink more wine. He sips some of his own, taking his sweet time in a way that's both sexy and infuriating.

"Okay, smarty," he says after a while. "Since you're so well traveled and knowledgeable, why are most European wines named after the region and not the varietal like in the United States?"

I roll my eyes. "The belief over there is that the unique landscape and climate where the grapes are grown is a better reflection of how the wine will taste than the varietals themselves. I swear you're convinced I'm a hack."

"Did you ever consider I'm purposely being easy on you?" he says, the heart-stopping grin returning on his face. "But I can go harder if you'd prefer."

I'm sure the double entendre was accidental. Still my breath quickens. I feel Ryan's gaze on me, but I refuse to acknowledge it or show how much he rattles me.

Leaving my glass of wine on the bar—I've had enough Wild Abandon for one night—I pull my shoulders back and say, "Can we move this along?"

"You can end the tour anytime," he says. "Simply answer a question wrong."

"And lose? Not an option."

"Then let's go," he says.

I follow Ryan upstairs, into the production area, and out into a courtyard. The color is draining from the sky. Soon the stars will be a glittering sea above me. I hear laughter and the buzz of conversation coming from the veranda that's hidden from view.

"That's the bottling line," he says, waving to a smaller limestone building across from the barn. "We're one of four wineries in Wilhelmsburg whose wines are exclusively estate grown and bottled, though with the way we're expanding, we may have to resort to purchasing fruit from the High Plains or other parts of Hill Country. Land is scarce these days."

We walk to the vineyard, the leafy canopy cloaked in

soft, diffused light. Ryan finishes his wine and places the glass at the start of a row of vines, which are bare except for a few straggling grapes.

"This is the Born to Run Block, which consists entirely of Tempranillo," he says, popping off one of the stray berries and handing it to me. Sweet juices burst in my mouth, the seeds almost dissolving. "And beyond that is the Pretender Block made up of Cab Sauv." Most wineries map out their vineyard sections with a simple A, B, C or 1, 2, 3 method, but of course Ryan decided to name his after classic rock songs.

He glances down at my shoes. "The ground is a bit uneven. Are you sure you can navigate in those after the porch debacle?"

"I'll manage," I say, my wedges rocking unsteadily on the foliage littering the path. I stumble a bit, and it's monumentally unfair that the world seems to conspire to knock me on my ass whenever Ryan is present. He places strong hands on my waist to keep me from teetering right over, the gesture reminiscent of the way he caught me the night of the Gansey house prank. My body relaxes, and I find myself leaning into him, as if it's something I've done a thousand times before.

"Careful there, Marge," he says. "All right, I'm waiting with bated breath for your next question."

Picking a leaf off the ground, I twirl the stem between my fingers and look at him. Everything about Ryan seems happy, free. I wonder what his secret is, because there must be something that weighs on him, something he's too proud to reveal. "Tell me your biggest regret."

"I don't have one," he says fast and without hesitation. "Regret's like speeding along the highway while only looking in the rearview mirror. It's unproductive and dangerous and why I dedicated a wine to the notion of living without it. I've found that if I focus on what's in front of me, regardless of where I end up, I'm never worried about how I got there."

"And what's in front of you now?" I ask, knowing I'm breaking the rules but curious anyway. What does a guy like Ryan want out of life?

"Half the fun is in not knowing and embracing the unexpected." Ryan stares at me as if he understands something about me that I don't, and I force myself not to fidget under the scrutiny. "But these days I mostly think about the winery and where to take it next."

"Oh? Grander plans than all this?" I glance around, taking stock of everything he's accomplished in so little time. I could never have guessed at the level of Ryan's success—or that I could envy him so much. For the first time I realize how success and happiness aren't as closely entwined as I've been raised to believe.

He shrugs. "Several bigger commercial wineries have been sniffing around. I could sell out to them, maybe return to France and start over there," he says, pinching off a few droopy leaves from the canopy overhang. "Or I could stay the course. We have a successful boutique operation going, and that doesn't have to change. But mostly I'd love to watch the winery grow and achieve its full potential."

What would it be like, I wonder, to be uncertain about your future but still know that no matter which path you choose you'll end up in the right place?

Motioning to a hill dotted with resting cattle, I ask, "Is that part of Grammy J's property or yours?" The segue is too easy, and besides, it's now or never.

"All fifteen acres belong to Joy," he says, coming to stand next to me.

"How long would it take to get there if you went through the vineyard?"

"On foot?"

"No, driving," I say.

"Five minutes, give or take."

"Good. It's my turn to show you something."

He raises an eyebrow as one side of his mouth curves higher than the other. "That sounds promising."

"I figured you'd be interested in a little adventure." I walk toward his Blazer parked beside the smaller limestone building. To my surprise the interior is absent of dog hair and dirt, the seats vacuumed, and the dashboard glossy with that Armor All shine. *Did he clean because of what I said?* I shake my head, erasing the foolish thought.

"Buckle up," Ryan says, starting the engine and putting the SUV in gear. "It may get bumpy."

As I guide him to the spot, the Blazer jolts and sways over the path that runs between the rows of grapevines and the grassy, rutted fields of Grammy J's property. We don't talk much, which I prefer, because the nervous excitement humming through me would no doubt come through in my voice.

"Over there," I say, pointing to a nondescript wooden door built into the side of a hill. Ryan parks, and before he has the chance to stop me, I steal the keys out of the ignition, pocketing them, then walk over to the new padlock I purchased earlier today and enter the sequence of numbers.

The hinges creak when I open the door. Immediately I'm hit with a wall of chilly, damp, stale air. I find matches and light a few of the lanterns dangling from hooks drilled into the walls. The soft yellow glow casts shapes around the cave.

"I've lived in Wilhelmsburg almost my whole life and

never knew this place existed," Ryan says from close behind. I feel his breath on my neck and his body heat against my back. Moving forward a fraction of an inch, he reaches around me and touches the rough indentations in the rock, his chest brushing against my shoulder blades. A shiver runs down my spine—I'm sure he felt it. It'd be so easy to turn around, so easy to fall into him, but I sidestep away.

"My grandfather stumbled upon it when he was a teenager," I say with a slight shake in my voice that I hope is concealed by the wind whistling through the gaps in the cave. "It's always reminded me of Ariel's secret grotto in *The Little Mermaid*, especially because Poppa Bart kept barrels of homemade bourbon and random valuables in here."

"It's incredible."

I look at Ryan. There's both awe and hunger on his face, and I imagine he's wishing this were on his land so he could use it as a cellar. "You may want to wipe away the drool," I say. "Who knew eroded limestone would be such a turn-on for you?"

His expression changes, and the fire that ignites in his eyes is so intense it could engulf me in flames. "Remember what I told you about the Cabernet? How one taste and her seductive pull becomes undeniable?" He steps toward me and slides a palm over my cheek, cupping my jaw. My breath catches in my throat. I should back away, stick to the plan, but I'm transfixed by the feeling of his thumb dragging across my lips, the way they part without my permission, how my heart is beating so hard it echoes in my ears. "I bet it's even truer about you."

The deep timbre of his voice coils tight and tense in my stomach, as if I'm a high-octane tank ready to explode. I'm not sure of anything anymore—all I know is that I need his hands, his mouth, all over me. Ryan suddenly pins me against the wall, and before I'm able to process anything, he's kissing me. It's slow, and scorching, and desperate, as if he's memorizing the taste of me.

The air has left my lungs, but I feel more alive than ever. Ryan has one hand on my waist, the other under my blouse, his fingers exploring my skin, hot and urgent. Clutching the soft material of his shirt in my fists, I draw him closer, and his grip on me tightens, a soft groan rumbling from deep in his throat. Breaking away, Ryan whispers in my ear, "*Je suis content d'avoir raison*"—*I'm glad I was right*—and holy shit he *does* speak French—then he dips his head and places openmouthed kisses along my jaw, down the curve of my neck, across my collarbone. His teeth lightly graze the hollow of my throat.

Tiny noises escape me, but I don't care, my concentration is focused on the way his tongue causes a current of energy to shoot straight to my nerves, how every part of me is crying for more. He reclaims my mouth and nudges a knee between my thighs, lifting one of my legs and wrapping it around his waist, pressing farther into me. I gasp when I feel him where I need him most, my body grinding on its own accord. Ryan lets out a small chuckle that vibrates against my lips, and it's like a physical blow, knocking sense back into me. *You're here for revenge,* I tell myself, *stop kissing the hell out of him.*

Pushing out of his grasp, my chest heaving, I stagger out of the cave and into the night air. Before he weaves another spell around me, I slam the door shut and reattach the padlock. Immediately there's pounding, dust flying everywhere from Ryan banging the old wood. Hopefully it holds.

"Clever, Marge," he calls out, his voice muffled.

"I guess this time *you* got beat," I shout, repeating what

he said all those years ago, moments before we were arrested. "Maybe you'll have better luck in the future."

Retrieving my phone from my pocket, I dial the local police and report a trespasser on the edge of Grammy J's property, then hop into his Blazer and return to the winery for my car.

Ryan may have compared me to private reserve Cabernet, something valuable and rare, but what he doesn't understand is when you take too many risks with wine, when you mishandle it, you end up with sour grapes.

10

Three days pass and not a peep from Ryan. Payback was supposed to rid him from my system, but instead I'm antsy, unsettled. Because that kiss—there was so much left unfinished in it, so much left to discover. He's like a scar that won't stop itching.

And if I'm honest, I didn't figure Ryan as the type who gave up so easily, and as much as I hate to admit it, I thought maybe he saw something in me worth pursuing.

I exit Pirouette, a French-inspired bistro on the main strip of Wilhelmsburg, a stack of glossy to-go menus in hand. All morning I've been speaking with store and restaurant owners, introducing myself, collecting brochures to display at the Inn, and discussing potential collaboration opportunities. I thought gaining people's support would be difficult—in Dallas business connections aren't established through goodwill and niceties but rather cutthroat networking and schmoozing over fifteen-dollar cocktails—but everyone in this town is so welcoming, so eager to help.

Ms. Wilde over at the Mockingbird Coach House even offered to host a weekly afternoon tea service in the bed-

and-breakfast's main dining room as long as Grammy J guaranteed eight participants at each sitting. And for no extra charge. "I'd have partnered with Joy years ago if only your grandmother had asked," she told me as I sipped a cup of Earl Grey. "Please let me know when's a good time to start. I have the most delicious cherry and pistachio scone recipe she'll love."

If only developing the Inn's new website were as accommodating. Like the porch, it's under construction, and creating it on Grammy J's ancient computer hasn't helped the process. In my haste to get the hell out of Dallas, I forgot my laptop in my condo. I hope to have the basics—background about the bed-and-breakfast, the list of accommodations and amenities—finalized and online by the end of the week. The reservation calendar, online booking and payment, and the section about vacation and tour packages can be added later.

Crossing the street, I enter the Vintner's Collective—a tasting room where several boutique wineries in the area rent space to showcase their wines—with the hope of talking to the manager about hosting a special wine tasting specifically for guests of the Inn. To my surprise, Bon Bon is behind the bar. I search the massive signs hanging overhead and notice Camden Cellars is listed as a member. She must split her time working here and at the winery.

She smiles when she spots me, and I wonder what she's aiming at with the gesture. On the surface it reads warm and genuine, but underneath I sense something purposeful that hints at an ulterior motive.

I stuff the to-go menus into my tote bag and walk toward her. "A pleasure to see you again, Bonnie," I say, sliding onto a creaky stool between a lumberjack of a man enjoying some sherry and a group of overloud women celebrating individual midlife crises—their conversation a mesh of dating-site antics and plastic-surgeon procedures. Replicas of Samma, Faye, and Piper in twenty years.

And me, if I'm not careful.

"You've been productive," Bon Bon says, using a rag to wipe off the bar.

"How so?" I toss my hair over my shoulder and cross my legs. My shorts climb up my thighs, causing my skin to stick to the seat. Ordinarily I'd wear a pencil skirt and blouse when meeting prospective clients or partners, but I thought the people in town may be more receptive to my ideas if I were dressed casually.

"Hiring Moose to fix Joy's porch. Befriending the locals. Sending Cricket to lockup. Like I said, productive," she says without sarcasm or disdain, nothing that indicates she thinks I'm an outsider weaseling my way into her tight-knit community. In fact her voice is almost amused, conspiratorial even.

"We had unfinished business," I say. Perhaps I should've stuck around to see Ryan's reaction when the police broke him out of the cave and handcuffed his wrists. I'm sure it was pure entertainment.

She places a large glass in front of me and grabs a bottle of wine from the fridge. The label consists of a handlebar mustache framed around the words NO HOLDS BARRED in retro font. I'd bet my trust fund this is another Camden Cellars blend, and I imagine if Ryan were here, he'd pontificate about how all is fair in love and war.

"The whole staff's been waiting for Cricket's moment of reckoning. It's only fitting you should drink the blend he created for when the gloves come off," she says, validating my suspicions. Bon Bon pours some wine, swirling the glass so the burgundy liquid moves up the sides, and passes it to me. "Compliments of Camden Cellars."

Sniffing the wine, I breathe in the aromas of strawberries and cocoa. The distinct scent of violets hits my nose. I take a taste. The flavor is structured, yet vivid, the tannins lingering long enough that I know they're serious. Like a first date that ends with breakfast. A mix of Sangiovese and Syrah grapes, if I had to put money on it.

"Well, we're even, so I wouldn't count on any more altercations between us," I say.

"Too bad," she says. "Things were getting exciting around here."

Spinning the stem of the glass between my thumb and index finger, I study her. There's no mistaking the humor in her wide-set blue eyes. What happened to the possessiveness, the jealousy she demonstrated at the party? What am I missing?

Bon Bon leaves me with the bottle and heads to the other end of the bar. I watch as she chats and laughs with customers, topping off their wine and closing out checks. In a way she reminds me of Lillie—the comfort in her own skin and carefree attitude, the joy in serving people, the camaraderie among those around her. I wish it all came so effortlessly for me. My whole life has been so focused on how others perceive me that it's difficult for me to lower my guard, make myself vulnerable. There's a reason hard exteriors provide the best protection.

Bon Bon swings back around as I finish jotting notes on my to-do list that's meant to bring the Bluebonnet Inn into the twenty-first century. Though most of the fixes—painting the kitchen cabinets, deep-cleaning the bathrooms, staining the hardwood floors—resemble the Band-Aid approach as opposed to true solutions. The B&B is lacking budget for anything else, but if Grammy J hopes to still be in business in the next five years, *something* must be done to save it.

"Another glass?" Bon Bon asks, picking up the bottle of No Holds Barred and tilting it toward me.

I shake my head no. "Actually, if available, I was hoping to speak with the manager."

"Gina went home an hour ago, but she always joins us for ladies' karaoke night at Axel's Off Main. You're welcome to catch her then."

Karaoke? I'd rather have cellulite dotting my thighs than sing off-key cover songs to a crowd of strangers. Standing, I gather my bag and toss a tip onto the bar. "Thanks, but no. I'll try her again later."

"You really should stop by," she says. "Our group can always use some fresh blood."

My internal alarm blares, now certain there's a hidden agenda at play. You don't go from bitchy and territorial to friendly and joking unless you want to gain an advantage. I would know—I invented that move.

"As much as I want to hear no-talent wannabes belt out renditions of 'Don't Stop Believing' that would make Journey cringe, I'll pass," I say.

I turn toward the exit, but her tone, somewhere between incredulity and pity, stops me. "You must not have many friends," she says.

I look at her, bristling at the truth in her words. My whole life I've surrounded myself with people who've claimed to be my friends, but none of them were real. All of it was as fake and meaningless as a padded bra.

"What would give you that idea?" I ask.

"Because you obviously don't recognize when someone's inviting you to hang out." Opening a drawer under the bar, Bon Bon pulls out a crumpled piece of paper and slides it over to me. It's a flyer for a local honky-tonk with an event schedule and a map at the bottom. "In case you're ever interested."

The confusion must be evident in my expression, because Bon Bon says, "Cricket and I were involved on and off a long time ago. I haven't always treated him the right way, but that doesn't mean I'm not still protective or have his best interests at heart." She corks the bottle of No Holds Barred and slides it across the bar to me, the humor in her eyes replaced with something softer. "After what you pulled, perhaps you're just the medicine he needs to shake him up a bit."

She's off helping another guest before I can respond. I stand there speechless—I have no idea how to interpret what she's said, it's so unexpected, but for the first time in a long time I'm willing to accept it at face value.

THAT EVENING I'm at the garden center picking up some things for Grammy J when Samma calls on my new phone that arrived yesterday morning. I consider ignoring it, but Samma's like a pesky gnat that won't go away—she'll keep redialing until I accept.

"Everyone's been talking. *Everyone*," she says the moment I answer. Her voice has a breathy, whiny quality that causes my eye to twitch. Meditation music filters over the line, and I wonder if she's at another spa retreat. Her husband must've attempted sex again and the experience was so traumatic Samma needed a vacation.

"I'm sure they have," I say, balancing two bags of soil, a box of seed packets, and a long-handled rake that won't behave. Sandwiching the phone between my ear and shoulder, I navigate a display of clay pots and walk into the greenhouse, where I dump the items into a shopping cart. The air inside feels like a dehumidifier that malfunctioned and smells like a jungle. At least the curls in my hair appreciate the boost in volume.

"The rumor is you've entered a treatment facility for exhaustion and depression, but everyone thinks that's code for substance abuse," Samma says. "Of course I tell anyone who asks that isn't the case."

"Which part? That I'm in a treatment facility or that I'm there because I have a drug problem?" I say as I hear a scampering sound behind me. Except when I turn to look, there's only a young couple perusing the hanging baskets near the back wall and a woman wearing a gardening apron helping an elderly man choose between two trays of identical flowers.

"Sweetie, let's not play dumb," Samma says in a patronizing tone. "Obviously I'm referring to the latter. We all noticed the signs, and after that outburst at brunch . . . Well, it was only a matter of time before you snapped. The girls and I are glad you've checked yourself in somewhere to deal with your issues."

"I didn't realize my grandmother's bed-and-breakfast in Wilhelmsburg was considered a rehab center, but it's comforting to know you're all so concerned," I say with a deadpan delivery as I envision the way she'll spin my words into salacious gossip. By tomorrow afternoon everyone in our social circle will believe I've been committed to a long-term program with no hope of escape.

I glance at the last item on the list—bee balm, which I can only assume is a salve that's rubbed on flowers to attract those stinging little insects. According to the notes Grammy J's scribbled in the margins, it's located in the greenhouse, but all I see are rows of plants. "Listen, Samma, I'd love to continue this conversation, but I'm busy 'dealing with my issues.' You understand."

I'm about to disconnect when she says, "That's not the

only reason I called. I thought you'd be interested to know what your former assistant has been up to."

Before I can reply just how uninterested I am, she launches into the story. I push the cart down an aisle in search of anything that resembles a jar of ointment, half listening as Samma prattles on about how my former assistant is now working as an event and media relations manager for Bill Heacock's firm, my biggest rival. Why this should matter to me, I have no idea—I fired the girl. She can gladly burden my competitor with her laziness.

I round the corner to the next aisle. The skittering noise I heard before seems to be following me. I peek over my shoulder, but I find only potted shrubs and small-scale trees that look more like twigs. Kneeling, I inspect the wheels on the shopping cart, expecting a leaf or a piece of stem to be jammed in one of the brackets. Nothing.

"Margaret, are you paying attention?" Samma asks.

"Like a raw foodist at a bake sale," I say, reading the product tags as I move past. The bee balm must be here somewhere.

"Then you're handling the news quite well." An undercurrent of skepticism runs through her voice, but she doesn't question me.

"How else should I react?" I ask, certain the scurrying sound is getting louder. *Where in the hell is it coming from?* I think, glancing around.

"I figured any mention of the Randy Hollis Band would upset you, so this is progress," she says.

I halt abruptly as her words finally register. The band is performing a small gig in Dallas to celebrate finishing the first leg of their tour and my former assistant has been put in charge of publicizing it.

"The therapy sessions must be helping," Samma continues.

"Yeah, the shrinks here are top-notch." I sit on a low metal bed, trays of brightly colored flowers encasing me, betrayal thick in my throat. I've cheered from the crowd during their local shows, watched from behind the scenes as the band struggled to country music stardom, clinked glasses of champagne at their weddings and bought bottomless shots after their divorces were finalized, and I'm not even deserving of an invitation or the opportunity to organize and promote the event?

When Nick and I broke up, I knew the guys would choose him over me—they wrote an album together, after all—and I was learning to accept it, but to have Samma reaffirm it in this way that highlights my failures both personally and professionally is an entirely different story.

"I'm sure your worthless old assistant will screw it up and the band will regret not hiring you in the first place, but I thought you'd want to be aware of the situation," she says.

How noble of her.

At her feigned sincerity, I feel the familiar clutch of resentment grab hold. Ironic how it seems to grow rather than dissipate whenever home resurfaces. "Because that's what friends are for. Right, Samma?"

I hang up, cutting her off midresponse, overcome with a sudden urge to do something foolish. Bon Bon's offer to join her at ladies' karaoke night is becoming more and more appealing, and perhaps it's time for me to venture out of my comfort zone, surround myself with different kinds of people. I silently make a promise to try new experiences.

Sliding the phone into my pocket, I start to get to my feet when I notice the skittering sound has paused, replaced by what I swear are teeth chattering. My skin prickles, and the hairs on my arms stand on end. Spinning around slowly, I peer into the mass of flowers, my gaze locking on a pair of dark beady eyes staring intently at me and a small gray furry body ready to pounce.

Oh no. No, no, no.

"Stay away from me you little tree rat." I scramble backward but not fast enough. The squirrel springs into action and attaches itself onto my shorts, sticking like Spider-Man on the side of a wall. I swat at it, but the evil kamikaze woodland creature won't budge, its nails clawing at the fabric, nearly scratching my hands and legs. My heart plays leapfrog in my chest, and it feels as if I'm on the verge of suffocating because I can't draw a breath. My whole body is tingling, breaking out in sweat.

A dog barks, and it's like a switch is flipped, because the squirrel loosens its viselike grip and jumps away from me, scurrying off. Sinking onto the cool floor, I practice inhaling and exhaling, waiting for my frayed nerves to settle and my heart rate to return to a noncritical level. It's overdramatic and ridiculous, but I don't care.

There's another series of barks, and I look to my left to see Bordeaux rushing toward me, tongue flopping out the side of her mouth. I flinch, bracing for impact. She charges into me, knocking me over and pawing at my ear. Lying down beside me, she feverishly licks my cheeks, my nose, my forehead. I should be disgusted, but all I can do is laugh because this is like icing on the banner year I'm having.

A throat clears. Blocking Bordeaux's tongue with my hand, I tilt my head to the side and make eye contact with Ryan. He's standing a few feet away with a smirk on his face.

"Has anyone ever told you that under certain circumstances, especially those involving squirrels, you do an impressive impersonation of Chevy Chase in *National Lampoon's Christmas Vacation*?" he says.

Of course Ryan had to witness the vermin attack.

Walking to where I dropped the shopping list, he retrieves it and does a quick scan. "The bee balm is right there by your feet," he says, gesturing to a group of potted plants bursting with bunches of tube-shaped flowers in brilliant neon purple. So much for an ointment.

Groaning, I let my head fall back against the ground. Bordeaux resumes her frantic licking.

Like I said, banner year.

11

Ryan helps me to my feet, a string of slobber dangling from my chin. I wipe it away. His gaze travels over me, slow and attentive, as if I'm someone worth watching.

"No visible welts, marks, or blood," he says as Bordeaux walks a figure-eight pattern around us. "Only a bruised ego, but a good meal will cure that."

"I didn't realize my body language screamed I was desperate to be wined and dined by an ex-con." I pick up a pot of bee balm and wedge it into the cart's lower rack, trying to regain my bearings. I thought Ryan forfeited, so what is he doing here? And why is he looking at me more determined than ever?

"Marge, be assured you're buying. It's explicitly stated in the fine print on my release papers."

I snatch the shopping list out of his grasp and toss it into the basket. "Hilarious."

"Turnabout's fair play," he says, then puts two fingers in his mouth and whistles. Bordeaux stops pacing and settles down next to me, leaning her full weight against my leg and staring at me with big brown eyes.

Oh, quit it with the begging, I silently chastise, but I pet her head and rub behind her ears anyway. She groans and sighs, lost in pure delight. When I remove my hand, Bordeaux rolls onto her back, stretching out to expose her belly. *Absolutely hopeless.*

"Did you train her to act like this as a means to seduce women?" I ask.

"Is it working?"

I roll my eyes. Ryan grins, then whistles again. Bordeaux pops up off the ground like she's pulled this trick a hundred times before.

"Our reservation is in thirty minutes, so you should check out," he says, guiding the cart toward the cash registers at the far end of the greenhouse. His voice is easy, convincing, as though we've had this date scheduled for weeks.

I catch up to him, Bordeaux sniffing at my heels, and step into his path. "Typically you're supposed to consult with the person before committing them to dinner."

"Marge, we both know running errands is the only thing you have on the agenda."

Touché. I was also going to watch reality television, maybe soak in a bubble bath, but I don't share that with Ryan lest he think I'm a whole new level of pathetic. Steering the cart around me, he walks to an open register and unloads the items for the clerk to ring up.

"Grammy J's expecting me at the Inn," I say, sounding like a teenager afraid to break curfew.

"Not anymore," he says. "I told her about our plans when I dropped off the wine for the evening social hour."

Did he think of everything?

"I doubt the restaurant considers on-the-go chic

proper attire," I say, gesturing to my plain cotton top, dirty chino shorts, and sneakers I borrowed from Grammy J's closet. Compared to Ryan in jeans and a form-fitted collared shirt with the sleeves rolled up, I resemble someone who fell into the bargain bin and barely escaped with her life. My mother would murder me if she discovered I went out dressed like this. Hell, even I'm embarrassed.

"The executive chef is an old friend, he'll let it slide. And before you protest, I'll drive. Your purchases will be safe in your car, and Bordeaux will be fine in the Blazer while we eat," he says as the cashier totals the order.

I pay and shove the receipt into my wallet, following Ryan as he pushes the cart through the exit to the parking lot before stopping at my Audi. "Well, Marge, it appears you're all out of excuses, so how about it? It might be the best meal you'll ever experience, if you'd put aside your preconceived notions."

Maybe Ryan's right. After all, I did promise to branch outside the safe and familiar.

"Come on," he says, the slowly sinking sun bringing out the gold flecks in his hazel eyes, reflecting the dare in them. "What's letting go for one moment going to hurt?"

More than it should based on history—I give in anyway.

―――

THE HOSTESS SEATS us at a table that faces the open kitchen, where I'm granted a front-row view of the team of chefs preparing dishes. Neutral tones, repurposed barn wood, and concrete are woven throughout the restaurant. The Edison bulbs hanging from the ceiling illuminate the space in a soft glow, and the tempting scents of simmering sauces wafting through the room cause my stomach to growl. I'm hungrier than I thought.

Browsing the appetizers and entrées displayed on a large chalkboard, I ask, "What's delicious here?"

"Apart from you?"

I glance at Ryan and arch an eyebrow. There's an amused expression on his face, as though he could spend all evening entertaining himself with his own quips. "Well, I know I won't be having the side of truffle mac since the cheese has already been served," I say, but silently I savor the insinuation that I'm something to be devoured.

The server arrives and greets Ryan by name, then delivers his spiel about the special multicourse tasting menu with wine pairings.

"We'll do it," I say, interrupting him. With the dishes emerging from the kitchen looking as if they've jumped off the glossy pages of *Food & Wine* magazine, I'd be an idiot not to fully indulge. The server nods and departs with our order.

Ryan leans back in his chair. "It's seven courses," he says. "Can you handle that?"

"Why? Are you scared of the commitment?"

"Marge, you can guarantee that when I devote myself to something, I give it my undivided attention," he says, his voice dipping low, and my stomach does a flip. "You're the one who has difficulty following through."

His gaze flicks to my lips, and I wonder if he's remembering our kiss like I'm remembering his taste and the sensation of his body pressed against mine. My heart flutters like a bird trying to break free of a cage inside my chest, replacing the anxiousness from the past few days. I don't know why I continue fighting him. It's obvious the invisible string tugging me toward him hasn't severed.

"I think the police officer who arrested you would disagree," I say.

Ryan shakes his head, a slight smile lifting a corner of his mouth. "You know, usually when a girl introduces handcuffs into the relationship, it's a bit more fun."

"How *was* your night in lockup? Homey? Familiar?" I say, wearing my smugness like a well-worn leather jacket. "Did you get in some quality snuggling with Big Fred and his gimpy leg?"

"I was only there for a few hours. The deputy who answered the call was fresh out of the academy and hellbent on establishing his authority. The sheriff released me when he learned about it."

Smoothing the napkin over my shorts, I say, "I noticed nobody contacted Grammy J regarding the incident."

"That's because everyone knows Joy can be triggerhappy when it comes to trespassers. Her shotgun is cocked and loaded at all times."

"Then I guess it's a good thing I didn't mention it to her either," I say as the server returns with half a glass of champagne for each of us and the first course—celery root soup dotted with hay-infused oil and rye croutons. Stunning in presentation. The smell alone is enough to put me in a trance, and the taste of the soup is creamy and decadent, the richness balanced by the champagne's dry style and acidity.

"I know the food is impeccable, but don't keel over from slurping," Ryan says, his voice threaded with its usual charm. "There's still a long way to go."

I lick the last bit of soup off the back of the spoon. "I was swooning, not slurping."

A member of the waitstaff removes our bowls and empty champagne flutes and sets the table with new cutlery in time for our server to deliver the next course—

roasted heirloom carrots with brown butter and hazelnuts, complemented by a bright, crisp Sauvignon Blanc. Delicious, yet dangerous in its simplicity.

While we eat and the courses progress, we lapse into easy conversation. We talk about the destinations we've traveled to and the spots we'd still like to explore, books we've read recently, and which sports teams are the most overrated (Ryan's choice being the New England Patriots and mine the San Francisco Giants). During the course of fluffy ricotta gnocchi with mushrooms and spring peas, we get into a heated discussion about the merits of risotto versus homemade pasta—Ryan is adamant that "risotto is rice that had faith in itself," and therefore trumps fresh pasta and its tender, satiny texture and delicious egginess. I not so respectfully disagree.

As the server clears our places in preparation for the next dish, Ryan fills me in on how the winery has started the fermentation process on the recently harvested grapes, and I tell him about growing up in Dallas. When I gloss over my career in PR, he stops me with questions.

"Marge, given your rather limited tolerance for people, how'd you end up in PR?"

"I don't hate all people." I smile. "Just the lazy ones with bad taste. And as my clients have the good sense to hire me, I give them the benefit of the doubt."

Ryan shakes his head, not in an exasperated way, but as if he truly appreciates my snark. "Really though, what was the draw?"

Brushing away crumbs blemishing the starched tablecloth, I say, "It seemed like the natural path. I'm good under pressure, I'm familiar with the social scene, and I love knowing that every time I take on a new client, I'm starting with a clean slate—no two projects are the same.

Things are always changing, and I love the challenge that presents."

"So do you miss it?" he asks, moving the water glasses out of the way so the waiter can set a steaming plate of braised short ribs atop vanilla-scented polenta in front of each of us. "I find it hard to be away from the vineyard for more than a day. Any more and I'd be micromanaging everyone from a distance and generally driving people to drink."

"At least it'd happen in a convenient setting." I smile, but Ryan raises a question I haven't considered. The truth is, I haven't missed any of it, and that doesn't trouble me as much as it should. "But to answer your question, no. The time off has been . . . necessary."

"Ah, you're experiencing burnout syndrome," he says.

"More like disenchantment."

"Got sick of acting like a glorified party planner for the rich?"

"Something like that."

"Then you've come to the right place to respark that interest. Sunshine, fresh air, and an abundance of wine. You'll clear your head and return to Dallas, ready to plan the next socially expected soiree." He levels me with a look heavy enough to pin me to my seat. "Unless, of course, you find that socially expected isn't your scene after all."

I laugh, uncomfortable with facing the idea that I may not ever want to go back. It's ridiculous and impossible, and what would I even do instead?

"And what, stay here?" I ask. "I suppose I could run for mayor, keep all of you country hooligans in line. My reign shall be fierce, but fair."

"I'll order the bronze statue for the center of town tomorrow," he says, sliding his licked-clean plate off to the side. "You know, Marge, we're at the point in the night where you admit I was right. An impossible task for you, but I'm sure you can manage just this once."

While the food has been exceptional, rivaling the best of Dallas's culinary scene, it's Ryan's company that's been the most memorable. He has this uncanny ability to make a single moment stretch and expand until two hours have passed.

I take a drink of the southern French red paired with the short ribs and say, "Fine. You win this round. The meal was incredible."

His eyes widen a fraction, both eyebrows rising in surprise—he clearly wasn't expecting that response. "Well, since you're obviously in a generous mood, care to revise your statement about my wine tasting like cough syrup?"

Always so overzealous. "I'm allergic to flattering the quick-witted and overly proud."

Ryan laughs, deep and a little hoarse. "But seriously, if not for the wine, then why Wilhelmsburg? Why aren't you taking time off at some snooty five-star resort in the Caribbean pestering the hotel staff?"

"I didn't realize I needed an excuse to visit my grandmother," I say, keeping my tone light despite the warning bell going off inside me.

"You don't," he says with a shrug. "But based on the phone call I overheard between you and your mom—she seems pleasant, by the way—it sounded as though she didn't agree with you being here, so I was curious why you chose to come anyway."

The moment bursts and reality clicks back into focus, his statement a reminder that I can't hide in this town forever. Eventually I have to return to Dallas, face the consequences of my leaving, rebuild my life and career.

The server whisks away our dishes and cleans our places with a table crumber in preparation for dessert. I should end dinner now before he unearths all of my secrets, but there's something disarming and open about Ryan that holds me here and causes me to lower my guard.

"Honestly, it was the first place that popped into my mind when I got in my car," I say. "I just wanted to be somewhere else. Somewhere away from . . ."

For the first time in my life I'm tempted to say exactly what's on my mind, to confess to another person the depth to which my mother has, and continues, to destroy me. That she's the reason for almost everything I do. Why I'm never satisfied with myself or with others. Why happiness —and more so, love—seem like foreign concepts. Why it's so hard for me to open up and make myself vulnerable. Oh yes, I'm tempted to tell Ryan all of those things . . . but I'm not ready to hear his response. Or for him to learn that side of me.

"From that guy you mentioned the other night?" Ryan finishes for me.

"Yes, in part," I say, glad to focus on anyone other than my mother. Once I start, I can't stop, and my entire history with Nick tumbles out. "Nick never tried to make it work between us. He was constantly pulling away, never letting me get close. After all the support I gave him, everything I sacrificed, he at least owed me that much." I hate the bitterness in my voice—the last thing I want to be right now is bitter. Not when everything about this evening has been so uncomplicated.

Ryan scratches his jaw, carved and covered in stubble, and studies me in an unnerving way that feels too probing, too intimate. The buzz of neighboring chatter, glasses clinking, and forks scraping across plates surround us. Finally he says, "Isn't that the risk of loving someone? Giving a piece of yourself without the promise of reciprocation?"

"Not if you've earned it." And I *did* earn it.

His gaze remains fixed on me. I want to ask him what he sees, but I don't. I'm too afraid of his response. "I believe you have to earn the privilege to tell someone you love them, but you're not entitled to be loved in return," he says.

The possibility that what Ryan says is true—that the effort I put into winning Nick's heart, gaining my mother's approval, achieving the utmost success in my career, has all been for naught terrifies me. Because that's not how life is supposed to operate.

"With determination and perseverance should come great reward," I say.

"It should," he says with a single, decisive nod. "Maybe you haven't gotten to the end of your race yet."

Wiping a thumb across the condensation dripping down my water glass, I ask, "So, if you're right, then what do I do?"

"You're already doing it—practicing your renovation skills, experimenting with using handcuffs, getting frisky with squirrels." He winks. "The point is, Marge, you've got to relax, live a little recklessly. Quit worrying about everyone else and figure out what brings *you* happiness. No regrets, remember?"

His words tip my world on its axis. I hadn't realized how long I've waited for someone to speak them aloud and grant me permission to act on them. Bon Bon thought I could be just the medicine Ryan needs, but she has it reversed. It's time I engaged in some good old-fashioned, no-strings-attached antics, and Ryan is the perfect reset button.

An hour later, we're the last diners in the restaurant, too

Sour Grapes

caught up in conversation to even notice. The owner pays our bill, probably to get us to leave so the kitchen staff can begin breaking down the cooking area. With his palm on my lower back, Ryan escorts me outside. Save for his Blazer, the guest parking lot is empty. The only sounds are our shoes crunching on the gravel and an owl hooting in a nearby tree.

The night has taken on a dreamy quality, and it feels as if I'm buzzing in a sort of tipsy state that has nothing to do with the wine I've consumed and everything to do with my renewed sense of confidence.

Ryan is staring at me with an expression I can't quite read. It's part contemplative, part desire, part something else. I wait for him to speak, but he remains quiet.

As I start moving toward his SUV, he grabs my hand and draws me around to face him. We're standing so close I can smell the remnants of his aftershave and feel his breath on my forehead. Ryan brushes an errant strand of hair away from my cheek, his callused thumb ghosting over the sensitive spot below my ear. I swallow, my chest tight, as though there isn't enough space for my heart to fit inside my rib cage.

Ryan slides his hand around to cradle the back of my head, while the other travels down and settles on the curve of my hip. "If I kiss you again, is there going to be a jail cell on the other end of it?"

"Only one way to find out," I say with a breathless laugh.

He pulls me flush against him, and then his lips are on mine. An electric jolt shoots through me as the pressure of his mouth changes from tender and coaxing to needy and demanding.

And I'm right there with him, matching everything he's giving. My palms skate over his broad shoulders and arms, his shirtsleeves stretched over the hard muscle beneath. He tastes like the chocolate cake we shared for dessert. Like something I could eat every day for the rest of my life.

I weave my fingers into the soft hair that curls slightly at the nape of his neck, tugging gently at the roots. Ryan lets out a sexy grunt that I want to hear over and over again. He lifts me off the ground, and I hook my legs around his waist. He steps backward until I'm pressed against his car. With the dark surrounding us, it feels as if we can do anything and not get caught. A rush of heat shoots through me at the idea. I reach for the buttons on his—

Sudden loud barking makes us jump apart, our chests heaving.

I sway a bit before regaining my balance. I glance at Ryan, who looks as disoriented as I feel. Sticking her head out the open window, Bordeaux paws at the inner door handle.

Ryan pushes on her nose and mutters what sounds like, "Great timing." Snorting, Bordeaux ducks back inside and drinks from the water bowl on the floor mat. Ryan turns to me, rubbing a frustrated hand down his face. "She's a resource guarder, and I'm her favorite toy."

I let out a shaky laugh, my whole body vibrating with pent-up energy. "Or maybe she's warning us that we're about to have an audience," I say, gesturing to the hostesses emerging from the side entrance of the restaurant. They walk around the building to the service lot.

Ryan's expression morphs from slightly irritated to focused and determined. He leans in close to me, his lips grazing the hint of collarbone peeking out from beneath my shirt. Air catches in my lungs and my skin prickles, but I force myself not to fidget, not to move for fear I may collapse right here on the gravel. Skimming his mouth up my neck, his breath stirring wisps of my hair, he whispers in my ear, "What happened to living recklessly?"

My brain is a fog, so I only manage to blurt, "Show me."

A devastatingly wicked grin spreads across his face. "Follow me."

Without hesitating, I buckle myself into the passenger seat of his SUV as Ryan slides behind the wheel. While he drives, I study his profile and how the moonlight casts him in shades of gray, as though he's been caught in a flashbulb. It's easier to absorb him this way rather than in vivid color, which can be too bright and blinding, like staring at the sun.

Ryan must sense my eyes on him because he looks over at me, his gaze lingering a little too long everywhere. I wonder if he's contemplating parking on the side of the road and hauling me over the center console so I straddle his lap. The thought does nothing to calm my racing heart or ease the tension building like a slow boil in my stomach.

He turns onto a cobbled path that leads to a large cottage constructed of limestone and wood and accentuated with a copper roof.

"I expected you to live at the winery," I say.

"I did for a while, but once we expanded, I bought this place and tore down the residence on the estate. We needed the space for the bottling line." Ryan pulls into an open-air garage and cuts the engine. Bordeaux pants and whines over my shoulder, scratching at the headrest. "Chill out, you neurotic beast," he says, petting her head in an effort to quiet her. "You'll be lying in bed in two seconds."

So will we, if I'm lucky.

Hopping out of the car, Ryan releases Bordeaux from the confines of the backseat. She barks and darts through the doggie door. We enter the house to find Bordeaux has already curled into a ball on an oversized pillow in a corner.

For a moment, Ryan and I stare at each other in silence, his gaze dark and so intense it triggers a flutter of nerves in my chest. But the good kind. The kind filled with anticipation and longing. He clears his throat, and I think he's about to suggest a glass of wine or a quick tour, but instead he crosses the distance between us in two long strides.

"C'mere." Then he's kissing me again with hot, drugging kisses. His hands are all over me, one buried in my hair, the other traveling down the length of my back, over the slope of my hip, around the curve of my butt, learning the contours of my figure.

His shirt is clenched in my fists as Ryan drags his mouth down my throat, tracing my pulse with his tongue. A moan falls from my lips, transforming into a gasp when his teeth bite the sensitive part where my neck meets my shoulder. I feel him smile against my skin, the stubble on his jaw brushing my cheek.

Oh, he's fighting dirty. But I crave it—ache for it even.

Ryan recaptures my mouth, his fingers slipping under my shirt, trailing up my stomach to my bra. And it's as if thunder cracks, desire rattling deep in my bones, because we're tugging at each other's clothes, removing them in between kisses as we stumble through the house, bumping into furniture, toward what I assume is his bedroom.

We make it as far as the great room before we collapse on a large sofa in a tangle of limbs. Ryan bats impatiently at the throw pillows, and they land with a soft thump on the floor. There are no lights on in here, but there may as well be. Floor-to-ceiling windows take up one wall, and the moon, huge and luminous in the sky, bathes the room in a silver glow.

Ryan hovers over my naked body, his strong arms anchoring him above me. The heavy ache between my legs is unbearable—it's been *so* long.

His gaze roams over every inch of my exposed skin, drinking in the swell of my breasts, the dip of my stomach, the Alaska-shaped birthmark above my left hip. My chest expands and contracts with labored breaths under his appraisal.

"You're so gorgeous," he says, his voice rough. It's all the incentive I need to pull him to me, our lips meeting in a frenzied kiss, tongues stroking and teasing. I run my fingers over his sculpted shoulders, across the faint smattering of hair on his chest, down to the ridges lining his stomach, and lower.

He lets out a string of curses, and an overwhelming surge of lust and power shoots through me because he's not the only one skilled at making a person come unhinged.

Ryan trails his mouth along my body, nipping and sucking and caressing places that shouldn't leave me squirming but do—the hollow of my throat, the crook of my elbow, the spot above my anklebone. I don't even attempt to censor the desperate noises I'm making.

I grab the back of his neck, unable to handle any more, and Ryan moves over me until I feel him *right there*. Then he pushes into me, both of us groaning as we find our perfect rhythm. Slow, deep, and so intense, my toes curl and my nails scrape along his shoulder blades, slick with sweat.

I grow dizzy, murmuring unintelligible words as our bodies move together. I feel a flush spread across my skin, the pressure building. Everything inside me is a throbbing, pulsing nerve.

Pressing an openmouthed kiss to his collarbone, I lick Ryan's skin, tasting the earthiness I've come to associate with him. He catches one of my earlobes between his teeth, and that's all it takes for me to unravel completely.

Color explodes behind my eyelids as I arch off the couch with a sharp cry. I clutch his shoulders, his muscles strained as Ryan reaches his own release, his whole body shuddering under my fingers, his breath hot in my ear.

As I lie there beneath Ryan, sweaty, breathless, and exhausted, floating in a weightless bliss, I wonder how I ever doubted him.

Turns out, messy *is* the best form of fun.

12

The next morning I wake up alone and naked in Ryan's bed with only a duvet covering me. At first I think he may be in the bathroom, but the house is silent, almost loud in its quiet. I touch his pillow. It's cold, despite the warm breeze drifting in through the open window. He must have disappeared hours ago.

Groaning, I roll onto my back, staring at the sunlight that cuts across the ceiling. I glance at the clock and my heart skips a beat when I spot the note propped against the lamp.

> *At the winery with Bordeaux—there's no rest for the wicked. A pot of coffee is ready for brewing in the kitchen, and breakfast awaits you in the warming oven. I parked your Audi out front. Your keys are under the floor mat. Stay as long as you want. If you feel the need to steal anything, the wine cellar is located directly off the pantry. And, Marge? You're no less alluring in your sleep.*
> *—R*

Smiling, I stretch out like a cat on the sheets, remembering his firm kiss and firmer touches, the sounds he murmured as our bodies moved together, the weight of him collapsing on top of me, sweaty and drained. Never in my life have I felt so sexy, so desired, so in control than I did watching him come undone.

No regrets.

Climbing out of the bed, my hair a tangle of knots from his fingers, I ignore my clothes piled neatly on the dresser and pull on one of his button-downs draped over a chair, the fabric feather-soft against my skin. Lifting the collar, I inhale his scent—soap and a hint of sweetness, like grapes ripened from the sun. No sign of cologne. Snippets of last night flood my vision. The ache between my legs returns, and I squeeze my thighs together to alleviate it.

I pad barefoot into the great room, which is immaculately decorated in a rustic style—wide-plank wood floors, exposed beam ceilings, and neutral earth tones mixed with simple patterns. I notice Ryan has straightened the couch cushions and coffee table. *Interesting.* It's something I would've done, but not something I'd expected from him with his carefree, relaxed demeanor.

As promised, in the kitchen I discover the coffee machine with cream and sugar beside it and a mug already under the drip. A sticky note tells me to press the small button on the top. I do as instructed. Immediately the aroma of roasted hazelnuts swirls around me. I remove the plate from the warming oven, and my mouth waters at the sight of scrambled eggs, bacon, and a stack of fluffy pancakes with maple syrup.

It's all so . . . domestic. I wonder if Ryan does this for all of his women, if a warm breakfast and a fresh cup of coffee are his way of saying, "Last night was fantastic, I'll call you." Somehow, I doubt it. There's something warm and genuine, almost special and intimate, about the gesture that makes me question if Ryan has more in mind than a predictable, no-strings-attached summer fling. I realize if I'm not careful Ryan will pull me in, make me comfortable in his life and his town. That's a risk I'm not sure I can afford. My life, my career, my future, is in Dallas, just as Ryan's future is here in Wilhelmsburg.

I eat standing at the counter, enjoying the view of the rolling countryside and vineyards. So serene. What would it be like to wake up to this every day? To have that one perfect moment each morning to appreciate a beautiful view? And how much better would my day be because of it?

I wash and dry the dishes but hesitate to leave them on the counter, so I scour the cabinets and drawers until I find where each item belongs. Everything inside the cottage is clean and tidy—the opposite of what I encountered the first time I rode in Ryan's Blazer. Perhaps he keeps his work chaos isolated to vehicles and the winery. That, or he's a study in contradiction.

There are no shoes kicked in a corner or dog toys scattered about, no junk mail cluttering surfaces or loose coins thrown in bowls. I shiver, thinking of my condo back in Uptown Dallas. Everything there is sorted and categorized, stored and shelved. Everything has a purpose and a place. But unlike Ryan's house, which feels lived in and comfortable despite its lack of clutter, mine has always felt a little bit cold. I convinced myself I prefer it that way, but now I'm not so sure.

And unless it's hidden behind art or a mirror, he doesn't own a television. Just rows and rows of books lined up on built-in shelves that encompass an entire wall in the great room. Running my fingers along the spines, I scan the titles and authors for anything I recognize. My eyes trail over resource volumes about vinification and the history of winemaking, out-of-date travel guides, the entire collection of Roald Dahl children's stories, and a set of Marvel graphic novels. He's like a ten-year-old trapped in a man's body, endearing in a way that's surprising.

It makes me curious about his other quirks, his passions, his secrets, but I resist the urge to snoop, wanting to discover them from him.

And what his intentions are in pursuing someone like me.

I ARRIVE at the Inn as Moose and his crew are demolishing the remainder of the porch. The air is filled with a cacophony of sound—saws whirring, hammers banging, pieces of wood crashing to the ground—and smells as if a mold-infested dust storm has passed through. I picture a migraine-afflicted Grammy J pacing inside the bed-and-breakfast, waiting for me to walk through the door so she can strangle me.

I unload the items I bought at the greenhouse into the newly organized shed. It takes three trips, and by the time I'm done, my hair is a mat of red curls against the back of my neck and my day-old clothes cling to my skin worse than a wet plastic bag. The temperature today feels like a searing, throbbing sunburn. Yet it's still more bearable than summer in Dallas with its soaring skyscrapers that trap in heat and pollution like a microwave container.

Moose waves when he sees me approach. Pushing the protective mask down onto his chin, he maneuvers around what remains of the foundation. Covered head to toe in paint flecks, dirt, and bits of rust, his face red and sweaty around safety goggles, he steps forward and embraces me in a hug tight enough to crack my spine.

"How was your sleepover?" he asks in a voice loud enough to be heard over the noise. He grins widely, a dimple dotting one cheek. "Worth doing again?"

Bristling, I pull away, hurt and betrayal spreading through me. I never imagined Ryan was the kiss-and-tell type, nor did I expect Moose to mock me about it. Is nothing private anymore?

"I'm glad my personal business is now fodder for town gossip," I say.

His smile fades. "I only knew you were over at Cricket's because he called me this morning to help him get your car. He didn't say anything else about you," he says quickly, as if trying to dismantle a bomb before it blows. "I meant it as a gentle ribbing between friends, but it obviously didn't come across that way. I'm sorry."

The apology catches me off guard, and guilt twists in my stomach for misjudging him—and more important, Ryan. I'm so used to Samma, Faye, and Piper's spiteful teasing that I didn't recognize Moose's attempt at a light-hearted joke. Not to mention he already considers me a friend even though we've spoken only a handful of times.

"It looks like you're making progress," I say, nodding at the porch.

Moose visibly relaxes, his shoulders slouching, the sigh of relief small but apparent. "Joy's not happy with the mess and current decibel level. She's only allowing us to work midmorning to early evening—after the guests have left for the day and before they get back from the wineries."

"So I take it I should sneak in through a window and hide in my room until the renovation is finished?"

"It's certainly advisable."

We chat awhile longer about the rebuild and other inconsequential things—the new line of fishing rods

Moose plans to stock at Hodgepodge, the PR work I'm doing for Grammy J, this year's county fair complete with pari-mutuel horse racing and a carnival—before the conversation turns to how I got Ryan thrown in lockup. I tell Moose the story, and as it progresses, his laughs grow louder and bigger, his entire body shaking.

When I reach the part about tricking Ryan and trapping him in the cave, Moose hiccups. "I can't believe Cricket fell for that stunt or that you pulled it off," he says. "He's never going to live this down—I won't let him!" Lifting his safety goggles, he wipes a hand under his eyes. "Oh that's great, but it's time I sledgehammered more rotted boards." Moose squeezes my arm, then positions the protective mask over his mouth and returns to the demolition.

From the backseat of my car, I grab the brochures and other materials I collected from the shops and restaurants around town and tiptoe through the front entrance. The entire bed-and-breakfast groans as I step inside, despite my efforts at being stealthy. The shared living spaces are empty. For a second I think I'm alone, but that crumbles when Grammy J's stern voice echoes from upstairs.

"Child, you can be certain the linens aren't goin' to change themselves," she yells, her accent more pronounced with the increase in volume.

Cringing, I deposit the promotional items on the console in the sitting area and climb the stairs. The old wood moans under my feet. As I walk down the hallway in search of Grammy J, I hear muttered curses emanating from the master suite. I peek in to find her struggling to put a fitted sheet on the king-sized bed. She manages to attach a corner around the mattress only to have the opposite one spring free.

When she notices me, Grammy J straightens up. Her

chest rises and falls, as though the simple act of breathing consumes all of her energy. I wonder how much of her day is spent carrying out tedious chores like this.

"You're responsible for the right-hand side," she says, all business, pointing to the bed. "After we're done with this one, there are three more that need our attention."

With a "yes, ma'am," I fix the corner that popped off and grab the other end of the sheet, pulling it toward the headboard and securing it around the mattress. The scent of fresh laundry hits my nose, and it instantly evokes an image of Nick and me in the grocery store, arguing over which fragrance of fabric softener he should buy for bed linens I would rarely sleep on. My chest tightens. I shake my head, dislodging the memory.

"I assume since you're only now getting back to the Inn that you had fun on your date with Ryan?" Grammy J asks, aligning the flat sheet over the fitted one, ensuring equal overhang.

My cheeks flush with embarrassment. "It was really nice. Dinner was delicious," I say, tucking in my respective side.

I don't know why I sound so sheepish—I'm an adult, not a teenager with a curfew—but I feel as though I should've called to tell her I'd be staying at Ryan's. Growing up, my mother never bothered to concern herself with my social calendar, always presuming I was in the appropriate place with the appropriate people, but the annoyed edge in Grammy J's tone indicates that maybe she waited up for me. The idea that she cares about my whereabouts, my safety, is so alien that it never crossed my mind to contact her.

She *mmm-hmms*, but a faint smile creeps onto her face.

"So, I established some good contacts in town yesterday and have great things planned for the Inn that

I'm excited to discuss with you," I say in a not-so-subtle ploy to change the subject.

Grammy J tosses me a pillowcase. "And exactly how much are these 'things' going to cost me?"

"Nothing. Everyone I've spoken to has been eager to collaborate. All I had to do was ask."

We finish making the bed in silence, arranging the down comforter and throw pillows. I trail behind Grammy J into the next room—this one with a queen mattress and a rollaway shoved against a wall—and watch as she fluffs the newly washed linens clumped into a ball on the storage bench.

The sunlight filtering through the sheer curtains softens her already striking features, and once again I'm overcome with the feeling that I'm staring at an older version of my mother. Grammy J's strawberry blonde hair is wrapped in a bandana à la the retro pinup style of Rosie the Riveter. Dressed in holey jeans cuffed at the ankle and a baggy plaid shirt that once belonged to Poppa Bart, she's the epitome of on-trend fashion.

I remember how on the night of my grandfather's funeral, my mother and Grammy J packed all of his belongings into boxes to send to charity. I wonder why Grammy J saved this particular shirt as a memento.

"Poppa Bart's clothes suit you," I say.

"Child, everything about that man suited me," she says with a chuckle, but sadness dulls her bright green eyes. It breaks my heart to think about how much she must miss him and their life together.

We repeat the same procedure as before, and in short order the remaining beds look like they could be featured in a home decor catalog, albeit an outdated one. A woman on a mission, Grammy J moves into the hallway and retrieves the bucket of cleaning supplies from the closet.

I follow her into one of the en suite bathrooms and cringe at the sight of dried toothpaste on the faucet and strands of dark hair stuck to the faux marble counter. People are careless and disgusting when it's not their own property.

Handing me rubber gloves, Grammy J asks, "Did you speak with your mother yet?"

I nod, keeping my focus on the pushed-aside shower curtain, which seems to be the only item not in need of a good scrubbing. "I'm sure you can guess how well it went."

When she doesn't inquire further, curiosity gets the better of me. "Will you tell me about what happened with you two? Please? Mother nearly bit my head off when I mentioned it."

Grammy J hesitates, as if contemplating how much information she should divulge. After a minute, she settles on the edge of the tub and pats the spot next to her. "Have a seat."

I sink down beside her and wait.

"Poppa Bart wasn't your mother's biological father," she says without easing into it or cushioning her words. "Just because he wasn't blood didn't make him any less of a parent—and a damn fine one at that. I told your mother the truth the night of your grandfather's passin', after you'd disappeared. She was . . . upset, as you can imagine."

Oh, I *can* imagine. My mother has never approved of sudden surprises or changes, so I'm sure she didn't react particularly well to a one-two punch of both. No wonder she looked as if she'd been crying the night she and my father claimed me from the backseat of the police car.

"But . . . why?" I ask, unable to articulate an appropriate response. I have no idea how to process her confession. My body is consumed with shock.

"Why did I wait so long to tell her or why did I tell her at all?"

"Both?"

It's no doubt a question my mother also asked, though probably not as diplomatically. *Why would you tell me something like that?* I envision her admonishing Grammy J. *What would I have to gain from learning that information?*

The air-conditioning kicks on, masking Grammy J's sigh. "Poppa Bart and I decided early in the pregnancy we weren't goin' to share that bit of history with your mother for reasons I'd prefer not to get into, but when I saw her sortin' your grandfather's things into piles, the secret spilled out of me in a way I couldn't contain. I think I just wanted her to know what an incredible man her father was." She picks at an area of dried shampoo on the tile with her fingernail. It's the first time I've ever seen her unsure, as if my mother's opinion of her matters more than she lets on. "But in the heat of the moment, my understandin' of Nancy was clouded by grief over your grandfather. I should've known the confession would unearth memories your mother had worked hard to leave behind."

"How do you mean?" I ask.

"Rumors are one thing, child, but confirmation is another," she says. "The moment I got pregnant there was speculation about who the father was, and people around here made certain to let your mother know that. She didn't take well to that kind of attention. And then for me to validate those rumors all those years later . . ."

More questions flood my mind. "So who is . . . ?"

"In truth, I'm not sure. I wasn't the most cautious teenager, but I refuse to apologize for it. My actions cost me my relationship with your mother, rightfully so of course, but I've accepted that." Her voice is firm yet carries a tone of absolution, as though she's forgiven herself even if my mother won't. "The only thing I truly regret is that my choices colored your mother's childhood, and her memory of this place."

For the first time, my mother makes sense outside of the cold, condescending box I've held her in for so long. What must it have been like to grow up in such a small town, constantly the source of gossip? I finally understand why she's so controlled and concerned with public perception, why she's so quick to squash any rumors about our family and why she holds her reputation above all else. She is what she allowed her childhood to make her. I wonder if we all must follow the path our childhoods lay out for us, or if we can choose another way. My mother's example says my future is inevitable. But maybe it doesn't have to be.

"Enough about that." Standing, Grammy J busies herself with wiping down the mirror, as if we've just been discussing the best way to eliminate soap scum.

There's an entire lifetime I need to learn about this woman, and more important, about my mother.

LATER IN THE EVENING, after I've scrubbed a thousand bathroom tiles, I retreat outside for some fresh air. Every inch of my skin smells like cleaning products, and my body feels like it could collapse, overcome with exhaustion, but it's the satisfying kind you feel after a hard day's work. I see now why Grammy J enjoys washing windows, mopping, dusting. Frustration, stress, anger—it all dissolves with the physical activity that housekeeping requires.

The sun has descended below the horizon, the stars appearing stitched together in the sky, but the heat hasn't dissipated. The front parking spaces are all vacant, guests of the Inn enjoying dinner at one of the many restaurants in town. Climbing onto the hood of my grandmother's beat-up truck, I lean back against the windshield, the metal pressing like an iron into my legs from baking in the sun all day.

My mind is still reeling over my exchange with Grammy J. I can't help but think about how I would react if I were in my mother's shoes. Would I feel angry, betrayed? Would I consider Grammy J selfish for telling me the truth? Would I even *want* to know the truth? Sometimes being honest serves no purpose other than to hurt someone. Sometimes ignorance really *can* be bliss.

A huge emotion swells inside me, one I've never felt for my mother—sympathy. Maybe, just maybe, if I broach the topic the right way she'll let me in, show me a different side of her. Maybe this could be the first step to tearing down the wall between us. Maybe this could mend our relationship, make it not so toxic and filled with strife. Before I can second-guess myself, I dig my cell out of my pocket and dial my parents' home number.

"Hello, Margaret," my father answers with a cheerful lilt.

I expected him to be at the office working late, so his greeting catches me off guard. He doesn't sound still upset with me, but then I remind myself that he's not like my mother, who holds grudges.

"Hi, Daddy," I say. "You're home early."

"Downtown had a power outage," he says. "I'm headed out to meet a client at the club in a few moments. Are you back in town? I'm sure your mother would appreciate a visit."

"No . . . I'm still in Wilhelmsburg," I say. "Have things been okay?" Of course what I'm really asking is if my mother has been taking out her anger on her only available target.

He pauses a moment. "You know, honey, I've come to realize that things are never really okay around here." Another pause. "But that doesn't mean it has to stay like that."

My father has never sounded so upbeat about my mother or the state of our family. Resigned, yes. Placating, yes. But hopeful? That's new, and I wonder if there's something going on he's not telling me about.

"Anyway, I've got to get going," he says. "I'll pass you off to your mother."

I hear the patio door opening followed by the telltale ruffling of a hand blocking the mouthpiece and muffled conversation. Then my mother's voice, hard and sharp as broken glass, comes through the line. "I'm not sure why you're calling us—our stance hasn't changed. You won't receive any financial support until you return to your responsibilities in Dallas."

Instantly I regret my decision to reach out to her, but it's too late to backpedal, so my only option is to move forward. "That's not why I'm calling," I say, sitting up and hugging my knees to my chest, as if that will somehow protect me.

"Oh? Then why?"

My throat feels tight and dry despite the humidity, and I wish I'd brought a bottle of water outside with me. "Grammy J told me about Poppa Bart . . . and you."

My mother goes eerily quiet. I envision her with an expression that on the surface seems nonthreatening, but underneath is simmering with barely contained rage.

Still I press on. "I know now why you cut Grammy J out of your life and why you won't return to Wilhelmsburg. And I . . . I was hoping you'd talk to me about it," I say, desperate to understand her better. Desperate to know her at all.

"How *dare* you bring that up." Her voice hums with a dangerous edge, like a power line on the verge of snapping. "The situation between your grandmother and me is none of your business, nor will it ever be. She had no right to share any of that with you. *No right.* When will you grow past this need to constantly pull at the curtain, to dabble in affairs that are best left alone?"

A gust of wind kicks up a mound dead leaves. They swirl in the air like a swarm of bees, and it's as if my mother somehow conjured them to attack me.

"This conversation is over, Margaret," she continues. "When you've finished acting like a selfish, spoiled child, you're free to come home. Until then, I don't want to hear from you. Or about your grandmother, ever again." Then she hangs up. She doesn't slam the phone onto the receiver, but still my ears are ringing.

Something inside me cracks. No matter how strong my desire is to establish a relationship with my mother, it will never, *ever* happen.

13

Setting up a reservation system and payment tool on the Inn's website is about as easy as finding an ounce of fat on a Victoria's Secret model. The software promised to revolutionize any boutique hospitality business with its seamless, drag-and-drop capabilities, but so far the only thing seamless is the transition from one error message to the next. Using an old computer in a cramped office only adds to my headache.

My muscles ache and my butt is numb from sitting in the same position for hours. Pushing the chair back, I prop my feet on the desk that's older than I am, stretching my legs, and roll my neck from side to side to work out the kinks.

"It seems like you need a break, Marge."

I jolt. Ryan is leaning against the door frame, hands tucked casually into the pockets of his faded jeans, looking sexier than should be allowed in a dirty, stained T-shirt, muddy boots, and with hair all disheveled. I didn't expect to hear from him so soon—I assumed he'd adhere to the three-day rule.

"And a glass of wine," I say, trying to ignore the girlish fluttering in my stomach. I notice a faint mark on his neck, and I wonder if it's from my teeth. The possibility only serves to intensify my nerves. I've never been the anxious type, especially around men, but Ryan makes me feel like I'm sixteen again.

"What's your stance on picnics?" His voice is easy, playful, without a trace of weirdness. I thought maybe things would be awkward when we saw each other again, but there's only that undeniable tug.

"Cliché and overrated." I stand and smooth my fingers over the simple jersey dress I borrowed from Grammy J. I hadn't anticipated being in Wilhelmsburg this long, and everything I brought is too dressy, too rigid. I suspect a trip to the shops lining Main Street is in my immediate future.

Ryan offers me a crooked smile that reaches his eyes. "I assumed that'd be your response," he says. "Which is why I packed us sack lunches to be eaten outside. But it's in no way considered a picnic."

"Cheeky," I say. "What happened to there being no rest for the wicked?"

"There's always time for sustenance."

Pushing off the door frame, he walks toward me and slides a hand around my hip, dipping his head to place a kiss below my jaw. For a second, I'm paralyzed by the feeling of his lips on my skin. But then my hands slip under his shirt, feeling the contours of his stomach, the defined, wide expanse of chest. His strained breath is heavy in my ear, which only feeds my desire. Without realizing it, I press myself into him until I feel the solid planes of his frame against mine.

Stepping us backward until my butt hits the desk, he lifts me slightly so I'm perched on the edge. His eyes roam over me like I'm a pinned target. Then he threads his fingers into my hair, almost desperate, and kisses me like I'm the last glass of Cabernet he'll ever consume and he has to get his fill. His hands travel the length of my body while his mouth tastes the column of my throat, his tongue mapping every dip and groove, as though he wants to ensure he'll find every pulse point, every flutter, every stretch of skin that makes me moan.

"But I suppose this'll hold me until we get to our destination," he says, nipping my bottom lip before pulling away.

The fluttering in my belly has turned frantic, spreading and migrating up into my chest, running wild. Ryan stares at me intently. "So, Marge, shall we?"

Nodding, I follow him out front still in a daze. The crew rebuilding the porch is resting in the shade, drinking sodas and devouring sandwiches. Moose is absent today, probably working at Hodgepodge.

I'm about to hop into Ryan's Blazer when I remember Grammy J is in the garden prepping the beds for the fall crops. "One second," I say. "I need to tell my grandmother I'm leaving."

It takes me a moment to spot her among the piles of ripped-out plants that have stopped producing vegetables with their roots sticking up in all directions. Grammy J's bent over a bell pepper plant, trimming all the branches except for those that still have fruit on them.

"Ryan and I are going to grab lunch. I'll be back later this afternoon to finish the website. Can I bring you anything?" I ask, gathering my hair in my hands to keep it from tangling in the wind.

Leaning back on her soil-covered galoshes, she tilts her chin up so she can see me from under the brim of her floppy hat. "Child, I have enough food here to last until Christmas," she says, pointing at the baskets filled with garlic bulbs, onions, green tomatoes, and okra. "But I appreciate the offer and you lettin' me know you'll be gone for a bit." She pats my calf a few times. My heart squeezes at the gesture—so simple, yet more significant than any touch I've received from my mother. "You still plannin' on attendin' karaoke tonight?"

I tell her I am, even though it goes against my better judgment.

Grammy J eyes me up and down. "That my dress?"

Shit. She said anything that belonged to her also belonged to me. Still I should've asked if I could wear it before barging into her closet without permission.

"It suits you, child," she says, surprising me with her answer. "Last time I donned that thing was when Poppa Bart took me line dancin' at the county fair. He'd be happy to see it on you. In fact, I reckon he'd be happy to know you're here at all and proud of the woman you've grown into. Just as I am." Grammy J smiles, then goes back to the bell pepper plant.

Her words are so unexpected, so damn . . . sincere that tears prick my eyes. There's no need to prove myself, no need to convince her of my worth. For some reason, Grammy J just believes in me, and I don't know what I did to deserve it.

"Thank you for that," I say, meaning it more than I've meant anything in my life.

With a good-bye, I head to the Blazer, nearly tripping when Grammy J yells, "Make sure you and Ryan use protection. You can never be too careful."

I spin around to face her, mouth hanging open. She's getting saucy in her old age.

"I'm not sure why you're lookin' so flustered," she says, cackling. "I was talkin' about sunscreen."

Ryan drives twenty minutes outside of Wilhelmsburg to a secluded area with natural springs. A metal sign warning DECAPITATION POSSIBLE dangles crookedly from a wooden post, the remaining available surface plastered with bumper stickers that proclaim things like HANGIN' WITH MY GNOMIES, KEEP AUSTIN WEIRD, and SWIMSUITS OPTIONAL.

"We're lucky because this spot is still a secret to most tourists," Ryan says, lifting the hatch on the Blazer. He grabs a blanket and a hard plastic, standard-issue cooler popular among tailgate fanatics and sorority girls who decorate them as a thank-you to their dates for being invited to a fraternity formal. I would know—I painted my fair share in college.

"This way," Ryan says, jerking his head in the direction of a narrow path several yards ahead.

He leads me through a grove of bald cypress trees strung with Spanish moss that provides shade from the blistering sun. Our shoes crunch against dead branches, upturned earth, and pieces of broken rock.

The trail opens to a wide, grassy knoll surrounded by clumps of misshapen limestone splashed with neon-orange lichen. I walk to the edge, mesmerized by the waterfall cascading over a cliff into a swimming hole thirty feet below. Hill Country stretches out below me like a living, breathing watercolor landscape.

Ryan comes to stand beside me. The sun catches the highlights in his hair, and my fingers itch to run through the silky curls.

"Beautiful, right?" he asks.

"Breathtaking," I say. Never in my life have I felt so small or seen something so magnificent. I'm usually so busy looking at what I have, especially as it compares to my neighbors, that I rarely appreciate what's around me.

Ryan holds two plastic stemless glasses of rosé in his hands and offers one to me. I accept, shocked at his choice. In some circles, rosé is often dismissed as unrefined plonk, a notch in class above boxed wine. And while the motto "real men wear pink" is widely accepted, the same can't be said for guys who enjoy wine that resembles shades of peach, salmon, or bright fuchsia.

My expression must betray my thoughts, because Ryan says, "I also eat soufflés and cry in movies, if that changes your perception."

I flash a wry smile, granting him that point. "Is this one of yours?" I ask. I take a sip, noting how the taste is fruity and floral with refreshing acidity and a vibrant finish.

"No," he says. "It's from the vineyard in Provence where I completed my apprenticeship."

"How long were you in France?"

"Almost two years, though I'd have stayed longer if I hadn't been called home." He strolls to where he's spread the blanket on the ground and kneels down.

I join him, kicking off my ballet flats and tucking my legs under me. "Why'd you pursue an apprenticeship if you already had a degree in viticulture?"

"Because it's the only way I could learn an artisan's approach to winemaking. Think of it like a language-immersion program. No amount of books or lectures can replace practical experience," he says, rifling around in the cooler. "Plus I graduated early, so I figured why not?"

My eyes are drawn to the way the hem of his shirt rides up to reveal a sliver of tan skin and two indents on either side of his spine above black boxer briefs that peek out of his pants. *Dear God, Ryan has Venus dimples.* My mouth dries a little, and I curl my fingers into fists to keep from touching him. I don't know how I didn't feel those when he was naked on top of me last night. Then again, my attention *was* diverted elsewhere.

"Did our lunch get lost?" I ask, my voice slightly hoarse from the memory.

Ryan looks at me as though I'm both insufferable and endearing. Closing the lid on the cooler, he passes me a brown paper bag. Inside are individual portion-sized containers of hummus served with pita bread and olives, Mediterranean shrimp and orzo salad, and peach halves drizzled with honey and cinnamon.

"Did you make all this?" I ask.

"Don't get carried away," he says, unwrapping a set of plastic utensils. "The only cooking I do is buying preassembled items from the market."

I lift the rosé in a toast. "Likewise."

"You know, I'm a little disappointed you didn't snoop or steal anything when I left you unattended in my house."

"How do you know I didn't snoop?" I ask, wondering if he has hidden cameras stashed in various rooms.

"Because you would've commented on my Monopoly token collection."

I shake my head, my lips curling in an amused half smile. He really is like a kid. "I did notice you're a bit of a neat freak, which doesn't explain why your Blazer was such a disaster that night you drove me to the Inn." I remove the lid on the orzo salad and pop a cherry tomato into my mouth.

"What can I say? I'm quite the conundrum." He finishes his wine and pours another glass. "Actually, during harvest time all bets are off. The days are long and relentless, and I end up living out of my SUV. Bordeaux making a mess of herself in the vineyards and dragging it all over the inside never helps."

We eat the remainder of lunch in comfortable silence, content to listen to the roar of water all around us and watch butterflies flutter in and out of the trees. My whole body feels relaxed, reenergized, and I have the urge to do something stupid like dive off the nearest cliff into the pool below. The idea alone is so unlike me that goose bumps pop up on my forearms. Perhaps this is what Ryan meant when he talked about living on the edge, and I don't even need to drink a bottle of Wild Abandon for encouragement.

Twisting my hair into a bun, I get to my feet and say, "I'm going for a swim. You coming?"

Ryan grins as he stands. "Only if there are no clothes involved."

"Not a chance."

"You are aware I've already seen you naked, right?" His gaze is steady on mine, flickering like a flame, and my heart trips a beat at his words.

Ryan grabs the collar of his shirt and tugs it over his head in one smooth motion, tossing it onto the blanket. My eyes rake over the corded muscle in his arms and shoulders, his defined pecs, sculpted from long hours laboring in the vineyard, and the V carved into his hips that disappears beneath the low-slung waistband of his jeans.

It was just dark enough the other night that I didn't get a full picture. But now, with his torso on display and the visible bulge in his pants, my whole body clenches, and a flush spreads from my face down my neck as sudden images of him moving over me, inside me, everywhere, race through my mind.

"I'm not a sculpture, Marge. The rule 'look but don't touch' doesn't apply," he says with a wink, then unclasps his belt.

Cocky ass.

Before he undresses completely and I'm unable to control myself, I walk to a rocky outcropping, moss and moisture slick under my toes. I refuse to glance down. If I do, I'll lose my nerve. I slip off my dress—Grammy J will kill me if I ruin it. The fine mist from the waterfall clings to the cotton fabric of my matching bra and underwear.

Then I close my eyes and jump.

My stomach lodges in my throat along with my scream. I plunge deep below the surface of the water. Coldness envelops me, stealing my breath but not enough to squelch the adrenaline pumping through my veins, and I wonder why I don't do this sort of thing every day. My body turns weightless. I listen for the churning, gurgling sound of the waterfall spilling into the pool, but all I hear is the beating of my heart echoing in my ears.

I break the surface in time to witness Ryan hurl himself into the air and land with an impressive splash five yards from me. Popping up, he combs a hand through his hair and swims over to where I'm treading water.

"I expected you to use the swing, but you went all in," he says, pointing to a frayed rope swaying from a tree near the crest of the cliff.

"And I was hoping you'd belly flop and deflate your overblown ego, but I guess we don't always get what we want," I say, smiling sweetly at him.

"Marge, it requires a personality like mine to contend with your snarkiness," he says, grabbing my waist, his fingers playing with the top of my underwear. The slight pressure is enough to lure me to him. His eyes are startlingly bright. Green with flecks of brown and gold, colors of the earth. Water droplets shine in his lashes, and his skin glistens.

Grasping his shoulders, my breasts pushing against his chest, I kick my legs between us to stay afloat, the fabric of his boxer briefs grazing my thighs. He guides us into an alcove behind the waterfall, the sun filtering through the fissures and crevices in the stone. Ryan uses a rock that juts out to keep us steady as I hang on to him. He slides his free hand along my ribs, over my bra. Moving the hair off my neck, he leans into me, and I suck in a shaky breath, anticipating his kiss.

Instead, he tilts his head back slightly and meets my gaze, a grin on his face as he twirls a piece of my hair. "You know, there's never been a time I haven't thought you were sexy. But there's something about the way you look now, with your hair tangled and fanned out, makeup washed off, and bare skin, that I can't get enough of . . . I'm bewitched." He wraps an arm around my waist. The weight of his palm feels warm and solid against my skin. "It makes me wonder, given what a powerhouse you are when you're all wound up and put together, what you'd accomplish if you unleashed yourself. What would you choose to do? Who would you choose to be? Whatever it is, I hope I'm there for it."

His words knock the breath out of me, and instinctively I pull away. I can feel my heart pounding in my ears, so loud I don't know how the sound isn't echoing around the alcove. I've been naked in front of a man plenty of times, but I've never felt more exposed than I do right now. So few have ever seen beyond my polished manners and careful expressions that it's impossible for me to process—let alone accept—praise like this.

And what does he mean he hopes he's there for it?

It hits me suddenly that this is the closest anyone has ever come to discussing commitment with me, and I'm so completely out of my depth I don't know how to interpret what he said. It seems as if Ryan has such a firm grip on his future, on his plans and where he wants to be—would it be so easy for him to envision me there with him? Is that what he wants? I'm desperate to know, but I'm too afraid of his answer.

"Margaret, wait, come here," Ryan says over the din of the waterfall, his brow furrowed. He glides toward me, stopping close enough for our bodies to almost touch. "Why do you have such a hard time accepting a compliment?"

His eyes travel over my face, and the way they tempt me, test me, read me, strips away all my pretenses. The truth flows out of me in a rush.

"I don't have much experience with flattery that isn't a guise for carefully crafted condescension," I say.

"I find that hard to believe," he says. "There's so much about you worth appreciating."

Of course in his world, unlike in mine, praise isn't a novelty you have to constantly second-guess. For as long as I can remember, my life's been a giant pressure cooker. The unrealistic demands for perfection and success. The constant parental criticism that shifts from grades and popularity in childhood to careers and social status in adulthood.

"I was raised to project a pristine image my mother can be proud of. Vulnerability has never been an option," I say, bobbing like driftwood as water laps around me. "And compliments, *if* they came, were backhanded and meant to point out my flaws and failures. The message was that I should be constantly striving to be better, work harder."

Ryan shakes his head no. "The problem with passive-aggressive criticism is that most of the time it only proves that the person talking hasn't bothered to look beneath the surface. Your mother certainly never has." He pulls me toward him, one of his legs sliding along mine. "And I know you *know* that. So why do you let her treat you as if you're beneath her or that you're a constant disappointment that baffles her? Where's the fearless girl who blindly snuck into a haunted house and told me off when we got caught?"

My chest tightens. I thought once all my secrets were out in the open, I'd feel free. But shame courses through me, holding me captive.

"Because she's my mother," I say automatically, as if it's that simple. As if that explains her behavior and my reaction.

An emotion passes over Ryan's face. I recall him mentioning that his father preferred using fists to words, and I realize he understands more than anyone—and especially more than I do—what it's like to grow up in an unforgiving environment. "Blood doesn't constitute loyalty or familial obligation—and it certainly doesn't mean what she says is true."

"It does where I come from. You're not born into money without strings attached," I say, not to brag but so that he understands. "And when you're raised with every advantage, every luxury, it's difficult not to feel as if you have to be worthy of the life afforded to you." I raise my eyes to meet his and whisper, "I want so badly to be worthy."

"Margaret," he says, his gaze like a magnifying glass on me. "The woman I'm looking at, the woman who doesn't seem afraid to stand up to anyone, she's worth *everything*. All she needs to do is believe it."

I want to tell him he's right, that I'm as strong as he thinks I am, but the lie gets trapped in my throat. Instead I kiss him, losing myself in the sensation of his mouth on mine, the feel of his wet, silky hair between my fingers.

Someday I hope I can prove his words true.

14

Axel's Off Main reminds me of the dive bars where I used to watch the Randy Hollis Band perform, back when they were still a bunch of college guys writing country music out of a grungy apartment and trying to break into the industry. Back when I mattered to them.

The drinks are dirt cheap, the faux wood paneled walls are decorated with kitschy art and rusty license plates, and the bartenders look like they've seen every scenario and then seen it all again. The air smells of stale beer and dirty mop water. Even the dartboards and pool tables with green felt that's faded and threadbare have the right amount of grime—a perfect balance between well loved and gross.

When Bon Bon invited me to ladies' karaoke night, I expected the typical boring setup—drunk people stumbling around on a stage while slurring out-of-tune hits, the audience pretending to pay attention but more concerned with snagging the random hookup.

Instead I'm a front-row spectator to Mad Libs karaoke where the crowd—a mix of young and old—is *fully* engaged. The only males in the place are the deejay and the bartenders.

Beside me, Bon Bon and three of her friends—Amber, Tiffany, and Gina, the manager of the Vintner's Collective and the woman I saw with Possum at the Camden Cellars party—flip through the book of song options. Rather than the traditional track listings, each page is a removable lyric sheet with lines where key words or phrases have been removed. I select "Ironic" by Alanis Morissette and spend the next fifteen minutes reworking the verses and chorus to make them *actually* ironic. When I finish, I give the paper to one of the servers to put into the queue.

Right now there's an older woman—Essie, as announced by the deejay—in a Western-style button-down and cowboy boots attempting a raunchy version of Amy Grant's "Baby Baby." She's replaced words like "heart" and "in motion" with "nipple" and "pumping." The audience roars with laughter and cheers as she dances seductively and does gestures with the microphone that will plague me with nightmares.

"If you think this is bad, imagine Essie gyrating while singing Salt-n-Pepa's 'Push It,'" Bon Bon yells in my ear.

I make a face. "That's horrifying."

Laughing, Bon Bon twirls a flimsy napkin above her head and launches it in the air so it lands at Essie's feet with the other junk cluttered on the stage—silk roses that were handed out at the door, wine corks, and coasters. The music fades out and applause erupts. Bowing, Essie exits into the crowd of regulars who greet her with high fives.

"Margaret, welcome to a standard night of depravity for us," Amber says as a waitress delivers enough lemon drop shots to our table to intoxicate a football team. The color is meant to be bright yellow, but under the horrendous overhead neon lights, the liquid appears blue. Amber takes one before passing the tray around.

She's strikingly gorgeous—big doe eyes, a heart-shaped face, and long brunette hair that has never touched dye—and it makes me want to pinch her to ensure she's real. Where I come from, natural beauty is as rare as an endangered species.

Tiffany slides three shots in my direction. "Bottoms up," she says, then informs me that because I arrived late to the festivities, I need to play catch-up. After Ryan brought me back to the Inn this afternoon, I spent five hours fighting with the online reservation system on the website until I finally got it functioning properly. Axel's was packed and spiraling into debauchery by the time I showed up.

Picking up one of the glasses, I lick the sugar rim and swallow the shot. The taste is reminiscent of limoncello—the burn of the alcohol, the sweetness of the simple syrup, the bitterness of the lemon flavor. Squeezing my eyes shut, I polish off another, my throat on fire.

"Thatta girl." Tiffany slaps the tabletop, rattling drink glasses. Liquid sloshes against the sides and onto the cracked wood surface.

She has a nose-to-ear chain, supporting a row of tiny gold medallions, and a Gothic style—black skinny jeans and black fitted blouse, sleek black hair that reflects purple in certain angles, pale skin—that reminds me of Angelina Jolie circa 1999. She's a loan officer at the only bank in town, and on the weekends does tarot card readings out of the shed in her backyard.

Bon Bon elbows me in the ribs. "Be careful. Tiff's the lush of the group. She'll drag down anyone who's stupid enough to fall for her antics." Tonight she's wearing a different Camden Cellars T-shirt, this one with the No

Regrets winking eye logo above the breast pocket. She must have come straight from the winery.

Tiffany dips her fingers into some ice water and flicks the droplets at Bon Bon's face. "Margaret, don't listen to her." There's a gap between her right incisor and canine, and it gives her speech a slight lisp. "I may be a lush, but I'm a helluva lot of fun, and you seem like you could use some of that." Tiffany wraps an arm around my shoulders, squeezing me against her, and slams back a shot of her own.

From the moment Bon Bon spotted me hovering in the doorway and waved me over, I've been treated as if I'm part of the group. In fact, when Bon Bon introduced me to her friends as "the girl who gave Cricket a taste of his own medicine," they actually *thanked me* for getting Ryan thrown in jail.

The deejay calls Gina as the next victim, and the entire bar breaks out into hollering and catcalls. Pushing back from the table, she pops the collar on her leather jacket, the tattoos covering her chest peeking out from beneath the fabric of her worn shirt. "Okay, ladies. Time to show you how it's done." With one hand on her hip and the other pointed toward the ceiling, she struts toward the stage like Mick Jagger.

Gina steps up to the microphone as the opening chords of Def Leppard's "Pour Some Sugar on Me" fill the room. As she sings, the crowd claps along. I'm so entranced by her voice, raspy and deep and soulful, equal parts Joan Jett and smooth jazz saxophone, that it takes a moment for me to process that she took Mad Libs karaoke to a whole new level and changed the lyrics into a parody titled "Pour Some Salsa on Me" about a horny burrito that wants to get stuffed with goodies, rolled, and have hot sauce smothered all over it.

The song is so absurd, so comical in its brilliance, that a laugh bubbles up. At first it's small, a tickle in the back of my throat, but it grows like a wildfire I can't control until I'm unable to breathe or make a sound, my stomach cramping from laughing so hard.

"Are you dying?" Amber asks.

But now I've infected Bon Bon, who's snickering beside me. "This is nothing compared to Gina's rendition of *The Fresh Prince of Bel-Air* theme song. She puts a Disney spin on it and calls her version 'The Fresh Princess of Beast's Castle.' It's famous around here. She even channels her inner Belle and wears a gold taffeta dress while performing it."

"And she always ends the song with a spot-on impersonation of the Carlton dance," Tiffany says, cackling, her green eyes bright, almost glowing like a cat's.

I picture Gina dressed in a poofy nineties prom dress, arms flailing, fingers snapping, and hips swinging in rhythm with the music, and laughter explodes out of me like water through a dam. Soon the three of us are all helpless, bent over and cracking up. Amber tries to keep a straight face, but eventually the giggles overtake her.

I can't remember the last time I laughed so loud and hard and with tears leaking out of my eyes, as though my body can't contain the joy flooding through it. If only life could always feel like this, exuberant and free and full of possibility. Though as I look around at the girls still guffawing like idiots, at Gina who's now mimicking playing an electric guitar on stage, at the audience soaking up every moment of the evening, I wonder if that's exactly how life is in Wilhelmsburg.

If that's how it could be for me.

———

An hour later Moose and Possum join us, and they come bearing dinner. Axel's doesn't serve food unless you consider the maraschino cherries food.

To my amusement, Possum has changed the color of his shaggy curls from carrot orange to My Little Pony pink. He gives me a two-finger salute in acknowledgment, then scoops Gina into his arms and plants a kiss on her mouth. They spend a solid minute making out, him cupping her butt with both palms and her grinding against his thigh. Bon Bon whistles, along with a few other people, and they break apart, flipping everyone off.

"So after that appetizer, who's hungry?" Moose asks with a bemused expression. Pushing aside the empty shot glasses cluttering the table, he places boxes of pizza, buckets of buffalo chicken wings and drumettes, silverware and paper plates, and various condiments in the center. I'm going to need to find a personal trainer or join a gym soon to combat the amount of calories I've consumed since arriving in town.

Then again, as long as I stay in Wilhelmsburg, I may never have to work out, with the amount of upkeep the bed-and-breakfast requires.

"I didn't picture you as the karaoke type," Moose says, ruffling my hair like he's teasing his baby sister. As an only child, I've never understood the sibling dynamic, but now I think I missed out on something special.

"I'm blaming it on peer pressure," I say, flicking his cartoon moose tattoo on its Rudolph-red nose in retaliation.

"The rest of us have already performed, but Margaret hasn't been called yet. It's coming though," Gina cuts in. She smiles at me in a way that feels genuine, but based on how she's scrutinizing my cotillion posture and navy sheath dress, it seems as though she's convinced I'll be the most uptight person to ever sing an off-key cover of a pop song. She's right, of course, but I promised myself to try new things and all that, so I refuse to back out.

"And we all know what Margaret's capable of, so imagine the trouble she'll cause on stage," Bon Bon says with a wink, like we're best friends sharing a private joke. It reminds me of how it used to be between Piper, Samma, Faye, and me, before competition and jealousy tainted our relationship.

At least Ryan isn't here to witness my future embarrassment, even if I secretly wish he was. It's unnerving how much I crave his smart-ass mouth and disarming personality—his approval—especially since he's supposed to be a fun way for me to forget the past. But I suspect I'm only fooling myself in that regard. He's already becoming more to me than anyone else ever has, and it doesn't scare me as much as I thought it would.

Possum dishes everyone slices of pizza, chicken wings and drumettes, and celery sticks that pretend to add nutritional value to the meal, while Moose steals two chairs from a nearby table. Wedging one into a corner for Possum and the other between Bon Bon and me, he takes a seat, his bulky frame pressing against our shoulders.

"So are you and Possum regulars at ladies' night?" I ask Moose while we eat. The sea of people has thinned a bit, but still the number of males can be counted on one hand, so unless they're rabid karaoke fans, I don't understand why they're here.

Across from me, Amber laughs around a mouthful of mozzarella and pepperoni. "They're here every week."

"It's not our fault the boss always schedules us on this night," Moose says.

"Oh, admit it. You both love being the only guys among all these women." She flings a packet of wet wipes at him that he bats away. Amber starts to say something else, but she spots someone she knows across the room and excuses herself.

Moose faces me. "Possum bartends and I deejay for the late crowd."

"Why do you work here if you have the store and your carpentry business?" I ask, spooning some ranch dressing onto my plate for the drumettes. I tear off a piece of chicken and pop it into my mouth.

Silence settles over the table. Everyone stares at me, incredulous and a little offended.

Possum clears his throat. "Most folks in Wilhelmsburg have multiple jobs in order to make ends meet," he says, and I feel like an out-of-touch snob, which I guess in reality I am. "I gotta get ready for my shift." He finishes his pizza in two bites, then heads to the bar, Gina following behind him, their fingers linked together.

"My mistake," I say too late for Possum to hear.

"Don't worry about the slipup. We've all shoved our foot in our mouths before," Tiffany says to me, licking some hot sauce off her thumb. She's eaten in record time, leaving only a mound of little bones and crusts on her plate.

"Ain't that the truth." Moose nudges my side, and I bet he's remembering how he did something similar around me recently. "All right, it's my turn to deejay. Margaret, I hope you're prepared, because I'm calling you up soon." He piles some chicken wings onto a stack of napkins and steals a sip of Bon Bon's lager.

"Hey! Buy your own," Bon Bon says, punching his bicep that's the size of a ham hock, which doesn't seem to affect him. She winds up like she's going to hit him again, but Moose steps out of her reach, snatching away her beer bottle in the process. Snickering, he swerves around servers and groups of inebriated women to the DJ booth.

"What a little shit." Bon Bon shakes her head in exasperation but smiles.

I so desperately want that tight-knit, easy friendship they all have with one another that it causes an ache in my chest. The pain must show in my expression, because she asks, "You okay?"

"I'm fine . . . You all are really close. It's nice."

Tilting her head to the side, Bon Bon gives me a measuring look, and I wonder if she's thinking about what she said to me at the Vintner's Collective—*you must not have many friends.* "We grew up in a town of three thousand people, so we didn't have much of a choice."

"Have you all always lived here?" I ask.

"Most of us went away to college," Tiffany interjects. "But eventually we ended up back home." She shakes the ice cubes in her lowball tumbler and swallows the last sip of a whiskey and Coke.

"And since then none of you have ever had the itch to experience other places?" I ask.

"No point," Tiffany says, shrugging. "We have everything we need right here."

"Not *everything*. I wouldn't complain if an actual salon with licensed professionals opened up," Bon Bon says, running her fingers through her hair. She attempted to style it tonight, but the humidity has collapsed the blond curls into limp waves.

I envy their contentment, the straightforwardness of it. In Dallas it's all about more money, more status, more ego —no amount of success is ever enough. People are stuck on a hamster wheel, sprinting at full speed but never getting anywhere.

Moose's sportscaster voice announces the next person

to the microphone, which thankfully isn't me, as Gina returns to our table, adult beverages in hand. She must've noticed I quit drinking after the lemon drop shots, because she distributes the drinks to Bon Bon and Tiffany and passes me a half-full glass of white wine. "No pressure," she says, the earlier tension gone. "It's in case you need some liquid courage for your performance."

Nodding in thanks, I take a sip. Immediately I'm hit with the flavor of Granny Smith apples, honeysuckle, and ripe, juicy pears. There's a prominent sweetness on the palate that I adore in a German-style Riesling. Even at a dirty dive bar in Hill Country, the wine is superb.

"So, what about you, Margaret? After only living in a big city, how are you finding our small corner of the world?" Tiffany asks, continuing our previous conversation. Reaching into the pizza box, she pulls another slice toward her. But by dragging it like that, she tears the toppings off the next slice, so all the cheese, sausage, and pepperoni lie in a clump on the cardboard.

"Aw, come on, Tiff. Why do you always do that?" Bon Bon says, her voice whiny and slightly slurred. "I wanted to eat that piece."

Tiffany shrugs. "You still can."

"Not if it's mutilated like that."

Gina leans over to me and whispers, "They have this fight every week," and I smile.

Rolling her eyes, Tiffany picks up the toppings from the destroyed slice and arranges them back on the crust, as if that somehow fixes it. "*Anyway*, as I was saying before I was so rudely interrupted, are you enjoying Wilhelmsburg?" she asks me.

I nod. "Everything's so relaxed, so wide open and beautiful."

I wait for one of the girls to crack a joke about me and

Ryan, something about how I better relish it here since I've been fooling around with the town's most eligible bachelor. But that type of callous comment is something I'd expect from Piper, Samma, and Faye, not these women.

"You should stick around for the holidays," Tiffany replies. "All of the historic landmarks on Main Street are decorated with lights, and the wineries participate in a tasting tour where visitors receive ornaments and hand-crafted items at each stop."

"And your grandmother creates a whole Christmas village on the Inn's property," Bon Bon adds in between bites of celery. I guess she decided against the mangled pizza. "The tourists flock to it, though not as much as in the past because the commercial vineyards with on-site guest lodging have begun copying her."

Gina's been watching a woman wearing a floral print shirt and atrocious khaki shorts flaunt across the stage singing her version of The Beach Boys' "Kokomo." I assumed she hadn't been paying attention, so it surprises me when she turns to me and says, "I didn't realize you were related to Joy. She's legendary."

"That she is," I say. "And a slave driver."

"It's a shame the bed-and-breakfast is struggling," she says. "In its current state, it's bound to be sold—too many people are clamoring for the land and the structure needs a major remodel."

My chest pinches at the idea of Grammy J losing everything she and Poppa Bart built together. As long as I'm here, I'll do everything in my power to prevent that from happening.

"It could definitely use some good TLC, that's for sure, which is why I'm trying to use my PR background to help revitalize it," I say.

"That makes sense," Gina says. "I imagine Joy's still

running the Inn the same way she did in the eighties and nineties. One of the reasons the Vintner's Collective started is because the boutique wineries realized they had to diversify and increase their audience in order to compete in a growing market."

That very dilemma—how to expand and stay relevant—has also been running through my head. As it stands, the Inn isn't succeeding as a bed-and-breakfast. Though the feedback I've heard from guests has been polite and mostly positive, they all agree the B&B could use some updates. Problem is, with no budget, bookings need to be the immediate priority.

"I've considered different options," I admit. "I've created a website, and I'm planning on hiring a photographer to stage some interior shots to post online."

Gina murmurs noncommittally, throwing back a stray lemon drop shot and returning her attention to the stage.

I can't blame her. Even I know catapulting the Inn into the digital age, professional pictures or no, is a quick fix at best. But if the Inn itself isn't enough of a draw for visitors, what might be? An idea sparks in my mind.

"Actually, I've been meaning to speak with you," I say. "The private events held at the Vintner's Collective, are those mostly just special wine tastings? Or do you have other types of events as well?"

"Mostly tastings, but we're always open to broadening our horizon. Why, what are you thinking?" Gina asks.

Swallowing the remainder of my Riesling, I put on my business face and say, "I'd like to run something past you. When I was building my firm in Dallas, I worked on some promotional efforts for a few microbreweries and farm-to-table restaurants located in the same area. As individual endeavors, PR was difficult because funds were limited. As a result, the companies agreed to band together and host a block party, where they each showcased their unique food and drinks for a crowd that paid a nominal entry fee. Since you're interested in expanding your current selections, this could be the perfect opportunity for you to do something similar."

"How so?" Gina asks, uncrossing her legs and leaning forward so we can talk without shouting over the music. By the expression on her face, I've got her full attention.

"We could collaborate on developing seasonal sample-and-savor events hosted at the Collective as part of various vacation packages that'll be available at the Inn. Maybe the events could incorporate demonstration classes centered on cheese making or charcuterie and how best to pair those items with wine. I also saw that you have mead on the menu," I say, referring to the alcoholic beverage that's created from mixing honey and water and fermenting it with yeast. "Perhaps you could invite a local beekeeper to discuss the process of cultivating and harvesting honey and how mead is crafted. Is any of this something you'd be interested in?"

As I pitch my idea, Gina nods and smiles, as if she approves of what she's hearing. When I finish, she goes quiet a moment, lost in thought.

Finally she says, "All of that sounds great—*really* great—but if your goal is to bring exposure to the Inn, I'd suggest hosting the events on the property and extending invitations to visitors staying at other places. That way the next time those people travel to Wilhelmsburg, they'll preferably reserve a room at the B&B and shop at the businesses represented. Not to mention spread the word."

She has a valid point. Perhaps my scope of focusing solely on guests booked at the bed-and-breakfast is too narrow. The real draw is this quaint country town with its wineries, farms and orchards, and local shops and restaurants. So maybe I need to concentrate more on how to market the destination and all it has to offer.

"That's a good idea," I say. "And as an incentive, Grammy J could give discounts to those people who reserve during the party."

"Exactly." Gina retrieves a business card out of the inner pocket of her leather jacket and slides it across the table to me. "Call me and we'll set something up."

Just like that. Without any more discussion or negotiations.

Moose taps the microphone and a squeal echoes around the room. "All right, it's my privilege to announce my friend Margaret to the stage," he says.

Once again the crowd lets out a roar of cheers and clapping. Their reaction must be standard operating procedure, because they're treating me as if I'm family rather than a stranger. Too bad I don't share their enthusiasm—right now my heart is jerking around in my chest and sweat is gathering in my palms.

I stand, wiping my hands on my navy dress, certain I'm leaving marks. "Apart from picturing everyone naked, any tips for a first timer?"

"You've *never* done karaoke before?" Tiffany asks, studying me with a dubious look. "Not even as a drunk college student?"

I shake my head, unable to reply. My stomach churns as though it could reject its contents at any moment. Why am I so nervous? I don't know the majority of these people, yet I feel the need to impress them. And why did I pick a song with so many high notes? Maybe if I'm lucky the alcohol will have dulled everyone's senses and trick them into believing I sound like Alanis Morissette and not a hyena on helium. At least I didn't choose a Mariah Carey ballad.

Tiffany rummages in her purse and pulls out a pair of oversized aviator sunglasses, tossing them to me. "Put these on. I promise they'll help."

Inhaling a deep breath, I slip them on, the overhead neon lights dimming. I make my way to the stage and step up, the surface sticky under my shoes. I gaze out at the audience. The sunglasses have added a dark layer, concealing people's facial expressions and body language, but it doesn't prevent my hands from shaking or my legs from wobbling.

The solo acoustic guitar and slow melody of "Ironic" start to play, the accompanying lyrics I modified appearing on the large screen set up beside me.

Here goes nothing.

The next moments are a blur. The words fall out of my mouth in a jumble, running together, as I grip the microphone, my posture tense. My voice is high-pitched and strained, as though someone's choking me with panty hose.

The crowd has quieted down, and I imagine they're all staring at me in horror, on the verge of booing or throwing peanut shells. But then I hear a familiar voice yell, "Come on, Marge. Show us some of that sass you're so proud of."

I push the sunglasses up on my head, searching for Ryan. I don't wonder or even care why he's here, just that he *is*. I spot him standing at the table beside Bon Bon, Tiffany, and Gina. He smiles and nods at me in encouragement, and the gesture immediately releases some of my nerves.

Exhaling, I clear my throat and turn to Moose at the deejay stand. "How about I try this again?" I ask.

Whistling and hollering swells around me. Moose grins and restarts the track. This time when I sing, I let go of all my inhibitions, belting out the lyrics the way I do when I'm alone in my car. I botch some of the lines I changed and nearly break into laughter at others, but I keep going. As I transition into the chorus, several women get to their feet, dancing and singing along with me at the top of their lungs, and by the end of the song, the whole room has joined in.

With a cheek-splitting smile on my face and the audience's applause ringing in my ears, I bow, consumed with adrenaline and pure euphoria. This must be how the Randy Hollis Band feels every night they perform. Like you can conquer anything and everything.

My eyes find Ryan. His gaze hasn't wavered, still focused on me with a searing intensity that feels too intimate, too private. Weaving through the room, he pulls me off the stage and into his arms. "I stop by Axel's to deliver a wine shipment, and what do I discover but my favorite redhead behind the microphone," he says. "What other surprises do you have hidden up your sleeve?"

"Enough to keep you guessing," I say with a wink, then head back to the table to select a new lyric sheet for the next round.

I'm just getting started.

15

I put the finishing touches on the trays of bite-sized desserts Grammy J so nicely prepared, eager for the festivities to begin. We're hosting a sort of mini Taste of Wilhelmsburg for nearly three dozen visitors from all around town, guests of the Inn included.

When I proposed a joint event to Gina at karaoke, I expected it to take weeks to coordinate. In Dallas, arranging even the most basic function requires at least a month of preparation. But between my organizational and party-planning skills and Gina's knowledge of the local businesses and wineries, we were able to pull it together in nine days. And while the last several hours setting up have been frantic, I've got my game face on and I'm ready to execute.

I hear the sound of tires crunching on the gravel outside. A familiar fluttering ignites in my belly, and sweat pricks up on my palms. I wipe them off on my dark-washed designer jeans, wondering for the fifth time if I should've opted for the more formal pencil skirt with my silk blouse. Reminding myself that the intent of the evening is to create buzz about the Inn and promote a brand—a casual, relaxed one at that—I inhale a deep breath and remove the ancient walkie-talkie I found in the garden shed from my back pocket.

I press the button on the side and ask, "Moose, are you handling parking?" A loud static noise fills the air. "Moose?"

Glancing through the kitchen windows, I search for him but only spot Grammy J on the lawn, directing traffic and greeting each person to the party with a glass of sparkling wine. When I broached the subject of hosting an event at the Inn, naturally her first question was how I intended to pay for it. After I explained that those attendees not staying at the bed-and-breakfast would be charged a nominal fee that'd cover the costs, she jumped on board much to my surprise. I expected her to be at the very least frustrated about me invading her turf, but then again, Grammy J's not my mother.

I try Moose once more. "Do you want your antlers mounted on the wall at Hodgepodge? Pick up."

The walkie-talkie crackles. "Margaret, he's not going to answer until you address him properly," Gina cuts in. She, of course, wasn't thrilled when I suggested using these "glitchy, pieces-of-shit communication devices"—her words—but Moose was *all* about it. Though he adamantly refused to loan me extra tables and chairs or lend a helping hand unless we followed "appropriate" procedure.

Rolling my eyes, I press the button again and call out, "Pirate Red to Rudolph."

His voice comes over the line. "Go for Rudolph."

"What's your twenty, over?" I say, referring to his current location.

"I'm unpacking the extra wine crates, over." Which means in reality he's busy sampling the product.

Since I need him sober and working, I say, "Rudolph, please step away from the alcohol and handle parking."

"Ten-four. I'm on it," he says, clicking off.

"Pirate Red to Gin and Juice," I say, switching gears to Gina. "Are all the vendors good to go?"

Tables have been stationed throughout the house and on the lawn, featuring everything from artisan cheeses to charcuterie to local honey to jars of jams and pickled vegetables. And to pair with the various foods are wines from vineyards around town, ranging in size from boutique to large operations. Had I known Wilhelmsburg was such a treasure trove of delicacies, I wouldn't have shown up to Ryan's party with a *fruit basket* like an amateur.

"Affirmative," Gina says, the annoyance in her voice broadcasting loud and clear. Next time I make a mad dash out of Dallas, I need to remember to bring my headsets and other equipment.

"Flying in with the mini desserts in a moment," I say. "Over and out."

Slipping the walkie-talkie into my back pocket, I prop the trays on my shoulders and pass through the swinging door to the main dining room. Immediately I notice that while the vendors are set up, the station with the self-serve plates and cutlery is in disarray. *How hard is it to manage one simple task?* I place the trays on the sideboard and head over to where Ryan and Gina are chatting at the Camden Cellars table.

"Gina, I thought you said you had things covered."

"I do." She gestures around the space where all the vendors are waiting patiently for the guests to enter from outside. Farmer Joe from Willis Orchards waves and gives a thumbs-up. "See, everyone's ready to start."

"Then what's the situation with the plates and cutlery? Since we're not in an enchanted French château in the woods, I don't think they're going to magically organize themselves. Get on that."

Gina's mouth drops open a fraction, her face reddening, her expression torn between astonishment and building anger, but before she can respond, Ryan interrupts. "Simmer down, Red. Drink a glass of wine or three, and remember why these people are here."

I sigh. He's right. I've snapped at her as if she's a crappy assistant rather than a valued collaborator. "Please excuse me, Gina," I say. "I can be a little high-strung when it comes to executing events."

Ryan nearly spits out a mouthful of Chardonnay, and I cut him a glare. Gina graciously nods and squeezes my arm. "It'll go smoothly. You'll see," she says. "Just have fun with it."

Wiping his chin with a napkin, Ryan leans in to whisper to me, his breath hot on my ear. "Rein it in for now, Captain. You can raid and pillage all you want later. In the meantime, I'll deal with the dishes and utensils." He playfully pinches my side before walking away.

"That's Pirate Red to you," I shout after him as a flood of people pile into the Inn from outside, Moose and Grammy J trailing after them.

After that, it's a whirl of activity—restocking bottles of wine and finding corkscrews, refilling the mini dessert trays and topping off water goblets, washing the dirty tableware and returning it all to the self-serve station before the next round needs scrubbing. Moose and Gina take charge of ensuring the vineyard and food shop owners have everything they need, while Grammy J mingles with the attendees, selling the B&B and all its kitschy charisma the best way she knows how—with her vibrant personality. Already we've had four new couples and a handful of current guests reserve rooms for next summer.

Before long, the sun has sunk below the horizon. I'm dumping ice into a bucket and Grammy J is chattering about what a fantastic party Gina and I put together, when Bob Hook, the owner of Hook & Arrow Cellars, approaches us carrying a mound of cured meats piled high on a napkin. From what Ryan's told me, Hook & Arrow is the largest commercial winery in Wilhelmsburg, distributed all over Texas and the Southwest, and I wonder if Bob is the person who's been wanting to buy Camden Cellars, desperate for the land like every other grape grower in the region.

"I sure hope you'll be making this an annual occurrence, Margaret," Bob says, placing a hand the size of a baseball glove on my shoulder. He reminds me of one of the weathered cowboys—white hair, bushy eyebrows and beard, tan face—from the old Westerns my father and I used to watch when my mother wasn't around to scold us.

"I'd certainly like to," I say, tying a knot on the bag of ice and setting it aside.

Despite my slightly neurotic start, this evening has been wonderful. Everyone's so relaxed and happy . . . so appreciative. The vendors seem to be thrilled with the publicity —they're booking tours and private demonstration classes like crazy—and the crowd is pleasantly tipsy and buzzing with enthusiasm. It saddens me to realize I won't be here this time next year. Though perhaps I could add Taste of Wilhelmsburg to my list of recurring projects. I could probably do most of the planning remotely from Dallas if Gina were willing to help, and I could drive down for the event itself.

"Well, it's a wonderful idea," he says. "A great way to attract new customers in an intimate, casual environment."

"Margaret's been full of great ideas since she arrived," Grammy J says in a proud tone, squeezing my wrist, and

I'm once again struck by the sincerity of it. "Did you know she built the Inn a fully functionin' website in only a few days?"

"That so?" Bob replies, then turns to me. "Care to share any other talents you have hidden up your sleeve? Maybe I can steal some of them to utilize at my winery."

Ryan meets my gaze from across the room and grins, though it quickly falls from his face when he notices Grammy J and I are talking with Bob. He weaves through the sea of guests to us. "What are you three conspiring about over here?"

Bob pops a slice of salami into his mouth and says, "I want to know what other wonderful ideas Margaret has in that pretty head of hers."

"Still after the best Wilhelmsburg has to offer, I see," Ryan says, sliding a possessive arm around my waist and pulling me against him.

"You certainly can't blame an old man for trying," Bob says with a laugh that's more belly shake than sound.

"Bob's been begging me to sell Camden Cellars for years," Ryan says to me, confirming my suspicions.

Grammy J pipes up, "He's also made a few bids for the Inn."

"Aw, Joy, you know I'd just as soon have a few other things as well." Bob winks.

"My virtue, much like this bed-and-breakfast, is not for sale," Grammy J says, then loops an arm through the crook of his elbow and leads him over to where Farmer Joe is passing out apple cider shooters concocted from the fruit in his orchards.

Ryan peers down at me. "Watch out for the vultures, Marge. They're already starting to circle."

"Are you comparing me to roadkill?"

As compliments go, it could use some finesse. Yet as is

so often the case around him, I'm pleasantly surprised and charmed. Everything about today should've been a vortex of pressure and anxiety, but it's been nothing short of superb. Typically at the end of an event I can't wait to get home, kick off my heels, and slide into a hot bath. But tonight I'm content to linger, to watch the guests enjoying the moment, to lean against Ryan and absorb his warmth.

IN THE TWO short weeks after the event, Wilhelmsburg changed from a convenient escape to something familiar and homey.

It's not the sort of small town that inspires wanderlust, yet there's magic and charm in its dirt roads that curve through farms and vineyards, in its sense of community and salt-of-the-earth residents, in its air that smells like spring water, ripe fruit, and soil. Things I never believed I would appreciate or enjoy when I arrived here a month ago, but once I let life unfold in its own natural rhythm, the simplicity of it all became my new normal.

I've filled the sun-infused days finalizing the vacation packages on the website and lending a hand in minor repairs at the Inn, my efforts evident in the fresh coat of paint on the exterior shutters, the refinished stairs and banister that lead to the second floor, the tended garden beds. The evenings I've spent in Ryan's company, exploring the area's hidden gems, getting lost in his vineyard, surrounding myself with his friends—maybe even my friends—who on the surface are nothing like me yet seem to accept me more than anyone in my past.

It's funny the way Ryan's crept up on me—slowly, then quick as a wink—his uncomplicated attention and easy approach to everything burrowing deep under my skin. I can't extract him, and I don't want to. Especially given how he's looking at me like I'm someone he wishes he could bottle and carry around in his pocket forever.

Our hair and clothes are drenched in mud from the fistfuls we keep flinging at each other as heavy rain beats down on us. The wind whips the trees, and against the monochrome gray sky, the leaves appear hyperpigmented, a vivid, electric green. The air smells fresh, heady, and a little sweet.

"You're going to pay for that." Ryan wipes the mud I smeared on his cheeks with the back of his wrist, but because he's coated head to toe in muck, his effort serves only to spread it around rather than remove it.

"I'm not the one who started this," I say as rainwater drips into my eyes.

We lazily wasted the day at the annual county fair with Moose, Bon Bon, and the rest of the group. The grounds were packed with locals from nearby towns, and when I inquired as to why, Gina explained that the four-day event is considered the biggest family reunion in Hill Country.

We left early afternoon when the storm blew in, and by the time Ryan parked the Blazer at the Inn, the world was underwater, as though it'd been desperate for catharsis, a healing purge from the intense summer heat. I wasn't out of the car ten seconds before Ryan fired the first shot, covering my T-shirt in sludge. Then it was on.

I throw another palmful of mud at him, and it hits the side of his neck with a satisfying splat. Laughing, I do a victory dance, gloating like I scored the winning touchdown.

"That's it, Marge. Playtime's over." Ryan stalks toward me, his expression a mix of determination and desire, and it sends a charged shiver down my spine.

"Is someone a sore loser?" I taunt, as though I'm not caked in mud, too.

He lunges for me. I dodge his grasp, but his fingers brush my arm, almost grabbing hold. I race for the porch, my sneakers squishing and sliding in the soft, wet earth, with Ryan close behind. We reach the front door in tandem, out of breath and soaked to the bone. Ryan shakes his head like a dog flinging off a bath.

I fit the key into the lock, but before I can unfasten the latch, his hands are on my hips, spinning me around.

"You can't run away that easily," Ryan says, his tone a low, controlled rumble, harmonizing with the chorus of rolling thunder.

With the exception of my harried dash to Wilhelmsburg, he's right—I have no experience in running. I've always toed the line and done what was expected of me. But now it feels as if I'm at a crossroads, and for the life of me I can't seem to figure out if staying here or heading back to Dallas is running. If I return to Dallas, step back into my old life and my familiar job, am I betraying the woman I'm becoming here? And if I stay in Wilhelmsburg, am I just avoiding everything I left behind?

"Even if I have spent the last month chasing you," he finishes.

"Anything worthwhile requires effort." I throw out the adage, half joking, half giving him an out. A small, nagging voice in the back of my mind—one that sounds suspiciously like my mother's—tells me that I'm *not* worth it, that to him I'm merely sport.

Instead, he says, "I'd be disappointed if you didn't make me work for it. But you're finally caught."

I gaze at him, at the gold-brown flecks in his eyes. "Why go after me?" I cringe as the words tumble out before I have the chance to stop them. Still I want to know the answer.

It's a question I never dared ask Nick, but maybe I should have. Maybe if I had, I would've realized much sooner that Nick didn't want me, and in turn I might have realized I didn't really want him either. Not in the way that matters, anyway. It's a little humbling, especially standing in front of the man who is teaching me to want more and believes I deserve better.

He's quiet a moment, studying me. Finally Ryan says, "Because when I look at you it feels like I'm experiencing a sunset for the first time."

A sudden intake of air expands my lungs, and my heart pounds wildly against my ribs. It's only now that I realize how much I needed to hear those words, no matter how cliché. That he feels as strongly as I do about this *thing* that's happening between us, even if I'm terrified to label it just yet. The moment I do, the moment I acknowledge that this could be anything other than a summer fling, more dangerous questions arise.

"And the best thing about sunsets, Marge?" he says. "They come every day, and I plan to be there to enjoy every one of them. If you'll let me."

Once again Ryan's thrown out a thinly veiled reference to a future he seems to see so vividly. And just like that day at the waterfall, he doesn't sound any less serious. I was too unsure of myself to ask him for details then, to ask him to explain what he really wants in direct words. Now I find the courage to face my questions—and his response.

"I asked you before what you wanted for your future. Have things changed?"

"Not changed," he says. "Just . . . expanded."

"How so?"

"You're going to make me say it, aren't you?" he asks with an almost shy grin.

"Yeah, I am."

Rubbing the back of his neck, Ryan inhales a deep breath and says, "When I'm with you it's challenging in a fun way and yet so damn easy. So damn *right*. And I don't know if that makes sense, but I know I want more of it. I look at you and see it all. So clear it's almost scary, so real I'm afraid to stare too closely at it." He trails a hand around my waist, flattening it against the small of my back, and pulls me closer. His other hand settles in the crook of my neck. "I see us sharing a bottle of wine while watching a meteor shower on a blanket in the vineyard. I see us arguing over the right answer for seventeen-across in the *New York Times* crossword and me distracting you from the fact that you're right with more interesting pursuits. I see us, Margaret."

But for how long? When will what he thinks is charming become annoying? When will I go from snarky to flat-out bitchy? When will pursuing me turn tedious rather than fun and challenging?

"You make it sound so uncomplicated, Ryan."

"That's because it is," he says, never taking his eyes off me. "You just have to stay."

You just have to stay. Such a straightforward, simple phrase, yet loaded with meaning.

I consider everything he's confessed. Wilhelmsburg was supposed to be an escape, an idyllic place for me to take a moment to breathe. I only ever intended to hit pause, not reset my entire existence, and that's what it'd require to remain in Wilhelmsburg permanently. A complete admission that my life in Dallas, the one I worked so hard to build, isn't what I want after all.

And while what Ryan says is a very desired thing, it's

also very dangerous. Real, unconditional love, as I've come to understand and Ryan has professed, is not something to be achieved and not something to be bought with hard work and determination. It's also not a guarantee of happiness. Staying here would mean placing my faith—and my heart—in Ryan's hands and trusting him not to break it. I've never given someone that kind of power.

"And if I'm not ready?" I ask quietly, wishing I were as certain as him, wishing I were as fearless.

"Then I'll just keep looking forward to those sunsets." Which is exactly what I needed him to say, though the undercurrent of sadness and disappointment in his voice is unmistakable.

Thunder cracks, loud enough to steal my breath, and lightning illuminates the clouds. We stare at each other in silence. Then Ryan kisses me. An urgent, rough kiss that tastes like rain and feels as destructive as the storm around us. As if he's afraid that if he doesn't hold on to me, I may blow away.

He fumbles for the doorknob, unlocking it, but I abruptly pull away when he starts to step inside. "If we track mud through the house, Grammy J will use our bodies as fertilizer in the vegetable garden," I say. Thankfully she's in Austin for the day, shopping with a friend from her bunco group, so at least we have some privacy.

Chuckling, Ryan kicks off his waterlogged boots and socks, and I do the same with my shoes. He strips off his destroyed T-shirt and tosses it over his shoulder. Recapturing my mouth, he picks me up, wrapping my legs around his waist in a move we've perfected, and carries me upstairs.

Without interrupting the kiss, we stumble into my room. Lightning brightens the sky and casts shadows across the bedspread and floral wallpaper. The wind blows dead, damp leaves and rain against the windows, the water beading and streaking across the glass.

"Where is the damn lamp?" I murmur against his lips, searching for it on the writing desk, only to come up empty-handed.

"Why are you whispering? No one's around," Ryan says as he leads us into the en suite bathroom. Shutting the door and flipping on the light, he sets me down and turns on the shower. I lean against the faux marble counter, my whole body shivering in anticipation.

I reach for the hem of my shirt, but Ryan stops me, taking charge. He slowly pulls the wet fabric over my head, dropping it onto the floor. My shorts and underwear follow soon after, as does my bra, until I'm standing naked in front of him. Steam fills the room, but it doesn't quell my trembling.

His gaze rakes over me, so thorough and intense it's as if his eyes are fingers. "Stunning," he says, and that one simple word shatters whatever fight I have left. I want him, right now, in the worst possible way.

As if reading my thoughts, he sheds the remainder of his clothes in record speed, and tugs me into the shower with him. We step under the spray, washing away the mud and the rain. Brown-tinged water gathers at our feet and swirls into the drain. The hot shower hitting my cold skin causes goose bumps to break out all over me.

Ryan grabs the bar of soap I brought with me from Dallas and creates a creamy lather. Its subtle fragrance of pink grapefruit, lemongrass, and sandalwood surrounds us.

"Now I know why you smell like citrus," he says as his sudsy hands travel over my arms, my hips, my rib cage. "And why I haven't been able to get your scent out of my mind." When his fingers ghost over my breasts, a breathy gasp escapes my lips and I arch into him.

How does he do that? Turn me into a quivering mess with only the smallest amount of contact?

Kissing my mouth, my jaw, my neck, Ryan moves to stand behind me, the solid planes of his chest pressed against my back. Pulling my wet hair over one shoulder, he nips the sensitive spot below my ear with his teeth, the stubble on his chin marking me with tiny scratches, as his palms slide around my waist, across my stomach, spreading the frothy bubbles in slow circles over my skin.

Hooking an arm around the back of his neck, drawing him closer, I twist my fingers into his hair and tug gently. He murmurs my name, a beg and a promise, and glides his callused hand down my body, but before things can go further, two swift knocks interrupt us.

The door creaks open, followed by the squeak of Grammy J's galoshes shuffling into the bathroom. "Child, there are rain puddles all the way up the stairs," she says, her tone laced with exasperation. "What have I told you about mopping—"

She cuts herself off. I picture her scowling as she eyes the heap of dirty, wet clothes on the floor, registering that I'm not alone. *What is she doing here?*

Ryan must be imagining the same thing, because he presses his mouth against my spine, and I feel his grin stretching across my tingling skin. His fingers dance over my rib cage, teasing. Glancing at him over my shoulder, I bat his hand away and shoot him a glare that indicates he must have a death wish.

"Anyway, you have visitors downstairs," Grammy J continues. "They're waiting for you in the sitting area, and they don't seem like the waitin' type."

Visitors? My thoughts race to my parents, and my throat constricts at the mere possibility. But no. My mother would never return to the Inn on her own accord.

"Okay," I say. "I'll be right out."

Grammy J *mmm-hmms* and I think I'm in the clear, that she's not going to embarrass me, but then she says, "I hope one of you is wearing a raincoat. It looks hot, wet, and slippery in there."

Ryan barks out a laugh. I jab him in the ribs but still crack a smile as I say, "Thanks for the weather forecast. We'll take it under advisement."

———

I NEARLY TRIP when I walk into the sitting area to discover Piper, Samma, and Faye perched on the edge of a sofa as though they think dust mites may crawl out of the upholstery and attack them at any moment, each with a glass of red wine in hand. A bottle of No Holds Barred is half empty on the coffee table.

Why are they doing here?

Dread sinks like a stone in my stomach—they're the last people I want to deal with right now. I feel my armor latch on to me once again, refortified and stronger than before.

As if announcing my entrance, one of the French doors slams shut from a swift gust of wind blowing through a partially open window, and the girls jolt in their seats. The thunder and lightning seem to have stopped, but rain still pours down in sheets, the world outside like a smudged charcoal drawing.

Taking a deep breath, I square my shoulders and say, "Well this is a shock." *And not the good kind.* "Welcome to the Bluebonnet Inn. Or as you all so nicely assumed, the rehab center where I've been 'dealing with my issues.'"

Samma misses my jab, standing to greet me with a demure kiss on both cheeks. "Sweetie, it's great to see you looking so . . . rustic," she says, scrutinizing my bare face and wet hair twisted into a messy bun. Compared to her expertly styled extensions and airbrushed makeup, I resemble one of those tragic "before" women on a makeover reality program. She swirls the glass of wine, then swallows a sip without remark or fanfare.

"Yes, Margaret, is there a reason you're dressed like a train conductor?" Piper asks, her gaze raking over my basic white top and denim short overalls faded and distressed from years of wear. Like much of my wardrobe these days, the clothes belong to Grammy J. I left Ryan to finish showering while I threw on the quickest semipresentable outfit I could scrounge together.

Normally Piper has no right to judge anyone's appearance, but she's traded her typical lululemon attire for a preppy shift dress, linen blazer, and strappy sandals. I bet she figured the B&B would be more of a miniresort and less of a ramshackle disaster. She's in for a rude awakening, especially when she learns the three of them will be sharing a room, since the rest are reserved.

"One of you should've called first," I say, skipping over Piper's backhanded question and jumping straight to the point. "Space is tight."

With the help of the revamped website, promotion from local businesses, and listings on sites like TripAdvisor, the Inn's booking schedule has slowly filled up. It's nowhere near capacity on a consistent basis, but perhaps by this holiday season that'll be a different story and there will be enough money in the bank to fund some of the more important renovations.

"And ruin the surprise?" Faye says. There's a pinched look on her face as she inspects her glass under the glow of a stained glass lamp on the side table, no doubt contemplating, the same way I did, how a wine from this area could taste so damn good. Or her expression could be from a bad reaction to Botox.

"Besides, this was a bit of an impromptu trip," Samma interjects, affronted, as though *I'm* the unreasonable one for suggesting they pick up the phone before barging in.

"So you all spontaneously decided to drive almost four hours to check on me?" I ask, skeptical. Thoughtful gestures are not in their vocabulary, so they're either on a reconnaissance mission for my mother or they wanted to witness the circus show, meaning me, firsthand so they can report back to our social circle at home. Most likely both. "Or were you just in the mood for a cheaper, Napa-esque vacation?"

The vacuum whirs to life upstairs, banging against furniture as Grammy J moves about—her familiar footsteps causing the floorboards to creak. She cleans when she's stressed or frustrated, though in this case it's unclear if it's a result of the shower spectacle or the girls' last-minute visit.

"Don't be ridiculous. Of course we're not in this Podunk town for the wine," Piper says. By the level in her glass, she has yet to take a sip. Otherwise she'd be singing a different tune.

"That's too bad, because the vintages being debuted this year may be the best yet," comes Ryan's voice from behind me. I've never been happier to hear his slow, musical drawl.

I turn to find him lingering in the doorway carrying a meat and cheese board. Moving into the room, he meets my gaze, a wry half grin tugging at his mouth, and sets the tray on the coffee table beside the bottle of No Holds Barred. Attractive as ever, he's combed back his damp hair with his fingers, and he's wearing a buttoned plaid shirt and old Levi's jeans Poppa Bart once owned. Both are too tight for his frame, which only accentuates his lean, muscular build.

The girls' eyes grow wide at the sight of him. I can't say I blame them.

"Are you here to collect our luggage?" Piper asks Ryan, dismissive as usual. "It's in the trunk of the BMW outside." She tosses her keys at him like he's a servant at her beck and call.

"They're designer, so be careful. The leather is sensitive to the elements," Samma adds, not even trying to mask her condescension, proud to be flaunting her wealth—her *parents'* wealth, to be more accurate.

He shoots me an *are-these-women-serious* look. He has no idea.

I wouldn't fault him if he flung the keys back in Piper's face. She's unaccustomed to being told no, so witnessing her resulting wrath would be worth it. But the last thing I need is a confrontation.

Before he can strike, I say, "This is Ryan Camden, a local winemaker whose blend you're drinking." *More like insulting.*

"What'd you do, import the grape juice from France and slap your label on the bottle?" Samma lets out a short, sarcastic laugh. Piper and Faye join in, though Faye's smile barely registers on her lips. *How has her body not yet revolted against all the cosmetic procedures?* "At least something around here is cultured."

My shoulders tense at Samma's words, reminiscent of the ones I spoke to Ryan the night we met at The Tangled Vine, and I feel a stab of shame at my behavior. Bluntness is not an excuse for rudeness.

Crossing his arms over his chest, Ryan considers the girls a moment and I watch the gears click into place. "You must be Marge's friends from Dallas," he says with more tact than they deserve, glancing among them.

"One and the same," Faye says, making no more effort at introductions, so I sigh and rattle off their names.

"Normally I'd be a gentleman and grab those expensive bags for y'all, but I was playing in the mud earlier and it'd be a pity if I got them dirty." He flashes me a look, eyes twinkling, and warmth spreads like a slow fuse through my body. Not caring that there's an audience, I slip an arm around Ryan's waist, tucking my hand into his back pocket, and kiss the side of his neck.

Silence settles over the room. The girls are frozen to their seats, eyes wide and mouths open. I notice a piece of dried apricot has fallen onto Piper's lap, her hand still hovering in midair. Samma recovers first and says, "Well, Margaret, it appears you've been sampling more of the local flavor than I originally suspected." To someone else, her tone might sound conspiratorial, like she's been let in on a secret, but I've been around Samma enough to recognize the catty undercurrent.

I start to tell her to stop acting like a twit, but a loud thud and sharp cry interrupt my retort. Panicked, I rush up the stairs to get to Grammy J. Before I reach the top, I see an upturned bucket of cleaning supplies with the contents scattered about, and my heart drops, anticipating the worst.

I find Grammy J doubled over in pain on the floor outside my bedroom, and instantly I know whatever happened is my fault.

16

A puddle ignored on the floor seems harmless. Not something worth making a big deal of, especially since it evaporates.

But the little things don't matter until they do.

If Ryan and I hadn't been so caught up in our escapade, if we'd been more cautious about dragging rain water through the B&B, if I'd cleaned up the mess we created, then Grammy J wouldn't have slipped and fallen. She wouldn't be at Hill Country Memorial preparing for hip-pinning surgery.

Guilt slices through me as I study Grammy J in a threadbare gown lying on a hospital bed that swallows her thin frame. Her personality's so big and spirited it's easy to forget how small and fragile she is. How vulnerable. A bruise is forming around her eye where her face connected with the door frame, and a splint protects the wrist she used to soften her fall. The artificial light overhead makes her appear washed-out and sickly.

How is Grammy J supposed to run the Inn? It's her life

*—her home—*and in a simple selfish act, I robbed her of that.

"The tracing looks normal," the cardiologist says, examining the pattern of spikes and dips on the EKG readout, while the technician removes the electrodes attached to Grammy J's body. "Okay, Joy. It's time to mend that fracture. Let me speak with your surgeon and anesthesiologist to verify everything's all set."

He raises the bed so she's situated upright before leaving us alone. For hours it's been a stream of doctors and nurses flowing in and out, taking X rays, collecting blood and urine samples, evaluating Grammy J's overall health to ensure the procedure goes safely and smoothly.

Now it's just the two of us.

Muffled pages over the PA system and the buzz of conversation among the hospital staff filter in from the hallway, filling the silence.

Gathering my courage, I open my mouth to apologize, to tell her I was stupid and careless, that I should have heeded her advice about keeping the bed-and-breakfast tidy, but Grammy J must realize what's coming because she cuts me off.

"Don't even consider it, child," she says, grimacing as she adjusts her position in the bed. "I was clumsy. Nothing more." Her voice sounds raspy and quiet, barely loud enough to be heard in the space between us, but sincere in a way that amplifies my guilt.

My throat feels tight and my eyes burn, but I suppress the tears, refusing to cry. This isn't about me. It's about Grammy J and her well-being. There's a knock on the door, and a nurse enters.

"The doctor's ready for you, Joy," the nurse says, lifting the rails and unlocking the wheels on Grammy J's bed. She turns to me. "Your grandmother will be in the best of care, sweetheart. I need you to head to the waiting room until after surgery."

I squeeze Grammy J's hand, a silent promise to be here when she wakes up. Her skin feels as dry and wrinkled as crepe paper. Grammy J returns the gesture with a warm smile and instructions for me not to fret. Which is an impossible order.

I follow as the nurse maneuvers the bed into the corridor bustling with activity and toward the operating area ahead. When Grammy J disappears behind large double doors with NO ENTRY printed in bold red across the center, I retreat to the crammed waiting room, which reeks of burned coffee and air freshener. People watch muted televisions mounted in wall alcoves, while others nap or read books. Newspapers and magazines are stacked on side tables cluttered with brochures offering guidance on injury and disease prevention.

I spot Ryan near the bank of vending machines, talking to members of Grammy J's gardening club. *How long ago did they get here?* Relief floods me. He stayed, even though he hasn't been allowed beyond the surgical waiting area or kept up to date on my grandmother's condition since arriving at the hospital hours ago. *He stayed.*

I left Piper, Samma, and Faye at the Inn with a key to their room and a list of restaurant options for dinner. In separate cars Ryan and I trailed the ambulance to Hill Country Memorial, located several towns over in Fredericksburg. It's not like the girls would've insisted on joining me anyway, and frankly, I think they were relieved not to be inconvenienced. I was hoping with my grandmother's health scare they'd cut their visit short, but according to Faye, "They didn't drive three hundred miles just to eat at a Cracker Barrel and sleep in some shitty motel off the highway." So they're sticking around.

When Ryan notices me, he excuses himself and walks over. "What's the diagnosis?" he asks. "Is it a fracture?"

I nod, remembering the X ray image lit up on the view box, confirming the break. "It was at the neck of the femur. The surgery should take less than three hours." Straightforward, easy. Except the physical therapy needed to help Grammy J regain full movement in her stride may take up to three months. Three months she can't afford, not when the bed-and-breakfast requires her constant attention. Not when it's one bad season short of bankruptcy.

"I caused this," I say, my voice thick with regret. The urge to cry rushes forward again. A deep, heavy ache that tears me apart. I bite my tongue to prevent the tears from coming, but they tumble fast and hot down my cheeks anyway.

"Margaret, no," he says, wrapping me in a hug.

I bury my face in his shoulder, breathing in his natural scent. He feels solid and strong against me. Ryan kisses my temple and whispers words of comfort and reassurance in my ear, but the wetness continues to blur my vision and dampen my face.

"It was an accident," he says, his hands firm on my waist. "Something that could've happened under a million different circumstances."

"But it didn't," I say. "It happened because of *me*. Because *I* failed to mop up a puddle of water." A mistake I'll never make again.

"You have to quit blaming yourself." Ryan cups my jaw in his palm, skimming his callused thumb under my eye and brushing away the tears. "I know Joy would agree with me."

His gaze bores into mine, imploring me to believe him. But right now warring emotions of remorse and worry and frustration are in control, and it's all I can do to hold it together. As if sensing my struggle, or fending off an argument, Ryan leads me to a pair of empty chairs beside the windows, and we sink into them. The upholstery itches the back of my thighs like the cheapest of fake cashmere, whatever cushioning it once had long gone—my butt will be numb in seconds.

Closing my eyes, I rest my head against the whitewashed wall and listen to the mindless, rambling chitchat of the people around us. Ryan leaves me alone with my thoughts, though his warmth and care remain. It's as if he recognizes when to push and when to pull back.

Suddenly I sit forward with a start, glancing at the clock above the reception desk. "Shit."

"What?" Ryan asks, his brow furrowed.

"Guests are arriving at the Inn tonight and nobody's there to check them in." Even if Piper, Samma, and Faye haven't gone for dinner yet, I doubt they'd bother to answer the door let alone greet any newcomers.

Chuckling, he says, "I'm not sure if it's the same level of creepy as finishing each other's sentences, but I'd already thought of that. One of the women in Joy's gardening club is dealing with everything."

"Definitely creepy, but thank you," I say, smiling. It should make me nervous how he reads me so well so quickly, how he knows exactly what I need without me voicing it, but it doesn't. Instead it makes me feel like I'm not alone, like I have someone on my team who supports me, watches out for me.

Like I'm something valuable to someone.

It brings out the brave part of me so that I ask, "Should I call my mother? Would you want to be told if you had a parent in the hospital if the two of you were estranged?"

Ryan peers down at his lap and scratches his jaw, carefully considering the question, and I wonder if he's thinking about his father. Or perhaps, given what he's overheard and I've shared, he's thinking about how a conversation with my mother will affect me.

He looks up, capturing my gaze. Whatever he sees there must convince him of his answer because he says, "Yeah, I'd want to know. It's never too late to set things right."

Set things right.

Nothing about forgiveness. Though I suppose you can't do one without the other.

"How about this," Ryan continues, standing and pulling me up from the chair. "I'll grab us some food while you call your mom." He touches my cheek, his palm rough in places where he's gripped too many grapevines, and kisses me. The tension inside me unravels, and for a moment I clear my mind of everything, savoring the gentle pressure of his mouth, the slide of his nose across mine, the breath we share. Then with a parting kiss, he exits the waiting area.

I do the same, moving out into the hallway and into a vacant patient room. Pacing back and forth, I dial her cell, my stomach twisting in knots, my unease resurging.

"You're home," my mother says into the phone. The background noise nearly drowns out her voice. It sounds as if she's at a rock concert, but that's impossible. Unless it's the symphony, my mother would rather get a full-body tattoo than attend a live music performance. Most likely I interrupted my parents at another one of their *functions*—their wealthy, pretentious term for an event or gala. "I'm glad the girls were able to reason with you. Stop by the house tomorrow and we'll have tea."

Only my mother would assume that orchestrating a

visit from my "friends" would persuade me to return to Dallas. Then again she made it clear she didn't want to hear from me otherwise, so why else would I be calling?

Before she can say anything more, I burst out with, "Grammy J's in the hospital. She fractured her hip and is in surgery now." I don't mention my complicity in her fall. Cowardly, maybe, but I can't handle being berated when the guilt I already feel is suffocating. "The physical therapy required for her recovery is extensive." Fortunately Grammy J's as stubborn as a red wine stain and would never accept defeat, no matter how much you scrub.

"And what do you presume I do about that?" my mother asks.

"Nothing," I say, tugging at a loose thread dangling from the hem of my overalls. "I thought you might want to know . . ." *I thought you might care.*

The background noise disappears, and I imagine my mother stepping out onto a balcony with hundreds of twinkle lights that sparkle like the sequins on her dress and the jewels dripping from her ears and neck. "So you're not suggesting that your father and I provide financial support for in-home treatment?" she asks. "Or that we move your grandmother into an assisted-living facility where someone can bathe her regularly and help her get around?"

I hold the cell phone at arm's length, flabbergasted at her insinuation, her audacity. "Of course not," I say, angry but controlled. I won't allow her to get the better of me or play off my emotions. "Why would Grammy J need *any* of that when she has me to take care of her? I simply wanted you to be informed."

"Well, I'm now informed." My mother's tone has turned cold, hard as a diamond and just as sharp, as though she's finally realized I haven't abandoned my foolish notions of remaining in Wilhelmsburg. That I'm no closer to coming home than the Dallas Cowboys are to winning another Super Bowl. "Congratulations, Margaret. For once you successfully accomplished what you set out to do. Relish this moment as I'm sure it will be the last of its kind."

My spine goes rigid as Ryan's question—*how can you let her treat you like you're nothing?*—echoes in my ear. I'm not a punching bag. I'm blunt and headstrong and flawed, sometimes even harsh enough to scab, but I'm also loyal and dedicated and caring.

And I have worth—the people I've met in this town have shown me that—which at the bare minimum means I deserve basic human decency. Not passive-aggressive reprimands or thinly veiled disgust from the one person who's supposed to love me unconditionally.

"You're wrong," I say to my mother. "It's unfortunate you're too narrow-minded to see all I've achieved, what I'm capable of, but perhaps someday you will."

It's the best I can hope for and the last thing I expect.

―――

Morning arrives too soon, but breakfast for eleven guests won't make itself no matter my level of exhaustion. I shuffle into the kitchen, showered and dressed and looking about as good as a road-slaughtered skunk.

I got back to the Inn well past midnight, intending to collapse into bed and fall fast asleep. Only my mind wouldn't shut off, my thoughts focused on my mother and her lack of compassion, on the B&B and all its responsibilities, but mostly on Grammy J and how best I can help her. She emerged from surgery groggy and in pain, but the operation was a success and had no complications. Now comes the challenging part—rehabilitation.

I hit the switch on the coffee machine and step out onto the rear porch. The sun is crawling over the horizon, weak and watery, chasing the stars away and lighting the sky pale blue. I ease into a rocking chair and gently sway back and forth, basking in the warm breeze drifting across my skin.

There's something wondrous about witnessing the world wake up—birds singing, squirrels scattering, a rooster crowing at a nearby farm. A mini rebirth I often take for granted. It reminds me of the Inn and its slow transformation, the way the worn siding and rebuilt porch merge old and new, imperfection with symmetry. For the first time, I realize how much I need this place, and more important, how much it needs me.

The smell of brewing coffee reaches my nose. I spend another few minutes soaking up the sunshine and fresh air before heading inside for a steaming cup, desperate for fuel. I lean against the kitchen counter, sipping my vanilla French roast, and sort the stack of cards listing the menu selections into two piles—guests requesting lemon ricotta pancakes with a side of bacon or those wanting scrambled eggs chilaquiles. Of course Piper, Samma, and Faye have to be difficult, dictating their meal choices be gluten free, even though the only dietary restriction they adhere to is consuming less than a thousand calories a day. Alcohol doesn't count, naturally. I bet the woman from Grammy J's gardening club has a permanent sour expression on her face from the few hours she spent accommodating them.

I tie an apron over my simple cotton dress, the fabric soft and worn between my fingers, feeling out of my element and overwhelmed but determined. Grammy J's usually the one who prepares all the food, but now it's up to me despite my limited cooking skills. Now everything regarding the Inn is up to me.

I locate the recipes in an old bread box beside the gas range and retrieve the ingredients from the fridge and pantry. Then I stare at the items scattered on the center island, unsure where to begin and short on time to figure it out. In two hours the dining room will be full of guests expecting a gourmet experience, and I refuse to disappoint them. Besides, I'm a master at multitasking and creating order out of chaos. I can handle this.

I'm formulating a plan of attack when I hear tires treading up the path to the Inn. It can't be Ryan—he's already busy at the winery. I tiptoe to the entryway, careful not to make too much noise so I don't wake anyone, and peek between the curtains to see Moose and Bon Bon exiting their respective vehicles. I slip outside, quietly closing the front door behind me. The ground has mostly dried up from yesterday's storm, but moisture clings to the grass, dampening my sneakers and sticking to my ankles as I trudge toward them.

"Hey, guys . . ." I let my words hang in the space between us, because for the life of me, I can't imagine why they've come, and at the crack of dawn no less.

"What? No snarky greeting?" Moose asks. "No comment about my lack of antlers or cloven hooves? No, 'What's up, Moose? Where are your buddies Grizzly and Raccoon?' "

"Leave her alone, you oaf," Bon Bon says, elbowing him in the ribs. "Margaret doesn't have on her protective gear yet. She can't be expected to deal with your asinine ramblings this early."

Moose frowns at her in such an exaggerated manner his bottom lip juts out. "They're not *asinine*."

Bon Bon raises an eyebrow in response while I continue to stand there, clueless.

"Guys, not that I'm unhappy to see you, but . . . why are you here?" I ask, glancing between them.

"To help you, obviously," Moose says, smiling.

"We're sorry about Joy," Bon Bon says. "Cricket mentioned the surgery went well. How's she doing?"

"Doctors are optimistic," I say. "A physical therapist is dropping by this afternoon to get her out of bed and have her moving around."

"She'll be causing trouble again in no time," she says. "You'll see."

Moose nods, then bumps my side and says, "So, show us the ropes, Chief. Order us around."

"Show you what ropes?" I ask, still not comprehending.

Gesturing to my apron, Bon Bon says, "You know, fixing breakfast, changing the sheets, cleaning the bathrooms. We're at your service."

For a moment, I'm stunned, speechless. Are they *pitying* me? Or is this their version of a handout? Because I don't accept either. "Thanks for offering, but I've got it under control."

"Quit being stubborn," she says. "We're not offering. We're insisting."

Grabbing my hand, Bon Bon starts to lead me toward the Inn when another car pulls up. Tiffany gets out and walks over to us, appearing flustered as she tries to balance the pastry boxes in her arms. She's tied her dark hair into a ponytail, the light accentuating the purple streaks, and switched out her all-black attire for all-pink gym clothes. The change is so drastic I almost don't recognize her.

"Sorry I'm late," Tiffany says, slightly out of breath. "I had to wait in line at the Ausländer for the cookies to finish baking." Moose scoots closer to her, lifting the lid on the top pastry box and inching his fingers inside, but she swats his hand away before he can snatch anything. Turning to face me, Tiffany embraces me in an awkward side hug. "I did a tarot reading centered on Joy this morning and drew The Star, which signifies a period of hope and renewal. It's a positive sign, like a beacon in darkness." Her eyes are bright with possibility, her expression optimistic, feelings I don't share.

"Okay, enough yammering and wasting daylight hours," Bon Bon says like a general rallying her troops. She glances around the yard at the broken branches, piles of leaves, and pecans littering the ground, casualties from yesterday's wind gusts. "Moose, you're in charge of beautifying out here. Don't forget the garden. The three of us will tackle inside." Then, as if ready for battle, she straightens her shoulders, marches up the front porch steps, and brazenly enters the Inn, leaving Tiffany and me scrambling to catch up.

We find Bon Bon in the kitchen, hands on her hips, peering back and forth between the menu calendar stuck to the fridge and the ingredients cluttering the island. "Okay, so we have our work cut out for us," she says.

"That's an understatement," Tiffany adds, placing the pastry boxes beside the sugar and flour containers. "I think we should split up duties by dish."

"Good idea. I'll handle the ricotta pancakes and you do the chilaquiles," Bon Bon says, rummaging through the pile of food. "Do you see where the package of bacon—"

"Everyone hold on," I interrupt, louder than I intended. I cringe, listening for movement in the guest rooms, then continue in a hissed whisper, "I don't need"— I wave a hand between the three of us—"whatever this is." It's sweet, their efforts, but the last thing I want is to owe anyone any favors. Worse would be to willingly acknowledge that fact. "I can deal with all of this on my own."

"I'm sure you can." Tiffany strolls over to the sink to

wash her hands. "The point is, you have people around you who won't let you."

"Exactly. We don't pity you or feel sorry for you or whatever else you're assuming," Bon Bon says, as though reading my mind from earlier. "We're here because that's what friends do—they band together. When one of us is down or needs help, the others pitch in. Grammy J's been a part of this community for decades, and now so are you. Accept it."

They're right, I'm acting ridiculous and selfish when all they want to do is help. "Okay, I'll prep the tomatillos for roasting," I say, my voice full of emotion, finally understanding what it means to belong.

17

"Well isn't this . . . quaint."

Samma's voice sweeps around the dining room, slathered in condescension, and every muscle in my body tenses. I finish clearing the table of a couple who recently left to visit an apple orchard. Piling the used silverware on top of the stack of fine china, I anchor the plates against my chest and pick up the partially full crystal water goblets, turning to face her.

She has sunglasses pushed over her eyes. She probably drank too much wine at dinner last night—a habit of hers—and now she's suffering from a raging headache. I don't care. Grammy J was in surgery for hours and Samma and the girls couldn't bother to check in with a simple text. *This is why you should never let your mother pick your friends.*

"You're late. Breakfast started an hour ago," I say, pushing past her to deposit the dishes in the butler's pantry on the other side of the French doors. I clean off the blueberry syrup stuck to my palm on a small towel draped over a cabinet knob.

Bon Bon catches my gaze from the kitchen, waving at

me as she flips the last batch of lemon ricotta pancakes—gluten included because Piper, Samma, and Faye can deal with their supposed IBS with Milk of Magnesia and large portions of kale like the rest of us.

The smell of bacon frying drifts across my nose, and my stomach rumbles. I've yet to eat anything today, unless you count a small piece of chorizo that escaped the frying pan, which I don't. But watching the guests' positive reactions to the food makes my hunger worth it.

Tiffany? I mouth. Bon Bon points to the ceiling and mimics vacuuming an . . . area rug? An upholstered piece of furniture? Or maybe she's acting out changing the sheets on the bed. Doesn't matter. I value the help either way. Now, if I could only convince some charitable soul to show Piper, Samma, and Faye around town and relieve me of the burden.

Last night at the hospital, Grammy J was insistent that I spend today with the girls. "Your friends traveled all this way to see you, so be a good hostess and entertain them," she said when I tried to protest. "Besides, it's going to be a lot of staring at the television between doctor and physical therapy check-ins around here." Even though she promised to have the nurses contact me with updates, I plan on dropping by Hill Country Memorial later anyway.

Moose steps into the B&B through the rear porch entrance, his face red and blotchy, his clothes stained with sweat and dirt from laboring in the yard all morning. "I'll tell you one thing," he says, wiping his forehead on his sleeve. "The Inn may be falling apart, but Joy sure does keep the garden in fantastic shape."

"That she does," I say with a smile. "You hungry? There's still plenty of—"

"Moose, get in here and wash up. The black beans for the chilaquiles need some attention," Bon Bon yells, speaking with the authority of an executive chef at a Michelin-starred restaurant.

Rolling his eyes, Moose squeezes my arm and goes to meet her in the kitchen. I reenter the dining room with a sterling-silver platter piled with the chocolate chip cookies Tiffany brought, and set it on the sideboard beside a vase of wildflowers.

Samma's claimed the table farthest away from where the light streams in through the windows, sunglasses still in place. Piper and Faye have joined her, and collectively the three of them are doused in enough perfume to clog the air filters. At least most of the guests have already departed and are spared from the overpowering stench of Chanel No. 5.

Grabbing the coffeepot, I walk over to the girls and fill their mugs. "Morning. Everyone sleep okay? I know you all aren't accustomed to sharing a room, so your sacrifice is appreciated," I say in a tone so sweet and fake saccharin can't compete. "My grandmother's going to be fine, by the way. Thanks for asking."

Piper takes a sip of coffee, wincing as the liquid scalds her tongue, glossing over my comments, while Samma brushes the hair off her shoulder and says, "Sweetie, of course she is. We assumed you would've called to tell us if that wasn't the case." Faye only stares, unblinking and with a scowl, at the creamer in the center of the table, as though wondering why the little porcelain container won't toddle over to her.

Samma gestures to my apron-dress pairing. "Nice Suzy Homemaker getup. All that's missing is the cherry pie."

"Maybe if you'd worn this kind of attire around Nick, he wouldn't have dumped you for Lillie," Piper says, hiding a grin behind her cup. That's rich, especially since she's decked out once again in lululemon and has never maintained a relationship that lasted longer than a manicure.

"No, it was always inevitable," Faye adds, finally contributing to the conversation. "Nick *clearly* prefers a woman who has talent and finesse in the kitchen, albeit a greasy, dilapidated one, and Margaret lacks even the most basic skills."

An ache seizes my chest at their total disregard for my feelings. "Nick didn't break off our relationship because I failed to hard-boil an egg or bake brownies." My voice cracks, but I hide the sound of my vulnerability with a laugh. "Though I understand your confusion, given how the three of you look at relationships as commodities ready for liquidation at the first sign of something new and shiny. It's no wonder you all shuffle through husbands and one-night stands like you do handbags."

I watch in satisfaction as their mouths drop open, one after the other like dominos, as though they've tasted for the first time the callousness they so easily assault others with. Before any of the girls can successfully work their way toward a witty reply, Bon Bon and Moose emerge through the French doors with steaming plates and deliver them to the table.

Samma pushes the sunglasses up into her hair and snaps her fingers at Bon Bon. "Um. Excuse me," she says, motioning to the fried tortillas in the chilaquiles. "Were these made with flour or corn? Because I have certain *sensitivities*."

"They're corn," Bon Bon replies, as though she fields these sorts of manners daily. She places a carafe of orange juice on the table.

"Organic?" Samma asks, clearly displeased that so far she has no grounds to object. "Because while I know these small farming communities are paid a great deal of money to grow genetically modified crops and that you're forced to ingest it, I'd prefer not to put that kind of poison in my body and risk sprouting an extra limb."

Bon Bon cuts her eyes over to me, irritation and disbelief at Samma's words warring for control of her expression. I shake my head, asking her to let it go.

"Your thumb really shouldn't be touching the plate so close to the food," Piper says, scrunching up her nose, as Moose sets a gorgeous stack of pancakes in front of her. "I mean, really, who knows where those hands have been."

"Milking the cows and molesting the chickens, no doubt," Faye chortles.

"I haven't let my fox loose in a henhouse in ages," Moose says with a grin, covering Piper's bare shoulder with his palm. "Maybe it's time I should. What do you say?"

She shrugs off his hand, a look of disgust on her face. "I'm not into tasting the local offerings, thanks."

"No, but Margaret seems to be. What was his name again? Ryan?" Samma raises an eyebrow at me. "You know, if you were so desperate for affection, you should've told me. I have the number of an agency, very discreet, very thorough. And I'm certain it costs less than however many bottles of wine you had to buy and choke down to court that man's attention."

I'm not sure which is worse, that she implied I'm the sort of woman who'd pay for sex, or that Ryan's my male escort. Either way, *enough is enough.*

"That's it. Stand up. You're done here," I say, my voice rising, my body quaking with anger, as I pull Samma's chair away from the table with her still in it. "You're all done here. You waltz into Wilhelmsburg under the pretense of 'checking on me,' abuse my hospitality, insult me and my friends, who, by the way, showed up to help me this morning because my grandmother just underwent *hip-*

pinning surgery, while you three were too busy sleeping off hangovers. And it's not surprising that none of you would know a good man when he greeted you. So move your spoiled, entitled asses upstairs, gather your things before I do it for you, and get the hell out of this bed-and-breakfast and out of my life."

Then, as Moose whistles and Bon Bon gives a long, slow clap and the girls stare at me in shock, I turn on my heel and exit the dining room without looking back.

———

THE CAMDEN CELLARS property appears even more majestic at night—the rows of grapevines that angle across the hillside, twisting and shifting directions like a maze; the live oaks, so old and craggy and awe-inspiring with their rough, wrinkled trunks, that look as though they were never saplings; the way the moonlight haloes the German stone barn in silver.

The winery is dark inside—the tasting room closed hours ago—but a soft, amber glow emanates from the veranda, warm and inviting. The wind carries the sweet, smoky remnants of a recently lit wood-fire grill and the sound of a dog barking mingles with the hum of cicadas.

I walk up the paved path that leads to the entrance and follow it around the side of the barn to the back. Stepping onto the veranda, I gasp at the sight in front of me. When Ryan asked me to meet him at the winery after I was done visiting Grammy J at the hospital, I expected to find him in the office, hunched over a pile of paperwork on the desk, not leisurely stretched out on a blanket, basking among the vines he works so diligently to cultivate.

"Hey, stranger," I yell, my voice ringing out crisp and clear in the quiet of the night.

Ryan glances over his shoulder. Even in the dark, I see a grin spreading across his face. He lifts a bottle of wine and beckons me with a jerk of his head, as if we've shared this ritual before. There's something about it that feels familiar. I cross the lawn, the white fairy lights strung through the trees illuminating my route, drop down beside him on the blanket, and kick off my shoes.

"Playing in the dirt again, are we? Those toys look a bit big for you," I say, referring to the seed drills stationed in a few of the alleys between the vine rows, which are used to disperse the cover crop into the earth.

"C'mere," he murmurs, putting a hand behind my neck and guiding me toward him for a long kiss that causes my stomach to flutter. His tongue slides over mine, and I catch hints of black cherry, pepper, and licorice, like a full-bodied wine I want to savor at first and then get drunk on.

We pull apart, slightly breathless. Ryan tucks a flyaway hair behind my ear and says, "I already told you, messy is what makes life fun."

No regrets and no strings attached.

Except my feelings for Ryan have developed beyond those two basic tenets into something raw and true. An emotion I've tried to deny, resist, yet one I can no longer ignore. Not anymore. He's captivated me, and I've let him. I've willingly put myself in a vulnerable position. Allowed myself to rely on Ryan. Maybe not in the same way I relied on Nick—with him I fell victim to the idea that his joy, his success, his *value*, equated to my own. But with Ryan, everything is different, effortless . . . an easy trap to fall into. My reliance on him is far more subtle, far more precarious. A smile from Ryan has the power to change my mood. A glance can strengthen me. The briefest of touches is electric enough to leave me buzzing for hours.

More and more I'm beginning to realize I'm happy

and truly myself, maybe for the first time ever, when I'm with Ryan. What does that mean for my future? Is this feeling I have when I'm around him something I can carry with me back to Dallas?

I suspect not. The thought of facing everyday life—work and social obligations and family pressures—feels so much more daunting knowing that Ryan won't be there with his ready grin and steady hands. I quash the ache that spreads through my chest and not for the first time wonder what the true cost of my trip to Wilhelmsburg will be.

Determined to enjoy every moment I can, I settle on my side, propping myself up on one elbow, and watch as he opens a bottle of private reserve Cabernet—the same vintage we drank the night of the cave incident—and pours us each a glass. I take a sip, and while delicious, the flavors pale in comparison to the taste of his kiss still on my lips.

"What varietal constitutes this block?" I ask, noticing how this part of the vineyard implements a T-trellis system rather a vertical one.

Ryan mirrors my position, facing me. The movement pulls up the hem of his shirt, and I feel an irresistible urge to touch the exposed slice of toned stomach, to feel his hard muscles beneath my fingers. "Viognier. The one you said resembles cat piss," he says, turning his wine glass in slow circles on the blanket. "The block's named Witchy Woman after the Eagles song, because although the grape can be a pain in the ass to handle, at her core she's as wild and mesmerizing as a seductive enchantress. Much like you."

My heart races, thundering against my rib cage. Every time I'm convinced his smooth-talking ways can't charm me any more, he surprises me with a new line that steals my breath away. Words that once felt disingenuous and designed solely to either irritate or seduce now feel welcome and soothing as a fresh rain. Refreshing, invigorating, and so very necessary to my survival.

I swallow a gulp of wine and say, "Where's Bordeaux? I was hoping she'd greet me with one of her slobbery kisses."

"She's chasing the peacock," he says.

"That's terrible. That poor bird must be traumatized."

"Nah. Merlot—that's the peacock—taunts Bordeaux. He'll swat at her with his tail and try to bite her. I try to tell Bordeaux it's Merlot's way of flirting with her, but she isn't hearing it."

"So that means you're out here, stroking your . . . ego and imagining your own private Bacchanalia?"

"I love it when you're a smart-ass, Marge." Ryan pushes his glass away and scoots closer, placing a hand on the dip of my waist, the perfect shape for his palm to rest. "Besides, as I recall, Bacchanalias were essentially giant, drunken orgies."

"Ah, so you got that all out of your system in college?" I tease.

"Well, there's that. But you know the problem with orgies?"

"They're sticky?"

Ryan smiles, but not the wicked one I expect. "The problem with orgies," he says, trailing a soil-stained finger along my jaw, down my neck, and across my collarbone, "is that I'd have to share the one person I find I'm entirely too possessive of." He's near enough for me to feel his body heat and see the intensity in his eyes. "And I don't share."

His words are designed to elicit a reaction, but I'm still shocked at the primal, pleased response they pull from my core. I know how dangerous it is for me to yearn to belong to this man, but as Ryan stares at me as if I'm the only thing he sees, as if I'm the only thing he may ever see, I find it impossible to quash the desire to be his and his alone. I barely resist the urge to say so, reminding myself that I'm here for a short time, that there's a whole life of responsibilities in Dallas I still have to face. I can't run forever; it wouldn't be fair to either of us.

"But I digress. And no, the reasons you mentioned aren't why I'm out here all alone." He stares at the stars winking in the inky darkness. Finally he says, "Life isn't always the storybook adventure you dream of as a kid. It can be exhausting and monotonous and disappointing. At times even cruel. Then I come out here when it's dark and peaceful and look around at the land that's never let me down, and I remember how damn lucky and grateful I am to claim this as my life."

A knot forms in my stomach at the truth in his words. Growing up I truly believed my life would be the privileged, romantic ride promised to me. But if these past several months of bitterness, heartache, and frustration have taught me anything, it's that you have to seek out your own happiness and take ownership of it. Treasure and protect it. Because you never know when it could all be ripped away from you.

"Not to mention, I was waiting for you to arrive so I could congratulate you on evicting your now former friends," he continues, squeezing my hip. "It's not every day someone gets the privilege of doing that." After the girls loaded their bags into Samma's car and drove away, I called Ryan and told him what happened.

"It was surprisingly easy to do," I say, remembering how Samma had not only missed the truth of Ryan's character, but had boiled him down to a plaything to be bought and paid for.

"Perhaps it was good practice," Ryan says, distracting me from the anger building in my chest.

"Practice? Do you need me to evict a few people from your life?" I ask. "Toss Moose and Possum to animal control?"

"I was thinking more along the lines of you getting a good feel for removing other cancerous relationships. The first one has to be the hardest."

Ryan's referring to my mother, that much is clear, and while the idea is tempting and something I've considered on more than one occasion, it's not realistic. Because cutting out cancerous cells carries a price—more often than not you have to take some healthy ones, too. Which means exorcising my mother from my life may damage my relationship with my father in an irreversible way, possibly even result in me losing him altogether. That's something I won't ever allow to happen.

Ryan's expression turns serious. "I'm sorry I couldn't go to the hospital with you. How's Joy? Is she making progress?"

The mention of Grammy J triggers a familiar pinch of guilt in my chest. I clear my throat and say, "She managed to cover half the distance of the hallway using a walker. She gritted her teeth and sweated the whole time, but she didn't complain once. Her surgeon said he's never treated someone more stubborn than my grandmother."

"Joy's feisty, that's for certain," Ryan says. "When will she be released?"

"Day after tomorrow, if she behaves and does exactly as instructed," I say. "And thanks for sending along Moose, Bonnie, and Tiffany today."

"I didn't. They came on their own because they wanted to. Because they care about you."

I nod, a half smile lifting a corner of my mouth. It still

feels strange knowing I'm surrounded by the kind of people who'd drop everything to be there when you need them. For several seconds, we're both quiet, looking off into the distance and listening to the wind sweep through the grapevines. Then Ryan laughs to himself.

"What?" I ask.

"Nothing," he says. "I was just imagining the conversation the girls must have had during their four-hour car ride back to Dallas."

"Oh, I'm sure it was filled with a rampage of insults directed at me. That, and spreading gossip, are all Piper, Samma, and Faye are good for."

Shaking his head and chuckling, he steals the wine glass out of my grasp and sets it on the ground. Rolling me onto my back, he lowers himself on top of me, relaxing into the cradle of my thighs. "You, Margaret Stokes, never cease to astound me. Your strength. Your ability to take a blow and come back swinging."

The warmth of his breath caresses my cheeks. I only need to raise my head a fraction of an inch for our lips to touch, but I hold off, allowing the anticipation to grow. Even though we're surrounded by acres of grapevines, miles from the nearest person, there's something reckless and thrilling about being in the wide open like this.

Ryan stares at me with barely contained hunger in his eyes, as though he's contemplating all the things he plans to do to me and knowing he has all night to accomplish them. Then his mouth covers mine, and *oh, the wait was worth it*. He kisses me, slow and tender, so different from the urgent, greedy ones I'm accustomed to, but no less capable of making me feel sexy and alive.

His tongue glides along my lower lip as I slip my hands under his shirt, my fingers tracing along the dip of his spine, the slope of his back, over his broad shoulders and down again, relishing in the smooth skin stretched over muscle and sinew. The earth is hard and uneven beneath me, but I don't care, my mind is solely focused on how good the weight of his body feels pressed against mine.

My hands travel farther down, drawing him closer. Groaning in approval, Ryan deepens the kiss, sweeping his tongue inside, tasting, teasing. He cups my breast through my dress, and involuntarily I arch into his palm. A low moan escapes my throat, goose bumps erupting all over my skin despite how hot it is tonight.

I thread my fingers into his hair, pulling at the roots, which elicits another groan from him, more strangled than before. "Do it again," he says. His voice sounds so husky it's more like a vibration. I comply, tugging more solidly on the silky strands and lightly digging my nails into his scalp. His breath fills my ear, just as ragged as my own.

Ryan breaks away long enough to yank his shirt over his head, tossing it aside, before bending down to trail kisses over the shell of my ear, along my jaw, across my collarbone. His teeth nip my tender flesh. Everywhere he touches is fire. My heart clangs like a bell against my ribs, strong and fast, and I wonder if he can hear it.

Reaching between us, my arms shaking with nerves and excitement, I unfasten his belt and release the buttons on his jeans. When I feel him *right there*, I gasp, which quickly morphs into a whimper. I buck up into him, scraping my teeth across his bare shoulder and tasting salt and something sweet on my tongue. Ryan lets out a sexy grunt in response, the one that drives me insane and makes warmth pool low in my belly.

Lifting himself up, he leans back on his heels and looks at me with dark, hooded eyes. "I've wanted you out here since I saw you sitting at the bar in The Tangled Vine, drinking my wine and pretending to hate it," he says, sliding his hands under the skirt of my dress and pushing the material up my thighs so it gathers around my waist.

"You wanted me on my back in the dirt?" I ask, my voice shaking a little.

"I wanted you beneath the open sky, smelling of fresh earth and curling around me, wild and hungry."

My breath hitches at his words, the desire no doubt evident on my face.

Crowned in moonlight, a breeze ruffling his hair, Ryan watches my expression as his fingers play at the edge of my underwear, hook around the elastic hem, and drag the thin, delicate lace over my hips and down my legs. His gaze locks on the part of me that's exposed, and I feel myself flush under his appraisal. Ryan murmurs what sounds like *beautiful*, then plants slow, wet kisses along my ankle, my calf, my inner thigh. I squirm as the stubble on his jaw brushes the sensitive skin.

Meeting my eyes again, he grins wickedly—Ryan doesn't play fair, and I love every second of it—then we are wrapped around each other. Everything fades away except the two of us touching, kissing, our bodies moving together.

Liquid heat boils through my veins, building and coiling in my stomach. Sounds of pleasure fall from my lips, echoing through the air, a plea for him to put me out of my misery. Ryan flashes another devilish smile but never lets up on his perfect rhythm.

He grips the outside of my thighs, and the change in angle is so deep, the feeling so intense, it sends my hands searching for something, anything, solid to hold on to, but there's only soft, heady earth under my palms.

My whole body trembles, tense and tight, consumed with a tingling sensation. I'm right there, hovering at the edge. As if suspecting I'm close, his thrusts grow harder, faster. That's all it takes. I cry out as I tumble over the cliff. Moments later, Ryan does the same.

My chest heaves with my labored, uneven pants, and my dress is damp with sweat. It takes a moment for my euphoria to calm, but eventually I push myself up on my elbows and stare at him. There's a smug smile on his face, which complements his messy, unruly hair thanks to my fingers. His stomach muscles contract with his ragged breathing, his skin glistening.

Ryan settles on his back, pulling me against him and wrapping an arm around me. I rest my head on his chest, slick with sweat, and listen to his heartbeat drum against my ear, almost hypnotic in its cadence. I idly trace a finger along the ridges of his abs while his hand runs the length of my spine, my arm, the curve of my hip, over and over in a circuit.

For several minutes we lie there in silence. Above us, the sky appears close enough to touch, the moon high and bright. A welcome breeze sweeps over us, bringing relief from the burning heat of our intertwined bodies and the outside temperature.

"What's going to happen with the Inn now?" Ryan asks after a while, his voice so deep and resonant I can feel the vibrations against my cheek.

"How do you mean?"

"While Joy recuperates."

"I'm managing it," I say, as if this should be obvious.

"And after she's fully healed? Are you staying?" He keeps his tone even, controlled, but there's something guarded underneath.

I fall quiet. Lying in the crook of Ryan's arm, warm and relaxed, I realize I can't possibly be objective in making such a huge decision, even if the idea has been whirling around in my head almost nonstop since Ryan brought it up during our mud fight. If I were to leave Dallas and move to Wilhelmsburg permanently—which I'm not at all convinced I'm ready to do—it'd be in large part because of the man holding me, the man who means more to me than even I understand. But no matter how wonderful Ryan is, or how amazing he makes me feel, I cannot, will not, run from one man to another or hide from my responsibilities forever. I'd need to be fully committed to something more than Ryan, something bigger and more permanent than the two of us.

"Margaret?" Ryan asks when I don't respond.

I look up at him, my hair draping over my shoulders like a veil. "And wreak havoc on your fall flavors?" My tone sounds playful—it's safer than confessing the thoughts racing through my mind.

His gaze searches my face, and it feels as though he's peering deep inside me and understanding my emotions without me needing to say anything aloud. "Funny thing about flavors, Marge, is that every now and again, one comes along and destroys your palate for anything else."

"Please," I say, affecting an air of casualness I don't feel. "I've seen your cellar. Your tastes are varied and eclectic. Each season there'll be something new to savor."

His eyebrows knit together. "How do you still not understand the depth of my feelings for you?" Ryan threads his fingers through my hair. His expression has gone soft and still, and the weight of his stare pins me in place. "I love you."

For a moment I can't breathe. My heart stutters before it picks up, pounding wildly against my ribs. No one has ever said those words to me. Not Nick, who engaged in an impressive display of verbal gymnastics to say anything but. Not my father, who, while supportive, has never been prone to verbal displays of affection. And certainly never my mother. Now that I've heard them, I'm unprepared for how dangerous and terrifying they feel.

Ryan rolls us, pinning me beneath him so he can stare into my eyes. "I love you, Margaret. I want a life with you. A future with you," he says, steamrolling right over any reply I may have. "I want you in Wilhelmsburg, in my home"—he cants his hips—"in my bed." He leans down, brushing a soft kiss across my mouth. "I want you to stay."

Full-blown panic grips my chest. I can see in his face how much he wants me to simply agree, to give in to him, to trust him. But everything that's happened between us, every captured look and purposeful touch and pointed conversation, has been too real, too fast, too . . . big. And I don't know how to process it, let alone handle it.

"Ryan . . . what you're asking for . . . I *can't*," I say, my voice strained.

He props himself up on an elbow, providing me much-needed breathing room. "Why not?" he asks, casual, as if he's wondering why I can't meet him for lunch.

I push at his chest and sit up. "It's easy for you," I say, trying to formulate my thoughts.

"Easy?" he repeats, his tone laced with frustration. "Believe me, Marge, nothing with you has been easy." Pulling away, he grabs his shirt and yanks it over his head, then buttons his jeans and buckles his belt.

"Don't kid yourself, Ryan," I say as I stand, brushing off the dirt on my dress. "This is much easier for you. You don't have nearly so much to lose—and nothing to sacrifice."

Ryan rakes his fingers through his hair. "I'm sorry, I didn't realize telling you I love you would be such a burden to you."

"Of course not! You don't have to change anything. I would just fall into your life. You aren't the one who'd have to sell his condo, give up his business, and move over two hundred miles away to start over. Everything stays the same for you." I shove my feet into my ballet flats. "That you don't understand that, that you can't see that you're pushing too hard, asking for too much, makes me wonder if you really know how you feel about me in the first place."

"How convenient for you to use my declaration of love as a way to keep avoiding what you need to fix in your life," Ryan spits out with a glare. "I'd hoped that telling you how I felt might make things easier, might make your faith in me and yourself that much stronger. But if you're determined to continue running away, by all means, don't let me and my misguided feelings stop you."

"And how convenient for you that you've never had to make such choices! You've never had to consider how your actions may affect your relationship with your family. You've never had to decide that everything you've worked for may in fact be worthless. You've led a charmed life, Ryan. You accuse me of having a silver spoon stuck up my ass, but all of this," I say, gesturing to the vineyard and stone barn, "was handed to you on a platter!"

"Well, I think you've made your feelings for me perfectly clear. So go ahead and go back to Dallas where you're so certain you belong. Just don't expect me to be here waiting for you when you finally figure out what it is that you want," he says. "Besides, if you're right, and I'm merely confused, then this shouldn't be anything a bottle of No Regrets can't help you get over."

Then he picks up his work boots and stalks away, beating me to it by seconds.

18

It's been a week and a half since Grammy J was released from the hospital and already managing the bed-and-breakfast feels like something inherent to me. Which, in a way, I guess it is, seeing as how the Inn has been in my family since before I was born. There's a rhythm to it that at first seemed daunting and overwhelming but now feels energizing, fulfilling.

It's a realization that always brings my thoughts back to Ryan and the harsh words we threw at each other in the heat of the moment. Because with every passing day, as the Inn begins to feel more and more like a place I belong, like a part of my future, the seed Ryan planted grows in me, blossoming into something real and tangible. The idea that I could stay in Wilhelmsburg to oversee the B&B has taken root.

So much of me wants to reach out to tell him this, but we haven't spoken since our argument. Now the quiet and distance have begun to feel permanent. The silence between us hurts in a way I never anticipated; a sense of longing and homesickness that follows me through the day, dogging my steps. And while I miss him and desperately want to mend things between us, he's made it clear that until I've figured out exactly what I want, who I am, there's no point.

I throw a load of sheets into the wash, grab the basket of clean, folded cloth napkins, and head downstairs, humming a country song I heard while shopping for gardening supplies at Hodgepodge yesterday. My legs and back ache from vacuuming, and my hands are wrinkly and raw from scrubbing toilets all afternoon, but I know tonight I'll sleep deep, satisfied I've provided the guests with a memorable stay. One I'd want for myself, even if I'm still on my quest for culinary prowess—though with the help of Bon Bon, my skills are improving a little more each day.

I put the napkins away, then retrieve the trays of canapés and charcuterie from the kitchen and place them on the table set up on the back lawn for evening happy hour. Connecting with the guests while they sip wine, discussing which vineyards they visited that day, offering restaurant recommendations, learning about their lives in a way that allows me to be an armchair traveler, has been my favorite aspect of running the Inn so far.

Like right now, I'm listening to an older couple from Colorado tell me about the incredible African safari their family went on last year, complete with elephant rides and a guided bike tour alongside zebras and giraffes.

"We also spent three days exploring the 'Spice Island' of Zanzibar," the husband says, which conjures up the image of cobbled alleyways brimming with the scents of vanilla, cinnamon, and nutmeg. "The Hamamni Persian Baths in Stone Town were especially breathtaking."

"As were the Sultan's Palace and House of Wonders," the wife adds. "Truly magnificent."

"It all sounds magical," I say as I pour them more Tempranillo, a perfect complement to the Serrano ham and manchego cheese croquettes they're sampling. We chat for a few more minutes before I excuse myself to top off the other guests' wine glasses.

The sun feels relentless, as though shining through a giant magnifying glass. But the sky is blue and cloudless, the breeze is fragranced with the scent of wildflowers and grape leaves, and the sounds of laughter and good conversation fill the air. I can't imagine anything better.

After happy hour ends and I tidy up, I retreat inside. It takes a moment for my eyes to adjust to the dimness. I hear Grammy J's voice coming from the office. Sticking my head in, I see a phone propped between her ear and shoulder. I knock lightly on the door frame. She spins on her heel and holds up a finger. Her eyebrows are knit together, and a frown pulls down her mouth.

I wonder how long ago her physical therapist left and if the session went well. Her gardening club is coming over to play cards in an hour, and I don't want her entertaining people if she's in pain. She's wearing loose, stretchy shorts and a tracksuit jacket with pockets so she can easily carry items like keys and medication. The wrist that broke her fall still requires a brace for stabilization, while the other has been wrapped with tape to provide extra support for when she puts weight on it. She's already progressed from using a walker to a cane.

While she finishes her phone call, I start organizing breakfast for tomorrow so the process of cooking and serving won't be so hectic. By the time Grammy J joins me in the kitchen, I've reviewed the guest menu choices, set out the cookware, utensils, and mixing bowls necessary to prepare each dish, and measured the dry and nonperishable ingredients into containers.

"Child, we need to talk," she says. "Let's move to my bedroom so we can speak in private." There's a different note in her voice, and not a good one.

An uneasy dread churns in the pit of my stomach, and I hesitate for a moment before meeting her there. I've been in Grammy J's room on multiple occasions to borrow an item of clothing out of her closet, drop off a basket of laundry, or sweep and polish the hardwood floor, and every time I cross the threshold it feels as if I'm intruding on something intensely personal and private.

The space is clean and tidy, the decor simple. Oil paintings of the rolling hillside of Wilhelmsburg hang on the walls. Stained glass lamps adorn wooden nightstands that are old but well taken care of. Framed photographs of Poppa Bart and their life together, a few of me as a child, and even one of my mother clutter the surface of an antique dresser. The colors in the floral pattern on the bedspread are faded from too much sun exposure.

Grammy J is waiting for me in the reading nook in the corner of the room. We had to replace her favorite comfy upholstered chair with a firm, straight-backed one that positions her feet so they lay flat against the floor. To guarantee her optimal recovery, Moose helped me injury-proof the bed-and-breakfast, removing tripping hazards like throw rugs and loose cords and adding safety handrails to the shower and grab bars beside the toilet in her bathroom. We rearranged some of the furniture to clear pathways between rooms and open up the shared areas to make getting around the Inn easier for her.

I sit across from her, careful not to bump into her cane leaning against the armrest. She's silent a moment, staring out the windows at two birds taking a bath in the water fountain in the garden, then she sighs and rubs her eyes with her fingers, smoothing out the wrinkles underneath.

Grammy J looks more exhausted than ever. Even her usually vibrant strawberry blonde hair is dull and limp. Once again a hot bolt of guilt shoots through me.

"That was a broker on the phone. The Inn's goin' to be sold," she says in her straightforward, no-frills way that never fails to catch me off guard.

Her words detonate like a bomb inside me, a hole blown through my heart, but I force myself to remain calm. "But this is your home. You *can't* sell it," I say. *Why would Grammy J consider something like this?* "If you're worried about what'll happen to the bed-and-breakfast while you heal, I've got it under control."

Her expression softens, her gaze turning almost sad. "Child, I know that," she says, patting my knee. "If I had my way, my bones would be buried under the large magnolia tree where we scattered your grandfather's ashes."

"Then why?" I ask, my tone mirroring the confusion that must be evident in my expression. "The B and B could earn a decent profit this year." In the last week alone, the Inn received a slew of bookings for the peak holiday season of October through December, many customers reserving one of the new vacation packages, which means my promotional efforts are reaching people. Now the trend just needs to last.

"Because it's not my choice. The property doesn't belong to me," Grammy J says. The wind sways a bush outside the window, blocking the slowly diminishing sunlight and casting shadows that zigzag across her face. "It belongs to your mother."

"What're you talking about," I say, still not believing it. "Why has she never told me?"

"I imagine she never deemed it important."

Of course my mother wouldn't deem that information

important. "But she purposely wanted to get *away* from Wilhelmsburg," I say. "Why would she own something that practically chains her to it?"

"When your mother and I still had a good relationship, before she found out about Poppa Bart, the Inn had a couple of rough years financially. Your grandfather and I were sure we'd have to shut it down, but your mother stepped in and offered to buy the property from us—your father's law practice had become hugely successful and they felt this would be the best solution." Grammy J shifts in her seat, pain flitting across her face, and once again guilt courses through my veins, nearly suffocating me. "Your grandfather and I took on the role of manager, and the money we earned from the deal allowed us to keep the Inn afloat."

"Once it was stable, you never saw the need to reclaim ownership?" I ask.

"Why would we? The arrangement was workin', and besides, the Inn was still in our family," she says, lifting a shoulder in a shrug. "After your grandfather died, I assumed your mother would finally rid herself of this place and cut all ties with me, but she didn't. I guess she and your father liked the income too much, and perhaps by permittin' me to continue runnin' things, it was her coded way of keepin' me away from Dallas and away from her. But it seems her attitude has changed."

My stomach twists, and I know with bone-deep certainty that my mother's rash decision to sell the B&B has nothing to do with Grammy J and everything to do with me. My mother's playing a game in which she controls all the pieces, and I have no idea how to outsmart her, let alone beat her.

The possibility that the Inn may no longer be a part of my life brings everything into sharp focus, solidifying what

I've been feeling since I came to Wilhelmsburg and realized how truly special this place is. For a long time I convinced myself I was happy in Dallas, confusing success and social status with contentment and belonging. But now I recognize those feelings were misguided and loaded with external expectations. Because while my life here has been simple and often repetitive, filled with a never-ending to-do list of cleaning, cooking, weeding the garden, and general guest management, there's also a sense of purpose and gratification. I finally let myself consider what that really means. Staying here won't just be challenging, it'll be painful and risky and exhausting. But I know this is where I'm supposed to be. Where I *want* to be.

I only wish my relationship with Ryan wasn't so fraught. He has this power to take my most frenetic thoughts and concerns and boil them down to something manageable. To take what feels difficult and overwhelming and lay it out in a path that makes those first steps easier. And more than anything, when he stands with me, quietly encouraging me, I feel more confident in my abilities. But he isn't here, and I have to acknowledge the fact he may never be. For a split second I allow myself to wonder if that changes anything. With stunning clarity I realize it doesn't. No matter what happens between Ryan and me, there's no question or hesitation that I want to remain in Wilhelmsburg and run the bed-and-breakfast.

"No. This can't happen. I won't let it," I say to Grammy J with a certainty I've never felt before. "I'll find a way to prevent my mother from selling it." I *have* to. For both of us.

I refuse to allow my mother to get away with kicking Grammy J out of her home with such callous disregard or disposing of the Inn as if it's nothing more than an outdated handbag. The reasons my mother has for being estranged from Grammy J don't excuse her behavior now. In fact, going forward, I'm done making excuses for my mother's cold, heartless behavior period, regardless of the circumstances.

"Child, it's okay. I'll survive. I can rent a small duplex in town. I have some savings and checks from Uncle Sam rollin' in each month. I'll be fine," she says with a laugh, and to my surprise, it's not edged with bitterness or anger, as though she's accepted long ago that losing her home is a foregone conclusion.

"When is all this supposed to happen?" I ask, wondering how much time I have to develop a plan.

"Soon," she says. "The broker mentioned he already has a buyer lined up."

Which means the window of opportunity to solidify my own future is closing fast.

———

I GRIP THE STEERING WHEEL, my knuckles white—it's the only way to prevent the anger at my mother, the situation, the unfairness of it all, from spilling out of me—as I drive quickly through town on my way to see Ryan.

Even though nothing is resolved between us and the clock is winding down, I can't fight the urge to talk to him. Ryan's familiar with the area and the process of buying property. Maybe he'll think of a straightforward solution to my problem. If nothing else, I know I can trust his advice and opinion, assuming he's able to put aside his hurt to hear me out. Because while my commitment to the Inn is entirely separate from my feelings for Ryan, this could be an important step toward building a life we could potentially share. I just hope he considers it enough, for now at least.

I park my car in front of Possum and Gina's house—the gang rotates barbecue-hosting duties and September belongs to my favorite spunky couple. Ryan and I planned to attend together, but that was before our argument. My stomach is a tangle of knots as I push open the old wrought iron gate and walk up the stone path to the cottage with rocking chairs on the porch, gingham curtains in the windows, and a tie-dye flag hanging above the front steps.

The wind ruffles a note taped to the Grateful Dead dancing bear knocker, inviting guests to let themselves in and join the party. I follow the scent of charcoal through the quaint living area and kitchen to the screen door leading to the patio. Amber is manning the grill, turning hot dogs and flipping hamburgers. A few feet away, Moose hovers over a table crammed with platters of fixings, slathering melted butter on roasted corn on the cob and sprinkling them with cotija cheese.

Possum and Gina are playing horseshoes, both nursing what appears to be red sangria based on the orange and lemon slices floating in their glasses. Once again, Possum has changed his hair color from Jem and the Holograms pink to Gumby green. Gina's in the middle of telling a story to the group as she lets a horseshoe fly, successfully hooking it around the stake. I hear Ryan's familiar laugh, and I spot him kneeling in the grass, wedging wine bottles into a large metal cooler filled with ice—only in Hill Country will you find a barbecue where wine is served instead of beer.

At the sight of him, my anger toward my mother fades and my nerves flare up. I feel the heat rising on my cheeks, but I force it down. Inhaling a deep breath, I slide open the screen door and step out onto the patio.

"Margaret!" Moose calls, waving the basting brush

above his head in greeting. "Glad you came. Did you happen to bump into Tiffany and Bonnie on your way in? They've gone missing on an errand of great importance."

Gina huffs and blows the bangs out of her eyes, winding up for another toss. "For the fifth time, they're not missing. They'll be back with a six-pack for your plebeian palate in a few minutes," she says, wrapping another horseshoe around the stake.

As if reading my earlier thoughts, Moose says to me, "I don't suppose you have a beer in that fancy purse of yours? I keep telling them that wine is for getting laid and beer is for barbecues, but no one listens to me."

"That doesn't prevent you from talking, though, does it?" Amber says, laying slices of pepper jack on the patties, while Possum salutes Moose with a raised fist and says, "Hear, hear!"

They're treating me like I'm a welcome guest. Did Ryan not tell them about our fight? Or are they acting this way to make my presence less awkward?

Ryan stands, grass stains marring the knees of his jeans, and walks toward me. "What're you doing here, Margaret?" His tone is oddly formal, his expression reserved.

"I need to talk to you."

The mask slides from his face, replaced with concern, his eyebrows knit together. "Everything okay?"

I bite my lip, then burst out with it. "The Inn's going to be sold, and I don't know what to do."

Ryan tilts his head, scrutinizing me as if trying to discern the crux of my feelings. "I didn't realize you'd be so upset about that."

"Why wouldn't I be? It's Grammy J's home," I say, looking at him in confusion.

"Well, yes, but Joy did agree to sell," he says.

"She didn't agree because Grammy J isn't the one who owns it. My mother does, and she's decided that the best thing for Grammy J would be to abandon her to fend for herself. Or maybe, if my mother's feeling generous, she'll dump my grandmother into a retirement home," I say, my voice trembling in frustration.

"I know Joy pretty well, Margaret, and she doesn't do anything she doesn't want to. Much like someone else I know." Ryan gives me a small half smile. Perhaps that's why I don't see the ground being ripped out from under me. "And besides, the Inn will be in good hands. You know I'll take great care of it."

Everything goes quiet—the gentle swish of branches moving in the breeze, the crack and sizzle of meat cooking over hot coals, the hum of happy voices soaking up the summer evening—leaving me with a low ringing in my ears.

"What do you mean you'll take care of it?" I ask, hoping I misheard him. I can't fathom the alternative.

Frowning, Ryan takes me by the elbow and leads us around the side of the cottage, all while my mind is spinning. I braced myself for the reality of an impersonal investor rifling through my family's property, determining what's of value, and discarding the rest. But now, as Ryan's palm grows clammy against my arm, a far more insidious thought burrows in and settles. *It can't be.* The Inn can't have been purchased by someone I know. Someone I trusted. A friend. A lover.

As Ryan drops his hand and turns to me, his face a study in closely guarded neutrality, I know what he intends to confess before the words fall from his lips. And yet, when he says, "I'm the one who offered on the Inn," the world shakes me up, yanking me out of the pleasant bubble I've come to rely on and back into the world I've always known. The world where betrayal is cheaper than Two Buck Chuck and loyalty is something only children expect.

"I don't understand," I say, stepping away from him, desperate for distance and clarity. Anger is bubbling in my chest again, gaining strength. "How could you do something like this to me?"

"Margaret, I didn't do this *to* you," he says, his gaze boring into mine as though trying to convince me of something impossible to grasp. "I've never hidden that I want to expand the winery, but I'm unable to do that unless I acquire more plantable land for vines. Yes, I've inquired about the property the Inn sits on before, but that was years ago and I was always denied. Truthfully, I'd given up on the idea, and started exploring other options for land in the High Plains and in other parts of Hill Country. So when the broker called to notify me that circumstances have changed and the B and B was now on the market, of course I jumped at the opportunity. It's a sound business decision."

A sound business decision? Is he kidding? I think, as the old bitterness I've worked so hard to smother resurfaces.

"The Inn isn't some square on a Monopoly board that can be bought and traded at will, Ryan!" I say as the anger finally explodes out of me. "And what does that make me? Free parking? Is that all this summer has been to you? Fun and games? Pass go, collect two hundred dollars, screw the out-of-towner, and do it all over again?"

"Margaret, I told you I was in love with you, and you told me you didn't feel the same. Do you *really* think that's all this summer has meant to me?"

For a second, I see deep hurt in his expression, but I force myself to continue. "So because of that you didn't even consider coming to me first? Ask me what I wanted or if I may have a problem with you being involved?" I retreat farther away, eyeing him like he's the enemy.

Ryan rakes a hand through his hair and lets out a frustrated sigh. "Why would I need to do that? You said you were going back to Dallas," he says. "Which was verified for me when I asked the broker if anyone else from the family was interested in buying the Inn and he claimed there wasn't."

"Why? Maybe because you saw me breaking my back to keep the Inn running? Maybe because you know how happy I've been since I've been here? Maybe because, for just a minute, you cared more about my feelings than your limited property line?" I say. My voice is acidic enough to transform wine into vinegar. "I've been doing everything in my power to save it, Ryan, and now you want to swoop in and steal it away from me and my family?"

He winces slightly at my words, guilt flashing across his face, as a cold, firm fist squeezes my chest, the devastation at how similar this situation is to my relationship with Nick—and my mother—nearly choking me. How many times must I learn that investing in something, loving something, leads only to heartache? But maybe I shouldn't be surprised. After all, it was Ryan who informed me that no matter how much effort you devote to something, no matter how hard you work, you aren't entitled to anything.

"You've been here one summer in sixteen years, Margaret, and now all of a sudden the Inn is yours to save?" Ryan crosses his arms over his chest, jaw set, hazel eyes sharp and piercing in the fading light. "Even if I ignore the fact that you've had your entire life to express an interest in this place, I can't ignore the fact that you haven't once actually said you pictured a future here or that the Inn means more to you than an escape."

"The last time I was here I was sixteen. I had no idea

what I wanted for my life, what I would find fulfilling and meaningful," I say. "The whole idea that I *should* have known, without the benefit of experience, how much this place would mean to me is ridiculous."

How can you love something before you've truly found it? Ryan is a perfect example. A bundle of hormones at sixteen, one second I hated him, the next I wanted his hands on my hips and his lips on my neck. I couldn't have predicted then how much he'd come to mean to me years later . . . Or how much he'd hurt me. Yet that's exactly the sort of prescient thinking he's demanding of me. It's not fair.

He shrugs. "You conquered an old porch and cooked a few breakfasts, but you're talking about a *lifetime commitment*. And generally, when people want to commit to something for a lifetime, they have the stones to say it out loud. When have you *ever* had the guts to say out loud, to me, to your mother, or even to yourself, what you actually want? You don't get to stand here, all self-righteous and indignant over a betrayal only you perceive."

Shaking my head, I open my mouth to respond, but Ryan cuts me off. "Actions speak louder than words, but the words are still important, Margaret. I'm not rescinding my offer. You want the Inn? Fight for it."

"Thank you for the education, Ryan. In the future, I'll be certain to spell out my intentions," I say, moving around him. My anger, the humiliation for actually *believing* that he knew me, cared about me, is so visceral and raw it makes my hands tremble and my heart feel like it could pound through my rib cage. My eyes sting, but I inhale deeply, willing the tears away.

I quickly slip out to my car undetected. The drive to the Inn is a blur and soon I'm pulling my Audi beside Grammy J's truck. All the other parking spaces are empty.

It's still dinnertime, so I know the guests are eating in town, but it seems too early for the members of Grammy J's gardening club to have left. Perhaps with the news that she's about to be ejected from her home, Grammy J wasn't in the proper frame of mind to entertain people. Not that I blame her.

I get out of my car to find her on the back porch, pottering around on her cane and inspecting the flower boxes. She takes one look at my expression and says, "So, it didn't go well with Ryan."

"You *knew* it was him?" I ask as I join her on the porch.

She shrugs. "He's always had an interest in this place. He's even asked about purchasin' it a few times, so it's only logical the broker would contact him first," she says, pinching the head off a pink geranium and tossing it into a bucket. "I'm glad it was Ryan and not some complete stranger. I'll sleep easier knowin' that the land that brought me so much joy will now bring him the same. I've seen what he's done with his business. There's love there, and where there's love, there's success and happiness."

"But this is your home. I refuse to let you part with it," I say. "*I* don't want to part with it."

Grabbing the gardening pail positioned on one of the rocking chairs, she hobbles along the railing to water the hanging ferns. "Child, I've loved this Inn for a long time, but it hasn't been the same since Poppa Bart died. Perhaps it's time I lay this season of my life to rest." Grammy J turns to face me, her expression wistful. Not happy, exactly, but something I suspect I don't yet have the years to appreciate. "And don't you worry, I'll come home eventually."

"What do you mean?" I follow her, picking up loose petals and fronds that have fallen onto the wood boards and adding them to the bucket.

"The broker mentioned Ryan intends to write into the

purchase agreement that upon my death, I'll be buried under the magnolia tree," she says.

A fresh course of anger surges through me. Of course, *of course*, Ryan has to do something considerate, chivalrous even. But then, it's easy to give an old woman a patch of dirt when in exchange you snatch away her family legacy.

"And anyway," she continues, "I haven't had the energy the Inn needs in a long time. And frankly, I never expected to witness it again in its prime. Not until you came along, that is. I'm prepared to let the Inn go, child. But I understand why you can't. So what are you goin' to do?"

The only thing I can and the only option I have left.

I wipe my dirt-covered fingers on my shorts and say, "I need to go back to Dallas and speak with my mother."

Grammy J smiles, full and wide, and for a moment, I glimpse the formidable woman my mother fears, the woman my mother can't control. Grammy J's not orderly; she doesn't conform to my mother's rigid expectations. If only I had the same ability, the same certainty to always know what's best for me, and the fearlessness to make it a reality. "I knew you were more like me than your mother."

"You did?" I ask.

"I always have. But my opinion really doesn't matter, and neither does hers. It's up to you, child. Which is why I've arranged for in-home care and hired a service to come over to prepare breakfast and clean the Inn for the next several days." She slips an arm around my shoulders and pulls me against her, giving me a gentle squeeze. "So, go take care of what you need to. I'll leave the porch light on for you."

19

I JOLT AWAKE TO THE BLARING RADIO ALARM. IT TAKES A moment before I remember I'm lying in bed in my condo in Uptown Dallas. More than six weeks away and the mattress and pillow still conform to the shape of my body, but they no longer feel comfortable. Everything is too fluffy, too soft, too much like a hotel bed. I miss my mattress at the bed-and-breakfast that has more springs than foam and the pillow that deflates when I rest my head on it.

I switch off the alarm and sit up, kicking off the thousand-thread-count sheets. I forgot to close the plantation shutters before I climbed into bed, and now the room is flooded with sunlight, the air-conditioning unit failing to keep up. Outside, I hear the sounds of a typical traffic jam —cars honking, sirens wailing, people shouting at one another. I used to be able to drown out the incessant city noises and fall into a deep, dreamless sleep, but I tossed and turned most of last night—Ryan, our fight, and his betrayal heavy on my mind.

My heart squeezes, holding in the anger, the pain, the bitterness so tight I'm shocked it hasn't shattered. I still don't understand how Ryan could steal something as precious as the Inn away from me. How could I be so blinded by my emotions that I'd allow him to manipulate me for personal gain?

But I can't focus on any of that right now. I have to face my mother, convince her not to sell. Even after the long drive to Dallas with only my thoughts to keep me company, I'm still clueless as to how to accomplish it.

I skip coffee and breakfast—I'm already too hyped-up for caffeine, and my stomach is ready to revolt at any moment. Not to mention anything edible in the refrigerator and pantry expired a month ago. I shower and put on the skirt suit my mother custom ordered for me, the one she claims brings out the gray in my eyes and highlights my fair complexion and red hair. If there's any chance of her listening to me, I have to dress the part of a confident, determined, successful businesswoman who always gets what she wants.

I stare at myself in the mirror, at the crisp, dark navy fabric that shows off my curves in a way that's classic and polished, at the loose curls draped over my shoulders, at the heels molded perfectly to my feet. I resemble the pristine, put-together Margaret everyone would recognize, the Margaret from before Wilhelmsburg changed everything.

The Margaret I no longer wish to be.

With one final glance around my condo that somehow feels both impersonal and stifling, I grab my purse and head out to fight the usual gridlock to my parents' residence in Highland Park. As the skyscrapers of downtown shrink in my rearview mirror, the streets narrow, bordered by old Georgian-style mansions and Tuscan villas accented with gushing fountains and circular drives on lots barely large enough to contain them.

I pull my Audi into the visitor parking area flanked by

flowers and manicured shrubbery and kill the engine. I study the place I grew up in, noticing how the French provincial structure with its brick exterior, steep-hipped roofs, and symmetrical proportions seems more like a museum than a house.

At this time of morning, my mother has most likely finished her tennis lesson at the club and is about to sit down for a gourmet breakfast, while my father is probably already in depositions for a nasty divorce case. Ordinarily I'd want him to be present for this conversation—he's judicious and fair and acts as a mediator when needed—but this is something I should face on my own.

Inhaling a deep breath, I walk up the stone path to the front door and ring the bell, feeling like an unwelcome stranger standing on my childhood doorstep. A figure moves behind the textured glass my mother hand-selected from Paris—nothing but the best for home. I brush a hand over my hair, smoothing any untamed curls, and straighten my suit.

"Miss Margaret," our longtime family housekeeper says in surprise when the door swings open. "You are back." Her eyes are wide, her mouth slack. I wonder how much of my situation she's garnered from listening to my parents argue.

"Nice to see you, Catalina." I step into the foyer, the herringbone wood floor gleaming under the chandelier, and bend slightly to give her a hug. Her whole body freezes, and I realize I've never greeted her that way before. In fact, I've never greeted her with anything other than a simple hello. "Is my mother around? I need to speak with her."

Nodding, she turns and leads me into the dining area that overlooks the pool surrounded by gardens and art sculptures. The table has been set for one, complete with fine bone china, wafer-thin crystal glasses, and a fresh-cut arrangement of roses. "Will you be joining Mrs. Stokes for the meal?" Catalina asks.

"Since Margaret has finally decided to grace us with her presence, I suppose that would only be polite." My mother breezes into the room as though this is a normal day. "Please inform the chef of my daughter's arrival."

Given the way our last phone call ended, I figured she'd be shocked to see me, but her expression is neutral, not showing the slightest bit of annoyance. Perhaps my mother assumes that if I'm here, I must've come to my senses and finally recognized the error of my ways.

She's wearing an emerald green dress with an ivory cardigan and modest nude heels. For years, when I looked at Grammy J, I felt as if I was peering at an older version of my mother. They have so many similar features. The same elegant neck, the same high cheekbones, the same thick red hair. But as I stare at my mother now, I realize the resemblance is truly only skin deep. My mother bears none of Grammy J's warmth. Her eyes don't crinkle when she smiles, and her mouth never twitches in amusement.

Catalina pulls out a chair for my mother, and after she settles into her seat, Catalina drapes a linen napkin across her lap. Then she quickly arranges plates and silverware on the table for me and hurries off to the kitchen.

"Well, don't just stand there as if you're waiting for charity, Margaret. Sit," my mother says, taking a sip of coffee. The last thing I want to do is consume food, but I'd rather not provoke her temper by being disobedient over such a small thing. Especially when I'm about to ask her for something so huge.

Catalina returns, carrying a serving tray holding today's offering. She places a dish in front of each of us. "The chef has prepared eggs Benedict with fresh fruit and roasted potatoes," she says, removing the silver dome covers. She pours us grapefruit juice, refills our coffee, and scurries out of the dining area, as if she thinks she's about to get caught in a war zone.

We eat in silence for several minutes while I work up the courage to start the conversation. Finally, I say, "I wanted to speak with you about the Inn." Straight to the point. I'd be proud except for the apprehension in my voice. No doubt she hears it, too.

My mother glances at me, her shrewd gaze taking in my hair, my face, then sliding down, patronizing and judgmental, to my suit. I force myself not to fidget. "Is that the suit I bought you? I seem to recall it fitting differently. But then, I don't recall raising a daughter who'd run off to the country over something as trivial as a romantic embarrassment. So perhaps it's not the suit that's ill-fitting."

Her words are meant to pierce my heart where I'm most vulnerable, and in the past, they would've succeeded. But I'm tougher now, and I refuse to allow her to hurt me. Besides, she's right. I *don't* fit here anymore, nor do I want to.

Ignoring her comments, I push my plate aside and say, "Grammy J informed me that you intend on selling it."

"Don't be obtuse, Margaret. We're not *intending* on selling. We *are* selling—something your father and I should have done years ago." She cuts into a poached egg, the yolk oozing over the honey-smoked ham and English muffin.

"I came to ask you not to." This time my voice is strong and assured, lacking all trepidation.

"It was rather foolish of you to drive all that way just for this, but at least you're back where you belong," she says, then adds, "Given the Inn's no longer a profitable endeavor, that's not an option."

I pretend she didn't just refer to Grammy J's home as an "endeavor" as I say, "That may have been true before, but with the promotional work I've done the Inn is slated to make money this year."

"And that's supposed to impress me?" she asks with no inflection, no raised eyebrow, no disdain etched in her expression. Instead she dismisses me as easily as she dismisses the landscaper. "Your feeble attempt to save something beyond repair is cute, but you're too late. The buyer offered our asking price and the closing documents are being drafted as we speak."

"No, I'm not. The deal isn't finalized. So instead let me take on the burden of the bed-and-breakfast," I say, trying to keep the frustration out of my tone and failing. "The Inn belongs in this family."

"Please." It's the closest I've ever heard my mother come to scoffing. "It's hardly an heirloom. No one will miss it."

"You don't think Grammy J will miss her home? The place she married Poppa Bart? The place she buried him?" I ask, anger and agony burning my vision. It's not like my parents need the money, but it's just like my mother to see little value in something and presume it holds no value to anyone else.

I expect the mention of Poppa Bart to finally spark her temper, but she remains cool and collected, if not slightly bored, as if I'm not worth bothering with anymore. "Your grandmother has agreed to move, so that argument is moot," she says.

"*I'll* miss it," I press. "Let me handle the day-to-day operations, let me run the Inn. I *want* to run it."

My mother blots her mouth with her napkin. "You mean gift it to you," she says. "Because you certainly don't have the funds to afford the property. You're not earning an income because you've flushed your career down the toilet, and surely your savings have whittled down to nothing."

"I'll have the money if you allow me access to my trust," I say.

She laughs, high and clear as a bell tolling her disapproval. "Borrow against it, you mean. As you know, you have no right to it until you turn forty or find someone suitable to marry," my mother says, spitting out the words as if they offend her. "No, your father and I have provided you with quite enough already, and with such a poor return on our investment. I told you before you won't receive any more support from us. Or have you forgotten?"

"Okay," I say, drawing in a calming breath. Getting riled up will only serve to prove to my mother that I'm the emotional wreck she believes me to be. "Then I'll secure a loan from the bank and buy it."

"I'd like to see you qualify for one, what with a floundering business and no real assets at your disposal," she says. "But if humiliation is what you're after—and given your behavior the past several months, I assume it is—by all means, try. But I won't put the sale on hold in the meantime."

They're right when they say insanity is doing the same thing over and over and expecting different results. And I'm clearly insane, because I keep hoping my mother will finally believe in me, support me, not think of me as a constant failure, but her attitude toward me never changes. And it will *never* change—a sobering fact I now recognize.

"I'd be disappointed if you did. You've never shown me the least bit of consideration, so why break the trend now?" I say, pushing my chair back and standing. "Do what you need to do, Mother, and I'll do the same. After all, you're the one who taught me to never accept no for an answer."

I drop my napkin directly onto my nearly untouched plate of food and leave the room. I'm no closer to my goal of owning the Inn, and yet, I'm exhilarated as I breeze through the foyer, waving off Catalina as she rushes to open the front door for me. I can't help but feel as if I've scored the first, and perhaps most important, victory. Maybe Ryan was right and tossing my so-called friends from the B&B had merely been practice for the main event.

But now I wonder how my decisions will alter my relationship with my father, if I've done something to irrevocably harm it. He got mad when he learned I was visiting Grammy J in the first place, so how will he react when he discovers I plan to buy the Inn and stay in Wilhelmsburg permanently? We've always been a team, my father and I, facing the storm that is my mother's anger together. Now that I've stated my intentions and cut the strings holding me back, I worry I've incidentally severed more than I meant to.

As I strip off my suit jacket, tossing it carelessly into the back of my car, and climb into the driver's seat, I know there's only one way to find out. Fishing my cell phone out of my purse, I call my father's office to ask his secretary if she can squeeze me into his schedule.

It's now or never.

―――

MAGICIAN THAT SHE IS, Thelma managed to shuffle a few of my father's appointments around and, at my suggestion, booked us a reservation at the Petroleum Club. I thought the conversation might go better without any lawyerly distractions or a large mahogany desk between us.

I follow the hostess into the dimly lit lounge area with a spectacular panoramic view of downtown Dallas. The room is packed with members waiting for their lunch tables to become available.

When I catch sight of my father relaxing on his favorite couch near the grand piano, enjoying a gin and tonic and a bowl of mixed nuts, sweat pops up on the back of my neck and lines my palms, and I resist the urge to wipe my hands on my skirt.

It's hard to believe two hours ago I was high on the thrill of making the first of many new changes in my life. Now I'm bracing myself for the real possibility that I may lose my father because of my actions. Part of me is even expecting it, that if my mother decrees that I be cut off in every way that my father will agree and choose her. I can't really blame him. In so many ways over so many years, we've both been guilty of choosing my mother. Of choosing the easy, placating route. That I'm finally ready to tip the scales doesn't mean my father is willing to do the same.

"Margaret. What a pleasant surprise!" he exclaims, his entire face lighting up when he sees me. Standing, he squeezes my shoulders and kisses my cheek. "You're home."

Instead of responding to his statement, I order an iced tea and sit beside him. He starts to make the usual small talk—when did I return to Dallas, am I getting settled into my condo after being away for so long, what upcoming PR campaigns do I have lined up?—but I'm on a time crunch. I need to obtain financing for the Inn immediately—the closing papers could be ready for Ryan to sign at any moment—and since I'm unsure how long that may take, I don't have the luxury of chitchat, no matter how glad I am to see him.

"Daddy, wait," I say, interrupting his stream of questions. "I'm not here to stay . . ." Then I steadily explain what brought me back to Dallas and relay the events of the morning, stealing his expression of carefree joy in the process. The look he wears isn't angry, but more contemplative and a touch of something else. Reserved surprise, maybe.

"And your mother denied your request, I assume?"

I nod in confirmation. "I'm not asking you to defy her, and in any case, it'd take both of you to sign off on releasing my trust." I fight the urge to toy with the hem of my skirt. "I only wanted you to know, as she's likely going to be in a foul mood, and I rather doubt I'll be welcome in your home unless I change my mind."

"And you're certain you won't? Change your mind, that is?"

I study my father's face, trying to discern what answer could possibly preserve our relationship. Finally, I settle on the truth. "I won't."

He sighs and rubs his fingers under his tired eyes. For the first time I see the old man he will too soon become. That, more than anything else, causes the guilt to surge up for bringing my problems to him, for putting him in the middle once again.

"I was aware of Joy's fall and her subsequent surgery, but your mother didn't inform me that she put the Inn up for sale or that she'd found a buyer." Tugging at his silk tie, he takes a sip of gin and tonic and clears his throat. "But then your mother has never confided much in me anyway. Even less so as of late."

"Because of me?" I ask, drawing a pattern with my thumb in the condensation of my iced tea glass.

"No, honey. You are not, and have never been, the reason your mother is so . . . disagreeable," he says, shaking his head. "No, sometimes there comes a point between two people where the only thing left to discuss is who's sleeping in the guest room that night."

Before I can ask him to clarify or press for more information, he pats my arm and says, "So, share your plans for the Inn. Do you intend to renovate or rebuild?"

"I'd like to do a full-scale renovation. Bring the B and B into the modern era while preserving its original glory," I say, then launch into some of the design ideas floating around in my head. The four-hour drive to Dallas provided ample time for vivid daydreams of restored hand-scraped hardwood floors and copper pots that gleam in the sun as they hang from a rack above the newly installed kitchen island.

"Well, I must say," my father says, leaning forward and bracing his elbows on his knees, "I've never been prouder to have you as my daughter."

"You are?" I ask, floored by his admission, warmth spreading through my veins as effectively as his favorite scotch.

He nods. "I always have been, of course, but I recognize I haven't been the best at vocalizing it . . . or showing it." He flashes a smile that I feel deep in my chest. "You've found something that you believe in, something that you love, and you're going after it with your whole heart. There's bravery and strength in that."

I've been waiting a lifetime to hear that kind of praise from my mother—I've yearned for it even—but now I realize who I really needed to hear it from was my father. I've always gone to him first, quietly sought his support against my mother for the decisions I've made. And while his responses and opinions haven't always been positive or supportive, they've never been harsh. I suddenly feel foolish for ever thinking my mother could drive a wedge between us or damage our relationship. I should have trusted that our bond is stronger than that.

"Thank you," I say, trying to conceal the crack in my voice. "And you're right. I do love the Inn and the person I am when I'm there, too much to let it go. I have to try to save it."

"I could probably help you with that," my father says. For a giddy second, I let myself hope that he's going to convince my mother to grant me access to my trust, that this is the moment my struggle ends. "Part of me wants to, but witnessing the woman you're turning into before me, I wonder if my involvement would be more detrimental than beneficial."

My father reaches across the table, his palm open and inviting. Despite my disappointment, I grasp it. He squeezes my fingers. "You've come this far on your own, Margaret. See it through to the end."

"And if I can't? If I fail?" I ask, tears clogging my throat.

"That's not the girl I raised talking," he says. "You'll find a way. But I will promise you this, if you're able to secure the financing to buy the Inn, I will do everything in my power to prevent your mother from interfering."

He pulls his hand away and motions to a waiter hovering off to the side. "Now, let's grab a table and have some lunch while you regale me with stories of Wilhelmsburg." His lips curve up, his smile part mischief and part ruefulness, as he says, "Perhaps I can learn a thing or two from your example."

An image of my mother's smug grin shadows my footsteps as I exit the latest bank to politely but firmly inform me that I'm a bad investment. All afternoon I've been meeting with various loan officers, and all I've been hearing are the same reasons for why my proposal is being rejected—not enough liquid assets, not enough managerial experience running a bed-and-breakfast, not enough *everything*.

At least there's a silver lining: If I find an investor willing to provide a significant down payment and additional collateral or form a joint venture, then I may have a chance of securing a loan. The most logical solution is also the one I haven't let myself truly consider, the only solution that may actually be worse than asking my mother for help —asking Ryan. The winery is flourishing, and although he wants the acres of land around the Inn for planting grapevines, the house itself is more of a benefit than a hindrance. Almost every guest who stays at the bed-and-breakfast tours Camden Cellars and joins the wine club, so it'd be easy to put together exclusive sip-and-stay enthusiast packages or host country weddings via a partnership once the Inn's been renovated.

Except that would mean swallowing my wounded pride and forgiving Ryan, and I don't know if my head or my heart will allow me to do that. Where would I begin, anyway? Bitterness, I'm familiar with, comfortable even. But forgiveness? I have limited experience with that particular emotion.

I step onto the sidewalk, shielding my eyes against the slowly sinking sun as I head toward my Audi parked in the garage at Mockingbird Station, the outdoor shopping center across the highway from the Southern Methodist University main campus. But I stop short when I spot the four guys gathered beneath the unlit marquee of The Brass Tap across the street.

My heart drops into my stomach. For a second I'm certain I'm hallucinating. They're country music superstars who are supposed to be on tour, not hanging outside the bar/live-music venue where I first watched them perform in college. But no, it is them—Matt, Karl, Jason, and Tim. The members of the Randy Hollis Band. Friends I haven't spoken to in months, if I can still refer to them in that way given all that's happened since Nick and I ended. Since they shoved me out of their lives.

They look the same, albeit a bit exhausted from a relentless life on the road. As I stare at them, a flood of memories threatens to drown me, but I push them out of my mind. *I need to get out of here*, I think as I glance around for the nearest escape route. Weaving through parked cars, I keep my head down and try to blend in with my surroundings in the hopes they don't see me. But clearly the universe has other plans, intent on forcing an encounter that I'm not ready to have.

"Margaret!" Matt's jovial voice yells from across the sidewalk.

I quicken my pace. A rush of blood thunders in my ears, and my pulse beats frantically in my neck.

Matt calls out my name again, adding, "Quit pretending you don't hear me and get over here. We've missed you."

We've missed you.

The sincerity in his tone, the familiar lilt, makes me halt. I can't help but think about the bond of friendship all of us once shared, how I wish I could get it back. Steeling myself, I arrange my expression into neutral and spin around. The guys grin and gesture for me to join them. Inside my guard is up, but a small smile touches the corners of my mouth as I walk over to where they're standing outside the entrance of the bar.

They immediately engulf me in a group hug, offering hellos and kissing my cheek. For the first time I really feel, deep in my core, just how far apart I've drifted from them, how long they've been vacant from my life. How much I've missed them and their antics—Matt's outrageous fan stories and Jason's lame jokes and Karl's ridiculous yet hilarious Zoolander impersonations and Tim's calming presence and subtle ability to read people.

"You look great, Margaret," Karl says, taking off his cowboy hat and placing it on my head the way he used to. "But now you look better." He winks and pinches my earlobe. I laugh, then hand the hat back to him.

"I don't think this is our friend Margaret," Jason whispers conspiratorially to Karl, his gaze raking over me. "I mean the hair is the same, and she's wearing the suit and heels. But this girl's got dirt smattered on her nose."

"They're freckles!" I exclaim. In the past, I lathered on the SPF-50 and followed a diligent skin-care routine to ensure my complexion remained flawless, porcelain perfection. But this morning, as I stared into the mirror, preparing to face my mother, I contemplated obliterating them under foundation. Only at the last minute, I put the tube down on the counter.

Each one of those little dots holds a story, a memory of my time in Wilhelmsburg—a morning enjoyed on the porch with Grammy J, an afternoon spent shopping along Main Street with Bon Bon and Tiffany, an evening strolling through the vineyards with Ryan. Moments I don't want to conceal, no matter how painful some are to remember.

And the truth is, I'm so tired of hiding the parts of me that aren't perfect. So I'm choosing not to.

"Proof you're an impostor. Or better yet, Margaret 2.0. Twice as beautiful and half as snarky." Jason touches a finger to my cheek. "The freckles flatter you."

"I rather like them," I admit.

"Of course you do," he says with a sly grin. "What's dot to like about freckles?" Jason mimics twirling drumsticks as he does the *ba-dum-ching* rimshot sound effect to punctuate the pun. "Get it?"

"You should focus on playing actual percussion instruments. It's what you're good at," Tim interjects, flicking a bass pick at Jason's forehead. At any given time, Tim usually has at least five neon-colored ones in his pockets to toss into the audience between songs.

"I don't know," Matt says, scratching his jaw as though contemplating something important. "Perhaps Jason's dot a point about the freckles."

Oh, god. Here it comes.

"Don't even start you guys . . ." I warn.

"I haven't dot a clue what's going on," Karl says, eyes twinkling.

"I'm going to kill all of you."

"But we're dot ready to die," Jason says dramatically.

That's it.

I try to move around Matt to punch Jason in the shoulder, but Matt steps in my path. "You shall dot pass!" he shouts, as Karl and Jason break into belly laughs and high-five each other.

Tim, who's refrained from joining this asinine exchange until now, grabs my hand and presses it against his chest. "It's okay, Margaret, you've still dot a friend in me."

I shake my head, struggling to contain my laughter. "You've all dot to be kidding me with this crap." My pun silences the group.

"Wow. Aren't you shiny and new and quite funny?" Tim says, his voice playful, though there's a softness in it, too. I've always worn my bluntness and snark as a second skin, but I can understand why gentle humor would surprise him. Before this summer, I never would've felt comfortable enough to joke around so casually. "Where the hell have you been?" The other guys nod, echoing his curiosity.

For a moment, I'm at a loss for words, shocked that they'd noticed, let alone wondered about my absence. But as I search their faces, I realize they're genuinely intrigued. "I've been staying with my grandmother at her bed-and-breakfast in Wilhelmsburg." I don't tell them what prompted me to go there in the first place, though I suspect they already know.

"So that's why you bailed on us," Matt says.

I furrow my brow. "Bailed on *you*?" They're the ones that cut *me* out. They never once reached out. So what is Matt talking about?

"Yeah, for our gig tonight at The Brass Tap to celebrate the end of this leg of our tour," he says, nudging my side with his elbow. "We were hoping you'd work your PR magic and help us promote the show. And attend it, obviously. But we had to hire another firm because our usual go-to person skipped town to drink wine in Hill Country." I remember Samma mentioning how my former assistant, now a media relations manager for one of my rivals, was put in charge of publicizing an event for the band. I guess this is what she was referring to.

"Why didn't one of you call me then?" I ask, glancing around at the guys. "I was only a few hours away with adequate cell phone service, not in Western Sahara. I could've easily taken care of it. In fact, why haven't any of you reached out at all these past several months? I know you were busy on tour, but . . ."

But they chose Nick, I remind myself.

Matt shifts on his feet. Jason fidgets with the buttons on

his plaid shirt. Karl shoves his hands into his pockets. All of them refuse to meet my gaze. Everyone except Tim, who is staring at me with a serious, purposeful expression.

"We were wrong," he says. Just like that. "We thought that because of our friendship with Nick you needed some space from us for a bit."

"So you completely stopped speaking to me?" I ask, giving him an incredulous look. "Come on, Tim. We've been friends since college. You should know me better than to assume I couldn't handle the four of you remaining close with Nick."

"You're right," he says, then repeats it, removing his baseball cap and raking a hand through his sandy-blond hair. "We didn't give you enough credit."

"Or any," I say.

Tim nods, granting me that point.

"We thought it made sense at the time," Matt says, jumping in. "Which is a terrible reason, and we're all aware of it. We just didn't want to hurt you."

"But please don't think you were ever out of our minds, because you weren't," Jason adds.

Karl squeezes my arm. "We're sorry, Margaret."

Sorry.

I used to believe it was an empty word, but I hear honesty in their voices, see sincerity in their eyes, and I know this apology holds meaning.

"We don't deserve your forgiveness, but we value your friendship too much not to ask for it anyway," Karl continues. "Will you forgive us?"

I'm certain the universe functions like a cheeky Santa Claus, always watching and doling out life lessons with no regard for what you want, but rather for what you need. It's like the year I got a tennis racket instead of the roller skates I asked for—evidently Santa and my mother were in agreement about appropriate activities for young ladies. Now, without warning, I'm faced with a practical lesson on forgiveness, the very question I was contemplating earlier.

This time it's me who steps forward, who opens her arms and wraps the guys in a hug. Because I know I'll regret it if I allow them to drift away from me again, and I promised myself to live without regrets. And because it's enough to know that not every mistake, every slight, has to be cruel and final.

The doors of The Brass Tap open and Nick pokes his head out. "They're all set up for you in here. I told them you'd be ready for sound check in—" He cuts himself off when he notices me among the group. His eyes grow wide, but then a grin brightens up his face. The smile is so unexpected that it makes the breath catch in my throat.

Is he actually happy to see me?

"Margaret," he says, approaching me. "You're . . . tan." He leans in to hug me, but stops, as if thinking better of it. The sun dances off the platinum band on his left ring finger.

"Hello, Nick." I brace myself for the one-two punch of anger and regret, the familiar cocktail of bitterness that always accompanies being around him, but as he stands before me, eyes deep and blue as ever, unruly brown hair curling around his ears, and contentment tugging at his mouth, I feel none of those things. Though the memories are there, bittersweet and clear, I find the emotions Nick brings to the surface have nothing to do with him, and everything to do with Ryan. I push the confusing burst of sorrow, pain, and longing away, focusing on the here and now.

Matt rests a hand on my shoulder. "We need to prep for the show, so we'll let you two talk, but don't sneak away after. We want you to be there tonight." The remainder of the band offers their agreement, then they all slip inside The Brass Tap, leaving Nick and me alone on the sidewalk.

For several seconds we stare at each other in silence, neither of us sure where to start. But then Nick speaks. "You look happy, Mags. It suits you." Which is the exact opposite thing I expected him to say.

"Thanks." My voice sounds almost tender and oddly foreign. "So do you, but then that's not much of a surprise. I'm glad you and Lillie are doing well." I hadn't planned to say it, and even as the words fall from my lips, I recognize how alien they are, as they lack any venom, but are no less true.

Nick must hear the change because he gazes at me, as though understanding something, before he says, "Listen, Margaret, I don't know where you've been the last several months, but it's obvious when someone's in a good place. I never made you look this relaxed or this comfortable in your own skin."

I consider his statement, realizing he's right. It took an escape and a summer away, but I'm finally becoming the person I want to be. For so long I defined myself by what I could give to others and the value they assigned to me in return, but now I understand a good relationship is one that emboldens you to invest in yourself. Ryan taught me that when he encouraged me to live recklessly and *for myself*.

"I'm still working on being fully comfortable in my own skin, but it's something I'm dedicated to cultivating," I say.

"It's not worth going through life any other way. Something I spent far too long figuring out. Which you know, of course, because you were there while I was in the midst of it. I hope you know I owe you as much as I owe Lillie for helping me get to where I am now," Nick says, rubbing the faint scar above his left eyebrow. I used to wonder where he'd gotten it, yearn for the day he'd share the story with me. But now it's a fine white line that holds no more curiosity for me than the latest gossip circling the Dallas Country Club. "I know you expected more from me than I could ever give you, and I'm not sure if I'm making things better or worse between us, but you have to know that our friendship was one of the most defining points in my life and had a profound effect on the person I am now. I will *never* forget that, Margaret. Never."

I suck in a breath, as time seems to stop, affording me a moment of stunning clarity. I *did* want so much more from him during our years of friendship and months of dating —I *expected* his love, felt I'd earned it—but I realize what I really needed was to hear that I wasn't just a placeholder for Lillie. That I was important, even if not in a romantic sense. And in truth, I never should've required so much from him when he was so clearly disconnected, when it was apparent his heart always belonged to Lillie despite my best efforts to convince myself otherwise.

"I appreciate that, Nick. Thank you."

He nods and smiles.

"I'm glad I ran into you," I continue. "But I should probably let you get back inside. Tell the guys I'll be at their show tonight, okay?"

"Will do. And don't be such a stranger," he says, then enfolds me in a hug.

This time I nod and smile, and we part in a way I'd never hoped for—as friends. The way we started, but it's more balanced and with a level of understanding that was missing before.

It's funny, because not so long ago I could scarcely imagine my life without Nick, but now I hardly remember the life I'd envisioned for us. I guess the universe is working overtime today, because it suddenly dawns on me that not all relationships are equal. Some are lopsided, and sometimes they aren't supposed to last, but that doesn't mean they aren't worthwhile or significant. In the end the most you can hope for is that those people change your life in positive, meaningful ways.

Perhaps it's that realization that finally forces me to look beyond my frustration and hurt and recognize Ryan for the incredible gift he is. He's never demanded anything of me, never wanted me to be anyone other than who I am—even when that person can be sharp and condescending. He created room for me in his life, and in that room, he provided me a place to grow in ways I didn't know I needed—or wanted.

And now, as I watch Nick walk inside The Brass Tap, closing that painful chapter of my life, I'm able to admit it's not just the Inn I'm not ready to part with. I'm not ready to let go of Ryan either. Which means confronting my mother was only the beginning. I have to accept that Ryan was right. I never stated my intentions for him or the bed-and-breakfast. I've been too guarded, too afraid to trust, assuming if I allowed Ryan into my heart he'd see me for who I really am, and like my mother—and Nick, to the extent I understood at the time—deem me unworthy.

But it's like Ryan told me, that's the risk of loving someone—giving a piece of yourself without the promise of reciprocation. And if I have any hope for the future I so desperately desire, then I have to put my heart on the line and tell him how I feel.

It's time for me to go back to Wilhelmsburg. It's time for me to go home.

20

LIFE SHOULD NEVER BE WASTED ON UNREMARKABLE WINE.

It's a motto I've followed since I stole my first sip of Brunello di Montalcino Riserva at a Christmas party my parents hosted when I was seventeen. The flavor ignited my senses and helped me understand what made a bottle of wine remarkable. I'd been raised to believe from an early age that material things were only as valuable as others perceived them to be, and tasting the wine that night put me on a course of only appreciating the renowned offerings from regions such as Napa, Tuscany, and Burgundy, never looking beyond the label to determine a wine's worth.

Until I came to Wilhelmsburg, that is.

Now, as I wait on the front steps of Ryan's limestone cottage, preparing for a conversation I'm not sure I'll ever be ready for, I wonder what experiences I've missed out on because the label didn't impress me. Was there a hidden gem with dark fruits and velvety tannins in that little village in Greece I visited during my semester abroad? A smooth, robust palate adventure I could have embarked on when I passed through Chile?

I toy with the bottle of wine I picked up on my way over, rolling the neck back and forth between my palms—No Regrets. For so long I thought that phrase meant treading carefully in order to ensure as few mistakes as possible. But as I stare at the label with the winking eye, I realize I had it backward.

A lifetime of carefully planned experiences, and here I sit, a laundry list of things I wish I'd done—and very few I wish I hadn't. Not anymore. Tonight, I intend to take the first step toward a life well lived, starting with confronting the man who's driving up the cobbled circular path to his house.

Ryan gets out of the Blazer, carrying a bucket of broken glass wine thieves—long, cylindrical tools the winemaker uses to siphon wine from the barrel for testing—his sturdy work boots kicking up a cloud of dust. Brushing away the fear that he doesn't want to speak to me, I stand to greet him, drinking in the warmth of his tan skin, honey-blond hair, and the corded muscles evident beneath his shirt as though it's been months rather than days since I've last seen him.

Bordeaux leaps out of the SUV after him. The second her paws hit the ground, she dashes for the running sprinkler system in the grass. Tail wagging, her bark high and happy, she covers her mouth over the spinning head, obviously delighted by the hissing attacker. Soon enough, her fur is soaked. I remain frozen in my spot, hoping to avoid another incident where I end up flat on my back with sixty pounds of canine on top of me and a pair of muddy paw prints staining my blouse. Though perhaps my talk with Ryan would go better with wet, transparent silk drawing attention to my breasts.

Ryan whistles. "Bordeaux!" His gaze sweeps around the yard before landing on me. His eyes widen, then quickly become indifferent. He turns his attention back to the dog and calls out, "The sprinkler isn't an intruder!" His tone is rough and authoritative but holds a tinge of amusement.

Trotting over to him, a satisfied doggy grin plastered on her face, Bordeaux falls in line behind Ryan as he saunters up the walkway toward me. His expression conceals his thoughts, a carefully guarded mask.

"Hello, Margaret," he says, his face still revealing nothing. "How's Joy doing?"

"Feisty as usual, but still recovering faster than the doctors expected," I say, which feels formal and awkward because we're conversing as if we're acquaintances rather than . . . Well, I suppose I'm here to figure out just what we are.

I arrived in Wilhelmsburg early this morning after driving all night, too anxious to be in Dallas—I snuck out of the Randy Hollis Band's show early, but only because I was certain there'd be more opportunities to see the guys perform now that they were back in my life —and as promised, Grammy J kept the porch light on for me.

"Glad to hear it." Ryan nods at the bottle of No Regrets in my hand. "Interesting choice. I know you've only been gone for a couple of days, but I'd assumed it was enough time for you to remember your distaste for longhorn shit." His hazel eyes glint in the dying sun, almost mocking.

My heart twists in my chest with longing and hurt. "I believe I used the term 'manure,'" I say, as Bordeaux sidles up beside me, scratching my leg with a wet paw and whining. I pet the top of her head and under her ear until she lets out a groan and lies down across my feet. "Condescension doesn't fit you, Ryan."

"No, that's your specialty," he says, and I notice how his square jaw, usually so defined and strong, turns sharp and obstinate. "Though I'd like to think I've picked up a thing or two."

He's angry, and though the jab stings, I'm also relieved. Anger I can deal with far easier than cold disregard. Still, it takes a few attempts to swallow my pride and say, "You were right, and I'm sorry."

Since my talk with Nick and the band, I've learned there's a certain strength and humility in accepting blame and admitting to it. In putting yourself out there without the guarantee of forgiveness. In apologizing and trusting the other person to know you mean it in word and in action.

"Apology accepted," he says. "Give my regards to Joy." Propping the bucket of wine thieves against his hip, he moves past me and unlocks the front door. Bordeaux sticks her nose into the open crack and slips inside.

Before he can dismiss me completely, I blurt, "I never told you how I felt about the Inn . . . or about you. But I want to, now, if you'll let me."

He sighs, his back to me, his hand on the doorknob. I know if he crosses that threshold, I've lost my chance. "What's the point, Margaret? You made it clear we're headed in different directions, that your place is in Dallas."

I shake my head and press on. "You're the one who said that at the end of the day all you can do is put yourself out there and hope the other person will love you in return. I'm just asking you to let me put it out there. Please."

At first I think I've misjudged the level of his anger and he's going to ignore me, but then Ryan faces me, steals the bottle of No Regrets out of my hand, and says, "I've found that a bold, full-bodied red blend makes an excellent companion to a dish of crow."

I follow him inside, wondering if he expects me to eat the whole bird, feathers and all, or if he'll cut me the smallest bit of slack. He's fully aware that apologizing doesn't come naturally to me, so I'm sure he's enjoying watching me work for it, if only because he's finally witnessing me at my most vulnerable.

Ryan walks into the kitchen, which smells slightly of chili and wood smoke, and deposits the bucket on the counter before disappearing into the cellar and returning with two large, thin-stemmed wine glasses as delicate as my composure. He uncorks the bottle of No Regrets and pours me a hefty portion as though he senses how much I need the liquid courage. I take a sip, and the familiar flavors coat my mouth.

Ryan sits on a bar stool and drinks slowly, staring at me with a gaze that challenges me to astonish him. He's waiting for me to start, I realize.

I chew the corner of my lip. "I don't know how it happened. Or when," I say, my voice thin but gaining strength. "I can't pinpoint the single moment I fell in love with this place. All I know is that I did."

Ryan spins his wine glass on his knee, the stem rolling easily between his fingers, the deeply hued purple liquid barely disturbed, and I pray my confession makes him at least curious even if he's not showing it. "If you'd trusted me enough to share that with me, Margaret, I never would've offered on the Inn." A muscle ticks in his stubble-covered jaw. "But you didn't. You haven't trusted me with anything." His tone is no longer angry, just hurt, if not a little cautious, and it cuts clean through me like the sharpest blade.

I study him, noticing the dark circles under his eyes, his tense posture and firm mouth, the way he won't hold my gaze. He looks exhausted and defeated and braced for me to push him away, for me to hurt him all over again.

"It's not that I didn't trust you, Ryan. It's that I didn't trust myself . . . or my feelings. I came to Wilhelmsburg because I needed an escape." I peer out the windows at countryside that slopes down and then back up again, the last dazzling rays of sun casting symmetrical patterns across the lush landscape. "For so long, it felt like every time I trusted someone, every time I invested myself, I was the one who ended up wounded. I had to try so damn hard with everyone in my life—my parents, Nick, even my so-called friends. None of it was uncomplicated, and none of it brought me happiness. Not like the Inn." I shake my head. It still catches me off guard how effortless it was to fall head over heels for a ramshackle bed-and-breakfast I'd once dreaded visiting. "I blinked and it slipped inside my heart, as if it'd always been there . . . The same way you did."

A lump forms in my throat, but I force myself to swallow. "You gave me the room to be *me* for the first time in my life," I continue, my voice strong and sure. "And now I don't know how to be any other way."

He raises his eyebrows, his expression shifting from circumspect to surprise, his shoulders relaxing as if he's no longer steeling himself for the emotional blow he expected. "Yet it was so easy for you to believe I'd deliberately betray you, cause you pain, when I've never wanted anything *from* you. All I've ever wanted *is* you."

"Which was my mistake, Ryan, but I needed some time and space to grasp that you were different. That you *are* different. I've always held back, always saved a part of myself out of fear I wouldn't be good enough. But with you I went all in. I *am* all in," I say, setting my wine glass on the countertop and stepping closer to him. Wishing like hell he'd reach out and tug me against him, end my rambling in the way he's best at. "I'm *in love* with you . . . and admitting that out loud terrifies me."

"Loving someone is supposed to be scary. That's how you know it's real, that it's big and meaningful and life changing." He shifts on the stool and rakes a hand through his hair, appearing unsettled. "But it's not enough to be sorry or to say the words. You have to act on it. And you haven't been ready to do that."

"I am now," I say, taking another step toward him so his knee touches my thigh. "I'm ready for all of it. Because I'm staying in Wilhelmsburg. I want to restore the Inn, and I want to do it with you by my side."

"And if that's not possible?" he asks. "Are you able to build a life here with just me? Or am I only worth the risk if you have a safety net?"

How can I make him understand that if I were to choose one happiness to keep—him or the B&B—it'd unquestionably be the future Ryan made me believe was attainable. The future where I pretend to tolerate Bordeaux, where we tour off-the-beaten-path wineries together, where we become a crotchety old couple rocking side by side on a porch swing.

"Ryan, you're worth everything to me," I say. "*Everything*. All I want is you."

Simple, direct, but the truth nonetheless. It's all I have to offer, and I hope it's enough for him to trust the depths of my feelings for him.

Something dark and intense changes in his expression, but before I can process it, he places his wine glass beside mine and kisses me, cupping my cheeks with those capable hands skilled at tearing me apart in the most thrilling way then putting me back together again, that simultaneously set me free and bind me to him. His tongue sweeps across my bottom lip, slipping inside my mouth, and a gasp escapes my throat.

Breaking away, Ryan kisses my forehead, then looks at me, his eyes reflecting the golden hues streaming through the windows. "From the moment you insulted my wine, I knew you were it for me. I'm in love with you, Marge. All of you. The part that barks orders rather than asks politely. The part that stumbled into The Tangled Vine wearing expensive shoes and a scowl that could sour wine. The part that's warm and relaxed in the morning because you haven't remembered why you have to be so strong." He brushes the hair off my shoulder and smiles. "I love it all, from this freckle on your shoulder to the pink polish on your perfectly pedicured toes."

A slow, liquid heat spreads from my heart to my limbs at his words. Before I can respond, he kisses me again, the forever, languid kind where time and urgency don't exist.

"You realize none of this means I'll be any less of a pain in the ass," I murmur against his lips.

"I'm going to hold you to that," he says, hefting me over his shoulder and striding toward his bedroom. He runs a callused palm up the back of my leg, settling it on the curve of my butt.

"Seems like you're holding me to something else right now," I say.

Ryan drops me on the edge of the mattress, arms braced on either side of me, triceps flexed taut, gaze roaming over me in a way that causes every muscle inside me to clench. "Margaret, you have no idea all the things I plan to hold you to."

THE MOON IS FLOATING high in the sky like a tarnished silver coin when we finally separate hours later, satiated, our bodies spent and slick with sweat, our skin awash in metallic-gray light.

Ryan pushes himself up on one elbow and gazes down at me, a crooked grin curling his lips. His eyes have that glassy, drowsy look that speaks to equal parts satisfaction and desire. "Hungry?" he asks, his voice hoarse and a little seductive.

"Starved," I say, tangling my fingers into the damp hair at the nape of his neck. As if on cue, my stomach rumbles, and we both laugh. We skipped dinner, too busy discovering all the ways we could make each other gasp and moan.

"Stay here. I'll be back," he says, kissing along my jaw before slipping out of bed, tugging on a pair of boxer briefs, and exiting the room.

I study the shadows dancing across the walls while I wait for my heart rate to slow down. My head feels tingly and slightly fuzzy, a juxtaposition to my weak, heavy limbs. A gentle breeze tickles my face as it drifts through the large, cracked-open windows, carrying the scent of fresh-cut grass.

Ryan returns a few minutes later with the forgotten bottle of No Regrets and a tray bursting with a selection of charcuterie, cheeses, and accompaniments. I sit up, pulling the sheet beneath my arms, and wrap a slice of prosciutto around a chunk of Parmigiano-Reggiano and pop it into my mouth. I immediately follow it up with a piece of Brie drizzled with local honey atop a water cracker.

"How are you feeling about everything?" Rejoining me in bed, Ryan hands me my still-full glass of wine.

"Exhausted and achy," I say, remembering all the dedicated, thorough attention he provided. My eyes travel over his chest, bare and broad and defined with muscle, across the shadowed ridges lining his stomach, and down to the thin trail of hair that disappears into the waistband of his briefs.

"I've been told I have that effect," he says, his expression as playful as his tone. "But that's not what I was referring to. A lot has happened in the last few days. Fill me in. Did you talk to your mom?"

Sighing, I nod and lean back into the pillows propped against the headboard. "It went about as well as I expected, but at least I asked her not to sell the Inn and told her how I felt."

Even if it did blow up in my face, and even if, despite our recent admissions and declarations, I'm still nervous and uncertain how to approach Ryan with my idea. And what a reversal that is. Business deals and impersonal transactions have always been my forte, whereas personal entanglements have sent me running. Now I find myself delightfully entangled with this wonderful man with absolutely no idea of how to broach the subject of a joint business venture. Is it too much, too soon? Will he once again assume my feelings for him are tied exclusively to my feelings regarding the bed-and-breakfast? And if that happens, can I reassure him otherwise?

"You should know I intend on rescinding my offer," he says, resting a palm on my hip, his touch warm and firm through the soft cotton. He draws his fingers in a tantalizing path over my hip, up, down, and back again, skirting a bit farther in the hollow dip with every pass. "In fact, I've been planning to ever since you left for Dallas."

"There's no point. If you don't purchase the property, my mother will easily convince someone else. She's insistent on ridding herself of the Inn. Unless . . ." I tuck a hair behind my ear and swallow two gulps of wine, needing a minute to gather my wits and garner as much courage as possible. *No regrets*, I remind myself. "Unless you'd be interested in entering into a . . . joint venture . . . with me."

His fingers stop their skate across my body, his eyes locked on my face. I rush forward with the details before he has a chance to say no. "I know you need the land surrounding the bed-and-breakfast for grapevines, and I support that. You were right that it makes good business sense for Camden Cellars to expand. And while the land is beautiful, Grammy J hasn't done much with it over the years, so it's not really of value to the Inn itself. As a result, I'm sure it's only logical to tear down the B&B. It interferes with your plantable area and the structure is in terrible shape, but—"

"But it matters to you, and therefore, it matters to me," Ryan says, rubbing my arm, encouraging me to continue.

I nod, grateful he understands without any justifications. "So, what if instead we renovated the bed-and-breakfast together? I think if we returned it to its original glory and allowed the vineyard to grow around it, we could rebrand the property as an exclusive destination for events, weddings, wine tastings, and weekend getaways. Much like what the larger commercial vineyards in Wilhelmsburg are already doing, but our venture would be more boutique. Quaint, but still charming."

Ryan stares out the window, contemplating my proposal. The stars glow like pinpricks of light against the night sky. Looking back at me, he shifts his body closer to mine and says, "It'd be an investment, but the potential for dividends could be huge."

"Right," I say, taking another sip of wine. The warmth of the liquid flows down my throat, relaxing me further. "So what do you think?"

"I think you found yourself a partner. It's brilliant. But I may have a stipulation or two," he says with a wry grin.

"Oh, please do tell," I say, relief flooding through me.

"Well . . ." He pulls the sheet away from me, exposing my breasts, and traces a finger across my collarbone. "I get to pick the staff uniforms at the Inn. I have this great French maid outfit in mind for a particularly fiery redhead. She'd also be required to speak the language."

Quirking an eyebrow, I say, "Unless you want to hear the lyrics to 'Lady Marmalade' repeatedly, I suggest you amend that last part."

He presses an open-mouthed kiss to the crook of my neck, eliciting a shiver. "*Au contraire.* The outfit won't work without the accent," he whispers, his tongue moving up the column of my throat to my ear.

"Quit playing dirty," I say, halfheartedly pushing against his unyielding chest. The slow, sweet ache that causes me to become unhinged is spreading through me. Once again I wonder why I bother fighting him when he gets his way every time. "We need to finish discussing this. There's still so much to sort out."

"Shhh, Marge," he says, grabbing the wine glass out of my hand and setting it on the nightstand. Then he rolls me onto my back and gently bites my shoulder. "I'm about to instruct you in the fine art of negotiation."

EPILOGUE

One Year Later

STREAMERS FLUTTER AND FLAP IN THE WIND, GREETING visitors and locals alike to the grand opening of the renamed Bluebonnet Inn at Camden Cellars. The October sun shows no inclination of giving way to fall, yet the attendance for the event is massive. Wildflowers adorn the lawn, their vibrant hues adding to the celebratory feel of the evening. Everywhere I look, people mingle, sip wine, and snack on hors d'oeuvres Bonnie helped me prepare.

Finally, the Inn personifies the warmth and welcome Grammy J herself inspired for so many years. Everything from the marble countertops in the kitchen to the herringbone tile floor in the bathrooms to the carefully selected color scheme has turned out better than I imagined, due in no small part to Ryan. Originally, I'd intended on a stark, pristine white for the siding of the bed-and-breakfast, but Ryan negotiated, rather expertly, for a creamy pale yellow with charcoal-gray shutters.

The renovation started right after the New Year and

included adding two smaller guest cottages so we can properly host midsize weddings and other events. The entire process took nine months to complete. Nine months with no customers and no income and a house in various stages of disarray. But instead of spending the time worrying, Ryan and I focused our attention on rebranding and promotion, trusting that it would all work out. Our efforts seem to have paid off, because the Inn is fully booked until April, and the property will host its first marriage renewal ceremony next weekend.

And all around rows of young grapevines line the hillside, the heady scent of soil, sunbaked earth, and lush green leaves so heavy on the wind I can almost taste them—smells I now associate with Wilhelmsburg. The new plots won't come into commercial production for three years, and already Ryan has promised to create a dry rosé blend using Grenache and Syrah grapes. Ginger Snap, he insists on calling it, with an icon of a redhead on the label. I wanted to suggest something snarky in return like a Riesling named Sweetie Pie with a picture of his face on the bottle, but Ryan has softened my edges.

A bass riff reverberates in the air as the members of the Randy Hollis Band take their spots on the stage set up adjacent to the vegetable garden—Grammy J, of course, threatened to dismember me if any cords, wires, or equipment trampled on her plants. Grabbing four large waters from a cooler, I toss one to each of the guys.

"Hydrate, guys," I say. The temperature outside is still beyond brutal. "My insurance doesn't cover death by heatstroke."

Tim tips his cowboy hat in thanks, unscrewing the cap and sucking down several large gulps.

Matt tucks the plastic bottle under his arm while he

finishes adjusting the microphone. "Yes, Mom. I mean, ma'am," he says with a wink.

"Cut her a break," Jason says, poking Matt in the shoulder with his drumsticks. "Margaret's not quite yet domesticated, so let her practice."

Karl only shakes his head, tuning the pegs on his Gibson Les Paul electric guitar for one final check before the show begins.

When I told the band about our plans to revive the Inn, they insisted on playing a mini concert at the celebration in support. Their tour ended six weeks ago, and since then they've been holed up in a studio in Dallas with Nick, writing and recording new material for their sophomore album, *Even the Streets*.

I notice Amber, who's in charge of the dessert table, drop a slice of rhubarb and strawberry pie on a member of Grammy J's bunco group because she's too preoccupied gawking at the band—Tim in particular—for the hundredth time in a few hours. She and the majority of the crowd. It's too easy for me to forget that to everyone else the guys are considered out-of-reach country music stars rather than regular people who happen to be my friends and perform songs for a living.

And even if I hadn't known the band before they were famous, only one man draws and keeps my attention these days. From across the yard, where he's hauling cases of wine and restocking the bar, Bordeaux nipping at his heels, Ryan catches me watching him and grins that smug, wicked grin that causes electricity to thrum through me. His gaze rakes over my face, the length of my body, and his grin grows wider. I can't wait to see that smile fall from his mouth when he finds out what I have in store for him later. While I've never conceded to his request that I wear a French maid uniform—polyester, tacky or otherwise, will never be a part of my wardrobe no matter how much I've learned to relax—French Chantilly lace lingerie in a black-and-white motif, however, is another story. One I expect to have an explosive ending after our party wraps.

"Margaret, come settle something for us," Moose yells above the noise from the rear porch. He and Possum are meant to be acting as sommeliers for the festivities, but right now they're lounging in rocking chairs chatting with my father, abandoning Gina behind the makeshift bar to pick up their slack and serve the awaiting guests.

As I cross the lawn over to them, dodging boisterous partygoers gesturing with their hands and weaving around cocktail tables scattered with glossy brochures detailing the Inn's improvements, I'm greeted with cheers and praise for a job well done. A grin stretches across my face, my heart full of pride for all Ryan and I have accomplished.

I spot Nick and Lillie in the crowd, and they both wave. When I invited them to the grand reopening, I expected them to graciously decline—four hours is a long way to drive for a party for an ex—but much to my joy and surprise they accepted, even bringing a framed watercolor painting of the remodeled Inn with them as congratulations. Though I doubt the three of us will ever be truly close, it's a relief to feel as if that part of my past is resolved.

I pass Tiffany balancing a silver tray of curried deviled eggs, crab cakes, and purple-hull pea cakes. "Stay sharp, buttercup," she says, pinching my ass and cackling before scurrying off inside the bed-and-breakfast where Bonnie is busy working in the kitchen. The whole gang has been amazing—Bonnie especially—pitching in wherever needed, allowing Ryan and me to enjoy the night as hosts instead of scrambling around to ensure everything is running smoothly. But then, that's what true friendship is

all about—lifting up one another, changing each of us for the better.

"What do you misfits want?" I ask Moose and Possum, jogging up the porch steps to join them.

Moose takes a long pull from a sweating bottle of Shiner Ruby Redbird and says, "Suppose you were browsing through different men's profiles on Match.com—"

"And why would I have an account on a site like that?" I ask, leaning a hip against my father's rocking chair and resting a hand on his shoulder. He reaches up and squeezes my fingers. After he and my mother separated during the holidays last year, I thought he'd feel somewhat lost, if not a little sad, but he seems more relaxed and carefree—happier—than I've ever seen him. And when I told him I was officially moving to Wilhelmsburg, he didn't even blink an eye, offering to help me sell my Uptown Dallas condo and dissolve my public relations firm.

"Hypothetically," Possum interjects. His hair resembles traffic cone orange again and is still just as shaggy, though the Inn's updated logo, a whimsical bunch of grapes, has been shaved into each side of his head. Payment for losing a bet to Ryan. As it turns out, Possum *can't* name the entire catalog of wines Camden Cellars offers like he claimed.

"—and suppose you stumbled upon a profile that contained only poses of the same business headshot as photographs and listed watching live coverage of the senior PGA tour and reading law journals as interests," Moose continues. "Would that strike your fancy?"

"Sure . . . if I liked those sorts of things," I say, which I don't. Like most other women, I imagine.

"I told you gentlemen my daughter would agree with me," my father says, his voice loud and jovial. Dressed in a casual blue polo shirt and khaki pants, nursing a scotch on the rocks that's now mostly melted ice in this heat, he looks like he belongs here. "My profile's only been posted for two months. The ladies will come around."

"Though it couldn't hurt to add more variety," I say, glancing at my father and smiling. The poor man, so clueless and so out of his element in today's online dating world, but at least he's trying. "Perhaps uploading some other pictures that aren't so"—boring, staged, lacking all personality—"corporate would be a good idea."

We don't discuss my mother much. What's there to talk about anyway? The last time I had contact with her was when Ryan and I signed the paperwork to finalize the deal for the Inn. I thought her absence might sting—she's still my mother—but I've found removing that kind of toxicity from my life has been therapeutic, healing.

"Our point exactly," Possum says, clinking beer bottles with Moose. He looks at my father. "Roger, my man, you need to loosen up a bit. It's a dating site, not a professional services advertisement. Women want an adventure."

The screen door opens—the hinges so quiet they whisper—and Grammy J walks out onto the porch carrying fresh-washed silverware and plates for the food station. "I seriously doubt the two of you could fill a thimble with your combined knowledge of women," she says, dumping the lot into Moose's and Possum's laps. I laugh. "Now, get on with makin' yourselves useful. And, Possum, shame on you for leaving Gina behind the bar to fend for herself against opportunistic drinkers. You know what shenanigans occur when free wine is involved." She shoos them away, then sits next to my father. "Roger, let me tell you a thing or two about what a mature woman wants."

Grammy J relaxes into conversation, blithely ignoring Moose and Possum's grumbling and my father's terrified expression. She's wearing a skirt and makeup for the occasion, and the sight of her nearly knocks me off balance. I'd been so worried for months following her surgery. So much had changed so quickly I was concerned the events would age her. But she looks younger and healthier than I ever remember seeing her, her hip even stronger than the doctor predicted. It helps that she can sit in her favorite rocking chair and boss me around the Inn rather than doing the tasks herself.

The opening chords of "Shadow and Dust" fill the air, the first track off the band's debut album, *Resolution*. "You folks ready to get this party started?" Matt asks into the microphone, strumming his guitar. He's answered by cheers and applause. "We're the Randy Hollis Band, and we want to wish our friends Margaret and Ryan congratulations and much success on their new venture. We couldn't be happier for you both." Whistling and hollering erupt around me. "Now let's play some music."

Jogging over to where I'm standing, Ryan wraps an arm around my waist and says to Grammy J and my father, "Mind if I borrow Marge a moment?"

"Go have fun you two. Enjoy your night." Grammy J squeezes my wrist, smiling, while my father only nods at Ryan, though I can tell from the way his mouth puckers around a sip of scotch that he finds Ryan's nickname for me distasteful. Still, my father swallows his drink and any comments he may have.

Ryan leads me over to the dance floor in front of the stage, twirling me into a spin. A kaleidoscope of color whirls in my vision before I'm flush against his chest, breathless and a bit off center—just the way he likes me.

As the world settles, firm and real, I say, "We pulled it off."

"That we did," he says, his day-old stubble brushing

my temple, his palm pressed flat against my back. "Hard to believe, isn't it, that a guy with dirt on his clothes and purple stains under his fingernails and a girl with a silver spoon stuck up her—"

I pinch his shoulder, cutting him off before he gets himself in trouble. "Always so cheeky."

"As I recall, you have a particular affection for my cheeks." Peering down at me, he wiggles his eyebrows and grins.

I roll my eyes, but there's no denying it. I have a particular affection for everything about this man.

"It's safe to admit it, you know," he says.

I tilt my head back to look at him more clearly. "You know I love you." *Do I not say it enough?*

"And I love you," Ryan says, his voice serious. Only the fine lines at the corner of his eyes give away his game. "But there's another admission I want to hear from you."

"It's never going to happen."

"Never is an awfully long time, Marge." He trails his fingers down my spine, evoking a fresh wave of desire. "Come on, confess. I won't tell anyone else. Promise."

I kiss the side of his jaw and put my lips against his ear. "Your wine is"—extraordinary, delicious, one of a kind—"passable."

Ryan laughs, twirling me around again. "I'll have you singing a different tune about my vintages soon enough."

"Not even if you had three lifetimes."

He pulls me close, nuzzling his face into my hair and breathing deep. "I guess I need to make this one with you count then."

I sigh, still so unaccustomed to promises of the future. For so long everything in my life felt precariously balanced, as if a simple blink could topple the house of cards I'd built my happiness on. But now, as I dance with Ryan in the warm October air, the sound of music and laughter and conversation around me, I know I'm on the right path, traveling with the man who will keep me grounded, yet fearless.

And I'm comforted by the understanding that in friendship and in love, like wine, there will be years of drought and years of hardship, years where the grapes sour and years where they freeze, but when the rain and the heat finally come and the vines blossom with rich, ripe fruit, those can be the most exquisite and rarest vintages of all, growing only stronger and better with age.

Throughout all the ups and downs, the important thing, I've learned, is to savor life in the moment, bottle and cork the memories to enjoy later, and share exceptional wine with those who matter most.

THANK YOU

THANK YOU for reading SOUR GRAPES! I hope you loved Margaret and Ryan's story as much as I loved writing it.

If you enjoyed this book, please consider leaving an honest REVIEW at the outlet of your choice. Reviews are wonderfully helpful to every author, big or small, and are both welcome and appreciated.

For the latest NEWS, SALES, and SPECIAL OFFERS for all of my current and upcoming novels, friend me on my Facebook Author Profile, like my Facebook Page, and follow me on Twitter and Instagram. For more information on all of my bookish happenings, head to my website: www.rachelgoodmanbooks.com

Keep reading for a sneak peek of FROM SCRATCH, book 1 in the Blue Plate Series, a down-home, feel-good Southern romance. On sale now!

THANK YOU

THANK YOU for reading SOUR GRAPES! I hope you loved Margaret and Ryan's story as much as I loved writing it.

If you enjoyed this book, please consider leaving an honest REVIEW at the outlet of your choice. Reviews are wonderfully helpful to every author, big or small, and are both welcome and appreciated.

For the latest NEWS, SALES, and SPECIAL OFFERS for all of my current and upcoming novels, friend me on my Facebook Author Profile, like my Facebook Page, and follow me on Twitter and Instagram. For more information on all of my bookish happenings, head to my website: www.rachelgoodmanbooks.com

Keep reading for a sneak peek of FROM SCRATCH, book 1 in the Blue Plate Series, a down-home, feel-good Southern romance. On sale now!

FROM SCRATCH SNEAK PEEK

BLUE PLATE SERIES BOOK 1

Chapter 1

LIP SMACKIN' DELICIOUS flickers in red neon above the diner's door.

Salivating addicts are crammed in the entryway and spilling onto the sidewalk, all vying for their Blue Plate Special fix. The chalkboard menu posted behind the register says today's offering is the James Beard—a dish dripping with enough cholesterol to clog even the healthiest arteries. Served all day and only seven dollars.

I elbow my way through the horde, careful not to maim someone's toe with my stiletto. The air inside feels as heavy as sausage gravy and smells of it, too. The sounds of my childhood surround me: forks clanking against plates, snippets of conversations, and a Bob Seger tune blasting from the Wurlitzer jukebox.

Scanning the crowd, I search for the familiar mop of black hair that belongs to my father. All I can see are shiny bald heads, gray hair, and baseball caps as they line the stainless steel counter, obstructing my view of the kitchen.

But I know my father is there. I can hear his boisterous laugh booming over the noise.

Turner's Greasy Spoons is my father's pride and joy, his existence. He's been running the joint for the past twenty-five years. The regulars have dubbed him Old Man Jack. Right now, he's on my to-die-painfully-by-butter-knife list.

Weaving around tables, past servers carrying pitchers and balancing dishes, I spot my father standing over the flat-top grill, flushed and grimy from oil splatters. He wipes his forehead with his sleeve. I march toward him, and when he notices me, a grin spreads across his face.

"Folks, Lillie Claire Turner, the best damn cook in Dallas and my only child, has arrived," he says, gesturing at me with a metal spatula.

Swiveling around on stools, patrons nod and tip their hats.

"Your only child wants to know why you're not in emergency surgery," I shout as my father disappears from view. A beat later he steps out from the kitchen and meets me behind the counter, wrapping me in a hug. I inhale the scent of hash browns and coffee. I pull away. In my five-year absence, he's aged tenfold—deep creases around his mouth, salt-and-pepper hair, tired hazel eyes, lanky build.

"I went to the hospital and the house, and this is where I find you?" I try to quell the frustration and anger sweeping through me.

He furrows his brow. "Course it is. The surgery isn't happening for another three weeks."

I shake my head. "You're unbelievable." Fishing my cell phone out of my suit pocket, I put his voice message on speaker.

"Hey, baby girl, I don't want to worry you, but I'm here at the doctor's office. I've been feeling run down lately and my bum knee's

been giving me trouble again. Anyway, he's saying I need surgery . . . Ah, Doc's back with the paperwork for the hospital. I gotta go."

"See," he says. "I never said it was scheduled for today."

I huff in exasperation. "I called you seven times, Dad. *Seven times* without an answer."

"I got busy with the breakfast rush," he says, then *shrugs* at me, as if this whole thing is a simple misunderstanding. I have a brief, out-of-body moment where I see flabbergasted, crazy-eyed woman about to kill her father.

"You scared me," I say, recalling my dash through O'Hare, the restless flight to Dallas, my panicked drive around town to locate him. "You made it sound like this was an emergency."

A bell rings and plates appear in the kitchen window. My father trays the order. "Well, listen, I'm sorry about that, but I told you not to worry."

I throw my hands up as a fresh wave of anger swells inside me. "You mentioned hospital paperwork, and then you didn't pick up your phone. How could I not envision the worst?"

"Easy there, baby girl. Calm down. It's just a simple operation to fix me up," he says, tapping his kneecap with his knuckles.

"So it's not even serious?" I ask.

"Doc says after some intensive therapy, I'll be shining brighter than a freshly minted penny. Now let me look at you." My father clutches my arms. "You're skinny as a green bean. Don't people eat where you live? And why are you dressed like one of those stuffy lawyers on *Law & Order*?"

"Because I was at work prepping for an important meeting," I say, my voice rising. At this very moment, I should be on the thirty-eighth floor of the United Building, overlooking the Chicago River, presenting to the executive board of Kingsbury Enterprises about their product launch. I'm the senior consultant on the account, the success of which determines if I make partner. "I dropped everything to be here, and you're acting as if I'm the irrational one."

"You don't belong in that job anyway. It's about time you came home. Five years in that frozen tundra is long enough. Now, how about some real food? No more of that bird crap you've been eating." He winks, and his lips curve up into a bright smile.

The fire burning inside me dies, replaced with exhaustion, and I slump against the counter. "I'm not hungry."

"Sure you are." My father pops his head into the kitchen window and speaks to Ernie, his right-hand man and short-order cook. "Can you plate up a James Beard for Lillie?"

"Coming right up, boss."

"Make sure you add extra syrup and bacon."

I cross my arms. "Dad, no. I—"

"You love this stuff." He pats my wrist.

"I'm not a little girl anymore."

"I know that. But you're never too old for tradition," he says, pointing at the wall on the far side of the diner.

Intermixed among rusted diner signs—with phrases like *If you're smoking in here, you better be on fire; Unattended children will be towed at owner's expense;* and *Jack Turner's diet plate: half the food, half the calories, full price*—are candid photographs from years past and framed high school newspaper columns written by yours truly.

Most normal parents tape their children's accomplishments to the refrigerator. Not my father. No, he creates menu items about them. Like today's Blue Plate Special, for instance. Inspired by my first column for *The Bagpipe* about legendary food pioneer James Beard's famous quote, "I've long said that if I were about to be executed and were given a choice of my last meal, it would be bacon and eggs," the special consists of three strips of bacon piled atop eggs scrambled with cheddar cheese and fresh vegetables, all drizzled with Vermont maple syrup.

The column was part of a monthly feature called "The Yummy," which focused on simple, delicious foods. Of course, I wrote those columns back when I cared about things like developing the perfect hush puppy recipe or discovering the key ingredient that made a pasta dish unforgettable. Back before I outgrew the diner and cooking altogether.

Ernie rings the bell and places a steaming dish in the window. The scent of hickory smoked bacon tickles my nose, and my stomach rumbles. *Traitor.*

Before I can protest, the plate is on the counter in front of me and a fork is in my hand. "Dig in," my father says.

I stare at him, refusing to cave.

My stomach rumbles louder. Bacon has always been my kryptonite. I've never been able to resist the mesmerizing sound of it sizzling in the skillet, the way its intoxicating down-home aroma wafts through the air, how the succulent flavors of juicy fat and crispy meat explode on the tongue.

"Go on," my father says. "I know it's your favorite."

My mouth waters until I can't handle it anymore. I take a bite. My eyes flutter shut and a moan slips from my lips. *Double traitor.* Somewhere around my fourth strip of pork heaven, I faintly recall my promise to eat no more than one.

"Slow down. Nobody's going to snatch it from you," my father says. "Heck, when you're in charge, you can sneak as much bacon as you want."

Freezing midbite, I look at him. "What?"

"You're taking over the Spoons."

His words hit me like a sucker-punch pie in the face. Usually I can sense when my father's about to hurl one my way—trickery and unwelcome surprises have been his standard operating procedure for getting his way since I learned to crack an egg on the edge of a mixing bowl—but I guess I'm out of practice because I never saw this one coming.

Once upon a time, the diner was as familiar to me as my own heartbeat. I said my first word, "cookie," crawling across the stainless steel counters. Lost my first tooth when I tripped and collided face-first with the walk-in pantry door. Solved my first fraction while measuring ingredients for a boysenberry crumble.

As a little girl, I gravitated toward the diner's kitchen, basking in the sweet and savory smells swirling around me. For hours I'd sit on the prep counter watching my father chop, dice, and slice, mesmerized by the careful cadence of the knife. As I got older, my life *became* food—experimenting with it, creating it, indulging in it—and a deep-seated passion for forming something with the palms of my own hands took root.

But that's my past, a past I duct-taped in a memento box hidden underneath my childhood bed five years and a lifetime ago.

The fork slips from my hand and clatters on the counter. I push the plate aside. "Are you delusional? I'm not managing the diner."

"Yes, you are." My father says it so matter-of-fact I almost believe him.

"No, I'm not," I say, anger building inside me again.

He steals my last strip of bacon and eats it. "Doc says with my surgery I'll be out of commission for a long while, so you can't expect me to run things while I recover."

"You can't expect me to do that either," I say through gritted teeth, thinking I really will stab him with a butter knife.

My father pretends he doesn't hear me, rambling on as if this was always the plan. "You can spruce up the joint a bit if you want. Do some small renovations. But keep the red booths and the checkerboard tile. The jukebox is a classic, so don't even think about getting rid of it. Though I suppose you could paint the walls a different color and replace the counters. Maybe order some new neon signs. The kitchen could use a new icebox—"

Pressing my eyes shut, I breathe in deep and count backward from ten. "I'm not moving back to Dallas. My career, my life, is in Chicago," I say, thinking about how far I've come.

When I first arrived in the city, heartbroken, scared, and alone, I took a thankless position as a receptionist in a dentist's office to pay the rent and studied for the business school entrance exam at night. After two years of grueling coursework and a massive amount of debt, I graduated with an MBA at the top of my class from Northwestern, landed a job at White, Ogden, and Morris—the best consulting firm in the area—and worked my way up from a lowly analyst. Now I'm the youngest senior consultant being considered for partner, assuming I haven't ruined my chances.

But I won't let that happen. I love my job: the satisfaction of winning a new client, the excitement of finding the missing puzzle piece to a complex problem, the thrill of closing a deal—it gives me a rush.

"My daughter shouldn't be living in a place with a baseball team that hasn't won a World Series in over a century. Those Cubs look more like a bunch of high schoolers, if you ask me."

"I'm happy there, Dad."

My father twists his mouth so that the whiskers of his mustache touch his nose like he does when he disapproves of something. He grabs the coffeepot and walks down the line, refilling people's cups.

Trailing behind him, I continue, "I love that it has four true seasons and deep-dish pizza and Oprah. I love the fog that rolls off Lake Michigan, its crystal-blue waters, and the fact that I'm minutes away from Oak Street Beach. I love how the river turns green on St. Patrick's Day and that the city's residents are unpretentious people who never sugarcoat their words with fake southern politeness and 'bless your hearts.' "

True, with my career taking off the way it has, I don't experience these things as much as I'd like, but I still love them on principle.

"Nonsense. Nothing's better than Texas. We even got the best state fair and Tex-Mex in America to prove it. Ain't that right, folks?" my father says to the patrons at the counter. They nod and murmur their agreement between bites of greasy burgers and slow-cooked pot roast.

I step in front of him. "Drew is in Chicago."

Frowning, my father returns the coffeepot to the burner and tosses a dishtowel over his shoulder. "You're still with that boy? I told you he ain't right for you." He always says this. My father thinks I belong with someone who's not a blue-tie-wearing, *Wall Street Journal*–reading, Cubs-cheering accountant. Someone more like Nick—my first love, the man who shattered my heart, and one of the driving forces behind why I left Dallas. But my father only remembers Nick as the vibrant, passionate boy I fell in love with as a little girl, and not the bitter, angry man he's become.

Besides, my father hasn't even met Drew. He doesn't see the way he complements me. He doesn't understand that we prefer to spend fifteen minutes shuffling through stacks of delivery menus, contemplating our dinner options, promising to one day stock our fridge with something other than bottled water and yogurt, rather than prepare a home-cooked meal. Or how our idea of a fun Saturday afternoon is sitting on the couch working on our laptops with work documents scattered around us and the History Channel on in the background.

"Yes. You know we're still together," I say. What my father isn't aware of is "that boy" recently proposed and I accepted. It's not as bad as it sounds, I swear. I just haven't been in the mood to listen to my father's grumblings. I will tell him, but not right now when I want to strangle him.

My father crosses his arms. "Well, I get what you're saying about . . . all that, but since you're already here, you should reacquaint yourself with how we do things at the Spoons. Three weeks will be here sooner than you realize."

"Dad," I say, softening my tone. I move closer to him so that maybe he'll see me—*really see me*—and finally grasp that I can't do what he wants. "Please don't ask me to do this. This place isn't me anymore. You have Ernie, and I'm sure there are plenty of people around town who would love to help out while you recover. All you—"

He quiets me with a look—the one I received countless times as a child—that indicates if I don't shut my mouth, I'll be on permanent potato-peeling duty. It's embarrassing how, at almost thirty years old, that look still strikes fear in me.

"The Spoons has been in our family since before you were born. I'm not trusting it to anyone else but flesh and blood. You're still a Turner, even if you live in a different zip code."

The firmness in his voice, his insistence, sets off an alarm in my head, and an uneasy feeling settles in my stomach. "There's more happening here than what you're telling me," I say, now certain that whatever is really going on is the real reason he called me this morning and why he wants me to manage the diner. "What is it?"

"I'm not sure what you're referrin' to, baby girl. I'm having surgery in three weeks and need you here to run things. Simple as that," he says, but I don't believe him. Over the years, I've come to realize that my father is a vault of secrets. Whatever his true motivations, he won't share them until he's good and ready.

"I'll work from Dallas until your surgery"—*or at least until I find out what you're hiding*—"but that's it."

"We'll see," he says, then picks up another James Beard special from the window. I notice the slight limp in his stride as he delivers the dish to a little girl in pigtails spinning around and around on a stool taller than her. Maybe it is just his knee, and this whole thing is some convoluted way of bringing me home permanently.

Around me, the life of the diner goes on as usual. People crowd the doorway. Servers hurry by, carrying pitchers of sweet tea and delivering orders. Several patrons lounge in booths, rubbing their stomachs as clean plates sit discarded in front of them.

My gaze drifts to the dent in the counter where I banged a rolling pin after messing up a piecrust. I spot the doodles I scribbled on the wall in the prep area. The tile grout under my feet is stained from when I spilled beet juice.

When I refocus my attention, my father's prattling on about how folks have been begging for my recipes. "Just the other day Gertrude Firestone commented how she misses your four-napkin Sloppy Joes," he says, straightening a pair of salt and pepper shakers. "And none of the regulars like my version of your mother's peach cobbler as much as yours."

My heart drops to my stomach as anger rises up. It happens anytime my mother is mentioned. Someday I'll learn to brace myself for it.

I have few memories of my mother, each one fragmented and fuzzy, as if I'm seeing them through a glass Coke bottle. I recall skin that smelled like honeysuckle, the soft swish of her apron, and long, graceful legs gliding about the kitchen.

I used to miss her in a bone-deep aching kind of way. When I was younger, I'd imagine what her voice sounded like. Soft and gentle as a whisper? Or maybe bright and lyrical with hints of mischief. Either way, I'd pretend I could hear it in my head, keeping me company, guiding me. "That one looks delicious," her voice would say, as I flipped through the pages of a cookbook. "Or maybe try the recipe with the clementines instead." No matter the task, her voice followed.

At night, in the silence, I'd curl up in my twin bed and wish she were there next to me, combing her fingers through my hair and humming pretty sounds until I drifted off into dreams. It was easier than wondering what I'd done wrong to make her disappear all those years ago and never return.

But as I got older I realized I couldn't miss someone I didn't remember.

"Time to prep for the dinner rush," my father says, ripping me from my thoughts. "Go get washed up. There's an apron for you in the back room. The carrots need chopping."

My chest tightens. Only my father can make me feel like everything I've worked so hard for is slipping away. I squeeze my eyes shut and force deep, steadying breaths into my lungs.

"You coming, baby girl?" my father calls over his shoulder on his way to the kitchen.

He expects me to follow. I don't. I can't. I may have been raised in this place, but that doesn't mean I belong here now. Instead I make a beeline for the exit, careful not to knock into anyone or anything on my way outside. I don't want to add another mark. I've already left too many.

OTHER BOOKS BY RACHEL GOODMAN

Blue Plate Series
FROM SCRATCH

A down-home, feel-good Southern romance, *From Scratch* explores one woman's journey back home to Dallas, Texas, where her family is cooking up a plan that doesn't quite suit her tastes…

Thirty-year-old Lillie Turner grew up with maple syrup stuck to her skin and bacon grease splattered on her clothes, courtesy of working in the family diner. Thank goodness she escaped all that when she moved to Chicago five years ago. Now a successful strategy consultant and newly engaged to a man who complements her like biscuits and gravy, she has everything she wants.

When an urgent phone call about her father's health pulls Lillie back to Dallas, she soon learns it was a ruse to bring her home so she can run the diner she'd rather avoid and compete in the Upper Crust, an annual baking competition, with no option to withdraw. Lillie is furious and ready to run back to Chicago, but her father's haggard appearance makes her wonder if he's hiding something. Things go from bad to worse when Nick, her handsome ex and the only man she ever truly loved, reappears, looking as scrumptious as ever.

Lillie's trip home forces her to question the path she's chosen, find her place in the family she abandoned, and wonder if the life she left behind is what she really wants after all.

ABOUT THE AUTHOR

RACHEL GOODMAN is the critically acclaimed author of the Blue Plate Series (light women's fiction/contemporary romance/chick-lit). She was raised in Colorado on Roald Dahl books and her mother's award-worthy cooking. Now an engineering professor at her alma mater, Southern Methodist University in Dallas, Texas, she has not lost her passion for culinary discovery or a well-told story. A member of RWA, she continues to hone her craft through the Writer's Path at SMU while seeking to create the perfect macaroni and cheese recipe.

Follow Rachel
www.rachelgoodmanbooks.com

facebook.com/RachelGoodmanBooks
twitter.com/mojitomaven
instagram.com/mojitomaven

Made in the USA
Las Vegas, NV
14 May 2021